Fated Winds and Promising Seas

Also by Rose Black
Til Death Do Us Bard

ROSE BLACK

Fated Winds
and
Promising Seas

HODDERSCAPE

First published in Great Britain in 2024 by Hodderscape
An imprint of Hodder & Stoughton Limited
An Hachette UK company

1

A CIP catalogue record for this title is available from the British Library

Hardback ISBN 978 1 399 72473 9
Trade Paperback ISBN 978 1 399 72474 6
ebook ISBN 978 1 399 72476 0

Typeset in Plantin by Manipal Technologies Limited

Printed and bound in Great Britain by Clays Ltd, Elcograf S.p.A.

Hodder & Stoughton policy is to use papers that are natural, renewable
and recyclable products and made from wood grown in sustainable forests.
The logging and manufacturing processes are expected to conform
to the environmental regulations of the country of origin.

Hodder & Stoughton Limited
Carmelite House
50 Victoria Embankment
London EC4Y 0DZ

www.hodderscape.co.uk

For the misfits, the damaged,
the dreamers. You belong.

CONTENT WARNINGS

Murder (not on page but described)
Death of a parent (not on page but described)
Self-harm (act not shown)
Abuse (physical not sexual) by a parent to a minor
(some description)
Attempted murder of a child (no death, some description)
Panic attacks, agoraphobia (described on page)
Death and dismemberment of a mythical creature
(on page, gory)
Suicidal ideation and considered attempt (on page)
'Violence'/ 'Graphic bodily threat'
(p 100 - 'force-feed you your own kidneys')

PART ONE

Chapter One

The four walls of his cell had become Lucky's closest companions. Four grey walls, cold hard stone. A small window with bars – iron – and a view of the sea below. One door. Heavy. Only opened for food and his daily sojourn outside. He hated most things about the prison, but the walls were constant, at least.

They never yelled or hit or accused.

His fingers traced the marks scratched on the wall. Thin vertical lines to denote the days of incarceration, given up after one year and seventeen days. On the wall by the window, he'd scratched his name, over and over, three years into his sentence, afraid if he didn't, it would disappear. The rest of the cell was covered in images of birds, shells, fish, anything he could remember, etched into the stone with the blunt knife they gave him to eat.

One time it hadn't been as blunt as they thought, and he wrote his name on his arm. His name was important, though he couldn't say why, only that he couldn't allow himself to forget it.

Under the bed was the sketch he kept hidden. The face of a boy, long hair, a scar above one temple. Lucky didn't know who he was, but his heart ached for him. When the thunderstorm shook the castle and the waves crashed against the prison walls, Lucky would climb under his bed and wonder who the boy was, if he would ever see him again.

Footsteps down the hall. Outside time.

Lucky sat on his bed.

'On your feet.' The guard's words were resigned, tired. They both knew what was coming. At least this was the one who was merely fed up with him, rather than the one who would take any opportunity to kick and punch.

Lucky stayed seated.

'Come on, don't be like this. We both know how it's going to end.'

Once he'd tried to remember the guards' names, match the shifting faces with those patterns of sounds, but after a while, it stopped mattering. They were all the guard, whether it was the bearded one, the kind one, the one who shouted. Guard. Walls. Inside. Outside. The details were irrelevant.

The guard sighed and unlocked the door. The lock went clunk. The door went creak. The footsteps went thud, thud, thud, exactly as they always did.

Lucky stayed seated.

The guard sighed again, and put a hand under Lucky's arm, hauling him to his feet. Lucky tried to stay seated, but it didn't matter, just as the guard said. They both knew how it was going to end. Still, the ritual felt important.

Ritual was about all he had left.

And he truly didn't want to go outside. As the guard pushed him up the steps to the walled courtyard, he pulled back, his nails digging into the wall.

'Nearly there,' the guard said with a grunt. 'I don't know why you put up such a fight. If I had to spend all my time in a stone box, I'd treasure every moment of sunlight.'

Lucky couldn't explain. Couldn't express how much the sky terrified him, so far away. The four walls were safe, familiar. The sky changed. It sucked at him, hungry. The guard gave him a shove and he fell to his knees on the flagstones, clinging to a small plant that had pushed through the gap. He kept his eyes on the ground, his fingers tight around that speck of green. The sky pulled. One day it would pull him right out of here.

Away from the guard. From the walls. From everything that made sense.

Lucky didn't want change.

The guard was on his arm again, pulling him to his feet. 'Walk.' He dragged Lucky a couple of steps. 'It's good for you. Do you want your muscles to waste away completely?'

Lucky kept his eyes firmly on the ground, on the line between the wall and the flagstone. He took one uncertain step, and then another. The air smelled of salt and the salt reminded him of blood and the wind was as cold as her smile.

Lucky shuddered at the thought of her. The girl with white hair who had destroyed his life. Ten years in solitary had made his memories crumple like wet paper, but he remembered her. Remembered that day. His mother bending down to examine something in the rock pool. The girl with white hair creeping closer. She'd smiled, a cold smile like a crescent moon, and she'd brought the rock down on his mother's skull. Lucky couldn't move, couldn't speak. Couldn't scream, even as she handed him the rock still dripping with his mother's blood.

They'd found him there like that, shaking and sobbing. There was no sign of the girl, and no one would believe him. At his trial they called him moon-touched and locked him away to be forgotten.

'Good, keep going,' the guard said, oblivious to Lucky's whirling thoughts. He blew on his hands and then wrapped his arms around himself. His tabard with the lattice threads of the church ruckled over his chainmail. 'Got a bite in the air today, huh.'

Lucky ignored him and walked. One step after another. Three times around the courtyard. That's all he had to do, and then they'd let him go back to the cell. It was safe in the cell.

He started the second circuit. There were forty-eight steps from each corner to the next. A hundred and ninety-two steps per circuit. Five hundred and seventy-six steps in total.

And then he'd be safe again.

'Sea's loud today,' the guard said. 'Bet there's a storm brewing. That's going to be fun tomorrow.'

Lucky said nothing. He carried on counting the steps. Two hundred and sixteen. Two hundred and seventeen.

The ground shook. Lucky stumbled, his shoulder slamming into the wall. He moaned, gripping with his fingernails to the damp wall, clinging on with all his strength. The wide sky beat down on him.

'What was that?' The guard rushed past him, leaning over the wall. Lucky stopped. The door to the cells was open, unprotected. He could go back.

He stopped, frozen, waiting for the guard to notice he wasn't walking. The man's attention was focused on something over the wall, out to sea. Lucky took a step towards the door. And then other. And another.

The ground shook again, throwing Lucky to the floor. He landed badly, slamming his hands against the flagstones.

'Threads of fate, protect us,' the guard murmured, his voice laced with horror. 'Leviathan!'

As he bellowed the last word, a bell rang out. Lucky clapped his hands over his ears. He lay flat on the ground, waiting for either the ringing to stop or the sky to suck him up, but neither happened.

Slowly, he lowered his hands – they were doing nothing to drown out the noise – and looked around. The guard remained staring out over the wall at the sea. Lucky pushed himself to his feet and sprinted for the stairs. There was no shout from the guard, no attempt to stop him.

By the time he reached the bottom, his lungs burned and his legs ached. Above him, the guard yelled, then screamed, and Lucky couldn't stop himself from turning around.

Something immense, scaly, and drooping towered over the wall. It had a huge maw, far bigger than any of the doors in the prison, surrounded by swaying fronds like seaweed. Seawater washed off the gleaming green-gold scales, pouring on to the prison yard. The guard backed away on his hands and knees, scuttling like a beetle. The thing swayed; an eye the size of the full moon stared down at him.

Lucky fled.

He sloshed down the passage, the cold water lapping at his ankles, slowing him down. The cold, lidless eye persisted in his mind, staring into his soul.

It was only when he reached the comforting solid wood of his cell door that he remembered the water wasn't normal.

It flowed through the barred window of his cell, splashing down into a pool on the floor that reached halfway up the legs of the bed.

Lucky backed away.

His head throbbed as he stared at the cell, trying to process what he saw with the safe, constant cell he knew. Sometimes in the winter the rain came in and made puddles. Sometimes a bad storm whipped the waves up and they did the same. But not like this. Never like this.

Lucky sat on the bed.

He pressed his fists into his stomach. It hurt, worse than he could remember. He moaned, hoping it would bring the guards. He didn't like the guards but they were normal, and normal was safe, or at least familiar, which was a form of safe.

But the guard was outside, under the watch of that eye.

Lucky wrapped his arms around himself, rocking slowly. He didn't know what to do. His life was the cell, the routine of the guards, meals, outside walk. No one else came, except the doctor twice a year, occasionally more when he was ill. Other people had once, but not for many years.

The water was up to the edge of the bed now and he knew if he stayed here, he'd die. Would that be so bad? He'd get to see his mother again.

He closed his eyes.

An unearthly wail filled the air. It raced down Lucky's spine, making the hair on his arms stand on end. The eye filled his mind again and he shivered uncontrollably, his hands slapping against his thighs.

Leviathan.

It reminded him of her, of the girl with the cold smile. Lucky shook his head. If he lay down and died now, he'd never learn who she was. The leviathan had given him a chance he may never get again. He stumbled to his feet, the water sloshing around his knees. The leviathan wailed again and Lucky wailed with it.

He staggered to the door, and pressed himself against the wall, listening for the guard. A slap, slap, slap sound made him tense, but when he peered around, the corridor was empty, just the rising water lapping against the walls, licking at the stone. Devouring them slowly. He turned towards the courtyard, out of habit, but there was nothing for him that way. No exits, no freedom.

Not that way.

The other way had more cells. All empty now, though he remembered that wasn't always the case. Sometimes there had been others. He'd heard them shouting or crying. But they never stayed, unlike him, and he'd hear their absence in the silence.

He pushed on. The water dragged against him, trying to pull him back. Lucky squared his shoulders and kept walking.

At the end of the corridor was a brick wall, with a window looking down on the sea. The water, much higher than it normally was, lapped at the window. Lucky avoided staring at it, afraid the leviathan would stare back. On his right was a room with a table and chair, an inkwell, and an open ledger. To his left, another set of stairs rose up to the unknown.

Lucky paused, uncertain. Stairs that went up would go to the sky and the leviathan. But there was nowhere else to go. He started up the steps.

The wall exploded inwards, showering him with shards of brick. The impact knocked him off his feet, slamming him into the steps and knocking the breath out of his body. He lay, gasping, covered in dust, as water rushed into the hole.

The water rose higher, coursing up his body as he fought to get air back in his lungs. It sucked at him, dragging him from the steps. Lucky scrabbled at the stone, trying to get a grip, but they were smooth and slippery and his nails cracked and broken.

A wave washed over his head and Lucky lost his grip, disappearing under the cold, murky water. He broke the surface with a gasp, coughing out the salty seawater, and another wave pushed him under again. The stone step smacked into the side of his face, slamming his teeth together.

He was too dazed to fight back as the water dragged him towards the sucking gap in the wall. Lucky closed his eyes as the water rushed over his head again. The current forced him through the remains of the window, out into the sea beyond.

Out into the wide world.

Under the sky, Lucky panicked. The water pulled him down, gripping his ankles with cold tendrils, smashing him into the rocks. Then the sky would yank him the other way and he'd break the surface, gasping and choking. The two grabbed at him, pulling him this way and that, each one refusing to give up their prize.

Lucky didn't want the leviathan to take him. He didn't want the sea or the sky to, either. He wasn't ready to meet his mother yet. Not before he'd found her killer.

He thrashed his arms, struggling to keep in the boundary of sea and sky. Deep in the back of his mind, a memory awoke, a memory of going into the sea voluntarily, of splashing around with others. Of movements to keep you in that space between the air and the waves.

He kicked, spraying water with wild abandon, but it helped keep the sea from dragging him down. A strange sensation, light and tickly, moved through his chest. Out across the sea, something floated, bobbing up and down on the waves. His first thought was leviathan, and he almost went under when his limbs froze in horror, but as he blinked through the spray, he realised it was a tall ship.

More shapes moved in the water, slipping quickly between the waves as they came towards him. Lucky tensed, but what could he do? He couldn't go back to the cell, could barely keep his head above water. If these were guards, at least they'd be able to tell him what to do. Give him back routine.

He was so focused on the approaching figures that he didn't spot the wave building until it struck him, smacking him into a rough, barnacle-encrusted rock. Bright colours went off behind his vision, and pain blossomed down his right side.

Lucky sank beneath the waves.

Chapter Two

The girl grabbed his hand, hauling him out of the water. Lucky struggled, swinging his arms, desperately trying to break out of her grip. Her white hair whipped in the wind, like sea foam in a storm.

She grinned, cold and hungry.

'Whoa, easy there!' The voice was strange, sharp and high and alarmed and angry. The vision of the girl faded from view and Lucky found himself staring at a woman, short dark hair jagged around her face, small mouth tight in a frown. Lucky let his arms go limp. It wasn't the girl with the white hair who had him.

She called over her shoulder, 'You want to give me a hand here, Golden Boy?'

More hands on him. He stiffened, his fists clenched. He didn't like it when the doctor prodded and poked him twice a year, and he could prepare for that. These were strangers. The water shifted, the hands pulled, and rough wood bumped up against his back. With a yelp, Lucky found himself lying in a small wooden boat. Beyond it, the ship grew closer.

Two figures peered at him. Lucky pushed himself back, waiting to see if they'd yell or hit.

The man leaned forwards, a gentle smile on his face. The sun gleamed off his blond hair. He held out a hand to Lucky.

'Hey. Are you all right? Anything hurt?' He looked the same age as his companion, a young adult, maybe early twenties. Much younger than any of the guards. They both wore loose linen shirts and brown trousers, with sturdy calf-length boots.

Before he could get another word out, Lucky's stomach rebelled, and he spewed a mouthful of seawater over the man's fingers.

His companion roared with laughter. The man eased his shoulder so Lucky was leaning over the edge of the boat.

'Shut up, Sienna.' He turned to Lucky. 'Back in the sea, mate. That's where it belongs.' He waved his clean hand, and a wave washed over the one Lucky had soiled. His nails were painted a shade of lilac. He muttered something under his breath, until he caught Lucky watching him. 'Not your fault.'

Lucky's stomach clenched again, and he retched, salt water and bile burning the back of his throat. He closed his eyes, fighting back the tears from the shock and pain. A hand rubbed circles on his back.

The motion of the boat changed suddenly. Lucky gripped the edge of it, pressing his forehead against the wood. He was rising, being sucked up with the vessel into the sky. He moaned, digging his fingers into the boat, setting off a jolt of pain from his jagged nails. It didn't make sense.

Then there was a thump and the motion stopped.

'Here we are,' the man said. 'Safe and home.' He tried to ease Lucky's hand away from the boat, but Lucky dug in harder.

'What you got there, Gabe?' Another voice. This one higher, older, commanding. Guard? He tensed, wanting to flee, but there was nothing but the empty sea around him. He'd escaped his prison, something he'd never thought of doing. He couldn't be caught by guards so quickly. It wasn't fair.

Lucky raised his head. The boat hung against the edge of the ship. Sienna, the woman with the short hair, had already moved over to the larger vessel, and now stood beside a second woman. Tricorn hat, braided hair, pistols on her belt. She didn't look like a guard, but she stood like one. Glared like one.

'We found him in the water, Captain,' Gabe said. 'Guess he got swept off the castle battlements or something. The leviathan completed destroyed the wall. He's banged up pretty badly.'

Her expression softened a little. 'Get him cleaned up. Was he the only one?'

They didn't know he was a prisoner. Fear prickled at him. What would they do when they found out?

'That we found,' Gabe said grimly. 'What about the leviathan? What happened to it? Why did it do that?'

'We turned it towards open water,' the captain said, pointing out across the sea. 'But now you're on board, we need to get after it. Something's not right.'

'I'll say,' Gabe agreed.

Lucky didn't really follow any of this, but from what he could understand, the leviathan had gone away. He sagged against the boat, relief draining any energy he had out of him, like the water running back to the sea.

Gabe was close again, one hand resting gently on Lucky's arm. 'Let's get you on the ship and get those wounds fixed up.'

Lucky shook his head. The sky above was too wide, too large, too high. He didn't know this man, didn't trust him. Didn't understand why he was so soft and gentle. He pressed his head against the wood, squeezed his eyes shut. He'd survived this far. He wouldn't let the sky take him.

On the ship, the captain shouted orders and sailors scrambled to obey, pulling ropes and calling out in rhythm. The massive sails tumbled down, billowing in the wind.

Lucky expected Gabe to try and drag him, pull him around like the guards did, but he sat down, leaning back against the boat. From this angle, Lucky found his hair was not just held back, but bound in a long braid that ran to his waist. He'd never seen anything like it before, couldn't drag his eyes from the way it swayed gently with the man's movements.

'Impressive, isn't it?' He gave Lucky a grin. He reached behind him and held it out to show Lucky. The hair was dark gold, soaked with seawater. 'I'm Gabriel. Do you want to tell me your name?'

Slowly, cautiously, Lucky released his left hand from the boat. He turned it, showing the scarred word on his forearm. Gabriel's eyes widened as he took in the jagged letters.

'Lucky.' He swallowed, and the smile came back, though smaller this time. 'I guess you are, given that we spotted you.' He held out a hand again. Lucky shuffled back. 'Come on. You don't want to stay on the boat. There's a nice cabin with a bed on board. You'll feel better for a rest.' Lucky eyed the hand cautiously. Gabriel didn't seem afraid of falling into the sky, and maybe the cabin would be like his cell. Four walls. Safe.

He reached his fingers out, snatched them back, and then reached out again. Gabriel's hand was warm and rough beneath his.

'Good.' Gabriel gave him a bright smile, and stood, pointing towards the ship. 'Just over the rail, and across the deck.'

Lucky tried to follow him on to the ship, but shivers wracked his body and his legs wouldn't move, and in the end it took Gabriel, Sienna, and the captain to help him. He made the mistake of looking up, once his feet were on the deck, past the expanse of sails to the grey sky above. Immediately he was on his knees, pressing his palms into the deck.

'It's all right. Nothing will hurt you now.' Gabriel's face filled his vision. Calm and confidence enthused his voice. 'Come on, Lucky.'

'Lucky?' Sienna sniggered and Gabriel shot her a dirty look.

Lucky took a deep breath. He could do this. Across the deck. It couldn't be further than the distance around the courtyard.

He could do this.

Gabriel's fingers rested on his arm in a butterfly touch, a barely present sensation, keeping him walking straight. He led Lucky down some wooden steps, and then the sky was gone and the dark wood of the ship covered him. He let out a sigh that came out as more of a sob.

'Here we go.' Gabriel opened a door. The room was the same size as his cell, only without any window. Gabriel lit a lantern and set it on a hook on the wall. There was a blocky wooden chest in the corner, and some blankets folded up next to it, and that was it. 'Sorry it isn't much, but I thought you'd want somewhere private and there isn't much of that on the ship. You stay here. I'm just going to get a few things. I'll be back in a moment.'

Lucky settled in the back of the room, his shoulder and hip wedged into the corner. Four walls. Low ceiling. This would do. It wasn't his cell, but it would do. He could be safe here, if he could keep his secrets. He watched the open door, longing to shut it, but unable to bring himself to move.

Gabriel returned, carrying a tray with a bowl of water, a glass jar, and several strips of white cloth. He was dry, now, his white shirt no longer clinging to his skin, and his hair a bright gold. He set the tray down and closed the door behind him. Lucky drew his knees up and wrapped his arms around them. He watched as Gabriel laid out the medical supplies, trying to understand the man. He was tall, with broad shoulders and muscular arms, not brawny like the guards, but easily capable of overpowering Lucky. But his tone was soft, gentle, encouraging, not ordering.

'What did they do to you in that place?' Gabriel asked, a frown pinching his brow.

Lucky shook his head. He couldn't say anything. Couldn't admit anything. If they found out what he was, what he'd been accused of . . .

'You need to get dry.' Gabriel gestured to the pile of blankets. 'Take your clothes off. Do you think you can do that?'

Lucky didn't move. Gabriel should leave. The guards always left. That's what they did. Why wouldn't he go?

But Gabriel didn't move like a guard. He moved slowly, as if he was afraid of something too. He didn't shout or order, either. Lucky put his head in his hands. Exhaustion spawned a headache that pounded between his temples and nothing made sense. He didn't understand.

Gabriel cleared his throat. 'You're going to catch a chill if you sit there dripping.' He held out a blanket. 'Please?'

The guards never said please. Twice a year, they'd strip him down to his small clothes, hold his arms while the doctor poked and prodded and mumbled under his breath. Then they'd throw a couple of buckets of water over him, cut his hair and beard, and leave again.

'Please?' Gabriel said again. The blanket brushed against Lucky's forehead, raking over the place where the rock had grazed his skin. The pain, suppressed by fear and confusion, leapt up and Lucky cried out. He tried to back away, but he was already pushed into the corner.

'Let's try something different.' Gabriel put the blanket down and reached a hand towards him. Lucky shook his head, sending a splatter of blood on to the floor of the cell. 'It's all right. I'm not going to hurt you. I'm just going to touch you, there.' He pointed at Lucky's arm. 'And I'll stop as soon as you tell me to. Just shake your head and I'll stop.'

Lucky shook his head, and Gabriel froze, hand outstretched towards him. But when Lucky stopped moving, Gabriel started again, his hand coming closer. Lucky shook his head again, and Gabriel paused once more. This time, Lucky bit his lip and held still and Gabriel pressed a hand against Lucky's upper arm.

Gabriel's palm was warm and rough. Lucky tensed, every muscle locked, ready to flee, but he didn't shake his head. Gabriel moved his hand in a circle, then drew it back slightly, bringing his fingers down to touch his palm. He did this several times, and something shimmered around it.

Water.

It flowed around Gabriel's fingers, looped around his wrist. The more he moved and gestured, the more the water expanded. It was coming from Lucky's own body. From his skin, his clothes, his hair. He watched, unable to even blink, until every inch of him was dry, and there was a swirling sphere of water around Gabriel's hand, hazy brown from blood.

Gabriel stood up and without another word left the cell. When he returned, the water was gone.

'I . . . er . . . don't normally show off to strangers,' Gabriel said, sitting down again. 'But this seemed like a special case.'

Lucky had never seen anything like that before. None of the guards could control water, or at least, not that they'd ever shown him. He'd never even heard of such a thing. But perhaps that was what life was like outside the cell?

Gabriel spread a couple of blankets on the floor, and held up another one, so he was hidden from view. 'I still need to take a look at your scratches. Take your shirt off. Lie down when you're ready.'

Lucky didn't want to do anything more than sleep, but the pain in his side was sharp and uncomfortable, and blood trickled down the side of his face.

I'll stop as soon as you tell me to.

And he had. That had felt stranger than the water in a way. Someone giving him control like that. So he pulled off his bloodstained, ragged shirt he'd worn every day for as long as he could remember, and lay down.

The blanket covered his back. He winced as fresh pain lit up across his skin, but didn't move. That was how he'd dealt with such things at the prison. Keep still; keep limp. Don't make anyone angry. It would end soon.

Gabriel knelt down next to Lucky, rolling the blanket back so only his shoulders and arms were exposed. With a cloth dipped in the bowl of water, he cleaned away the blood.

'Next bit is going to sting a bit,' Gabriel said apologetically, picking up the jar. 'But there's nothing better for healing up scratches, I promise.'

He dipped two fingers into the jar and they came out coated in something thick and yellow that smelled of old fish.

'Shake your head if you want me to stop, all right?'

He smeared the stuff across the back of Lucky's shoulder. Immediately the skin burned with a new and different pain. He whimpered and shook his head. Gabriel's touch lifted and Lucky felt him waiting.

The burning sensation from the yellow salve was intense, but when it faded, it took away the older, deeper pain, too. Lucky lay for a moment, waiting for it to return, or for something else to go wrong, but it did not. He looked up and caught Gabriel's eye, then nodded.

Gabriel's face lit up in delight and for the second time that day, Lucky felt the strange lightening sensation in his chest. He laid his head down on the blanket and gritted his teeth as the other man went to work.

As Gabriel finished tying off the last bandage, someone knocked on the door.

'Grub's up, Gabe!'

'Thanks,' he called back. 'Fancy some food?' he asked, turning back to Lucky. 'You can meet the rest of the crew.'

Lucky shook his head. His world had been turned upside down. He'd been half drowned, smacked into rocks, forced on to a ship, prodded and poked. He wanted his cell and to be left alone. If that meant going without food, then so be it.

He pulled the blanket around him.

Gabriel said nothing, but opened the door and called out to someone Lucky couldn't see. A few moments later Sienna appeared and handed Gabriel a tray. She peered over his shoulder and he waved her out the room.

Gabriel set down a bowl of something steaming on the floor, and a plate of green-flecked bread next to it.

'Don't worry, it's not gone bad. It's seaweed bread,' Gabriel said, pointing at the plate. He looked up, and his eyes widened as he took in Lucky's appearance. 'Oh, hey, you don't want to wear that old rag. I'm sure I can find you something better.'

Lucky dug his fingers into the shirt and Gabriel held up a hand.

'Fine. I get it. Too much change, right? You eat. I'll come back in the morning, but if you need anything, I'll be out on deck.'

Lucky met his gaze and nodded, once.

'Night, then.'

He closed the door, leaving Lucky alone.

Chapter Three

Sleep did not come easily. After eating, he dozed for a while on the blankets, but things were just too different to get comfortable. He kept glancing at the door, expecting Gabriel to come back, but he didn't and Lucky couldn't decide if that was good or bad. He wasn't like any of the guards, not cruel or angry or annoyed or indifferent. His soft tone was calming, and there was something about his face that tugged at Lucky's mind.

After a while, he gave up on sleep. They hadn't given him a knife with his food, but the wood was softer than the stone of his cell and if he pressed hard with the edge of the spoon, he could make an impression on the wall.

When the door opened, he was engrossed in creating an image of swirling water over an open palm.

'Morning,' Gabriel said. Lucky started, freezing with the spoon pressed against the wood. Gabriel's eyes widened as he took in the room and the images Lucky had created. 'You've been busy. Didn't you sleep at all?'

Lucky's heart raced, his chest tightening. The guards never paid any attention to his scrawling, and he'd taken to drawing as he always had to calm his nerves. He pressed his hands against the scratches, trying to cover up what he had done. He couldn't get into trouble, couldn't risk himself.

'How are you feeling?' Gabriel didn't sound angry. 'Does the motion of the ship bother you?'

Lucky shook his head. The ship rose and fell in a gentle rocking motion that was strange, but not unpleasant.

'That's good. I was so sick when I started living here. Spent most of the first week hanging over the rail. Oh, here. I brought you some breakfast.' There was a soft chink of plates or bowls knocking together. Lucky turned slowly, still pressed against the wall, as Gabriel set a tray down on the floor. Two bowls, steaming slightly. Two cups that did the same. Two plates of the flat greenish bread.

Two.

'I thought you might like some company this time.' Gabriel squatted by the tray. 'Do you want me to stay?'

Lucky thought about it. He didn't want Gabriel looking at the sketches. But he didn't want him to take the food or drag him out of the cell. His stomach rumbled loudly, betraying his hunger.

'Good.' Gabriel dropped down, crossing his legs, and began lifting things off the tray. His braid hung over his shoulder, reaching down to his lap. 'Right. We've got porridge here, some of yesterday's bread, and this.' He held out a cup to Lucky.

Lucky let the spoon fall. Gabriel gestured with the cup again, and Lucky edged over until he was sitting opposite. He took the cup, warm, and sniffed it. A bitter scent tickled his nose, unlike anything he'd ever smelled before. He looked at Gabriel in confusion.

'Coffee.' Gabriel took a sip of his own and let out a happy sigh. 'Careful, it's hot though.'

Lucky took another sniff. The warmth that spread through the cup to his fingers was comforting, so he dipped his tongue into the liquid. The bitter taste was far worse than the smell, but very quickly the heat scorched his tongue and he couldn't taste anything much. The cup slipped from his hand as he reached up to cover his mouth, shattering on the floor.

'Whoa, hey, careful!' Gabriel reached forwards and Lucky flinched back. Gabriel pulled his hand back. 'I did say it was hot.' He waved a hand over the pool of dark liquid, and it floated up and over the empty stew bowl from yesterday. Gabriel flicked his fingers, and it rained down into the bowl.

Lucky curled in on himself. Now he'd done it. He ducked his head, waiting for the shouting, for the blows.

'It's all right,' Gabriel said, his words soft. Strange. 'It's all right. I'm not angry. It was an accident. No one's going to hurt you.'

Lucky lifted his head, found himself staring into Gabriel's eyes. They were deep brown, like the wood of the walls, wide and filled with concern and sadness. He offered a hand, and then closed his fingers again and pulled it back when Lucky didn't move.

'What did they do to you?' he said softly.

Lucky couldn't answer. He didn't understand the question.

'Here.' Gabriel handed him the bowl of porridge, and then picked up the shards from the cup and placed them on the tray. He used his hands this time, picking up each piece and setting it down again, rather than making them rise and fall with a gesture.

The porridge was closer to the food he was used to. Faintly salty, sloppy, beige. His tongue was still numb from the coffee, but the pain had faded to a tingle. He glanced down at his arm as he ate, white bandages and scattered flecks where the red-brown scabs were visible. But it didn't hurt.

'Told you that stuff was good,' Gabriel said, as Lucky poked at one of the marks. 'The slime from the leviathan skin numbs pain like nothing else. Speeds the healing up, too.'

Lucky shuddered, visions of the cruel yellow eye filling his mind. Gabriel didn't seem to notice, as he was focused on the other bowl of porridge. For a while, they ate in silence, Lucky cautiously and Gabriel with gusto.

'Is that me?'

Lucky raised his head to see Gabriel pointing at the wall, the empty porridge bowl abandoned at his feet. Heat rushed into his face and his stomach lurched, threatening to lose the porridge he'd consumed.

'It is, isn't it?' He approached the wall, running a finger over the grooves Lucky had carved, a swirling pattern down the wood to represent the braid. 'Don't be embarrassed. This is good. And you did it with a spoon!' He picked the tarnished metal spoon off the floor, twirling it around his fingers. His nails were a blue-green colour this morning.

Before Gabriel could say anything further, someone knocked at the door. Gabriel took one last look at the wall, then turned and opened the door. Sienna on the threshold. She poked a finger towards Gabriel's chest but didn't touch him.

'Captain wants to see you, Golden Boy.' She turned away, then peered over her shoulder at Lucky. 'Wants to see both of you.'

Gabriel's shoulders slumped. 'Fine. We're coming.' He shut the door before she could say anything else, and after a moment her footsteps stomped away. 'Guess we better go. The captain isn't someone you want to keep waiting.'

He put his hand on the door handle and Lucky shook his head. Why wouldn't they let him be? The more time he spent with people, the more chance that someone would work out who he was.

He backed away, pushing himself into the corner.

'Please?' Gabriel said, rubbing a hand over his forehead. 'You don't know my . . .' He cleared his throat. 'You don't know the captain like me.'

Lucky shook his head again. His gut twisted at the way Gabriel looked so downcast. How to make him understand? It wasn't just the captain. He couldn't go outside again. Couldn't face the wide sky sucking at him. He braced his back against the wood, solid and safe.

Gabriel dropped down to the floor and wrapped his arms around his knees. His braid fell over his shoulder again, and he fiddled with the end idly.

'If only I understood what happened to you,' he said. 'What bothered you most. Maybe I could help you understand it won't affect you here.'

Lucky bit his lip. Gabriel had been kind to him, and he didn't understand. No one had been kind to him in years.

Gabriel sighed and stood up. 'Maybe I can get her to come here. I should get you some clothes, at least.' He peered at Lucky. 'Think you'll fit some of mine? Hmm, they'd probably be a bit big on you.'

His braid swayed in front of him, and Lucky reached out a finger. He snatched it back quickly when he realised what he was doing.

'You can touch it if you like.' Gabriel's frown hadn't faded, but his mouth twitched at the corner. 'It's just hair. I trust you.'

Lucky reached out his hand again, let a finger brush against the loose hairs beneath the leather tie. It was softer than he expected, softer than his own hair, which was dry and straw like. Gabriel pushed it further into his hand.

'Maybe,' he said, chewing the pad of his thumb. 'Maybe you could hold on to it. Then, you know, anything that might happen to you, happens to me, right?'

Lucky glanced down at the braid in his hand, and back up to Gabriel.

'And nothing's going to happen to me,' Gabriel added quickly. 'Please? Just give it a try.'

Lucky closed his eyes, closed his hand tightly. Gabriel's hair tickled his palm. He could do this. If Gabriel wasn't afraid of being sucked into the sky, maybe Lucky would be safe too. Maybe this would make up for the coffee, for the kindness.

He opened his eyes and nodded.

Gabriel gave a noisy sigh of relief. 'Great, thank you, great.' He clapped his hands together. 'Whew. I appreciate it, really.'

Lucky got to his feet and shuffled after Gabriel, through the door, holding tightly to the end of his braid. The leather thong that bound the end pressed into his palm and he focused on the sensation as if it alone could hold him in place. They reached the steps and Gabriel paused.

'Ready?' he asked, and Lucky took a deep breath. He could do this.

When they stepped on the deck, he was less sure. He kept his eyes focused on the lines between the planks of wood that made up the deck, but the waves breaking all around buffeted his ears, and the smell of spray on the air brought back memories of the water smothering him.

The girl's hands on him.

He froze and Gabriel let out a yelp as he tried to take another step but was pulled back.

'Hey,' he said softly. 'There's nothing wrong. This is what the ship is like. This is normal. Come on, we're almost there.'

Lucky bit his lip, tasting blood. He looked down at his hand, at the end of Gabriel's braid. Gabriel gave him an encouraging nod.

'Just a little bit further. See, that door over there. You're doing really well.'

Lucky counted the steps on the deck, focusing on the numbers, until they'd reached a door on the other side and Gabriel was knocking, sharp and hard. A voice called for them to enter and Lucky stepped in to meet his fate.

Chapter Four

Stepping into the room, away from the sky, should have been a relief, but Lucky found his shivers growing worse. The room was far bigger than his cell, either cell, and a vast window dominated the back wall. He dug his feet down, feeling the light pull at him. In front of the window was the woman in the tricorn hat, though the hat no longer sat on her head, but rested on the desk next to her. She stood, leaning against the desk, her eyes fixed on Lucky.

He made the mistake of meeting her gaze, and it bored into him. He focused his attention on a knot in the wood of the deck.

'You, er, you wanted to see us, Captain?' Gabriel said, breaking the silence that pressed against Lucky's ears.

The woman stood up straight. She was shorter than Gabriel, but taller than Sienna. Her skin was white, but tanned, especially across her face, her hair dark and bound in many small braids, silver shining at the ends.

'Welcome to the *Dreamer*,' she said. 'I'm Captain Haven.' She gave Lucky an expectant look.

'I don't think he talks,' Gabriel cut in. 'He hasn't said a word to me.'

The captain frowned, and Lucky shrank back.

'Does he understand?' she asked.

'I think so.'

'This ship is on a mission, and we cannot afford the time to take you back to shore,' she continued. 'The best I can do is let you have a dinghy. Does that suit?'

Lucky considered his options. He didn't know what a dinghy was, but he understood enough to know it meant away from here. On the sea. With the leviathans. The creature's haunting yellow eye filled his mind, the memory of its scream turning his blood to ice. He shook his head harder, gripping on to the end of Gabriel's braid.

'You can't send him off on his own. Whatever happened to him back in the castle, it obviously hurt him pretty badly, here.' Gabriel touched his forehead. 'Please. Let me keep an eye on him.'

'Don't give me those puppy eyes, Gabriel. I'm running a ship here, not a home for waifs and strays.'

'Could have fooled me,' Gabriel muttered under his breath. 'That's pretty much what the ship is.'

'It's dangerous.' The captain folded her arms. Her attention was fully on Gabriel and Lucky felt as if he'd been forgotten. Better that way.

'I'm not saying he should be out there pulling the quills off a leviathan!' Gabriel threw up his hands, the braid twisting in Lucky's grip. 'Let him work – he could clean or help out Poe.'

'Take on your least favourite chores, you mean?' She raised an eyebrow.

'That's not what I mean,' Gabriel protested. He shuffled, his face in that same dejected expression he'd worn in the cell, the one that made all his features run down. Lucky closed his hand into a fist, his nails digging into his palm. His fault.

His tongue felt large, awkward in his mouth. How did everyone else make it so effortless? But he knew the answer – practice. Lucky hadn't had any reason to speak to another person for years. His voice had dried away from lack of use. He had to try. The ship would have to go to port at some point and he could get off there. And he didn't want Gabriel to be sad.

He could do this.

'. . . W-work.' The sound came out more of a cough than a word, but both Gabriel and the captain spun to stare at him. He cleared his throat. 'Work.'

He didn't really understand what he was agreeing to, but it changed Gabriel's expression from downcast to excited and that was enough.

'You can talk,' Gabriel said, his eyes wide.

The captain held up a hand before either of them could say anything else. 'If you stay on my ship, you need to remember this is *my* ship. My orders are paramount. If I am not around, you take orders from First Mate Haven. Gabriel is bottom of the pile.'

Gabriel snorted and rolled his eyes.

Lucky nodded. Hierarchy he did understand.

'Fine. You're under Gabriel's care for the moment.' She turned away from Lucky. 'Get him started tomorrow, give him another day to recover. And until he's contributing, any costs are coming out of your pay.'

Gabriel rolled his eyes again. 'Fine.'

'You have a funny way of saying, "Yes, Captain",' she said, but her lip twitched. 'Dismissed, both of you. Oh, and Gabe, make sure he's got something better to wear than blood-stained rags.'

Gabriel turned away and Lucky followed him back outside. He lowered his eyes to avoid catching a glimpse of the sky.

'Sorry about that,' Gabriel said, rubbing the back of his head. 'She can be a bit intense.'

The captain still reminded him of his prison guards, sharp, hard. He didn't want to stay on the ship, but it was better than the idea of being out there alone under the sky. And it had made Gabriel smile. Something about the man itched at him in the back of his mind, and he found he wanted to know more.

'That's the mildest thing I've heard you say about her for a while.'

They both turned to see a sailor sat on the steps to a raised part of the ship. She gave them both a grin and a wave. Lucky dropped his gaze to the deck again.

'Eavesdropping again, Ma?' Gabriel called. 'Aren't you always telling me that's a bad habit?'

She jumped down the last few steps and walked around to stand in front of them.

'Ship's business is my business,' she said. 'Especially when it concerns my wife and my son.' She leaned up and brushed a kiss against his cheek, then turned to study Lucky. Her scrutiny made his face flush, and he raised his eyes to study her in return. Unlike the captain, who was sharp lines and angles, she was soft curves – her body, her face; even her hair was a series of wide spirals, held in place by a red bandana. Her skin was dark, and there was a smattering of freckles across her nose. She smiled at him. 'Amala Haven, first mate.'

He wanted to say something, but he didn't know the right words to say. She didn't feel like a guard. She reminded him a little of his own mother, and the thought awoke a painful grief. Lucky forced it down.

'I'll let you get on,' she said, 'but don't be too hard on your mother, Gabe. She's got to think about everyone.'

'I wish she'd just trust me,' Gabriel muttered.

'She does trust you. But she can't be seen to be giving you any favours, so she's got to be extra tough on you. You know this.'

'Yeah, yeah. I know.' He rolled his eyes, then turned to Lucky. 'Come on, let's go.'

'Looking forward to getting to know you,' Haven called as they walked back towards the cell.

'They're not my mothers by blood,' Gabriel said as they started down the steps into the welcome gloom and the solid walls of the ship's interior. 'But that doesn't matter. They adopted me when I was fourteen. Sienna acts like it gives me perks, but really it means I have to fight twice as hard to be taken seriously.' He laced his fingers together and stretched his palms above his head. 'So, what do you want to do? Want to see the rest of the ship?'

Lucky couldn't fight back the yawn in time and Gabriel laughed.

'Understood. I guess you didn't sleep much last night. Oh, that reminds me.' He held open the door to the cell, then turned away, pulling the braid out of Lucky's hand. 'Back in a minute.'

Lucky settled down on the blankets. His head felt thick and fuzzy, as if someone had filled it with fabric as well. Nothing made sense still, but some of the tension pulling at him, dragging his focus from one threat to the next, had faded. He stared down at his hands, nails ragged, backs scuffed and cut. But steady. Not shaking.

'Here.'

Lucky looked up as Gabriel handed him a stick of something white.

'It's chalk. We use it to tally things in the hold. Probably easier to draw on the walls with than the edge of a spoon.'

Lucky took it, white dust smearing his fingers. He swallowed, throat rough.

'Why?'

Gabriel stopped, his outstretched hand frozen. 'Why, what?'

Lucky coughed and rubbed at his throat. The words were all there, in his head, but forcing them out of his mouth felt like wading through water.

'Why are you kind to me?' he managed. He gestured at the chalk, the bandages on his arm, the room around him.

'I . . .' Gabriel started, then closed his mouth. He stretched his fingers out and then drew them back to himself, once, twice, and then sighed. 'I think it's important to be kind. Not enough people are kind, and I want to make up for it.'

'Not used to it,' he mumbled.

Gabriel leaned in closer, enough that Lucky could see a small white scar above his temple. In exactly the same place as the boy in his sketch in the prison cell. Lucky blinked. The memory of the sketch and Gabriel's face blurred together. It was him. The boy he'd sketched and kept hidden under his bed.

'Lucky?'

He realised he was staring, open-mouthed. Lucky clamped his jaw shut.

'Nothing. I'm tired.'

'Get some sleep, then.' Gabriel gave him one more look, concern and confusion on his face, and then stood up, brushing down his slacks. 'We'll talk about tomorrow over dinner. Sleep well.'

The door closed behind him before Lucky had a chance to react. He lay down on the blankets, the piece of chalk gripped tightly in his hand. Now he'd seen it, he couldn't deny it. Gabriel was the boy he'd drawn – older now, his hair longer, his jaw more square. Real. Lucky couldn't remember how they'd known each other, couldn't remember anything but Gabriel's face and a sense of comfort.

He rolled over, laying an arm over his forehead, his thoughts spinning. It didn't make sense. How had they found each other after all this time? Did Gabriel remember him too? Why had the leviathan freed him, just in time for Gabriel's ship to pick him out of the water? He closed his eyes, picturing the boy with the golden hair, and tears rolled down his face.

Gabriel woke him later with a knock on the door. Lucky had come to recognise the sound, somehow bright and cheerful. Not that anyone else had any cause to knock on the door for him, of course. He tensed, wondering how to act, how much to say.

Gabriel handed Lucky a bundle of cloth – shirt, trousers, just like his own clothes.

'Get that on you. I spoke to Poe and he's happy to have you help out in the galley.' He breezed into the room, glancing at the walls. 'Do you want to come down and eat with the others?'

'Not today.' He wasn't keen on it tomorrow, and he didn't think that would change the day after, either. Gabriel was trying hard to keep the disappointment from his face, as Lucky added, 'Too many people. It gets . . . too much.'

His expression softened. 'Sure, I get it. Why don't you get changed, and I'll bring some food?'

He didn't get it, how could he, but Lucky bobbed his head and Gabriel left, closing the door behind him. Lucky held out the clothes. Linen shirt and slacks, both in a sandy colour, and a long strip of fabric in bright red.

He pulled his old shirt over his head, intending to drop it, but his fingers wouldn't release it. He turned the ruined fabric over in his hands, investigating the mottled bloodstains, the tears and holes. Ragged and broken. It felt like a fitting symbol of his old life.

He wanted to change, wanted to be the sort of person who could find out what happened to his mother. But he knew so little about what had happened, about who the girl in his memories was. Didn't know where to start.

Lucky dropped the shirt and picked up the chalk from his bed. On the opposite wall to the spoon-image of Gabriel, he began to sketch. He drew in long, sweeping strokes, hand moving in a blur.

He pulled himself back to that day, squeezing every detail out of the scene. The sky was overcast, the wind whistling around the rocks, racing ripples across the pools. His mother had her back to him, her hair tied in a bun that was steadily falling out. She was peering in the rock pools that formed under the cliffs, hands on the barnacles and limpets that encrusted their sides. She was saying something to him, but Lucky couldn't remember what, could barely remember her voice.

The girl stepped out from behind a black ridge of rock, her white hair whipping around in the wind. She was younger than him, slight, skin the colour of barnacles and sea foam, wearing a dress with serpents around the hem. She held the rock in both hands, creeping across the sand. Lucky couldn't move. An invisible hand had him gripped. She turned to him, and her smile grew, cold and hungry and cruel, and she raised the rock and—

'Lucky.'

He snapped back to the ship, the change leaving him dizzy and nauseous. Gabriel was holding his wrist, fingers not quite closed around it. He followed the line of his arm with his gaze, down to the fingers, the chalk, and then to the wall.

She stared back.

Lucky stepped back with a cry as she stared back, her cold white eyes, that hungry smile, white hair flying loose around her shoulders. As if she was standing there. As if she was seeing him.

'Hey,' Gabriel said softly.

'No. No, no, no.' The words bubbled from him in a moan that didn't sound quite human. He'd summoned her, summoned his mother's killer to the ship. To Gabriel. He stumbled forwards, pressing his hands against the wall, wiping frantically, smearing at the drawing to make her go away.

'Hey,' Gabriel said again, louder this time. 'What's wrong? Who is that?'

He put a hand over Lucky's, and Lucky lashed out, swinging his arm back. His fist struck Gabriel's face with a solid smack. They both froze, silence pushing in, heavy and oppressive. Gabriel touched his lip, his finger coming away bloody. His face paled at the sight, and he raised a hand to protect himself.

Lucky let out a moan and retreated. His back met the corner of the room with a thud, and he dropped to the floor, wrapping his arms around his knees. The action seemed to snap Gabriel out of his trance.

'Oh, no, it's all right. It was an accident. You didn't mean to hurt me.' Gabriel rubbed his hand on his slacks and held up the clean finger. 'See? Fine now.'

Lucky put his head on his knees and wept.

Chapter Five

When he raised his head again, the lantern had burned down low, and his eyes were raw and itchy. He rubbed them and yawned. Did he fall asleep again? Every muscle ached and his back clicked as he unfolded himself.

The chalk drawing had vanished from the wall. A chill rushed through him. Had he just imagined it? Then he spotted the damp rag at the foot of the wall, and Gabriel sat leaning against the door, his chin on his chest, fast asleep.

Lucky pulled himself to his feet. He shivered, and realised he was still shirtless. With a glance to check Gabriel was still asleep, he pulled on the new clothes. He wasn't sure what to do with the strip of red fabric, until he spotted a similar one around Gabriel's waist, though his was a pale blue.

Gabriel stirred, rubbing a hand over his eyes, and Lucky tensed. Gabriel raised his head, blinked, and gave him a small smile.

'You're awake again. And you're finally out of those old clothes.' He yawned, stretching his arms over his head. As if he was completely unbothered by Lucky's presence. As if Lucky hadn't struck him.

'D-did you do that?' Lucky glanced at the wall, not wanting to look at the red mark on Gabriel's lip.

Gabriel rubbed the back of his head. 'Yeah. I hope that's all right. You seemed really distressed by it.'

The wall was faintly discoloured by a smear of chalk that hadn't been removed, but all traces of the girl were gone. In his mind, he could still see the lines of her smile, sharp and cruel. He wrapped his arms around himself.

'Why don't you eat?' He indicated a tray that Lucky hadn't noticed. 'It's all cold now, but it's still good. You'll feel better for some food.'

Lucky didn't move, but Gabriel began setting out dishes between them. He hadn't eaten, either. Lucky didn't understand his continued kindness, his desire to stay after everything that had happened. But he'd said more words today than he had in years and now they'd all dried up, so he joined Gabriel, cross-legged on the floor, and shovelled cold stew into his mouth in silence.

When their bowls were empty, Gabriel collected them and set them on the tray. He met Lucky's eye, then looked away, pressing the knuckles of one hand against his lip. Lucky tensed, waiting for the words that would tell him that everything was broken. That Gabriel believed he was a killer too.

Gabriel took a deep breath. He shifted so he was no longer sitting in front of the door. 'I want you to know you're safe here,' he said slowly. 'I know that might be hard for you to accept, but it's true. You're in trouble, aren't you? Who is the girl?'

'You can't help me,' Lucky said quietly. The room pressed in on him, and for the first time, it felt too small. He glanced at the space Gabriel had made by the door. Giving him space to leave.

But where could he go on a ship?

'I can try. I won't pressure you, but . . . trust me, it helps to talk.'

Lucky stared at him, seeing the etched face that he'd lain awake looking at over so many years, overlaying the ketch of the boy and the man with the soft dark eyes. Fate guided everything, right? If they were here, together, it must be fate? Must be, right? He swallowed.

'She . . . she killed my mother.' He took a breath, knowing that he was about to throw everything away. 'They . . . they think I did it, but I didn't. I didn't.'

There. He'd done it now. Now Gabriel knew he was an escaped prisoner. He wouldn't believe him, and Lucky would be sent back to the prison, to the guards. To being alone again. He curled up on himself.

'I believe you,' Gabriel said softly.

'Why?' No one believed him. Not the guards, not the church official at his trial. Why would Gabriel? Unless . . . 'Do . . . do you know me?'

Gabriel cocked his head. 'I don't think so.'

Lucky's heart sank. Had he been mistaken? No, he'd stared at that face for so long it was etched in his mind. Then Gabriel didn't remember him. That almost hurt more than being wrong. To have come so close to someone who could help him. Like reaching out and brushing fingertips, but not being able to catch their hand.

'It doesn't matter. I'm going to find her, find out who she is. I won't cause any trouble, I promise. I just need to get back to land.'

'Maybe I can help?' Gabriel suggested. 'I lived in Ciatheme for a while and—'

'Why?' Lucky demanded. He smacked his fist against the floor, the pain and shock making him shiver. The impact knocked off several scabs and blood ran down his hand. Gabriel didn't know him. Didn't owe him. His eagerness only left Lucky feeling scared and suspicious. Who would help someone like him?

Gabriel sat back on his heels. He held up a hand, as if examining his reflection on the green-blue of his nails. 'Because . . . because I know what it is to be hurt. To need help and think it's never coming.' There was pain in his own eyes now. 'And I don't want to let anyone else go through that alone if I can help it.'

'But . . .' Words were turning to soup in Lucky's mind. He had feelings, so strong they were almost physical, but the words to explain them were dissolving. 'I don't know so much. What if . . . what if . . .'

'What if you don't like what you find?' Gabriel suggested. 'What if you feel you're in some way responsible?'

'What if I'm bad?' He stared down at the blood, the red stark against the white of his skin. 'What if . . .'

'I don't think you're bad. Let me put it this way.' Gabriel reached out a hand, leaving it hanging there. 'Do you want to hurt me?'

Lucky shook his head, hard enough that the room span slightly.

'You're safe here,' Gabriel said again and Lucky was caught between the desperate hope that he was right, and the crushing fear that he was horribly wrong.

He slept fitfully, dreaming of the white-haired girl, of a boy with golden hair sobbing, of the sound of the sea breaking against the rocks. After the third time waking up gasping and tangled in the blanket, he got up. Lucky sketched a starfish in the corner of the room, then rubbed it out again, like the tide coming in and erasing a sketch in the sand. He did this over and over until Gabriel arrived with porridge and coffee.

'I can't wait until we can hit port and stock up a bit,' he said, setting the tray down. 'I haven't had an egg in months.' He picked up one of the cups of coffee and settled down with it next to Lucky. There was no trace of the pain he'd displayed yesterday, and he seemed back to the bubbly persona he'd exhibited since they'd met. 'No spilling this one.' He pointed at the other cup still on the tray. 'Wasting good coffee is a sin.'

Lucky eyed the cup suspiciously, memories of a bitter tingling tongue dancing in his mind.

'So,' Gabriel continued. 'Got to get you out of this room today, start making you part of the crew. Poe's happy for you to help him in the galley, or if you'd rather get some fresh air, I can find you some cleaning tasks on deck.'

Lucky bit down on the spoon in his mouth. 'Inside.' He'd seen too much of the sky recently. Even the idea of leaving the room made him queasy. But he had to try, if he was going to find her. And he wanted to help out, help Gabriel. It felt easier to accept his kindness and support if he could do something in return.

'Yeah?' Gabriel frowned at him over the steam coming off the coffee. 'It's a nice day today. Much better than yesterday. You can't be stuck inside all the time, right?'

'I like inside,' he said softly. He had a thought of staying here forever, these four walls becoming his new companions. Gabriel bringing him meals. It didn't sound too bad.

'But there's so much you can't do when you're inside.' Gabriel finished his coffee and eyed the second cup in an unsubtle manner. Lucky nudged it towards him.

'I don't think I like it.'

'It will grow on you.' Gabriel wrapped his hand around the second cup. 'About the only thing my mother and I agree on these days is the necessity of a good coffee in the morning. Anyway, as I was saying, outside is good. Have you ever been fishing? Swimming around a reef?'

'Couldn't do much of that in prison,' Lucky pointed out. 'And I don't remember much about what happened before.'

Gabriel flushed. 'Ah, right, yeah. Well. All the more reason to start living again. And the crew is great – well, most of them.'

Lucky wanted to explain, but when he tried to put it into words, it sounded daft.

'I'm not used to being outside,' he said slowly. 'The sky . . . the sky feels too big.'

'Huh.' Gabriel regarded him over the cup, his expression a mixture of curiosity and sadness. 'I can't imagine what that must be like.'

Lucky shrugged. 'It's . . . not good.'

'Well, we can work on it over time,' Gabriel replied, certainty solid in his voice. 'For now, let's get you over to Poe.'

Poe turned out to be a man older than the captain, with skin darker than the first mate's, and tight white curly hair. He stomped across the deck with a strange rhythm until Lucky realised one of his legs was wooden. He met Lucky's gaze with an impassive expression and Lucky stepped back behind Gabriel.

'Lucky, this is Poe, the *Dreamer*'s cook and treasure chest of stories.' Gabriel bounced on the balls of his feet. His enthusiasm washed over Lucky, and he peered over Gabriel's shoulder. 'Poe, this is Lucky.'

That was it. One word to define him in front of this stranger. But it wasn't prisoner. It wasn't dangerous. It wasn't moon-touched or killer. Just 'Lucky'. He wondered if he'd ever feel that way.

Poe grunted, rubbed a hand on his apron, and held it out to Lucky. Lucky let it hang there, as he'd done with Gabriel's hand.

'You can trust him. He won't hurt you,' Gabriel whispered in his ear. 'Hold it and shake.'

Awkwardly, Lucky closed his fingers around the other man's and Poe moved his wrist up and down. Like Gabriel, the skin of his palm was rough and calloused, but cooler, drier. After a moment he let go.

'You better get going,' Poe said, turning to Gabriel. 'Sienna was looking for you. And your mother wants you to help with the charts when you're done.'

Gabriel nodded quickly, the action sending ripples down his braid, and made for the door. He turned back and fixed Poe with a questioning look.

'I'll look after him,' the cook said, and Gabriel nodded again.

'You'll be fine,' Gabriel called over his shoulder. Then he was gone, and Lucky was left alone with a stranger.

The galley was a long thin room. On one side was a big black stove, warm enough that Lucky could feel the heat from the doorway. Beside it was a stool fixed to the floor. There were thick workbenches on the opposite side, pitted with knife cuts and stained with reds and greens. Sacks and crates nestled under the counter, held in place by a wooden rail. Pots, pans, big wooden spoons, and spatulas hung from a series of hooks above.

Poe stomped around him and pointed to a big tub on the floor and a crate of dirty cooking implements. 'Brush, soap, pans,' he said, pointing from item to item. 'Do a better job than Gabe.' Then he stomped back to the stool he'd been perched on when they arrived and returned to peeling carrots.

For a while, neither of them said anything. Poe focused on peeling, though he barely glanced at the knife or the vegetable in his hands. Lucky scrubbed at the stack of pans and bowls and cups. In the water, scrub, examine, repeat. The repetitive action reminded him of counting steps, and it had the same calming effect. He was able to push aside the fears and the dreams and concentrate on cleaning. Wash the past away, leave it clean and new. Poe said nothing and for a while, Lucky felt as if he were alone.

Occasionally, noises from above or outside the room reminded him that he wasn't. Footsteps, shouts, the sound of singing floated down from the deck above. Once, the shrill voice of the short-haired woman floated past.

'What's wrong with you? More than usual, I mean.'

Gabriel responded, but Lucky couldn't make out the words.

'Who the fuck let you have more coffee?' she yelled, and rapid footsteps charged past the room. Poe snorted.

'So,' Poe said to the room, the knife in his hand flashing and the peel spinning around as it fell. 'The *Dreamer*'s picked up another stray.'

Lucky said nothing, but he put down the pot he'd been washing. He tensed, his heart rate quickening.

'That's what she does, you know,' Poe continued.

'The . . . the captain?'

Poe snorted again. 'No, the ship. Draws in weirdos and misfits and, well, dreamers. People who don't belong anywhere else. You might not feel like it right now, but you'll fit in around here soon enough.'

Lucky pushed the pot back under the water. He wasn't sure he believed it yet, but he found he didn't *disbelieve* it, either.

'It's nice to have some decent company.' Poe slid off the stool and stomped over to a wooden counter, where he began hacking the peeled vegetables into chunks. 'Some of 'em don't know how to shut up and get on with the job.'

Lucky had barely met any of the crew, but he somehow suspected that comment was mostly aimed at Gabriel. The tension began to drain away again. Poe didn't seem inclined to shout or insult any more than Gabriel had. When Lucky finished washing and moved on to drying and polishing the pots, Poe peeled an orange and set it down next to Lucky.

'Wouldn't do for you to get scurvy, now, would it,' he said gruffly.

Lucky bit into a segment, the sweet juice exploding in his mouth. The intensity of flavour took his breath away, and he had to nibble it to prevent being overwhelmed.

'What . . . what does the ship do?' Lucky asked, hoping that wasn't a stupid question.

'No one told you that?' Poe raised an eyebrow and Lucky shook his head. 'She chases sea monsters, lad. Leviathans.'

Chapter Six

Lucky almost dropped the pot. It slipped in his hands and he struggled to get a grip on it, leaning dangerously over the tub.

'W-what?' he stammered, his throat tight. The vision of the yellow eye filled his mind, and his hands shook so much he almost lost the pot again. He set it down by the tub before anything else could happen. Lucky remembered the long, serpentine head, the cold and hungry eye, the way the ground had shaken. The way the guard had screamed.

'She chases leviathans,' Poe said again, as if this was the most normal thing in the world.

'Why?' The word burst out of him. Who'd want to chase after monsters?

Poe rubbed his chin. 'Because if no one did that, the leviathans would attack ships, disrupt trade. And you can harvest useful things from them. The slime that coats their skin numbs pain and aids healing. The quills around their jaws ease fever. Some even claim they can neutralise poison. And so it goes on.'

'Do you kill them?' he asked in awe.

'Course not.' Poe slammed the lumps of vegetable into a clean pot. 'Leviathans do no harm – well, mostly. Killing them would be a cruelty.'

Lucky wasn't sure the leviathan would have the same consideration for them.

He watched in astonishment as Poe waved a hand, and a silvery trail of water emerged from a barrel behind Lucky. It floated gently across the room and landed in a splash on top of the vegetables.

'Gabriel could do that. Can everyone do that?' Lucky asked. Perhaps he could do it too, he'd just never thought to try it. Perhaps it was like speaking or walking calmly under the sky. Something he'd forgotten how to do. He waved his fingers at the washtub, but the water remained flat, leaving him feeling a little foolish.

'Magic? No, not everyone can do it.' Poe's voice was laced with something Lucky couldn't quite place. Not sadness, and not anger, but something smeared between them. 'It's a choice you have to make, one with a price. It's not for everyone.'

'Why not?'

'People don't understand the price. Don't understand what it's going to cost them. You can't cheat it. Can't avoid it. It will always come. Always.' He cleared his throat, scratching at his thigh above the wooden prosthetic. 'Let it go, lad. It's not something you need to worry about.'

'I don't understand,' Lucky said, but Poe held up a finger to his lips.

'Hush. You've been good company so far. Let's go back to that.'

Lucky washed, scrubbed, rinsed, and dried until the pile of dishes dwindled on one side and grew on the other. Next, Poe helped him put everything away, and then showed Lucky the ship's stores of salted meat, root vegetables, grains and flour, and a chest of little drawers, each of which contained a powder with a pungent odour. Poe explained their uses with enthusiastic gestures. Lucky watched in awe of his knowledge and passion, but there were so many new words that they washed into his mind and out again.

'You can't expect to learn everything in a day,' Poe said cheerfully as Lucky bit his lip. 'You've done well so far. It will come to you, if you want to learn. If not, she's a big ship. You'll find your place soon enough.'

Later, Poe taught him how to make the flat rounds of bread, how to knead the dough and set it to cook on a hot pan. Lucky slid the golden-brown rounds on to a platter, over and over, a sense of warm satisfaction spreading through him.

'It's good, isn't it?' Poe eased himself on to his stool and gave Lucky a grin. 'I like creating things. I find it satisfying. Whatever happens, we can bring something new into the world. Something good.'

Lucky felt a smile tugging at his own mouth. He let it slip away. Would he say the same if he knew what Lucky had been accused of?

'Try one. They're better warm.' Poe picked up the latest round of bread and tore it in half. He handed one to Lucky. 'Listen, I don't know your past, who you were, who you think you were, but that doesn't matter anymore. You're on the *Dreamer*. You have the choice of who you are now. Remember that.'

Lucky stared at him, the words soaking into him, the way the oil had soaked into the flour. Changing it. His stomach flipped like the bread in the pan.

'Is something burning?'

They both turned to see Gabriel leaning against the door. Poe sniffed and his eyes widened. He snatched the pan out of Lucky's hand and slid the round of blackened bread out.

'Remember this, as well. Never take your eyes off the pan.'

Gabriel grinned and Poe gestured at him with the pan.

'I don't know what you're smiling about. He's done a much better job than you did on your first day. Or your fiftieth.'

Gabriel gave him a flourishing bow. 'Some men were made for more than mere bread.'

Poe picked up the burned bread and flicked it across the room at Gabriel. 'Some men are going to go hungry unless they get over here and help out.'

Gabriel sauntered over and helped Poe move the big cooking pot off the heat and over to a closed hatch. Lucky picked up the platter of flatbreads and followed them. Poe undid the latch on the hatch, revealing a room beyond with several large tables and a mass of people milling around. Immediately they formed a line.

The sound was like nothing in the prison. Bright conversation, laughter, backslapping. It hit him like a wave, making him cringe instinctively, but it was warm and cheerful, unthreatening, so he uncurled again.

Poe ladled out stew into two bowls and pushed them at Gabriel. 'Go on, get. You can owe me later, Gabe.'

Gabriel touched two fingers to his forehead. 'Appreciate it. Come on, Lucky.'

Lucky grabbed a couple of rounds of bread and headed for the door.

'You did well today,' Poe called after him.

'Eat with the crew today?' Gabriel asked hopefully, pointing to the room on the other side of the hatch. 'We're right there, so it makes sense.'

Very little made sense to Lucky still. Not a ship that stalked sea monsters, or people who made a trade to control water. But choosing what kind of man he wanted to be, that resonated with him. He wanted what the crew had. That comfort in other people's presence. The easy connections. Friends.

'I ... all right.'

Gabriel's face lit up with a grin, and Lucky's heart lifted. He gestured with the bowl, slopping a little of the food over his fingers. 'This way!'

As they entered the room, the chatter and laughter faded and every person turned to look at him. Lucky took a step behind Gabriel. What were they thinking? Were they judging him? Did they suspect? He turned to leave.

Gabriel's hand hovered just above his shoulder. 'Sailors are just curious folk. That's all. They don't mean any harm. They've all been where you are at one point or another. So have I.' He leaned in close, his breath warm on Lucky's ear. 'We can leave any time you want.'

Lucky swallowed down his fears. He'd have to get used to it sooner or later. 'I want to stay,' he whispered and was rewarded by another sunshine smile.

Gabriel walked over to a table and sat down, licking the stew off his fingers. Lucky hurried to sit down next to him. No one joined them, but the other tables were filling out fast. He glanced around the room, and spotted Sienna. She caught him staring and scowled. Gabriel gave her a wave.

'You've met Sienna. She's got the personality of a weasel with its tail on fire, and she desperately wishes she was me, but she's not actually as bad as she likes people to think she is.' He scanned the room and pointed to a red-headed pair who were sitting beyond Sienna. 'Cass and Erin, the twins. They're water dancers, like me and Sienna. And Poe and Mum, but they don't dance anymore.' He flushed. 'I mean Captain Haven. Grace, the woman arguing with Poe about portion size, is the quartermaster. Most of the rest are just sailors. They'll try and prank you, get you to complete impossible tasks, but it's all in good spirits. Give as good as you get, that's the way to handle it.'

'What's a water dancer?' Lucky asked.

Gabriel flicked his fingers and Lucky's stew rose out of the bowl, and then settled back down with a plop. 'Those of us who can control water.'

Lucky thought about Poe, and how he'd said it wasn't for everyone. He wondered what it was that made Gabriel and the others different. 'Do you power the ship? Steer it or something?'

'Nah, the wind does that. We've got a special task. Maybe I'll get to show you sometime.' He gave Lucky a wink.

'Is this everyone on the ship?' There were about fifteen people in the room. He couldn't see the captain or the first mate.

'This is about a third. We run three shifts, so there's someone up and awake at all hours to deal with anything that comes up. The sun might sleep, but the wind runs on its own time.'

Lucky shrugged, unsure what to make of that. He turned his attention to the stew, amazed that it tasted so different to the last two meals he'd eaten. Everything in his old life had tasted the same, bland and moist and miserable. People drifted by, and Gabriel introduced them, but as with Poe's recipes, the information refused to stay in his mind. The noise of the conversation blurred until it was little more than a dull roar that chewed at the back of his mind.

'Lucky?'

He flinched at the sound of Gabriel's voice, suddenly intruding on his consciousness.

'You all right?' Gabriel waved a hand in front of him. Lucky looked down to check the stew hadn't been waved from his bowl and found it already clean.

'You've been putting an empty spoon in your mouth,' Gabriel said and Lucky's face flushed.

'Sorry. It's . . . noisy,' he finished, feeling ashamed. 'I think I'd like to go back to my cell now.'

Gabriel shook his head. 'You can't call it a cell, mate. It's not a prison. You're not a prisoner.'

Lucky looked away. 'Sorry.'

'Why don't we try outside?' Gabriel ran a last piece of bread around the inside of his bowl and tossed it into his mouth. Every movement he made was precise, effective. Attention-grabbing. He made Lucky feel as if his hands were sponges, thick and clumsy. At the same time, Lucky couldn't take his eyes off him. He raised an eyebrow at Lucky. 'Well?

Look, it's night now. The sky's not so big at night. Everything blends in a bit more.'

'I don't know . . .'

Gabriel stacked the bowls and took them over to the counter.

'Give it a try?' he asked, giving Lucky a look with wide, hopeful eyes. 'You've done so well today.'

'Maybe I shouldn't push it . . .' His head ached from the noise, and the idea of stepping outside had made his heart pick up.

'It's your choice,' Gabriel said, a note of disappointment in his voice. 'But you're missing out. The stars will be out tonight, and the weather looks like it's about to change. They might not be there tomorrow.'

Lucky took a deep breath. Gabriel's hunger to show Lucky his world and everything that went with it was endearing, if exhausting. 'Maybe for a moment, then.'

They stepped back out into the corridor and turned for the stairs. Gabriel offered Lucky the end of his braid.

'Just for a moment. And if you want to turn around and go back in, then just let me know. We don't need to stay long.'

Lucky nodded, though his heart was pounding in his ears. He tightened his grip on the leather band around the end of Gabriel's braid. Just for a moment. He could do this.

They walked slowly up the steps and out into the dark. Lucky forced his gaze down on the wooden planks of the deck, a sickening, swirling feeling taking hold in his chest. Beside him, Gabriel took a deep breath.

'It is a beautiful night. Take it slowly. There's no need to rush on a night like this.'

Gabriel's confidence pushed against Lucky's fears. Lucky clenched his fist around the braid, nails digging into his palms. He closed his eyes, letting his other senses take things in first. The gentle rocking motion of the ship, rising and falling with the swell of the waves. The thud and slosh of the sea hitting the side or breaking over themselves. The scent of seawater in the air, spray on his skin.

The curve of her smile, hanging in the air.

Lucky's eyes snapped open and he gasped, the air rushing out of him as if he'd been punched. He doubled over, and Gabriel cried out as he was dragged down too. Lucky let go of the braid and dropped down to his hands and knees, panting. An iron band constricted his chest, crushing his lungs. Sweat ran down his face and the world swayed in and out of focus.

'Talk to me,' Gabriel said softly. His hand lingered on Lucky's shoulder, a touch without pressure. 'What do you see? What are you afraid of?'

'I thought . . .' Lucky coughed, nausea swirling his stomach. 'I thought I saw something not real.'

'That's right. It's not real. What is real?'

Lucky dug his fingers into the wood. 'Th-the deck.' He pushed against it, solid and ungiving. Real.

'Keep going,' Gabriel urged.

'Waves,' Lucky said. 'The waves are real. My shirt.' The band around his chest eased. He took another breath, able to breathe in deeper now, fill his lungs. 'You.'

Gabriel settled down next to him. 'That's good. That's really good.'

Lucky kept his eyes closed, but he sat upright. The night breeze brushed the sweat from his face, making him shiver.

'I'm sorry,' Gabriel said. 'I pushed too hard. I shouldn't have done that.'

Lucky shook his head. 'It wasn't the sky. I . . . I have been seeing her again, the girl who killed my mother. She can't be here, but sometimes it feels so real, like she could reach right out and snatch me away too.'

Gabriel said nothing, but his shoulder brushed against Lucky's. Lucky leaned back and opened his eyes.

The sky rushed away from him, dragging his breath with it, but Lucky pushed his focus into the hard deck, the sound of the waves, the warmth of Gabriel's shoulder. His vision spun for a moment, and then slowly things came back into view. The tall mast, draped in fluttering sails, and above it, an arc of soft blackness, sprinkled with tiny white lights that sparkled like dewdrops in the sun.

'Hey,' Gabriel said softly, and Lucky realised he was crying.

'It is beautiful,' he said, wiping his eyes.

They sat in silence for a while, while Lucky drank in the view of stars for the first time he could remember. He had to keep closing his eyes when the expanse grew too much, but with the solid wood beneath him and Gabriel at his side, he could go back to it. It wouldn't drag him away, wouldn't swallow him up.

'How did you know?' Lucky asked.

'Hmm?'

'How did you know what to do?' he asked. 'How to bring me back?'

Gabriel stretched his arms out behind him, leaning back and looking up at the stars. 'That's down to my mother, really. When she found me, I was in a bad way. My father . . .' He swallowed and when he continued, it was with a noticeable tremor in his voice. 'My father had always been cruel when he was drunk. And my best friend, the one who helped take my mind off the beatings, left without saying goodbye. It only got worse after that. I tried to run away, and my father came after me. Put his hands around my neck and choked me. Mum saw us and she . . . she shot him dead, right there.'

'I . . .' Lucky started, but the words wouldn't come out.

Gabriel gave him a sad smile. 'Don't. We both know there aren't the words. But I know what it's like to see things that aren't real. To feel like you're back in a moment you can't escape. And I know it gets better.'

Lucky lifted his hand and let it rest against Gabriel's, their fingers brushing. At first, the touch was awkward, uncertain, and then Gabriel lifted his hand and settled it on Lucky's. And Lucky found he didn't hate that feeling.

'I meant what I said,' Gabriel said, 'about helping. You don't have to deal with it alone.'

'Thank you,' Lucky murmured. 'I'd like that.'

The wind picked up, making him shiver again, and the ship dipped and rose higher and faster on the waves. The motion made Lucky's stomach roll. He was about to suggest heading back into the ship, when a voice called out from above:

'Leviathan!'

Chapter Seven

Gabriel leapt up at the word and ran to the rail, leaning out over the waves. Lucky stood up and followed more slowly, struggling to keep his balance as the ship moved.

'Can't see it,' Gabriel muttered, peering out into the gloom.

'Make yourself useful and go fetch the captain,' the lookout called down.

'Oh, right. Yeah.' He turned to leave, then turned back to Lucky. 'Will you be all right here? Or do you want to come with me?'

'You go,' Lucky said, gripping the rail tightly. 'I'll be all right here.' Each little step gave him a bit more courage for the next one.

'I'll be back soon,' Gabriel said, before sprinting across the deck.

Lucky watched him for a moment, then turned back to the sea. The spray stung his eyes as he stared over the choppy water. As he squinted, he could make out something in the far distance, that at first looked like a wave, but moved differently to the others.

Leviathan, or trick of his mind?

Out there, whatever it was didn't seem threatening. Just a splash on the horizon. It was hard to correlate it with the vast, serpentine thing that had smashed a wall and eaten a man alive. He shuddered, pulling his arms around him.

Gabriel returned at a run, the captain following at a more sedate pace. She wore a loose-fitting shirt and slacks this time, rather than the blouse and jacket she'd worn the day before. Her hair was free from its braids and hung in spirals around her face.

Lucky wondered what Gabriel's hair looked like unbound.

She joined them at the rail without a glance at Lucky and raised a thin brass cylinder to her eye. After a moment, she handed it to Gabriel.

'What do you think?'

Gabriel's visible eye widened for a moment, and then he frowned, leaning out in the direction of the shape Lucky had spotted.

'It's . . . female, the same one that attacked the castle. Must be fifty feet long. Swimming fast on the surface. That's unusual for this time of day.'

'Good.' She took back the cylinder and Gabriel pushed out his chest. 'Course of action?'

'We should . . .' Gabriel started but stopped and bit his lip. 'We shouldn't get too close, not at night.'

The captain gave him a smile. 'You're learning. Maintain this position,' she called out to a sailor standing behind a large wooden wheel. 'Don't let it out of your sight. If it changes course or depth, fetch me immediately. We'll make a closer investigation at dawn, find out what happened at Ciatheme castle.' With that, she turned on her heel and strode back to her cabin, seemingly oblivious to the motion of the ship.

Gabriel watched her leave with a grin on his face. 'Hear that? She said good.' He clenched a hand into a fist.

'What's happening?' Lucky asked.

'We caught up with the leviathan that attacked the castle. We need to find out what happened, what caused it to behave like that. I've never heard of a leviathan acting that way.'

'Poe said they sink ships,' Lucky pointed out.

'That's different, isn't it?' he replied, shaking his head. 'Ships are in their territory. It's understandable. But striking at something on land, something like a castle?' He rubbed at his temple. 'It's a mystery and no mistake. But don't worry, we'll get to the bottom of it.'

Gabriel's easy confidence tugged at Lucky, who longed to believe that things would work out. But this was another mystery, like the girl, like his connection to Gabriel. All these questions swirling around him like a vortex.

He glanced at Gabriel leaning over the rail, straining to see the leviathan in the dark. Through the long, lonely time in the prison, the face had comforted him. But if he didn't remember, couldn't help Lucky understand, then there was a distance between them, one he could never explain.

When morning came, Lucky slipped out of the room without waiting for Gabriel. There was a tension in the air, like a thunderstorm, and it affected every inch of the ship, as if the *Dreamer* herself sensed something was going to happen. Today he'd try on his own to face the sky. Above him, voices shouted and called, excited. Nervous. He could make out Gabriel's voice amongst the others.

Lucky approached the stairs leading out on to the deck, the sky visible up ahead. At once, his stomach lurched, and he stumbled, clutching at the banister. His heart pounded in his ears. Stu-pid. Stu-pid. Stu-pid.

'We're ready, Captain.' That was Gabriel, and Lucky felt his heart settle at the sound.

Lucky forced himself to take a deep breath. He could do this. He had to do this. He dug his nails into the banister, and focused on the smoothness of the wood, worn by many hands before him.

Real.

He gritted his teeth and pushed on up the steps and out on to the deck. Even though the light was low and the sky cloudy, the difference from the gloom of below deck struck him like a slap to the face. He closed his eyes and his fists, pushing his feet down as if he could root himself into the wood.

'Out the way!'

Someone pushed past him, knocking him as they barged on to the deck. Lucky stumbled, everything twisting, unable to suppress a cry.

'Steady.' A hand nudged his shoulder, gently urging him upright. Lucky opened his eyes to see Captain Haven regarding him with a cool expression. 'Come to watch us tackle a leviathan?'

He forced himself to nod. She took her hand away slowly, as if concerned he might fall again.

'You don't have to be here,' Gabriel said, coming over. The captain gave Lucky one more glance, then turned away and began barking out orders.

'I want to.' Lucky forced himself to raise his gaze from the deck to the rail. This felt like a safe place – not looking up, not fully aware of the sky, but giving him enough vision to be aware of those around him. 'I don't think I could sleep knowing one of those things was nearby.'

The serpent swam ahead of the ship, its long body undulating along the surface, cutting through the water. It had a crest of deep green spines that started at the back of its head and ran all the way down the length of its wide, scaled body. The tail ended in a fin that shone as it caught the sun, changing from green to gold as it swayed.

'They're something, aren't they?' There was a note of almost fondness in his voice, as if he was speaking about something that wasn't a fifty-foot serpent. 'First time I saw one, it gave me nightmares for weeks. But they're not cruel. They don't hurt for the sake of it. They're not the real monsters out there.' He rubbed at his neck absently, then flashed Lucky a grin. 'They're actually pretty beautiful.'

'How do you know they won't attack the ship?'

'We won't take the ship close enough to make her feel threatened,' Gabriel replied.

'Then how—'

Gabriel gave him a wink. 'That's where I come in.'

'Approaching safe distance,' called the sailor at the wheel.

'Right,' the captain snapped. 'Drop anchor. No risks,' she added, turning to Gabriel. 'Just get close enough to take a look and see if anything's off. Maybe an injury or a parasite. No collection this time. We don't want to provoke it, especially after what happened. Ready?'

Gabriel turned to the others around him: Sienna and the red-headed twins Lucky had seen in the mess. 'You heard the captain. Let's go!'

Sienna said something Lucky couldn't make out, then all four ran to the side and dived overboard.

Lucky gasped and hurried over to the rail. He peered into grey-blue water, but there was no sign of Gabriel or the others. Not even ripples on the water. A chill gripped his insides. Where had they gone? The leviathan wasn't close enough to have consumed them, right?

He raised his gaze, tracing it across the water, until he saw them.

Four figures streaked across the waves, running across as if it were as solid as the deck. With each step, the water rose up and pushed them forwards, so they travelled at speeds impossible on land. As they moved further and further away from the ship, avoiding the sky became impossible. Lucky dug his fingernails into the rail, unable to tear his eyes away.

A wave surged towards them as the serpent turned. Lucky got his clearest look yet at a leviathan. The head was scaled, a mottled mixture of ivory and gold, with two immense, forward-facing eyes, each as tall as a human. Its jaws were squarish, the upper one larger than the lower one, and two fangs protruded, dripping seawater. Around the jaws, it had a beard of the same greenish frills it had on the top of its head.

The four water dancers – and Lucky understood the term now – reacted and split into two groups of two. The monster twisted its head, looking between them, and then turned after the twins. Lucky let out a sigh of relief.

Gabriel and Sienna approached the leviathan from behind, keeping pace as the thing struck out after the other dancers. They seemed to hover effortlessly above the water, hands and arms turning in a complex series of motions. The twins split apart, and again the serpent paused, trying to decide a target.

Gabriel pointed to something on the leviathan's neck. He made a gesture at Sienna, but she shook her head. Even at this distance, Gabriel's irritation was clear. He sliced his hand, spraying water at her, and the serpent turned. Gabriel floundered, pinned under the leviathan's gaze.

Lucky wanted to help, to throw himself into the water, but he couldn't command the waves. He'd sink like a stone. On deck, sailors watched, but none of them moved to take the ship closer. The captain stood near the wheel on a raised part of the ship, the brass cylinder to her eye, and her lip twisted in a snarl.

'Dammit, Gabe,' someone whispered behind him, and he turned to see the first mate.

'Do something!' he said, and she shook her head.

'Nothing we can do. We can't get any closer to the leviathan, or it will go for the ship, rip it to pieces, and drown every soul on board.' The cold horror in her voice told him this wasn't mere speculation.

He turned back to the rail, not wanting to watch his first friend in ten years get eaten, but unable to look away.

The leviathan opened its jaws and Lucky screamed out a warning. Then Sienna barrelled into Gabriel and they both disappeared under the waves. The serpent let out a furious sound, part roar, part shriek, and Lucky clamped his hands over his ears. It dove into the depths after them.

Lucky scanned the empty sea. The twins stood on the water nearby, looking confused and alarmed. He waited, his heart heavy in his ears, drowning out the sound of the waves, the murmurs from the crew, the mumbled chanting from the first mate next to him.

The sea boiled, then erupted, and Sienna and Gabriel shot into the air, followed by the leviathan. They hung in the air, drops of water spiralling around them, a sparkling halo around a tableau of horror.

Sienna pushed Gabriel away, twisting to the left as he fell to the right. He righted himself awkwardly, standing on one leg, arms pinwheeling. The serpent turned on him, but it was too close to twist itself fully to engulf him, and ended up smacking him with the side of its head.

Sienna, Cass, and Erin rushed into its line of sight, twisting around each other in an elaborate dance. The serpent let out another shriek and turned on them. They raced away from the ship and Gabriel, movements coordinated and beautiful.

On the surface, Gabriel picked himself up and shook himself, spraying water and sending his braid twisting.

'That's it, son,' said the first mate softly.

Gabriel set off after the leviathan. Lucky expected him to join in with the others, but he remained behind the monster, creeping up to its neck. He seemed focused on a spot behind its immense jaws. Lucky leaned out as far as he could, every muscle tense, fear sending tingles running up and down his body.

Then Gabriel put two fingers in his mouth and let out a piercing whistle. All four water dancers disappeared under the water.

Lucky held his breath as the serpent gazed about, then ducked under the water. It came up again further from the ship, peering around, and ducked under again. Behind Lucky came a rush of water, and the first mate rushed over to the other side of the deck. Lucky found it took him a moment to unlock his fingers from the rail before he could follow her.

The four water dancers stood on the deck, dripping and shivering. Each of them was breathing heavily, exhaustion clear on their faces. Someone handed out thick brown blankets, and the first mate offered Gabriel her shoulder to lean on. He shook his head and rested a hand on the rail behind him. The other hung limply at his side.

'Report,' the captain barked.

'Mel, let them rest a minute,' the first mate said quietly, but the captain shook her head.

'It's fine, Ma.' Gabriel took a deep breath and stood up straighter. 'I found something on the leviathan, but it doesn't make any sense. Someone marked it.'

'Marked, like a scar? Was it from a fight with a ship, or maybe from prey?' she asked, and he shook his head again.

'It wasn't a scar.' He sounded sick. 'It wasn't a scar, it was a brand. Someone burned the image of a bird on to that leviathan's neck.'

Chapter Eight

The assembled crew broke out into astonished chatter at Gabriel's words. Some stared out to sea, trying to catch another glimpse of the leviathan. Others bombarded Gabriel with questions.

'Quiet!' Captain Haven barked, and the noise dropped away. She turned to her son. 'You're sure, Gabe? You took a heavy blow from the leviathan.'

'I didn't imagine it,' he protested.

'I saw it too,' Sienna put in and Gabriel gave her a grateful smile.

He sagged slightly, gripping the rail again. The first mate straightened the blanket around his shoulders.

'I believe you,' Captain Haven continued. 'But it doesn't make any sense. I don't know how to begin going about branding a leviathan, let alone why anyone would want to do it. With what happened three days ago, I don't think we can ignore this. Set a course for Sea Hall. Let's bring this to the council's attention.' She turned away, then called over her shoulder, 'Gabriel, with me. We need to discuss what happened out there.'

His face flushed. 'What? No. No, you are not chewing me out because Sienna refused my order.'

The captain turned on him, her eyes flashing. 'Do you really want to do this out here in front of everyone, Gabriel? Because we can.'

He looked away.

'That's what I thought. What are the rest of you waiting for? Get this ship turned around!' With that, she strode off.

Sienna gave Gabriel a concerned look, then hurried below deck before he could say or do anything. Gabriel took a deep breath, then let the blanket fall and flicked the water off himself with a hand gesture. He headed slowly after the captain, muttering to himself. Lucky watched him leave, unsure what to do or say.

'If you sit on the third step to the quarterdeck, it's amazing what you can hear,' the first mate whispered in his ear. He turned to her in surprise, and she gave him a sad smile. 'He's going to need a friend today.'

She patted his shoulder before heading off. Lucky had no idea what a quarterdeck was, but he remembered where she'd been sitting the day he'd first met the captain, and headed over.

He climbed to the third step and sat down. Voices floated up, muffled, but given the volume of the speakers, he had no issues making out the words.

'You promised me.' That was Gabriel. Lucky could picture him, fists clenched, shoulders bowed. 'You promised me I could lead that job to investigate the leviathan.'

'And I kept my word.' The captain sounded more tired than angry now. 'I let you lead. But you messed up, Gabe. And I can't afford that. People die in those circumstances.'

'I didn't! Sienna refused an order.'

'And she was right to. You were supposed to observe, not get close enough to get smacked. I know what this means to you. I know how much you care about the leviathans, want to study them.' She sighed, and the sound of liquid being poured filled the space in their silence. 'Here.'

'I don't want it.'

'You're refusing coffee now?' The captain laughed. 'You really are mad at me.'

'Because you don't believe in me.'

Another sigh, and the creak of a chair being sat on. 'I do believe in you. I also believe you're young and hot-headed. There's time, Gabriel. Time to learn and do it right. You're an excellent dancer and you'll make a good captain one day. But only if you stop rushing in headlong. You don't need to keep pushing yourself.'

'You never wanted me to learn in the first place.'

Even from outside, Lucky felt the temperature of the room drop.

'No, I didn't. I didn't want you to risk yourself. I didn't want to sit there for days wondering if my son was ever going to open his eyes again. And I didn't want you to pay the price. But you didn't listen to me.'

'I can do it, when it comes,' Gabriel said sullenly. 'I chose my price carefully. I'm strong enough to deal with it when it happens.'

'It's not about strength!' she shouted back. 'You have no idea what it's going to do to you and neither do I. And now I can't stop it. I just have to sit here and wait, knowing someone I love is going to face some incredible pain and there is nothing I can do to change it.' The chair creaked again. 'Get out, Gabe. Just go.'

Lucky scrambled to his feet as the door to the captain's cabin slammed shut. He caught up with Gabriel at the steps to the deck.

'I'm guessing Ma told you how to eavesdrop,' Gabriel said without turning around.

'She said you'd need a friend,' Lucky said.

Gabriel sagged. 'Yeah, I think I do.'

Instead of turning towards the cell – despite Gabriel's words, Lucky couldn't break that habit – Gabriel turned towards the galley. Poe took one look at them as they entered and poured two cups of steaming liquid.

'You can start work when you're done with that,' he told Lucky.

They took a seat at one of the tables in the mess. The room was mercifully empty, and Lucky suspected Gabriel also appreciated it.

'Is there something wrong with your arm?' Lucky asked as Gabriel picked up his cup. It hung limp at his side, and he'd made no attempt to move it since returning to the ship.

He gave it a dismissive glance. 'Probably got a massive bruise building, but it doesn't hurt. It literally doesn't. I got coated in enough leviathan slime that I won't be able to even feel it for hours.'

Lucky thought of the monster slamming into Gabriel and shuddered. 'What did she mean, pay the price? Poe said something like that, too.'

Gabriel took a drink of coffee. For a moment, Lucky wondered if Gabriel had not heard him, and was about to ask again, when Gabriel set the cup down with a sigh.

'To be granted the powers of a water dancer, you have to go to the shrine to Promise at Sea Hall. It's underwater most of the time, only revealed once a year when the tides are right. There you promise something. A sacrifice. If it's considered worthy enough, and if you're strong enough to survive the process, then you gain the abilities. The price is taken from you sometime later in life. Might be a week, might be a day, but for most, it's decades down the line.'

'And there's no way to avoid it?'

Gabriel shrugged his good shoulder. 'You can't outrun a promise.'

'What . . .' Lucky swallowed, his throat dry. 'What did you promise?'

'Not polite to ask, mate.' He waggled a finger at Lucky. 'Sorry, but everyone's sacrifice is personal. It's not fatal, though, despite the way my mother behaves. I offered something I can accept losing. Poe offered up his leg, and he's fine.'

Lucky glanced over his shoulder at the cook stomping around, his uneven footsteps echoing in the galley.

'I just want her to respect me,' he said in a small voice. Gabriel rubbed his temple, looking tired, worn. 'We've been fighting so much this year, and I hate it. She wants to protect me, I know. But I'm not a child anymore. I'm not who I was when she found me. I want to use what she's taught me. I want to help.'

'You helped me,' Lucky said softly. His face burned, and he took a sip of coffee to cover his embarrassment. The liquid was still bitter, but there was something comforting about that mixture of bitter and warmth.

'I suppose I did.' Gabriel rubbed at his shoulder. 'I . . . My mother – my birth mother, that is – died when I was very little. They didn't have medicine, you see. Maybe . . . maybe if there had been a better supply, maybe she would have had a chance. Maybe my father . . .' He sniffed. 'Maybe things would have been different.'

Lucky stretched his fingers out on the table so they just brushed against Gabriel's hand.

'Do you want things to have been different?'

Gabriel's eyes widened. 'That's a question.' His hand tightened around the cup. 'It would have been nice to not have my father try to kill me, got to admit. But then I'd never have met my mothers, and I'd never have ended up on the *Dreamer*. Maybe never met you. So . . . I don't know, is the honest answer.'

'That's fair.'

'What about you?' He watched Lucky over the top of the coffee cup.

Lucky took another sip. 'I think . . . I think the same as you. I don't know. Maybe things would be better. Maybe they would be much worse. Who can say?'

Gabriel held out his cup and knocked it against Lucky's with a soft chink. 'Who can say?'

'Need a hand in the kitchen,' Poe called. They both stood up and Poe shook his head. 'Not you, Gabe. Go and rest, before your mam yells at the pair of us.'

'I'm fine,' Gabriel muttered.

'Sure, but you're not going to be much help to anyone until you get the feeling back in your fingers. Besides, Lucky and I have got it covered, haven't we?'

'Go and rest,' Lucky told him. 'I'm fine here.' He wanted to offer Gabriel that same gentle comfort and care he'd given when Lucky was hurting, but he didn't know how to help with leviathan-induced numbness. He could do this, though.

'I see how it is,' Gabriel said, shaking a finger at Lucky. His eyes crinkled with a barely contained smile. 'Ganging up on me when I'm hurt and vulnerable. All right, all right, I'm going.' He finished the coffee and headed off while Lucky hurried to the kitchen.

'What do you need help with?' he asked.

Poe pointed to a stack of vegetables. 'You could peel and chop those for me. But first, tell me what you think of this?' He pushed a little bowl over.

Lucky looked down at the contents – stewed fruits, still steaming from the pan. He took a tentative taste. It was sharp yet sweet, flavoured with something warm and woody. Poe raised an eyebrow.

'It's . . . good.'

'Yeah? Not too sweet, not too sour? Enough cinnamon?'

'I . . . I think so.' He took another small taste and Poe laughed.

'Eat it up, it's yours.'

Poe turned back to the fish he was skinning, humming to himself. Lucky finished, then busied himself peeling and chopping, enjoying the lingering taste of fruit on his tongue. He'd made his way through most of the vegetables when a long piercing whistle filled the air, followed by three short blows. Poe laid his knife down carefully.

'Stay here, lad,' he murmured.

'What's going on?' Lucky asked, his heart hammering. 'Is it another leviathan?'

'We should be so lucky,' Poe grumbled. 'Don't worry yourself about it. I'm sure it's fine.'

Lucky started after him. 'Please. What's happening?'

'Sorry.' Poe stopped in the doorway and gave him a sympathetic look. 'It's no fun being in the dark, is it? The long whistle means sail spotted. The three short ones mean it's a church vessel. And that could be a problem.'

'Have they come for me?' He hugged his arms around himself, a chill running down his spine. He thought of the guards, who shouted and hit and never believed him.

'Could be,' Poe said. He put a hand on Lucky's shoulder. 'But the captain won't hand you over. That's not how Mel works. She might act cold, but she'd put her life on the line for this ship and everyone aboard.'

Lucky leaned against the cook, breathing in the scent of cinnamon and stewed apples, fear turning his legs to jelly. 'I don't want anyone hurt because of me. I . . . I don't deserve it.'

'Let us be the judge of that,' Poe said firmly. 'Besides, everyone on this ship has a reason to hate the church, so it's not all about you. You should stay down here, though. Hide in a cupboard. Just in case.'

Four walls. Small. Safe.

'No.' Lucky shook his head. 'I don't want to hide away anymore.'

Poe frowned, but Lucky stood up straight and squared his shoulders. Poe sighed. 'Come on, then. But we're staying out of sight at least.'

Lucky followed Poe out of the kitchen and over to the stairs leading up to the deck. The crew were assembled on the deck, with the captain and first mate closest to the rail. Behind them stood Cass, Erin, and Sienna. Lucky glanced around the crew and spotted Gabriel towards the back.

From his vantage point, he could see another ship approaching. This one was a little smaller than the *Dreamer*, but armed with numerous cannons. The sails were decorated with the same lattice threads that had adorned the guards' tabards and his breath hitched in his throat as he stared at them. He pressed his palm against the wall, grounding himself on the feeling of the wood beneath his skin.

On the top of the mainmast, a black triangular flag flew. It had a symbol stitched on to it that looked like a long flat wooden sword with a rounded end.

'Beaters,' Poe said gruffly. 'The church's enforcers.'

On the Beaters' ship, a figure in black clothes stepped forwards. 'Hail, the *Dreamer*,' he called, his voice warm and cheerful. It didn't match his face, though, which bore a barely concealed sneer. 'Permission to come aboard.'

'Permission denied,' Captain Haven called back and he shook his head sadly.

'Ah, that's a shame, because I wasn't really asking. My name is Yale, of the Beaters, and I'm here looking for a missing prisoner. Your vessel was seen in the vicinity of Ciatheme castle, where the prisoner escaped.'

Lucky cowered down, his heart rattling in his ears. Poe put an arm around his shoulders.

'Wouldn't know anything about that,' she replied with a shrug. 'It's fate who is supposed to know everything. Our business is with the leviathans. Speaking of which, you should be aware there's a particularly bad-tempered one out here. Would hate to offend you by saving you with our heretical powers.'

There were sniggers and jeers from the assembled crew.

'Let's not make this difficult, Captain,' Yale said, as if talking down to an obstreperous child. 'Let me and my team have a look on your ship. If you haven't done anything wrong, then you've nothing to fear.' His voice was calm, reasonable. Lucky held his breath, waiting for the captain to seal his fate.

'You have no jurisdiction here,' Captain Haven said. 'You can threaten us, but the sea is our home and she responds to us. You're an interloper here, and you know it.'

'It seems we're at an impasse then.'

He folded his arms, staring down the captain. Lucky thought about the cannons, thought about them ripping into the ship. Tearing apart this home. He closed his eyes and bit back a sob.

'I should go up there,' he said to Poe. 'It isn't right. I can't let you all get hurt because of me. I'm going—'

A bell rang out on the Beater ship, cutting him off.

'Leviathan!' someone called. Yale glared at Captain Haven and rushed over to the other side of the ship. He came striding back a few moments later, a scowl on his face.

'This isn't over, Captain. You'll be seeing me again.'

'I look forward to it,' she replied with a cold smile. The two ships peeled away from each other, and Lucky slumped down against the steps, shaking.

'See,' Poe said softly. 'I told you, you're safe here.'

'How did she know?' Lucky asked. The relief had turned his whole body to water, and he didn't think he could stand. 'How did the captain know about the leviathan?'

'Hmm? Oh, I don't think she did. I think we got lucky there.' Poe grinned. 'Maybe you're a good omen.'

Chapter Nine

After that, things settled down into a kind of routine – not as fixed and sparse as the one he was used to, but a routine nevertheless. Every morning, Gabriel would bring him breakfast, and then he'd be passed on to one of the crew. For the first few days, it was Poe, and Lucky learned the basics of cooking. But as the days passed, and his confidence grew a little more, he worked with others. He learned how to mend a sail and tie a dozen types of knots. He learned the various parts of the ship, from the quarterdeck at one end to the bowsprit at the other. The quartermaster taught him how to do the inventory in the hull, marking the walls and the ledger.

He had the feeling he wasn't the first to be brought on like this. Some, maybe most of the crew, were career sailors, but given what Poe had said about misfits and weirdos some had been through this ritual.

It was hard – so much information fell through his mind like water through fingers. And sometimes the noise or the space grew too much, and he'd have to retreat. But there didn't seem to be any judgement from the crew, at least not to him directly, and he went to bed each night exhausted but satisfied.

He declined the mess for meals, though, preferring the peace of his cell after a busy day. And he found he liked the opportunity to spend time with Gabriel alone, too.

In those moments he had to himself, he sketched with the chalk all the things that stood out to him. Dolphins, leaping out of the water at sunset. A long thin fish someone had caught one day on a line, its mouth full of tiny, needle-like teeth.

Gabriel riding the waves.

He'd gone over the spoon-made indents with the chalk, and added to the image, making it dynamic. It occupied most of the wall, but he hung a blanket over it when he wasn't working on it. He couldn't quite say why – it wasn't like he thought it was bad, or he was ashamed in any way. He told himself Gabriel would find it weird to eat beside an image of himself. But looking at it set off a strange sensation in Lucky's chest, too.

Around three weeks after the day Gabriel pulled him out of the sea, he burst into the cell without any breakfast. Lucky, still lying on the blankets, raised his head in surprise.

'Come on, get up!' Gabriel urged.

Lucky groaned and pulled on his clothes. 'How much coffee have you had already?'

'None.'

'Who are you, and where's Gabriel?' he teased and Gabriel grinned.

'Plenty of time for coffee later. You've got to see this.' He bounced on his heels at the door, and Lucky wasn't sure he believed a word about no coffee. Lucky followed him up on to the deck and took a breath.

The coastline was visible off the bow of the ship. Lucky hadn't seen dry land in weeks, and somehow the sight of cliffs and trees and buildings seemed stranger to him than the open sea. Gabriel rushed up to the prow, earning a glare from one of the sailors who was working, and leaned out over the water.

'Sea Hall,' he said, pointing ahead. Lucky followed his gaze and saw a huge wooden gate set over the water ahead. On the side of the gate was an immense statue, twenty feet high, wearing long, flowing robes, carved beautifully by the artist as if they were flapping around her in the wind. She held one hand out to the sea, and the other above her head. She'd been painted at one time, and traces of colour remained in the shadowed crevices, but now she was mostly a pale alabaster. The tips of her sandalled toes had worn away, and spidery cracks marred one ankle.

As the *Dreamer* approached, the gates swung outwards across the waves, making a creaking, groaning sound as if they were in pain.

'I'm looking forward to getting some time on land,' Gabriel said. 'Gonna eat a whole load of things that aren't fish. Gonna check out the markets. Gonna get drunk.'

'Drunk?'

Gabriel's grin grew. 'Allow me to introduce you to the wonders of the port-side inn.'

Lucky shrugged, trusting in Gabriel.

The sailors guided the ship through the great gates and into a wide harbour, where the waters were still and calm. The *Dreamer* pulled up and ropes were tossed down to those waiting on the wooden docks. Once she was secured, the captain stepped into the middle of the deck.

'Lots for shore leave,' she called, gesturing to the first mate, who held a cup full of thin sticks. One by one, each of the sailors chose from the cup. Those who had a black mark on the end cheered, while those who had plain sticks looked sullen. Gabriel approached and Lucky followed, not sure if this ritual applied to him or not.

Gabriel closed his eyes, his hand hovering over the sticks.

'You can't tell, Gabe,' the first mate said with a laugh. 'It's all random.'

'Haven't been wrong yet,' he replied and plucked out a stick with a flourish. 'Hah! See?'

He stepped aside and Lucky reached out, but the first mate shook her head.

'It's your first time. Everyone gets their first time for free.' She leaned in close. 'Make sure he behaves himself, would you?'

'I will,' Lucky said, but he wasn't sure he could stop Gabriel doing anything he wanted. They filed towards the gangplank past the quartermaster, who handed each sailor a pile of coins. She held out a stack to Lucky, who stared at them.

'Your wages,' she said, raising an eyebrow.

'You worked, mate, therefore you get paid,' Gabriel said, pocketing his own coins. 'Come on, we've got spending to do!'

When they reached the bottom of the gangplank, the captain was waiting for them. Gabriel held up a hand.

'I know, I know. I promise to behave.'

She rolled her eyes. 'You're a grown-up, I'm not going to lecture you. Not that it ever did the blindest bit of good. I wanted you to come with me to the council.'

Gabriel's eyes lit up. 'Really?'

'You want to be a captain one day, you want to know more about the running of things, then this is a good place to be. I warn you, it's probably going to bore your socks off, but I thought I'd offer.'

'Thanks, Mum. Oh, what about Lucky?'

'Bring him along too. Probably better for him than getting lost or pickpocketed on his first shore leave.'

'What do you say?' Gabriel asked. 'Want to come along and see what the council have to make of the leviathan situation?'

Lucky shrugged. He didn't want to be separated from Gabriel. The town was noisy, full of people milling around, shouting, calling. Strange scents filled the air, some pleasant, most unpleasant. Streets led off the main harbour in multiple directions, going to places unknown.

'Right, that's settled then.' Gabriel put his hand gently on Lucky's shoulder, his touch light and unthreatening. 'Let's go.'

The captain led them up a steep street, away from the water. Unlike down on the harbour, where most of the buildings appeared to have their doors open, and signs hanging above them, these were all closed, no goods or signs. Houses, Lucky told himself. People lived there. A memory tickled the back of his mind, of being small and knocking excitedly on a red door.

By the time they reached the top of the hill, Lucky's legs ached and he was breathing heavily. Neither Gabriel nor the captain seemed bothered. He leaned heavily against the side of a building, trying to force more air into his lungs. A stitch pinched at his side.

'Anytime I played up when we were in town, Mum made me run up this hill,' Gabriel said.

'I seem to remember that was pretty frequently,' the captain replied dryly.

'At least once a visit for a few years,' Gabriel agreed with a shameless grin.

When Lucky recovered – or at least enough that he didn't think his legs would collapse under him – they rounded the corner and came out on a wide courtyard. It was flat and open, paved with pale flagstones that reflected back the sky. Lucky shrank back.

'It's fine,' Gabriel said in his ear. 'Nothing's going to happen to you.'

Lucky breathed out. Working on the ship had eased the fears of falling into the sky, but even knowing it was irrational, he couldn't shake the feeling entirely, the swooping stomach and pounding heart.

The captain was already striding across the courtyard, and Lucky could see from Gabriel's jittery motions that he longed to join her. But he stayed with Lucky, close enough to touch if needed without pressing in. Lucky pushed down another breath and nodded again.

'Let's go.'

The courtyard had a low stone wall which gave views of the harbour and the sea down below. Lucky glanced over the waves, but there was no sign of leviathans out there. Around the edge of the courtyard were statues of men and women, much smaller than those at the harbour gates, barely larger than human.

'Old council leaders,' Gabriel said as Lucky peered at one. 'Boring.'

On the far side of the courtyard was a stone building. It was wide and low, only one storey, but it had an elaborate sloping roof that reminded him of two ships passing each other. It was covered in grey slate in neatly fitting lines, and at each peak was a stone leviathan head, as if the creatures were swimming away and pulling the roof up with them. As he got closer, he could see the stone of the building was carved, decorated with images of the sea – ships, fish, leviathans, seabirds.

He approached a panel showing a fleet of vessels, running a finger over the images. 'It's beautiful.'

'I guess.' Gabriel shrugged. 'Sorry, it loses a bit of its wonder after the fiftieth time you've been here. Your art is better.'

Lucky's face flushed and Gabriel laughed.

Inside, they found themselves in a large, open anteroom. Wooden pillars, carved with small birds – not like the seabirds that followed the ship – held up the ceiling. Solid wooden doors, marked with iron in abstract patterns, stood to his left, right, and straight ahead. A few people milled around, some dressed like the captain in shirts and long jackets, others more like the statues in long flowing robes of muted greens, blues, and reds.

'The council are convening in an hour,' the captain said, startling Lucky from his observations. 'I'm going to go and speak to a few people. Keep yourselves out of trouble until then.' She flicked Gabriel a coin.

'This way,' Gabriel said as the captain walked off, her heels clicking on the tiles. He pushed open the door on the left, which took them to a space like the ship's mess, only bigger and brighter. Huge windows on the far side of the room offered a view of the sea, which seemed to be the most popular place to sit. Lucky moved towards a table closer to the door.

'Hungry?' Gabriel called, heading towards a big counter. A woman in a short dark jacket stood behind it, her jet-black hair arranged in an artful style on her head, pinned back with a silk flower. Behind her, a huge array of bottles covered the shelves, filled with liquids in a range of colours. And on the counter in front of her, a selection of little parcels, some round, some square, some like delicate twists. Gabriel pointed to a few and handed over the coin. He returned with two cups of coffee.

'Council all drink tea,' he said, pulling a face. 'Tea is a coward's drink.'

Lucky frowned, not understanding at all.

After a few minutes, the woman walked over with a little wooden box which she set on the table. Gabriel opened the lid and there were the parcels he'd selected, glistening and steaming.

'Breakfast,' he announced with a flourish.

Lucky couldn't identify any of the flavours – much as Poe tried to teach him, he'd never been able to get his head around what went with what. He wanted to learn, though, wanted to understand how to bring people happiness through food. The little parcels were disappearing quickly, and Gabriel called for more coffee.

'You're not going to be able to sit still,' Lucky said, and Gabriel scowled.

'I get enough of that from Ma. I'm not taking it from you.'

'Sorry.' Lucky flushed, and Gabriel's eyes widened.

'No, me, too. I didn't mean to snap. I'm just fed up with having all my actions judged, but I guess that's what happens when your mothers run the ship.'

'Who is the statue on the gates?' Lucky asked, to change the subject. 'The great big one.'

'She's Promise,' Gabriel replied, his hand hovering over the steaming parcels. 'She's the goddess of the shrine, the one who helps humanity break away from the conformity of fate. Sea Hall operates under maritime law, unlike most of the country. The church doesn't like it much, but the leviathans mean they have to grudgingly accept the presence of water dancers – on the sea, at least.' He selected a pale pink dumpling, shaped like a cockle shell. 'You don't remember anything of this?'

'I don't really remember much,' Lucky replied. 'I remember my mother dying, and I have flashes of other memories. I think I played on a beach as a child. But most of it's gone. I guess I didn't need that part of me when I was locked up.'

'That's rough.' Gabriel rubbed his neck. 'I remember too much sometimes.'

An uneasy quiet settled over them, until the woman brought over fresh cups of coffee.

'Are there other shrines?' Lucky asked. 'Can you be something other than a water dancer?'

'As far as anyone knows, this is the only shrine,' Gabriel replied. 'I suspect if the church of fate ever found any others, they'd destroy them. And water dancer is the only option. But that's really to be expected. Promise is represented by water, by change. The dancers are an embodiment of that.'

Lucky picked up a dumpling, warm and soft between his fingers. He held it, enjoying the sensation. 'If you don't know what anyone's offered, what happens if two people promise the same thing?'

'You should be a priest,' Gabriel replied with a shrug. 'They love that sort of question.'

Talk turned to the ship, leviathans, the crew. Gabriel's rivalry with Sienna.

'She thinks I'm just riding on my mothers' coat-tails,' he complained. 'But Mum never wanted me to get the powers in the first place. She forbade it. I had to sneak off the ship to the shrine. And Sienna knows this. She's just being an arse for the sake of it.'

Lucky smothered a grin at Gabriel's vehemence. 'What happens at the shrine? Does it hurt, when you gain the powers?'

'So many questions,' Gabriel teased. Lucky lowered his gaze. 'Hey, it's fine. I like talking with you. The shrine is set in the cliffs on the other side of the hall, and is only accessible once a year. You have to walk down the cliff path and enter the cave. Then there's this long passage, which takes you to a statue of Promise at the end. You touch her hand and say your sacrifice; that's it. It felt like being punched in the gut.' He winced, as if reliving the memory. 'After that, things are a bit of a blur. The process takes it out of you, and apparently I had a fever for five days. I woke up and Mum spent the next day yelling at me and hugging me in turn.'

'Sounds like she loves you,' Lucky said softly. He thought of his own mother, wondering what type of parent she'd been. Had he loved her? Who would he have been if he'd been able to save her? Who could he be when he found the girl, got his revenge?

The girl's smile filled his mind. He felt the sensation of the rock on his fingers, still slick with his mother's blood.

'Hey.' Gabriel's fingertips brushed against his. 'Whatever it is, it's not real, remember?'

Not real. He remembered Gabriel's technique that night on the deck, and pushed his focus on to things he could trust. The solid table, and the coffee cup, still warm. Gabriel's touch.

'I'm all right,' he said, the roughness of his voice betraying him.

Before Gabriel could respond, the captain strode into the room.

'Ready?' she asked. Gabriel swallowed the last of his coffee and stood.

They followed her to the room opposite the entrance. The doors stood open currently, and people filed in. The room ahead was octagonal, with banks of seats that sloped down towards a central stage. The light came in from a series of skylights, illuminating the table and seats in the middle.

The captain led them to seats facing the front of the stage, about halfway down from the door. The room could clearly hold a couple of hundred people, but Lucky estimated that there were less than fifty in there at the moment. People shuffled and coughed, draping a tapestry of soft sounds over the place.

A bell rang out, cutting the threads into silence.

'Stand for the council,' a voice called out, and the assembled group got to their feet. Six people walked down the steps to the stage. They all wore robes of blue-green, which reminded Lucky of the sea, and appeared to be older, their hair greying or missing entirely. One walked with the same rhythm as Poe, which suggested a wooden leg concealed by their garment. Another had blank eyes and was helped down the steps by a younger person in a grey robe. They settled in their seats, and, without a signal this time, everyone else reseated themselves.

The captain had not been wrong about the proceedings being dull. Lucky tried to listen, but much of the language was related to ships and sailing and went straight over his head. Or they spoke of people and places he had never heard of. Beside him, Gabriel fidgeted in his seat, playing with the end of his braid, while the captain looked as if she was trying to resist snapping at him.

'Captain Haven?' one of the council members called out, looking around the room. 'I believe you wished to speak.'

The captain stood in a smooth motion. She addressed the council and explained about the leviathan they'd come across, occasionally conferring with Gabriel over details. If the quiet was anything to go by, the room was listening with a much greater intensity than they had been for other speakers.

'And you say you'd been pursuing this serpent after an attack?' one of the councillors asked and she nodded.

'When we first caught up with it, it was attacking the old castle at Ciatheme. We managed to attract its attention and draw it away. Once distracted, it left and headed out to the deep sea.'

One of the other councillors whispered something to him. 'Yes, we were aware of the attack, but not the full details. Captain Thomas, I believe you have a similar story?'

A man with thick blond hair and a full beard stood up. 'Yeah. I don't know if it attacked anything, but we encountered one with a similar brand. We didn't realise what the image was at the time, but now you've said it, it could well have been a bird.'

Murmurs bubbled up from the assembly.

'Are you trying to say someone's been branding leviathans?' someone called from the other side of the room. Lucky peered around Gabriel to see a burly man in a deep purple jacket get to his feet. 'Why would anyone do that? How would anyone do that? You must be mistaken.'

'We don't know if it's deliberate or something else is going on,' Captain Haven said, keeping her tone reasonable. Her hand hovered near Gabriel's shoulder. 'We're merely collecting information here.'

Another captain announced they, too, had seen a leviathan with the strange wound. But no one else reported any attacks on buildings.

'The events at Ciatheme might simply be a coincidence,' the councillor said, and Gabriel scoffed.

'Doubt it.'

The voices in the chamber rose, and the councillor called for quiet.

'Captain Haven. The council request that you return to Ciatheme and conduct an investigation of the events around the attack. See what people remember, and report back. The rest of you are obligated to keep an eye out for more strange behaviour and more of these markings. Perhaps this is nothing, and we are clutching at water, but I believe this warrants investigation.'

Lucky shivered at the thought of going back there, and Gabriel brushed a hand against his. Lucky looked up and Gabriel met his gaze. He didn't say anything, but the word 'safe' was written in his reassuring expression.

There was another speaker after this, but it was clear even the council had little attention left to give him, and he cut off his speech. The council stood and left, and the rest of the room filed out after them.

Captain Haven was one of the last to move, waiting until the chamber was almost empty. As they approached the doorway to the atrium, the blond captain turned back and approached them.

'Captain Haven, a word?'

'Captain Thomas,' she greeted him. 'Of course.'

'I wanted to compare notes on the wound you saw.'

'Gabriel can probably tell you more,' she said, gesturing to her son. 'He was the one closest to the beast.'

'Sure,' Gabriel agreed, drawing himself up. 'Do you want to come with us?' he asked, but Lucky shook his head. The two cups of coffee he'd drunk earlier weighed heavy in his bladder, and he headed outside. Behind the building, he found a patch of scrubby shrubs out of sight and relieved himself.

As he was tying up his trousers again, there was a strange, low rumbling sound, like several heavily loaded carts were trundling towards him. Afraid someone had caught him out here, that the guards were going to punish him, he looked around.

But there were no carts.

No guards.

Lucky gave a nervous laugh. Of course there were no guards, not here. This was Sea Hall, and neither the guards nor the church had any powers here. He was safe. He wondered if he'd ever truly believe that.

The ground shook.

Lucky was thrown to the hard stone floor, as the ground around him trembled with a shuddering motion. He dug his fingers down, trying to hold on, trying not to get shaken up into the sky.

Then, just as quickly as it started, the shaking stopped. Lucky couldn't bring himself to move. His fingers ached from clinging on.

Was it real?

They told him on the ship it was impossible for the sky to suck him up, but what was that? His heart was racing and so was his mind, and the speed of both left him feeling sick and dizzy.

Lucky couldn't breathe. A drumbeat pounded in his ears, and his chest seized, refusing to let in air. He clutched at his shirt, gasping and wheezing.

A stone dug into his knee and anew pain flared from the impact. Lucky clung to it. *Real.* Above him, a seagull shrieked. *Real.* In front of him, a pebble, smooth and oval and marked with white lines. He held it in his fist. *Real.*

'Lucky!'

The sound of Gabriel's voice gave him the strength to lift his head. His thundering heart started to slow. His throat was raw, but he managed to call out in a scratchy voice. Gabriel and Captain Haven appeared at the entrance to the courtyard and Gabriel hurried to his side.

'There you are. I was so worried when I couldn't find you. Are you hurt?'

Lucky pulled himself into a sitting position, keeping a grip on the ground just in case. 'I'm not hurt.' He looked up at Gabriel. 'What about you?'

'All good here. Everyone's a bit dazed, but I don't think there was any real damage.'

'Wh-what happened?' Lucky asked, his voice as tremulous as the ground had been.

'Earthshake,' Captain Haven said. She offered Lucky her hand and he allowed her to help him to his feet.

'Are . . . are they common here?'

She shook her head. 'I've never heard of one happening here. Ever.'

Chapter Ten

Captain Haven studied a crack in the ground, muttering to herself. Gabriel peered at Lucky, his frown deepening. 'Are you sure you're all right? You're really pale.'

Lucky ducked his gaze. He didn't want to think about the ground shaking or the sky or why these things were suddenly happening around him.

'Everything's just too big right now,' he mumbled.

Gabriel gave him a sympathetic smile. 'Come on, then. Let's head down into town. I'll show you the sights.' He turned to his mother. 'If you're done with us?'

'Yes. Go on, have fun. I'll help tidy up here. But we sail on the morning tide so don't come back too late or too drunk. And I'm not paying your jail fines again, you hear me?'

'That was one time!' Gabriel called back. 'Honestly, she never lets me live it down. Wasn't even my fault. I just picked up the wrong purse. The guy was salty because I beat him at dice when he thought I was an easy target.'

Lucky followed after him down the steep road as Gabriel grumbled to himself. Once they reached the bottom, Gabriel launched into a walking tour of the city.

He had an opinion on every inn, and most of the shopkeepers seemed to know him by name. Almost every street they walked down came with an anecdote of something that had happened to him or another crew member. The earthshake didn't seem to have affected the lower town much. People had heard sounds, felt a brief shudder, but nothing as dramatic as Lucky had experienced.

By the time they'd reached the harbour again, Lucky's feet ached and his mind buzzed with information. They sat on a wall watching the ships, eating battered crab dressed with a spicy sauce that made his lips tingle, all wrapped up in a flat round of bread.

'There's a whole world out there,' Lucky said suddenly. 'I don't know any of it.'

Gabriel shoved the last of his lunch into his mouth and chewed quickly. 'Stay on the ship and you'll get to see all of it.' He gave Lucky a concerned look. 'You are planning on staying on the ship, right?'

'I have to go back to Ciatheme. I have to at least try and find out what happened. But . . .' He leaned back, watching a bird soar overhead. 'Maybe . . . afterwards. I'm getting used to it. I like helping Poe. And I have my own cell . . . my own room.'

'You know it's a store cupboard, right?' Gabriel asked with a grin. 'Most of us sleep in the bunk room, or out on deck if it's nice.'

'It's mine,' Lucky replied. The concept of things that were his was new to him, and suddenly he wanted more. He fingered the coins in his pocket. 'I want . . . something else that's mine.'

Gabriel raised an eyebrow. 'What do you mean?'

'I don't know. I just want to buy something. Something I can keep.'

'Ah, first wages burning a hole in your pocket?' Gabriel gave him a wink. 'I understand. What do you fancy? Clothes, jewellery, tattoo?'

'I guess I'll know it when I see it.'

Gabriel leapt to his feet. 'Let's go shopping then.'

As Lucky got to his feet, he almost said no and sat down again. But Gabriel's enthusiasm was compelling, and he soon forgot the pain as they peered at shops and stalls. He turned down silk bandanas, glass bangles, leather belts marked with designs of leviathans. Nothing quite felt right.

After what had to be a couple of hours of walking, poking, and rejecting Gabriel's suggestions, Lucky was ready to pack it in.

'Let's walk down to the harbour and find dinner,' Gabriel suggested, and Lucky tried hard not to let the disappointment show on his face. 'You can buy me a drink. Maybe that's all you need?'

Lucky glared at him and Gabriel laughed. Lucky wanted to trap the sound in a bottle, so he could listen to it every time the world got too big.

Before they emerged on the waterside, they passed a stall and Gabriel paused. 'What about this?' he called, holding something up.

Lucky examined it. A small pewter feather, about an inch long, hung on a leather thong. The curve of it reminded him of Gabriel's braid. He ran his finger along it, the ripple of the metal tickling his fingertip.

'Yeah, I think that will do.' He handed over the coins and clutched his purchase tightly in his hand.

'Happy now?' Gabriel asked and he nodded. 'Good. Time for a drink.'

They settled in one of the inns Gabriel had pointed out earlier. Lucky took a seat at a table and Gabriel headed off to the bar. He turned over the necklace in his hand, the metal warm against his palm.

'You should put that on before you lose it.' Gabriel set a couple of tankards on the table. Lucky undid the clasp and after a couple of fumbling attempts, closed it again around the back of his neck. The metal feather felt very noticeable against his chest.

'Looks good,' Gabriel said, pushing a tankard over.

'Is this going to be like coffee?' Lucky eyed it suspiciously.

'Come on, you like coffee now.'

'I drink coffee. It helps me focus. I wouldn't say I like it.'

'Try it,' Gabriel urged. 'It's not hot, at least.'

Lucky took a small sip. It was bitter, pungent, but a very different taste to coffee. He took another, larger sip.

'Well?'

'I don't hate it,' he admitted.

'That's the spirit.' Gabriel grinned.

Food arrived – a plate of thick stew served with a dark brown bread slathered in butter. Lucky found he was ravenous after walking around all day, and very soon the dish was empty.

'Your turn,' Gabriel said, pushing the empty tankards towards him. Lucky headed towards the bar. The inn was only getting busier as time went on. Tables filled with men and women, drinking or playing dice and cards. He spotted several of the crew of the *Dreamer*, and they acknowledged him with a nod or a wave.

You'll fit in around here soon enough.

Poe's words floated back to him as he carried the now full tankards back to their table. Perhaps he already had. He worried that the comfort of the ship, of safety and companionship, was pulling him away from his task. But the ship was going to Ciatheme next and he'd make sure he found out what happened then. After that . . . he could be free. Free to cook and fish over the rail and drink coffee with Gabriel, watch him dance on the waves . . .

'What did the council say?' Sienna's voice cut through his thoughts, startling him. He sat down at the table and handed over the tankard.

Gabriel scowled at her. 'None of your business.'

She pushed into the seat next to Lucky. 'I rather think it is. Leviathan business is just as much mine as yours.'

Gabriel picked up his tankard and drank deeply, though Lucky wasn't sure whether it was because he wanted to avoid talking, or thought the ale would help him answer.

'What about you? Did you hear what they said?' she asked Lucky.

'I . . . um . . .' He floundered, unsure if he'd be putting his foot in it to answer.

She slammed her own tankard down on the table. 'You two are the worst. Fine. Well, will you tell me if I buy you both a drink?'

'Two each,' Gabriel said.

'Absolutely not. I'm not buying four extra drinks.'

'Gabriel can have mine,' Lucky said softly. The effects of the beer were already making themselves known to him. A lightness in his head, a feeling of relaxation spreading through him. Like the taste, he didn't hate it, but he didn't want it to get any stronger. Didn't want to risk seeing anything because of it.

'Fine. Two drinks, Golden Boy. You're on.'

She headed over to the bar, using her slight figure and sharp elbows to make it through the crowds. The way people parted around her reminded Lucky of a leviathan moving through the sea. She returned and slammed two beers on the table, slopping ale on to the wood.

'Hey, watch it.' Gabriel pulled the tankards towards him and settled back in his seat as Sienna sat down. 'The council want us to go back to Ciatheme. See if we can find out why the leviathan was attacking the castle, or anything related to the branding.'

She pulled a face. 'Haven't they got people for that sort of thing?'

Gabriel shrugged. 'Who knows.'

'I'd rather be out on the sea, protecting ships, working with the leviathans,' she said.

'Sure, same,' Gabriel agreed, surprising Lucky. 'But the captain's not going to argue with the council, is she?'

'Don't see why not. She argues with everyone else,' Sienna pointed out.

'I think she's worried,' Gabriel replied, and Sienna's eyes widened. 'We weren't the only ones to encounter a leviathan with a wound like that. No one seems to know what it means.'

'I can't understand who'd be stupid enough to take a brand to a sea serpent.' Sienna went to take a drink and pulled a face when she realised it was empty. 'It's just asking to get eaten. And why mark them, anyway? Why would you want to know if you've encountered a specific leviathan in the past?' She turned to Lucky. 'What do you think?'

'I don't know.' He spread his hands. Why ask him? 'I don't know anything about leviathans.'

'That's why I'm asking. You might have a different perspective.'

Lucky thought about it. 'What if they're not marking them for themselves? What if they're marking them for someone else to find?'

'See.' Sienna banged her empty tankard on the table. 'That's what I'm talking about. Golden Boy would have never considered that.'

'You didn't either.' Gabriel shook a finger at her, and she mimed biting. 'I don't know how it helps us, either.'

Her shoulders slumped and she sighed. 'I guess it doesn't.'

A gloomy silence settled over the table. Gabriel focused on his drink and Sienna looked sadly at her empty tankard. Lucky pushed his over towards her and she gave him a warm smile before going to work on it without a word.

'What's wrong?' Lucky asked as the atmosphere became oppressive.

'It's not right,' Gabriel complained. 'Someone doing something to hurt the leviathans.'

'But . . . but they're monsters,' Lucky replied, and they both turned on him with a furious glare.

'You take that back,' Sienna hissed, and it was Gabriel's turn to nod along. Lucky had never seen them agree so much. He wondered how much had to do with the drink. Gabriel was on his fourth pint, and there was a pink flush along the lines of his cheekbones. Lucky found himself studying it.

'They're not monsters.' Gabriel pointed a slightly wobbly finger at him. 'They're just creatures. I mean, sure, they'll bring a ship down if it gets too close, but that's what any animal does if it's threatened.'

Lucky couldn't imagine many other creatures bringing down a whole sailing ship, but he held his tongue.

'The water dancers work *with* the leviathans,' Sienna said. 'They guide them away from the path of the ship, keep everyone safe. Even a ship like the *Dreamer*, where we're using them for medicinal components. We're not there to hurt them.'

'On this ship, you have to respect the leviathans.' Gabriel slapped the table.

'I'll . . . I'll make sure I do,' Lucky replied, though all he could think of was the great golden eye staring down at him, the scream of the guard.

'We should probably get back to the ship,' Gabriel said, finishing the last of his drink.

'I'll catch you up. Gonna see if I can supplement my earnings with a little luck at dice.' She pointed over to a table surrounded by people shouting and cheering.

'Your loss.'

'She doesn't seem so bad,' Lucky commented as they headed towards the door.

Gabriel snorted. 'Oh, she's the absolute worst. But she gets leviathan, I'll give her that.' He took a step and stumbled. Lucky held out a hand, but he shied away from it. 'I'm fine.'

'How did she end up on the *Dreamer*?' Lucky asked.

Gabriel glanced back across the common room, but Sienna was engrossed in a game of dice and winning at it from the sounds of things. 'Her marriage came up in the tapestry. She didn't want to be married. I don't think he was a bad choice. He just wasn't her choice. I think that's why she admires the leviathans so much. Every one we've come across has been female, did you know that? They go where they want, do what they want. That's Sienna's dream.'

They stepped out into the cool night. The drop in temperature from the stuffy inn helped clear Lucky's head. They walked back towards the ship under a sky scattered with stars. The larger pinkish moon rose over the horizon, spilling a delicate light on to the sea. The smaller orange one would be up soon. Lucky fingered the pewter feather at his neck.

'You look happy,' Gabriel noted.

'I think I am.'

Back on board the *Dreamer*, Lucky headed to his cell, expecting Gabriel to say goodnight and head off to wherever he was sleeping. But he followed him, and they stood in Lucky's doorway, Lucky feeling more and more awkward. It felt like Gabriel had something to say, but he kept silent.

'Well, um, goodnight,' Lucky said, trying to push the matter to a resolution at least.

'Right. Sure. Goodnight.' Gabriel took a step towards him but stumbled and flung out a hand to keep his balance. He caught the edge of the hanging blanket. Lucky dived for it, but it was falling before he could reach it. The chalk picture stood exposed for the first time, and Gabriel's jaw dropped.

'I . . . I can explain,' Lucky mumbled, his face on fire.

Gabriel's eyes widened as he took in the picture of himself, striding across the waves. Spray swirled around the figure's ankles, and he stood, one hand outstretched, the other behind him, his long braid whipped by the imaginary wind. The chalk-Gabriel's shirt was unlaced, and his eyes were closed in a look of bliss.

Lucky wanted the floor to swallow him up.

'You . . .' Gabriel took a breath. 'You . . . did all this, huh?'

Lucky couldn't meet his eye. 'I can get rid of it.'

'What?' Gabriel turned on him. 'No, I mean . . . It's really good.' He swallowed. 'You . . . you must have thought about me a lot when doing that.'

Lucky bit his lip. The shame and horror enveloped him, but at the same time left him utterly exposed. Why wouldn't Gabriel just leave? He squeezed his eyes shut.

'Lucky,' Gabriel said softly. Lucky opened his eyes to find Gabriel's face close to his, his expression not angry or hurt, but . . . fond? 'I've thought a lot about you too.'

The emotions hit him like a fever dream. Like a hunger. He *had* been thinking about Gabriel. About the way his smile warmed the empty places in Lucky's heart. The way his braid hypnotised him with its movements. The way his touch, so cautious and gentle, could make Lucky's chest flutter with imaginary birds.

Lucky pushed his lips against Gabriel's, his body compelled by an instinct even stronger than his shame. Gabriel let out a happy squeak, a sound that made Lucky's heart leap. He stepped back and gave Gabriel a shy smile.

'I hope I did that right.'

Gabriel's eyes shone. 'I don't know. I think we better test it again.' He gave Lucky a wink.

They moved close, and this time Lucky raised his hand to caress Gabriel's cheek. Gabriel tensed and slapped Lucky's hand to the side, stepping away from him.

'Oh.' Lucky couldn't keep the sound of disappointment repressed.

Immediately, Gabriel held up his hands. 'Oh, no, I'm sorry. It's not you. It's me.' He pulled his arms around himself, shivering. 'I'm . . . I'm not great with people touching me, especially men.' He sat down on the blankets and Lucky sat next to him.

Lucky remembered what Gabriel had said about his father and felt a twist of guilt in his guts. 'I'm sorry. I should have realised.'

'I want it,' Gabriel said, his voice plaintive. 'I do. I really do.'

'We don't have to do anything that makes you uncomfortable. Neither of us want that.' Lucky moved his hand close, and after a moment, Gabriel moved his, so their little fingers brushed.

'I've been trying.' Gabriel stared at a sketch of a seagull on the other wall. 'I tried going to the brothel several times. I thought it might be different there, and with women too. But it felt all wrong, being intimate with strangers. You can't tell anyone on the ship this, though. I have a reputation to maintain.' He blushed. 'Each time I went and things . . . didn't happen, they ended up just playing with my hair. But I'd paid them money, so they screamed my name a bit to make it sound right. Stupid, huh.'

'Doesn't sound stupid to me,' Lucky replied, and Gabriel gave him a grateful smile.

'I want to,' he said again.

Lucky moved his hand so his finger was resting not beside Gabriel's but on it. 'We'll go slow. And if you tell me to stop, I will. Just shake your head.'

Gabriel kissed him, quick and hard. 'I can do that,' he said.

Chapter Eleven

Lucky woke to the familiar and comforting press of Gabriel's back against his. He sat up and looked around, a fluttering sensation in his chest. Gabriel slept, his hands tucked under his chin, the braid curling over his waist. He looked peaceful, so Lucky moved as silently as he could to get ready and slipped out the door.

Taking things slowly meant things hadn't changed much, except more kissing when they were alone. Both ship work and an unspoken agreement kept them apart for most of the day. Although Gabriel said relationships amongst the crew were common, Lucky suspected the captain might feel different when one was her son.

But the last three nights, Gabriel hadn't left after eating, and they'd settled down to sleep, back to back. The warm presence of another person next to him was a comfort like no other, and he slept each night in dreamless peace.

'Morning,' Poe greeted him as he stepped into the galley. The chef ladled out a couple of bowls of porridge and poured two cups of coffee without asking.

'Do you ever sleep?' Lucky asked and Poe grinned.

'Not as much as I used to, but I don't need it so much. Go on. We'll be reaching port later today. Lots to do before that.'

Lucky picked up the tray of breakfast and stepped out, almost bumping into Captain Haven, who stood, arms crossed, in the corridor. Lucky felt a chill run down his back. Her expression gave nothing away, but he doubted she was there to collect her own meal.

'G-good morning, Captain.'

'I know what you're doing.' She unfolded her arms, folded them again, and then pinched the bridge of her nose. 'Sorry. That came out harsher than I intended.'

'We won't cause any trouble,' Lucky said quietly, avoiding her gaze. 'We won't let it affect our work.'

'See that you don't.' She frowned, then sighed. 'Just don't hurt him, Lucky. He's been hurt enough in his life. That's all I wanted to say.'

Lucky shook his head. 'I would never . . .'

'Then everything is fine.' She turned on her heel and strode away. Lucky had the distinct impression the conversation was as awkward for her as it was for him.

He returned to the room as Gabriel stirred.

'Morning,' he said as Gabriel blinked and yawned. 'I brought coffee.'

Gabriel stretched and Lucky's eyes were drawn to the lines in the muscles of his back and shoulders. 'Mmm, this is a good way to wake up.'

Their hands brushed as Lucky handed over the cup, sending a rush of tingles up his arm.

'We should reach Ciatheme today unless the wind turns against us,' Gabriel said. 'How are you feeling about going back?'

'Scared. But I need to find out what happened.' Lucky sat down and pulled his arms around his knees. 'I wish I could remember more. I don't remember anything other than the prison, really.' He shivered, remembering his old cell, the bars on the window, the guards who pulled and yelled. The band closed around his chest, making his breath rattle.

'Hey,' Gabriel said softly. He rested a hand on Lucky's. 'Hey, you're safe. You're free. You're not going back to a cell.'

'What if they recognise me? What if they drag me back?' His stomach lurched and bile burned the back of his throat.

'Take deep breaths,' Gabriel told him. 'Count to five each time. It helps with the nausea. No one's going to take you back there, Lucky. Anyone tries, they'll have to go through me.'

Lucky leaned against him, and Gabriel moved his hand to Lucky's back, rubbing slow circles. He forced himself to count each breath in and out, and the band eased.

'I don't think anyone will recognise you anymore. You've got meat on your bones, for a start. You stand differently. But if you're worried, we can disguise you?'

Gabriel pulled on a shirt and hurried from the room. When he came back, he had a razor, a pair of scissors, and a hand mirror.

'Do you trust me?'

Lucky inhaled. He did trust Gabriel, even if he often didn't understand what he was on about.

'Right. Sit still then. I promise I'm not going to hurt you.'

It took a few attempts, as the presence of blades near his face set off a panic in Lucky, but eventually he controlled himself enough to let Gabriel snip at his hair and shave his beard off. When he'd finished, Gabriel held up the mirror.

Lucky didn't recognise himself. Couldn't recognise himself. He hadn't had access to a mirror since they locked him up, had never thought to ask for one on the *Dreamer*. Staring into the face of a stranger was disconcerting. He knew he wasn't a fourteen-year-old boy anymore, but seeing a man with his eyes left him feeling as if he'd been slapped.

'Hey,' Gabriel said. 'It's real. That's you.'

'I . . . I know. I know it's me. It's . . . I look so strange.'

'I think you look good,' Gabriel murmured.

Lucky ran a hand through his hair, now short around the back, but longer on one side. He stroked the line of his jaw, now visible.

'You look good,' Gabriel said again. He leaned in close, and Lucky tasted the coffee on his lips. 'You'll believe me soon enough.'

The *Dreamer* approached the port at Ciatheme. Lucky stood at the bow, watching the land come into view. The castle on the cliffs came into focus and he felt a strange emptiness. He'd spent nearly half of his life locked up there, and probably more in the area before that. A small sandy beach lay beneath the cliffs. Was that where his mother had died?

He shuddered, cold running down his spine. Was the girl still out there? Did she know he was coming back? Did she even know he'd escaped? He couldn't change what happened, but he wanted to know why. Why his mother? Had she wronged the girl somehow? Was she cruel like Gabriel's father? Or was it the girl who was cruel? He gripped the rail, forcing himself to look down at the waves, focusing on the shifting patterns of blue and white until the shaking stopped.

The ship docked, sailors calling to the harbour workers as they threw lines between them. Unlike Sea Hall, where the atmosphere had been convivial and the two crews had shared jokes and friendly banter, here it was all work. On the dock, huge signs proclaimed that magic was illegal, and any water dancing would be met with swift punishment.

The captain and the first mate stepped into the centre of the deck.

'I need volunteers this time,' the captain told the assembled crew. 'No dancers. I don't want to risk any trouble with the Beaters, not when they've already got their eye on us. Make enquiries about the events with the leviathan. See if you can find anything out and report back to me. Don't take any risks, though. If you get attention from the church, let it drop.'

She stood back. Three sailors stepped forwards, ones Lucky barely knew. Lucky did the same.

The captain frowned. 'Are you sure? You'd be safer staying on the ship.'

'I need to find out what happened to my mother,' he said, doing his best to keep his voice firm. 'I need to know.'

Gabriel stepped up beside him and the captain shook her head. 'I promised him, Mum. I promised I'd help him.'

'The Beaters can't touch us if we don't do anything,' Sienna said, stepping up to stand beside Gabriel. 'And Gabe and I were closest to that leviathan. Maybe we'll pick up on something others will miss. Don't worry, Captain. I'll make sure neither of them do anything stupid.'

The captain's frown deepened, but she sighed. 'That makes sense. Just . . . no risks. Come back to the ship if you need to.'

'We'll be fine,' Gabriel said, and she narrowed her eyes.

'Sienna is in charge.'

Gabriel opened his mouth, then shut it again. The two groups filed off the ship while the rest of the shore leave was sorted.

'Why is the captain so nervous?' Lucky asked as they stepped down on to the docks. The atmosphere was completely different to that at Sea Hall.

'Things are different on land,' Gabriel said. 'The church of fate controls everything here. Worship of Promise, water dancing, it's all considered heretical. They tolerate the dancer vessels because of the risk to trade, but if they could wipe us and the leviathans out, they would.'

Lucky shuddered. 'No wonder the captain didn't want to let you off the ship. Isn't it risky if people don't like the water dancers?' He felt guilty for not looking into the matter more, for accepting Gabriel's help without understanding the risk to him.

'They can't do anything to us if we don't use the ability,' Sienna replied. 'But they know every ship has at least one on board, so they watch us closely. Sometimes they try and bait us into it, so they can arrest us.'

'Not a good idea,' Gabriel agreed. 'They'll lock you up for sure, and if they think your actions are bad enough, the priest can call for an execution.'

Lucky shivered. 'Why, though? You help people?'

'The church doesn't like people going against their fate,' Sienna replied. 'And they can't predict the leviathans like they can other disasters. They need us, even though we go against everything they stand for, and that is a contradiction they just can't stomach.'

Lucky turned back towards the ship. 'You should go back to the *Dreamer*. Stay safe. This is my problem.'

'Hey. I said I'd help, and I will. We'll be careful. Promise.'

Sienna gave him a warning glare. 'Careful, Gabe.' She turned to Lucky. 'Don't worry, I'll stop Golden Boy doing anything dumb.' Sienna poked her tongue out at Gabriel. He rolled his eyes in return.

Unlike Sea Hall, which sprawled up the side of the hill, clinging like a limpet, Ciatheme made a slow spiral around to the outcropping where the castle stood. The houses were whitewashed here, with red tiled roofs rather than the dark slate of the previous town.

'What's that?' Lucky asked, pointing to a large structure that dominated an area on the hill up from the castle. It was stark against the sky, somehow brooding and cold.

'A church,' Sienna replied. 'We're best not going there. Being heretics and all.'

'That's where they hold this area's tapestry,' Gabriel explained. 'The proclamations come through from the mother church, telling each area everything they need to know, from marriages to impending disasters. It's supposed to keep everything safe. Ordered.'

It sounded to Lucky like another prison.

'Fuck that,' Sienna said firmly.

'You don't have to tell me twice.' Gabriel rubbed his neck. 'So, Lucky, where do we start?'

'Maybe the beach, below the castle? I think that's where she died.' He stopped in his tracks, suddenly uncertain about heading to the scene of the crime. What could he possibly find after all this time? Maybe it was better to leave things alone, leave *her* alone. His breath caught in his throat, the iron band tightening around his chest.

'Hey,' Gabriel said softly. 'We don't have to do this if you don't want to.'

'I want to.' He pressed his hand against Gabriel's. 'I need to. For my mother, for me. Otherwise it will weigh down on me like the sky for the rest of my life.'

Gabriel's hand closed around his. 'You're not alone.'

'You go on ahead,' Sienna said suddenly. 'We'll catch you up, Golden Boy.'

Gabriel paused and glanced at Lucky, who shrugged. With an answering shrug, Gabriel walked off. When he was out of sight, Sienna pushed Lucky against the side of a building.

She caught him off guard, before he could react to her touch, or she'd never have been able to move him. He shoved her hands away, every nerve tensed to flee. She took a step back, hands out.

'I want to make one thing clear,' she said, her voice soft, laced with tension. 'You hurt him, and I will hunt you down and force-feed you your own kidneys, do you understand?'

Lucky could only stare at her. 'I thought you hated Gabriel?'

'Can't stand him.' She stuck her nose in the air and gave a pointed sniff. 'Perhaps if he pulled his head out of his arse once in a while . . . However, the fact remains: hurt him, and it's going to be you, me, and a little kidney midnight feast.' She waved a finger in his face.

Lucky lowered it slowly. 'I have no intention of hurting Gabriel. I don't know why everyone thinks I would.'

'Everyone?' She frowned.

'I got a similar speech from the captain. She was less . . . explicit about what would happen to me, though.'

Sienna grinned. 'Oh, Captain Haven is far scarier than I am. If she's on the case, then I have nothing to worry about.'

She hurried off after Gabriel, leaving Lucky bewildered. The pressure of the moment drained out of him, leaving him suddenly tired and washed out.

'Come on,' she called. Lucky took one last deep breath to calm his juddering heart and followed after them towards the place where his mother had died.

Chapter Twelve

The tide was out as they walked down over the beach. Women with baskets on their backs hunted for shellfish in the damp sand. Perhaps his mother had done that? Perhaps that was what she was looking for in the rock pool the day she died. He glanced around, trying to locate that part of the beach, fit the memories in his head with what his eyes took in. Waves washed in and out in the background, a susurration tickling the back of his mind.

Lucky stared up at the ruined wall of the castle. The guard's scream echoed in his ears. Sienna took a step towards him and whistled as she took in the jagged hole left by the leviathan.

'I still can't get my head around what happened,' she said. 'What made it attack?'

'Do you know what that place is?' Gabriel asked, pointing up at the wall above the hole.

'The only thing that's there is the prison courtyard,' Lucky replied.

'Seems an odd place to attack if you wanted to actually break into the castle,' Sienna said.

'It's a leviathan,' Gabriel pointed out. 'They're not known for their tactical warfare. I wonder what they did to provoke it? Were they the ones to brand it? Poor thing.'

Lucky wasn't sure he'd ever get used to Gabriel talking about fifty-foot monsters as if they were puppies. He remembered the creature's maw and shuddered, then pushed the image out of his mind. That wasn't what he was here for. He carried on around the beach, shells crunching under his feet. The sound awakened memories, of running across the sand looking for crabs, sheltering from the wind and rain under the shadow of the cliff. The longer he stayed here, the more familiar it all felt. He ran his hand along the rock and found scratches etched into the black surface. As he peered at them, he could make out some letters.

An L and an R.

'Lucky,' he said out loud. 'But who is the R?'

'I think it's you,' Gabriel said softly. He brushed his fingers over the scratch marks, closing his eyes. 'Lucky was my nickname, when I was a child. Before my father died. I think that's why I was so drawn to you when we pulled you out of the sea. I thought you were like me. But I think there's more to it than that.'

He could remember now. Remember the little blond boy with the bright smile, despite his frequent black eyes and split lips.

'What happened?' he'd ask.

'Got unlucky,' came the familiar retort.

'Got to change that. Maybe I'll call you Lucky. See if that weaves into the thread.'

'I was your friend,' Lucky said in wonder.

'You were my best friend,' Gabriel agreed. 'I haven't cut my hair because you said you liked it when we were six. I thought . . . I thought you'd gone, left without saying goodbye, but you'd been arrested, hadn't you? I'm sorry. I had no idea. Everything around that time is such a blur.'

Lucky sat down in the sand, his head spinning. He felt a strange mix of warmth of finding an old friend again, and rage that Gabriel had been taken from him for so long. The emotions made him dizzy, and he leaned back against the cliff, solid and reassuring. Gabriel sat next to him, and Lucky rested his head against Gabriel's shoulder.

'She took so much from us,' Lucky said. 'If . . . if I'd stopped her, saved my mother, how different things would be.'

'You can't blame yourself,' Gabriel said softly. 'I'm sure you did everything you could.'

A tear rolled down Lucky's cheek, grief for the boy he could have been. Anger twisted at his guts again, bitter and cold.

'Get up!' Sienna called suddenly, startling them both. 'Get up, we've got to go, now.'

'What's going on?' Gabriel helped Lucky to his feet.

'Beaters,' she hissed. 'Coming this way.'

'We haven't done anything wrong,' Gabriel protested.

'You know that won't matter to them if they're in the mood for a fight. And if they recognise our friend here . . .' She let the implication hang in the air. 'We split up, keep their attention off Lucky.'

'I . . . I can't ask you to do that,' Lucky said and Sienna gave him a cold smile.

'Good, because this is my choice. Right, Gabe?'

'Yeah. We've got this. Get out of here, head to an inn called the Frog and Whistle on the far side of the harbour. They're sympathetic to sailors and dancers there. We'll meet you once we've lost them.'

Before Lucky could protest further, they'd run off, shouting at a group of Beaters who had just stepped down on to the sand. Sienna and Gabriel split off in opposite directions, as they had with the leviathan, and it had the same effect here, splitting the group, two going after Gabriel and one after Sienna. Lucky thought about going after them – he hated the idea of being alone – but he'd be throwing away their gift. He slipped around the rocky cliff and headed up the beach, looking for a way to get up the cliff.

Lucky scrambled over rocks, splashed through pools, listening for any sign that the Beaters were getting closer, that Gabriel or Sienna were in trouble. But there was only the sound of his breathing and the beating of his heart.

He found himself in a tiny bay, one that he suspected spent a lot of time covered by the tides, and froze.

There was a pool of water up ahead, and craggy cliffs that could hide a slim figure hiding with a rock. He blinked and saw his mother lying on the edge of the pool, the blood and water soaking into her hair.

There was something white lying off to the side of the pool, but Lucky couldn't make it out through his tears. He took a step forwards, rubbing at his eyes.

'Hello, little bird. Nice to finally meet you at last.'

Lucky turned with a yelp, his blood turning to ice. Standing behind him was the Beater from the ship, Yale. He gave Lucky a sneer and drew a pistol.

'I . . . I'm not going back,' Lucky said. 'I didn't kill my mother. I'm not a murderer.' He looked around, searching for an exit, or a weapon. Searching for anything he could use to save himself.

'Are you sure?'

The Beater's question reminded him of the guards, who had asked the same thing as they tormented him. *Are you sure? If not you, then who?*

'I am.' He stood his ground, raised his fists.

Yale grinned. 'You see, because I've been looking into you. Father left when you were a baby. Tut, tut, very naughty. Breaking the threads that bound him to marriage. And your mother, well, she did her best, but she was half blind and struggled with work. Did you know she sold you to the church?'

Lucky couldn't answer.

'Perhaps you resented that? Perhaps you wanted to be like your father, forge your own path. That's why you found yourself fitting in with the heretics on the ship. Perhaps that's why you brought the rock down on her head?'

'No!' His voice echoed off the cliffs. 'I didn't. It was the girl. The girl with white hair.'

'Are you sure?' Yale asked again. The sneer increased, inching hungrily across his face. 'Because the threads have shown me a few things, and I think you might like to take a look at one of them.' He pointed to the white shape behind Lucky. 'Go on, take a look.'

Lucky looked over his shoulder and then back to Yale. His feet were stuck to the sand.

Yale gestured lazily with the pistol, again. Lucky gritted his teeth. He needed to get out of there, needed to rush the man or something. Sienna would know what to do, but she wasn't here. He hoped she and Gabriel were safe, had made it to the inn.

He took another step towards the shape, dreading what he'd find. Was it another body? Had something happened to Gabriel in the time they'd been parted? He shook his head. No, no, that made no sense. He was letting the Beater get in his head, scare him.

It was a statue, half dug out of the sand. Small, not as tall as him.

No . . .

'The threads showed me where to find it,' Yale said. 'It might have been visible, say, ten years ago.'

A face stared back at him from the sand. A face that had haunted his nightmares for ten years. A face with a cruel, hungry smile and flyaway white hair.

Lucky's chest tightened, squeezing his breath out. 'No . . .'

'Do you understand now?' Yale asked.

She wasn't real. The reason no one had been able to find her, the reason no one had ever believed him, was because she wasn't real. He'd killed his mother and his mind had taken a fallen statue and made a monster to take the blame.

He staggered back, bumping into Yale.

'It's all right, little bird. You've served your time. I'm going to take you into the service of the church. That's your thread in life. There has been a delay, but let's get things back on track. What do you say?'

'No!' Lucky screamed. Yale put a hand on his shoulder and Lucky struggled in his grip. He bit down on the man's hand, and the Beater screeched in pain. Lucky shoved an elbow in the man's gut and fled.

'Wait,' Yale called, but the word came out more of a gasp as he struggled to breathe.

Lucky ran and ran, longing to get away from the beach, from the Beater, from everything he was. Everything he'd done. He came up from the sand and dashed down a street, bumping into people, who yelled at him.

He tripped and came tumbling to a stop against the side of a shop, curled up and sobbing. He wrapped his arms around himself and tried to make himself as small as possible. He'd found everything and lost it all at once. How could he go back to Gabriel now, knowing everything he'd told him about himself was a lie? *I thought you'd gone, left without saying goodbye.*

Gabriel had sounded so hurt by that. Lucky couldn't do it to him a second time. He had to explain, had to confess. And then he'd see what Gabriel said.

Lucky picked himself up, wiped his tears. He felt strangely empty, as if he'd squeezed every last emotion out of himself. There was no sign of any Beaters as he cautiously crossed the harbour to find the Frog and Whistle. By the time he reached it, every muscle was tense, ready to run at a moment's notice.

Sienna's voice guided him to the correct table and for a moment, he felt the relief and comfort of hearing a friend's voice.

'Gabriel Haven, if this is some sort of joke, I swear to all the threads that I will fill your bunk with brine shrimp every night for a month.'

Lucky pushed his way through the other tavern visitors. Sienna had her back to him, leaning over the table. Gabriel slumped in his seat, eyes closed.

'What's wrong?' he asked, his voice trembling. Any relief he'd felt was washed away by a wave of fear.

She turned on him so fast the chair almost tipped over. 'Where have you been?' She shook her head, her lips trembling. 'Not the point right now. Something's wrong with Gabe. He started slurring his words, and then he collapsed like this. I . . . I don't want to touch him. He doesn't like to be touched.'

'I know,' Lucky said. 'Is he drunk?' Maybe it was nothing. Maybe Gabriel was fine.

She fixed Lucky with a glare. 'He barely touched his drink. Too worried about you. He wanted to go back out there, look for you again. I was about ready to let him when he collapsed.'

Lucky tensed, a rock in his stomach, his mouth dry. He scanned the room, and sure enough, the sneering Beater stood near the door, watching him.

'Wait here,' he told Sienna, crossing the room before she could protest. She scowled at him, but didn't leave Gabriel. Yale stepped outside as Lucky approached, and he followed.

'Ready to behave?' Yale asked. 'You can't escape your fate, you know.'

'What have you done to him?' Lucky demanded. He reached for the Beater, and the man slapped his hands away with a dismissive snort.

'Your friend isn't very observant, is he? My colleague slipped a poison in his drink.'

He pulled a little glass vial out of his cloak and waved it in front of Lucky's face. With a snarl, Lucky launched himself at the man, his fist drawn back to attack. The man sidestepped his blow and gripped Lucky's wrist, lowering it almost gently.

'Now, now.' The Beater's smile grew cold and humourless. 'You wouldn't want me to drop this antidote, would you?'

Lucky froze. It felt like an entire leviathan rested on his shoulders. 'What do you want from me?'

'I want to put you back on the right path, where you're supposed to be. And I want you to understand that it's the right thing. You hurt people when you stray from the path, little bird. You killed your mother, and now your friend is in trouble because you didn't come along nicely when I asked.' He gestured to the tavern. 'Take your friend back to the ship. Tell Captain Haven you're leaving with me and you won't be back. I'll hand over the antidote then. I don't want the stubborn captain to cause me any further issues.'

Lucky glanced back through the door at the table. Sienna leaned over Gabriel, trying to rouse him with her voice. Lucky would be giving up a place that was becoming home. Giving up people who had been kind to him. Might have even been friends in time. Heading off with a dangerous stranger, one who was cruel and manipulative.

And then he thought of Gabriel's smile, the way it lifted his whole face. His hands, his touch, so light and tender. Gabriel's lips, never free from the taste of sea spray. And he made his decision.

Lucky had killed once, but he wouldn't let anyone else he cared about die.

'Fine,' he spat.

'You made the right decision, little bird. I'll be right behind you, in case you get any bright ideas.'

Lucky hurried back to the table. 'Let's get him back to the ship,' he told Sienna. He leaned down to Gabriel's ear. 'Gabriel? We're going to get you back home. Sienna and I will have to touch you for that. We're not going to hurt you, I promise.'

Gabriel stirred at the sound of his voice. 'Lucky? I . . .' He licked his lips, his voice dry as sand. 'What happened?'

'Shh, it doesn't matter. Can we touch you?'

Gabriel tried to push himself up, but his arm didn't seem to be able to support his weight. 'Please,' he murmured.

Lucky eased Gabriel's arm over his shoulder, one hand resting gently on his waist. Gabriel flinched at the touch but didn't pull away. Sienna came around and eased Gabriel's other arm over her shoulder.

'I'm sorry, Gabe,' she murmured.

'I don't feel good,' he moaned, resting his head against Lucky's.

'I know.' Lucky brushed his lips against Gabriel's cheek. 'Let's get you home, all right? You'll feel better on the *Dreamer*.'

Getting back to the ship was slow going. Gabriel was taller than Lucky, and much taller than Sienna. Despite their best efforts to keep him talking and conscious, he weighed heavily on their shoulders, barely moving.

The first mate was on the deck as they struggled back on board, and she rushed towards them.

'Gabe? What happened? What's wrong with him?'

Lucky and Sienna laid Gabriel down on the deck. His eyes were closed, and his skin was pale as sea foam, slick with sweat. Lucky kissed his temple, his lips brushing goodbye. Gabriel didn't react.

'Where's the captain?' he asked, standing up.

'Here.' She stormed across the deck, her heeled boots clicking like a pistol being cocked. 'What have you done to my son?'

'I'm leaving,' Lucky said. The words tumbled out of him, bitter and cold and fearful.

'And coming with me,' Yale said, stepping on board.

In a fluid motion, Captain Haven had her pistol drawn and cocked and pointed at his heart. 'Get off my ship.'

'Mel,' the first mate called. She knelt at Gabriel's side, her hand hovering over his shoulder, and didn't seem to have noticed the new arrival.

'Wouldn't you rather I handed this over first?' He held out the small vial of liquid with a smile that could have curdled milk. 'The little bird comes with me, and you make no effort to ever find us again. That's a very small price for your son's life, right?'

Gabriel's body twitched and he retched, spewing part-digested stew on to the deck.

'Mel!' the first mate called again. 'Help me, please! I'm scared he'll choke.'

Captain Haven fixed Yale with a look that could have pierced his soul, then held out her hand. 'You have my word.'

Yale flicked the vial to her and she caught it, then knelt down next to her wife. He gestured to shore, and Lucky walked away from the ship.

He didn't look back.

Chapter Thirteen

'Promise me he'll pull through,' Lucky demanded as they walked away from the ship. 'Promise me the antidote is enough.'

Yale raised an eyebrow. 'Antidote? That was a vial of water.'

Lucky turned on him, shoving him into a wall. The Beater laughed and pushed him off. In a blink, he had an arm around Lucky's neck, and a knife pressed against it.

'You're terrible, little bird. This is how you threaten someone.' He released his grip and patted Lucky on the head. 'Don't worry. Once you're a Beater, we'll teach you how to do everything properly.'

Lucky didn't want to threaten anyone, didn't want to hurt anyone. He didn't want to belong to the church. But he'd hurt too many people already.

'Will Gabriel live?' Lucky asked through gritted teeth. In the back of his mind, he knew the knife should scare him, but he felt cold and numb.

'Yes, yes.' Yale waved a hand. 'As long as someone makes sure he doesn't choke on his vomit, the effects of the drug will wear off by morning.'

A spark kindled in Lucky's gut. 'You lied to me. I could have stayed on the ship. It would have made no difference.' He turned, ready to flee, but the ropes were being released as the *Dreamer* prepared to leave port. If he ran, would he make it?

As if Yale read Lucky's mind, he said, 'You'll never catch it, and even if you did, Captain Haven's given her word. You'll never be allowed back on board.' He put a hand on Lucky's shoulder, and Lucky pushed him away. 'Never trust anyone unless they promise, little bird. That's your first lesson. I doubt you'll forget it.'

'What's going to happen to me?' The words came out sullen.

'Why, a great honour. You'll join the Beaters, act as a defender of fate. Protect the strings of reality against those who would seek to reweave them. The Beaters are everywhere. We defend all the cities.'

'I didn't see any of you in Sea Hall.'

The Beater sniffed. 'Sea Hall is different. Dive full of heretics and heretic lovers. The council of Sea Hall manage the waves and the sea traffic. The Beaters control the land, that's the important part.'

The Beater's knife was back in his belt and Lucky eyed it. He'd never be able to take out Yale himself, of course, and the man was right about the *Dreamer*. Captain Haven would hold him responsible for her son being hurt, and even if she hadn't given her word, that would be enough to make sure Lucky never stepped on board again.

But maybe it didn't matter. Maybe *he* didn't matter. Could he get the knife to his own throat in time? No one would miss him. He was a moon-touched murderer who didn't even know his own name.

His thread should have been cut long ago.

He lunged for the blade, fingers closing around the bone handle. Yale drove his knee into Lucky's gut, knocking him backwards. The breath rushed out of him in a gasp, and he stumbled, unable to fill his lungs with air. But his hand remained clutched around the knife, and he drew it up to his neck.

For the first time, Yale looked alarmed.

'Come on now, little bird. There's no need for that. Are you really going to throw your life away?'

'What life? I don't even know my name.' He might have had a life on the *Dreamer*. Might have had a life with Gabriel.

But that was all gone now. No one would want a murderer. He pressed the knife harder against his neck, the pain a promise.

Lucky closed his eyes.

The rumbling sound forced them open again. A cart rushed backwards down the road towards them, the driver desperately clinging on to the seat, screaming for help.

Yale slammed into Lucky, spilling the knife from his hand and pinning him out of the way of the cart. A wheel hit a pothole, jolting the whole cart and throwing the driver from his seat. He hit the ground head first with a sickening crack, tumbling over and over before coming to a stop.

Lucky stared at the body, seeing his mother.

'Is that really what you want?' Yale jerked a thumb at the corpse.

Lucky shook his head, feeling numb.

'Come on, then.' He sheathed the knife and pointed down the road.

'You know my name, right?' Lucky said. 'You know who I am.'

Yale shrugged. 'Yeah. I do.'

'Tell me who I am and I'll come quietly.'

'Your name is Robin Tress. You were no one important.' He shrugged again. 'What matters is that you were given up to church service, and that's where you belong.'

'Did . . .' Lucky cleared his throat. 'Was she a good woman?'

'How should I know? She wasn't a heretic, I can tell you that much.' He set off down the street at a quick march.

Robin. He tasted the word in his mind, tried to wear it and picture himself in it. It didn't seem to fit, and his mind rejected it. It didn't suit him.

'Come along, little bird.'

The fortress loomed from the top of the canyon. The Beater's training ground. His new home. High up in the hills, days from the sea. Watching him. Thick walls, grey, cold. Controlling. It whispered to him of bars and cells and guards. Trapped. Prisoner. Lucky stopped, digging his feet into the path that zigzagged up towards it. He groaned as his chest tightened. His legs turned to lead, too heavy to lift.

'We're not taking another break,' Yale snapped. 'Get moving.'

Lucky counted to five and released a breath, then drew another one in and held it for five more. Slowly, the feeling came back to his legs, the ache now merely the consequence of all the walking they'd done over the last few days. This was right. This was his choice. This was where he belonged.

He touched the feather dangling around his neck, thought back to the day in Sea Hall, where everything felt bright, hopeful. That day was past, and days like that would never come again. He was a Beater, or on the road to becoming one. He could never go back to the *Dreamer*. And he knew now what happened to his mother, though not why.

This was right.

'Move,' Yale called.

Orders. Obeying. Offering up control in return for certainty. That was how he'd survived in the prison. That's how he'd survive now. Yale made another gesture and Lucky walked towards him, one foot after the other. He counted his steps, knowing each one would take him away from the sky and back towards the walls.

Where he belonged.

At last they reached the entrance to the fortress, where huge wooden doors stared down at him. They were unadorned, reinforced with studs of black iron.

'They call it The Fell,' Yale commented as they approached. 'The fell is the edge of the new cloth, where the last weft gets beaten in. Fitting, isn't it?'

He marched up and stared at an opening high above the entrance.

'Open the fucking door.'

They creaked open, the grinding, scraping sound reverberating in Lucky's bones. He focused his gaze on the wide flagstones that made up the floor. They were smooth, polished by the passing of thousands of feet.

Voices hushed as Lucky and Yale stepped through. It reminded him of walking into the *Dreamer*'s mess that first time, and he pulled himself in, making himself as small as possible. No more cooking with Poe. No more meals with Gabriel.

'What you got?' Boots clicked across the floor, coming to a stop in front of him. Lucky raised his head slowly, to see a woman in Beater uniform glowering at him.

'Another acolyte.' Yale pushed Lucky's shoulder, sending him stumbling forwards.

'Old for an acolyte,' she noted, peering at him. Lucky felt like a lump of meat on display, being assessed for consumption.

'Yeah,' Yale replied with a dismissive wave of his hand. 'This one slipped out of our hands for a while. But he's been signed for and he's back where he belongs.'

'Your problem, Yale,' she said with a sniff, before spinning on her heel and marching off. Yale muttered something under his breath, then shoved Lucky's shoulder again.

'Move.'

Lucky moved through the room as if he were wading through water. Though room didn't really capture the place. It was a vast hall, held up by pillars wider than most tree trunks. Figures in black or grey stared at him as he passed, their expressions either callous or indifferent.

Yale took him through the hall and down some steps to a room with four beds. It looked out over the valley and smelled of damp.

'That's yours,' Yale said, pointing to a narrow cot close to the window. A grey acolyte uniform lay on the grey blanket, on the bed which stood on the grey floor. Lucky lay down on the bed, hard, scratchy. Like the cot in his old cell.

Four walls. Familiar. Safe.

Where he belonged.

PART TWO

Chapter Fourteen

The Beaters functioned on conformity. All acolytes wore the same dull grey, like a cloud pregnant with rain. They all cut their hair short. They moved in unison, every step identical.

They thought the same.

The Beaters functioned on cruelty. They beat down, pulled on every little thread of self-esteem. They punished everyone for a single person's transgression, and then the culprit was punished again in the dorms.

The Beaters functioned on faith. Sermons were daily, a spiel on the importance of the threads, on obeying. On not being out of place.

Lucky felt nothing but out of place. Six months he'd been here, and he'd never even considered religion before then. Everything was about obeying, keeping to the narrow path ordained. The Beaters pushed and pulled and dragged him without a care for his opinions or feelings.

This was his life now.

He tried to treat it like he had in his cell, back in the castle. But it was different this time. Deserved. Lucky was a murderer and this was his penance.

He tried not to think of Gabriel.

Sometimes he was successful. Sometimes he'd go for days and this would feel almost normal. Then a flash of gold, or a length of rope, or the spray on the washbowl would set off the memories all over again. And he'd hate himself all over again.

This was right. This was right. This was what it needed to be.

He repeated the mantra over and over, pushing down the memories of a time when people asked to touch him, spoke in gentle tones, didn't kick and hit. A time when he could have been happy.

It wasn't real. The time with Gabriel had been nothing more than a dream in between two waking nightmares. That was all.

He stepped out into the weapons yard. Of everything, this at least he appreciated. Especially when he fought Yale. In all his time here, he'd learned nothing more about the man, other than how much he hated him.

'Looking forward to getting your arse kicked, Robin?' Yale gave him an unfriendly smile as Lucky stepped into the yard. Lucky had given up trying to get him to call him anything else. At least Robin was better than little bird.

Without answering, he picked up the training dagger. The blades were blunted, but that didn't stop them bruising, and if the wielder hit hard enough, they broke the skin anyway. Lucky learned that the hard way.

Yale took up position opposite him. The weapons master would call in the fight, but Yale never waited for the call, and no one ever punished the Beaters for it. An acolyte couldn't get away with that shit, but they could be ready.

Lucky was ready.

The blow came in fast, an upward thrust that would have grazed his jaw if he hadn't been prepared. He turned the blade, then came in fast with his own attack, going in low with a slash across the gut. Yale danced back.

'Predictable,' he sniffed. 'You've learned nothing.'

The taunts were designed to enrage and destabilise and Lucky didn't care. You couldn't bruise the self-esteem of a man who had none. He took a step back, the dagger held in a defensive position.

'What are you waiting for? Come at me.'

Lucky didn't rise to it, and with a snarl, Yale pushed into an attack, his blade held out in front of him. He moved with a speed Lucky could never hope to match – lean and wiry, there was nothing to him but muscle. At the last moment, just before the dagger hit his chest, Lucky pivoted, one leg out. Yale crashed into it, stumbling forwards. Lucky swept his leg back, and drove the dagger down to Yale's kidney.

The weapons master dropped a hand. 'End. Point to the acolyte.'

Yale recovered his balance and fixed Lucky with a smirk that somehow carried less menace this time. 'Perhaps you have learned a smidge, little bird. Come, walk with me.'

Lucky wanted to refuse. He enjoyed the fights, wanted to improve his skills but he had no desire to spend any time with Yale that didn't involve almost driving a blade into his soft innards.

But he walked across the yard after him without question.

Yale took him up the steps to the ramparts that surrounded The Fell. He leaned out over the crenellations and looked down at the valley below. Scrubby bushes fought to stay anchored on the grey rocks as a constant cold wind whistled through. Out in the distance, spry goats clambered over seemingly impossible paths.

'You've done well,' Yale said, the words catching Lucky off guard. Praise wasn't something that happened here. 'I think it's time you said your oath.'

'Oath?'

'You didn't think you were a real Beater yet, did you?' The sneering felt more usual, more comfortable.

'Of course not.' The sky overhead was grey as the walls. It would rain soon, and the acolyte dorms would be even damper and colder than they normally were. He missed the sea, missed the air smelling of salt.

'Do you know what a Beater is?' he asked and Lucky shook his head. 'On a loom, it's the tool that presses the weft against the rest of the fabric. That's what you'll be for the church. Once you say your vows to guard the weft and keep the threads, you'll be out of the grey. Out of the shared dorms and the daily humiliations. Won't that be nice?' His smile held no humour, no fondness. It might as well have been painted on.

'What's it to you?' Lucky asked. Yale always had an angle.

'Why, I get my acolyte raised to full Beater faster than most and claim bragging rights. Sorry, little bird, I don't give a shit about you as a person. But I do want out of this place. Once you leave, so can I.'

'I don't want you to care about me.' He'd had that – kindness, respect. Losing it hurt and Lucky was tired of hurting. Better this way. 'What happens if I don't?'

Yale's eyes widened. 'What do you mean? What happens if you don't take the oath? You're here. You're becoming a Beater. That's your fate. It's written in the threads.'

Lucky thought back to what Gabriel had said about tapestries and proclamations. About the sailors who'd broken free of that path. 'So . . . I'd be a heretic?'

'You would indeed. And you know what we do with heretics, don't you, little bird?'

Lucky didn't really, but he could guess it wasn't anything good. Perhaps they'd put him back in a cell. Perhaps they'd kill him. Something pulled at his mind. 'How does it work? If I'm destined to be a Beater, then how does it work if I fail to sign on?'

'You will.' Yale met his gaze calmly. 'There is no other way. We find whatever it takes to make you sign and you sign. It might take time, but we do it. We always have. Time is something we have in abundance, Robin. You should remember that.'

'I don't believe you could.' Lucky stretched his arms above his head. For the first time, he found himself with a modicum of control. The sailors, the dancers, Sea Hall. The leviathans. All of them had stepped away from their threads. He couldn't do that, didn't deserve to do that. But he didn't have to capitulate to Yale's every whim, either.

'Is that a challenge, little bird?' Yale grinned. Lucky had never seen such a hungry look on the man, and a shiver ran down his spine. 'I know all about pain, about fear. I promise you, you do not want to test me.'

Lucky didn't back down, tried not to even blink. He was a murderer. Murderers deserved pain. At least it would be on his terms.

'Go. You'll see I'm right before long. You can't escape your fate.' With that, Yale turned and marched away, leaving Lucky on the ramparts. He thought about going back to the weapons yard, but the moment had sparked a rebellion in his heart, and he took himself down to the dorms.

All the beds in the room were hard and narrow, too short for Lucky and he wasn't the tallest of the group. He wondered how Gabriel would fare in a bed like that, and cursed himself, closing his hands into fists so his nails dug into his palms.

He lay down on his bed, pushing his face into the scratchy pillow. This was his reality. This was his life. There was no ship, no leviathans, no Gabriel.

Only the Beaters.

He woke later to darkness filling the room. No one had come to find him, come to punish him. Maybe the Beaters weren't so fierce after all. He stretched, trying to ease out the kinks in his back. He was stronger and more muscular than he'd been on the *Dreamer*. His hair had grown out of the style Gabriel had given him and now it was shorn close to his skull. Six months here, but he felt at least five years older.

As he approached the hall, he heard voices raised in a commotion. He hurried up the steps, wondering who had put their foot in it this time. There were any number of acolytes who struggled, and that made them easy targets. Lucky heard at least two of the members of his dorm crying at night from time to time.

He stepped into the hall, and as he passed through the doorway, there was a long rumbling sound, almost like a growl. Lucky tensed. He'd heard that sound before. Before he could react, the ground shook back and forth, knocking him to his knees. Around him, people shrieked and shouted, and the earth beneath the hall clattered and juddered in a drawn-out rattle.

As the earth steadied, Lucky got back to his feet. For a moment, there was only an eerie silence, and then the voices broke out again. He couldn't make out any words, but the mixture of fear, anger, and confusion was clear enough. Another earthshake. He'd never experienced anything like that at the castle in Ciatheme. And now twice in six months.

Someone shoved into his back. Lucky turned and found a Beater glaring at him.

'Out of the way, acolyte,' she hissed.

Lucky didn't move. 'What's going on?'

She moved to shove him aside, and then sighed.

'Strangers.' She pushed past Lucky and headed into the hall.

Strangers? That piqued his interest more than the earth-shake. The fortress was far from civilisation, reached only by taking a treacherous, rocky path, slippery at the best of times, lethal at most others. Plus bears and wildcats lurked in the hills, ready to pounce on the unwary. Once the acolytes took their oath, they'd be sent out across the country, to make sure everyone followed their fates.

He walked down the hall towards the crowd of people, curious to see who had made the journey, and stopped. A voice, louder than the others, carried on the air. Lucky recognised it instantly and his heart lifted. But it couldn't be. He forced the emotion down, smothered it as the Beaters had taught him. There was no place for hope here.

But as Lucky stepped into the wide room, pushed his way past the jostling mix of Beaters and acolytes, there he was. Lucky rubbed his eyes, blinked five times, closed his eyes and counted to ten, and when he opened them, Gabriel was still there.

He was a mess. Blood oozed from an open cut on his cheek, and there was more blood on his shoulder. Some of his hair hung loose, pulled free from the braid.

Sienna was in a worse state.

She lay unconscious in Gabriel's arms as he begged for someone to help.

Lucky pushed to the front of the mass. Gabriel caught sight of him and his eyes widened.

'Lucky! We found you.' The warm hope in his words wound its way around Lucky's heart. 'Help us, please.'

'You're not supposed to be here.' Lucky's voice came out cold and empty. Push down the emotions. Smother them. Drown them. It's better that way. Lucky was a murderer. He'd already got Gabriel hurt before.

This was right.

Gabriel bit his lip, pain creasing his features. 'Please. Please. She needs help.'

Lucky's gut twisted. Gabriel had come here, come looking for him. Maybe there was a chance to go back to the *Dreamer*, to throw off the Beaters and their casual cruelty. Back to where he felt safe, comfortable. His heart ached for people who asked before they touched, who treated him as a person rather than a means to an end.

Moreover, his heart ached for Gabriel, his soft words and understanding, his gentle touch, his lips that tasted of coffee and freedom.

Gabriel's earnest brown eyes met his, and Lucky's resolve faltered. He glanced around the room for Yale, caught the Beater creeping down the back of the room. Yale's hand rested on the knife on his belt.

And Lucky knew it would never work out.

Yale would never let him leave. He'd poisoned Gabriel once already. Even if Lucky could somehow convince the Beaters to let him go, Yale would come after them. Lucky was Yale's thread, until Lucky said his oath. That was his own thread and when he'd tried to break it once before, his mother had paid the price. And Gabriel would pay the price next if he did it again. The vision of Gabriel's pale face as he lay unconscious on the deck of the *Dreamer* swam before Lucky, and an icy hand wrapped itself around his guts.

He couldn't do it. Tears burned at the corners of his eyes, and he turned away from Gabriel, from his pleading expression. From his hope.

'Yale!' Lucky called. 'You wanted me to say the oath? This is my price. You help them. And then you send them away.'

'No!' Gabriel yelled, anguish shredding through his voice. 'No, Lucky, don't do this!'

Lucky didn't hear any more. He fled from the hall, his heart pounding in his ears.

This is right this is right this is right.

Chapter Fifteen

Two days later, and Lucky was almost ready to say his oath. He'd been left alone, spared all chores, training, harassment. It was supposed to be a day of quiet reflection and preparation. Lucky spent most of it pacing.

Gabriel was here.

Gabriel was here in The Fell and the knowledge ate at him. He'd spent six months trying to forget him, his old life, the *Dreamer*. Six months of learning to be cruel, callous, dismissive, in order to bury those feelings.

And now Gabriel was here to break all of that.

He paused mid pace as his stomach clenched. What was he doing here? Lucky couldn't go back. Captain Haven wouldn't allow it. And Gabriel wouldn't want to know him when he understood what Lucky had done.

'You're going to wear a hole in the floor like that.'

Lucky spun round at the voice behind him. Yale leaned against the doorway, watching him with a raised eyebrow. Lucky looked away glowering.

'Your uniform,' Yale said, holding out a bundle of dark cloth. 'You better get a move on if you're going to be ready.'

'How is Sienna?' he asked. He couldn't think of Gabriel, but Sienna had never done him wrong, and he couldn't help worrying about her.

'They're not your problem, little bird. Put them out of your head and move on.' He thrust the uniform towards Lucky again. Lucky crossed the room, but instead of taking it, he grabbed Yale's shoulder and pressed the side of his hand against his throat.

'Tell me the truth,' he spat in Yale's face. 'I want a promise. Promise me that they're unharmed, that Sienna's recovering.'

Yale swallowed, the action bobbing against Lucky's hand. He grimaced, and moved his palm back, just slightly.

'You didn't forget the first lesson. I'm proud of you.'

Lucky dug his hand back in and Yale winced.

'All right, all right. I promise you the heretics are fine. I made sure of it. Now, will you go and get ready, or do I need to carry you and dunk you in the pool myself?'

Lucky snatched the bundle of cloth out of Yale's hands and stormed out of the room. He was halfway down to the cleansing pool before he remembered he hadn't forced Yale to promise they'd be released. He'd made it a term of his oath, but he didn't fully trust Yale to follow through.

Still, when Lucky was a Beater, he'd see to the matter himself. Whatever possessed Gabriel to come here, it had already hurt both him and Sienna. Lucky was a bad force. It was better for them to stay apart, live their own lives. If a Beater was what Lucky was fated to be, so be it. Gabriel belonged on the ship, with his family.

He headed down, deep into the bowels of the hill, to the purifying pool. There was no sound down here. No voices, no wind, no birds. He felt like he was the only one alive. That might have been better for everyone, he thought, then he couldn't hurt anyone.

The pool was in a small chamber with tiles on the walls and a domed ceiling. On the far side, water tumbled down and flowed through a channel, before disappearing through the floor again. Several iron pegs hung on the wall, and Lucky used one to hold his new uniform, then stripped out of his acolyte clothes, leaving them scattered on the floor.

He scrubbed every inch of himself at least twice, to the point where even he knew he was trying to draw out the matter. His skin felt raw, as if he'd sloughed off a whole layer of himself.

Slosh. Murderer headed down the drain. Slosh. There went sailor. Slosh. He washed away hopeful.

This was right.

Lucky turned away from the running water and stepped into the round central pool. Small stone steps led the way to the bottom, and by the time he stood in the centre, it was waist-deep. The water was cold as moonlight and not nearly as beautiful, almost black in the dim chamber. He thought he was supposed to feel something profound while standing there, but he only felt cold and numb.

With a sigh, he stepped out and stood dripping on the cold stone floor, trying unsuccessfully to smother the shivers that wracked his body. The cloth they'd given him to dry off was rough, scraping over his body and taking off yet another layer of skin. Another layer of himself. Lucky wasn't sure how much more he had left to give. He reached for his uniform.

This was right.

The black clothes, wool and leather, slipped on to his form with a series of harsh whispers. They chastised him, just like the other Beaters and acolytes. The uniform hung awkwardly, as if it, too, knew this was all a charade.

This *was* right.

Whether it was penance, or justice, or just the inevitable threads of fate pulling at him, this was what he needed to do. He'd see Gabriel and Sienna sent away, and then he'd let the Beaters tell him what to do. Beaters, guards, it made no difference. He could let the weft of the threads carry him, and then he wouldn't make mistakes. He wouldn't hurt others and he wouldn't get hurt again.

This was *right*.

He bent over, tying the laces on the black leather boots, when the sound began again. It started almost imperceptibly, ripples radiating out from the centre of the pool. Then a rumble that tickled the soles of his feet, even through the boots.

Lucky started for the door, and the shaking grew in intensity, the floor rolling underneath him like the deck of a ship.

The whole room echoed with a grating, grinding sound, and Lucky decided underground was the last place he needed to be. He made a dive for the door, stumbling and falling several times before he made it. Dust fell from the ceiling, clouding the air like smoke.

The dorms were empty, nothing but shattered washbowls and broken furniture. In the dining room he found a similar scene of empty devastation. After the heavy rumbling of the earthshake, the silence was chilling. Was he the only one left alive? The thought of being alone in a prison made him feel sick.

He carried onwards to the main hall.

The door to the main hall was heavy wood, carved with a crow on each side, facing the ornate brass handles as if they wanted to pluck them out and fly away. Lucky pressed his ear to it, keeping one eye on the corridor. It was too quiet. The place was never deserted before curfew.

Even through the heavy wood, he could make out the sounds of cries and moans. As he cracked open the door, they grew louder. A section of the ceiling had caved in. Bodies lay in the ruins, some twitching, some crying. Lucky recognised one as from his dorm, one of the ones who cried often in the night.

He wasn't crying now.

Other Beaters rushed around, trying to tend to the wounded. Had they all gathered in here when the shaking started? It hit him. They'd been waiting for him to say his oath. Lucky's stomach turned. If he'd been quicker preparing, he would have been standing right there in the centre of it all.

He backed away, fighting the urge to retch.

'You!' Yale pulled himself to his feet. He was covered in dust and debris, blood on his face and hands. 'This is your fault.'

'How?' he stammered, retreating. Yale staggered after him, limping heavily.

'You brought heretics here. There were never earthshakes here. Never,' he spat. 'Now two? It has to be because of them.'

Lucky shook his head. 'They're water dancers. They can't do this.'

'Why take the chance?' Yale drew a knife out of his belt, a wild glint in his eyes.

Lucky was unarmed as Yale charged at him. He stepped back, tripping over the sill of the door and falling over the step. Yale swung at him wildly, narrowly missing slicing the new Beater uniform.

Yale came at him, slashing again and again, the same furious blur of motion he used in training, designed to overwhelm and wear down. Lucky rolled away, pushed himself to his feet and hurried towards the dining room, where there would be more space and more chance of finding a weapon.

Instead of following him, Yale turned towards the stairs to the dorms and below. To where the prisoners would be held.

Lucky was a murderer, but he wasn't going to let people die because of him.

He threw himself at Yale and they tumbled down the stone steps. They hit the bottom, battered and bruised, but Lucky landed on top. Yale lay stunned. Lucky grabbed his dagger, drove the pommel into Yale's temple, then slipped the weapon into his belt.

He fetched a sheet from one of the beds, and tore it to shreds, using them to bind Yale as tightly as he could. For good measure, he gagged the man and pushed him under a bed. Hopefully he'd rot there.

Lucky started back up the steps to the main hall, then paused. He could leave. He could go somewhere far away. But did he deserve to? He'd killed his mother, a cold and calculating act. He enjoyed the fights with Yale, enjoyed the violence. He was no better than the Beaters. He belonged here.

He took another step and stopped again. What happened if one of the other Beaters made the same decision, that the heretics were to blame? He'd dealt with Yale, but he didn't know how many others were alive upstairs.

Yale had promised Gabriel and Sienna were safe. Not that they were free.

He turned and headed past the dorms, past the purification pool, deep into the hill. Instantly, he was reminded of the cells in the castle. The atmosphere, the smells, were identical. The force of the memories made him dizzy, and he clutched his head, forcing himself to remember he wasn't in Ciatheme anymore.

'Gabriel!' Lucky called into the gloom. 'Sienna!' Visions of Gabriel and Sienna trapped, pinned under rubble, crushed and bloody, filled his mind. The earth shook again, grating, grinding against itself. The dust made it hard to see, hard to breathe. Larger pieces of the ceiling fell down, sharp chunks of rock, and he covered his head with his arm.

'Lucky!' Sienna's voice flooded down the corridor and he ran towards it. Despite the situation, he felt a stab of relief to hear her voice again. 'Get your arse over here and help us.'

He skidded to a stop in front of one of the cells. A Beater lay slumped nearby, blood running down the side of his head. The wall had a zigzag crack running up it, and the bars that formed the fourth wall had come free on one side. They'd fallen into the cell, pinning Gabriel's legs. Sienna crouched, trying desperately to raise them.

'Help me,' she yelled as he approached, and then her face twisted in fury. 'You're a Beater now?'

Lucky looked down at his uniform. 'Not the time.'

'You came,' Gabriel said softly.

'I'm just getting you out of here,' Lucky said, avoiding Gabriel's gaze. He bent down and wrapped his hands around the bars. Between the two of them, they managed to get the bars raised enough for Gabriel to wriggle free. He stood and gave Lucky a fond look, reaching a hand towards him.

'Lucky. I found you again.'

Lucky took a step back, ignoring the offered hand. His stomach roiled with emotions. He couldn't let them break free. Not here. Not now.

'Let's get out of here.' Get them out, get them free, and then he could go back to his prison.

Gabriel's eyes widened, and the pain in his expression stabbed at Lucky's heart, but he steeled himself. He'd get them out, and that would be that. It was right.

Sienna was the first out of the cell. Whatever her injuries had been, she seemed mostly healed, apart from a dull purple bruise down the side of her face. Gabriel still sported the long red scratch, but the blood had been cleaned off.

'Move it, Golden Boy,' she ordered. 'I'm not spending a minute longer in a Beater cell.'

'You don't have to tell me twice,' Gabriel replied, but his eyes were fixed on Lucky.

The ground had stopped shaking, but the building was creaking and groaning alarmingly. Lucky led them back up the stairs, past the dorms, but paused at the staircase leading up to the main hall.

'We're not going out that way,' he told Gabriel and Sienna as they emerged. 'But at least the Beaters are occupied. Let's try the training yard.' He cast a glance at the dormitory, but there was no response from Yale.

As he stepped into the yard, the damage to the hall was clear. As well as the roof, part of the south wall had collapsed in on itself, leaving a jagged gash in the building. The dark stone walls still standing were cobwebbed with cracks.

'I hope there were a bunch of Beaters in there when it went down,' Sienna said coldly.

'There were,' he replied, and her lip curled in a smile. His fault. They'd been waiting for him and they'd died because of it. Lucky doubled down on his resolve. He'd get Sienna and Gabriel away from here, away from any Beaters who might want to hurt them, but he couldn't stay with them.

His luck would only get them killed.

The main gate in the yard was closed and locked, but Lucky had never expected a door to be their way out.

'Up here,' he called, heading for the ramparts.

'Are you sure you know what you're doing?' Gabriel asked, peering over. The ground tumbled away in a steep cliff, the valley floor hundreds of feet below them.

'You shouldn't have come here. I never asked you to,' Lucky snapped, then he looked away, his lips pinched. Once, Lucky would have felt guilty, but it wouldn't affect him now. The Beaters worked hard to beat anything positive out of the acolytes, and Lucky hadn't resisted.

It was so much easier not to care.

He continued until the ramparts turned and he was standing above and to the left of the gate. It was still about thirty feet to the ground here, but that was much less of a risk than on the other side. The bricks were rough and uneven and Lucky had often peered down in a quiet moment and wondered if he could climb them. Now was the time to learn.

He took off the boots and tossed them over. They hit the ground with a thud that sent a jolt up his spine. They'd all make one big splat if he'd misjudged this. He pulled himself over the parapet, his feet probing the wall for suitable footholds.

'Um,' Sienna said, her voice cracking. 'I don't think I can do this.'

'You've climbed the rigging, right?' Gabriel said, his tone light. 'It's just like that, I'm sure.'

'One, only under duress, and two, you're an idiot. That's nothing like rigging.'

Lucky continued his descent. He just had to get them out of here. That was all.

'Let me go first,' Gabriel said. 'I'll tell you where to place your feet. You can do this, Sienna.'

She made a low growl in her throat. 'I better, Golden Boy, or when I fall, I'm taking us both out.'

Lucky was about halfway down as Gabriel swung himself over the parapet and started his descent. He glanced up, and then immediately back down again, not wanting to be distracted by the way Gabriel's braid swung as he moved.

What was wrong with him?

'Come on,' Gabriel called to Sienna. Lucky recognised the soft, persuasive tone he'd used on the ship. A rough heat itched through his chest as he listened to Gabriel use it on Sienna, coaxing her over the top and down the wall. It was better this way, though. Gabriel and Sienna belonged together.

It was Lucky who was the outsider.

He concentrated on scaling the wall, moving as quick as he could down the stones. The harsh surface ate at the skin of his fingers and palms, but the pain helped him focus and he moved hand over hand down the wall. He was a third of the way from the bottom now, moving quickly and easily. Nearly there. Then he'd be able to point them on the path and watch to make sure the Beaters didn't come after them.

Then it would be over.

He put his foot down towards the next stone, his hand already moving for the next hold. He misjudged the distance and his foot scrabbled against the wall, failing to find purchase. With only one hand still on the stones, his grip faltered. Lucky dug his fingers in, scraping his fingernails, but he couldn't hold on.

He landed on the ground with a thump, pain radiating out through his shoulder and down his side.

'Lucky!'

Gabriel's cry of alarm echoed around the valley. Lucky wanted to respond, but the air had been knocked out of his lungs. He lay there, trying to force himself to breathe, as Gabriel hurried down towards him. By the time Lucky was able to pull himself into a sitting position, wheezing still, Gabriel was at his side.

'Lucky, talk to me. Are you hurt? Can you move?' He knelt at Lucky's side, hands near his shoulder, but not touching.

'I'm fine.' He almost managed that in a normal voice, almost managed to suppress the pain from his tone. Gabriel clearly didn't buy it from his expression.

'Don't move,' he said. 'Take it easy until you're sure.'

It reminded Lucky of being in his cell on the ship, of the feeling of safety, of respect. Of hope.

Of all the things he had no right to have.

'Get out of my way.' He pulled himself to his feet, biting his lip to keep the moan locked up in the back of his throat. Another prisoner.

Gabriel's lip twitched. 'What happened to you? This isn't you.'

'Isn't it?' he snapped back, the pain reinforcing his anger. 'Maybe it is. Maybe this is who I was always supposed to be.'

Gabriel's eyes narrowed, 'It's not.'

'Gabriel, I killed my mother. She sold me to the church and I picked up a rock and I must have killed her. There was no girl with white hair. It was just a statue. Maybe I was your friend once, but I can't be now. I'm a murderer.' Saying it was a relief. It was out in the open now. Gabriel knew what he was. He'd understand why things had to be this way.

'I don't believe you. Lucky, I don't believe you. Not without proof.' He held out a hand but Lucky backed away. Gabriel's lip trembled. It made Lucky's heart ache to see him like that, but it was better than hurting him physically. This would heal, for the both of them.

It was better this way. It was better this way. It was . . .

'Hey!'

They both turned to Sienna, still high up on the wall.

'Do you think you could put aside your lover's quarrel for just a moment, and get me down from this fucking wall?'

'We're not lovers,' Lucky murmured as Gabriel flushed with guilt.

'Sorry,' he answered. He gave Lucky another glance – part hurt, part fear – and straightened up.

'What do I do?' she called, her voice laced with panic.

'Just climb,' Lucky called back and was answered with a series of expletives. 'Look, we did it. You do it too.'

'Neither of you are scared of heights,' she said, but she moved one foot down, finding a new place to rest it.

'That's it.' Gabriel clapped his hands. 'That's it.'

Lucky scoffed. 'Don't patronise her. She doesn't need pampering. She needs to move. She's got that far. The Beaters would never tolerate such weakness.'

'Yeah? Well, it's a good thing I'm not a fucking Beater, isn't it.' She moved again, coming down slowly and carefully. 'And if we were anywhere near a source of water, I'd drown you right now. What did Golden Boy ever see in you? You're feral.'

As if powered by her rage, she moved faster, grumbling threats under her breath as she went.

'You got cruel,' Gabriel said, sounding more shocked than angry.

'I got her down the wall, didn't I?' Lucky shrugged. 'I told you what I was. Why won't you see it?'

Sienna reached the bottom before Gabriel could reply, and her legs gave way from underneath her, dropping her in an undignified heap on the floor.

'Are you all right?' Gabriel asked, moving away from Lucky. He eyed him cautiously, as if Lucky were a snake waiting to strike.

'Fine. Fine.' She pulled herself to her feet, wobbled for a moment, then stood up straight. 'Well, Golden Boy. You found him. What now?'

'You're coming with us, right?' Gabriel asked, his expression pleading. He stretched out a hand, coming close but not touching Lucky's shoulder.

Lucky shook his head. 'I can't. This is where I belong now. It's better for everyone this way.' Murderers belonged in their prison. Murderers had to do their penance.

'You heard him,' Sienna said. 'What do you say we turn right around and go back to the ship, leave him to the Beaters he loves so much.' She walked towards Lucky, her hands clasped behind her back.

Gabriel bit his lip. 'I . . . I can't.'

'Yeah, I was afraid you'd say that.' Her arm flashed out, and she struck Lucky across the temple with something hard. The ground rushed up to meet him, but faded away to black before he hit it.

Chapter Sixteen

'. . . Believe you hit him with a rock.'

Voices broke through the fuzzy darkness that enveloped Lucky's mind. He pushed his battered senses out, trying to work out what was happening. His head ached, but he felt strangely floaty.

'Yes, Gabriel, for the fifth time. I hit him with a rock. You weren't going to leave him and he wasn't going to go, so it was that or spend the rest of our short lives camped out at the gate of The Fell.'

As his awareness trickled back in, Lucky realised the floaty feeling was because he was being carried. He twisted in his captor's arms, struggling to break free.

'Hey! Whoa, hey, stop that. I'll put you down.'

Lucky pushed away and tumbled to the ground. A tsunami of pain washed over his back and shoulders, and he couldn't bite back the groan.

'I'm sorry, I'm sorry, I'm sorry.' Gabriel leaned over him, face pinched in a mixture of guilt and concern. Lucky rolled away.

'Go away.' He closed his eyes against the pain and the nausea and the confusion. It didn't help much. 'Go away, Gabriel.'

Gabriel made a choked sound in the back of his throat.

'Right.' Sienna's voice cut through. 'Gabe, go get us some water. I saw a stream back there.'

'But . . .'

'Now, Golden Boy. Take your time. Lucky and I are going to have a little chat.'

There was a pause, then a sigh, and Gabriel stomped away. Lucky sat up slowly, waves of dizziness stirring his brain like soup. Sienna sat in front of him, idly twirling a knife around her finger.

'It's not midnight, but let's have a chat about why I shouldn't remove your kidneys right now.' She gave him a cold smile that sent Lucky scurrying backwards. 'What happened to you? You were quiet, shy, a little strange on the ship. But you weren't cruel. What changed?'

'You two should go. Leave me.' He avoided her intense gaze. 'It's better this way.'

She raised an eyebrow. 'Hurting Gabe is better now?'

'In the long run. He's better off without me.'

She tossed the knife from hand to hand. 'And you're the arbitrator of that, are you?'

'I killed my mother. I'm dangerous. You know this is true. By keeping me around, you're putting him in danger too.'

'That's true.' She sat back and slipped the knife back into its sheath. Lucky breathed a sigh of relief. He'd be able to take her in a fight normally, but right now he could barely see straight. 'But it's his choice. That's important. When he found out you'd left to save his life, he couldn't bear it. The only reason it's taken us this long to get here is because Captain Haven's had us under close watch and we couldn't find a way to sneak off the ship until last week. I'm not going to take that choice from him. I'm just here to try to minimise the damage.'

Lucky rubbed at his temples. Of course Gabriel had come after him. 'This is my choice. Doesn't that count?'

'Is it?' She raised an eyebrow.

He nodded and regretted it immediately. His vision swam his stomach roiled. Sienna moved back, looking alarmed. Lucky forced down several deep breaths and his stomach settled.

'Did you really have to hit me with a rock?'

'I was working with limited options.' She shrugged. 'You want to know what I think?'

Lucky did not. He wanted to go back to being an acolyte, to beating Yale in the training yard. To being hardened and empty.

'I think you don't know who you are, so you fill yourself in with whatever's around you. On the *Dreamer*, you let Gabriel shape you. Then you left him and became what the Beaters wanted you to be.' She pointed a finger at him. 'When are you going to start living as Lucky?'

'Robin,' he mumbled.

'What?'

'My name is Robin, apparently.'

She threw back her head and roared with laughter. 'Sorry, sorry. But it doesn't suit you.'

He couldn't suppress the slight smile on his own face. 'It doesn't, does it? Not sure Lucky is any better.'

'It could be, if you wanted it to be,' she suggested.

Footsteps approached and they both turned to see Gabriel walking towards them. His head was down, shoulders hunched. A stab of guilt poked at Lucky's ribs and he quashed it quickly. This was Gabriel's choice, not his.

'Time to make a decision.' Sienna's hand moved towards her belt. 'You want those kidneys left in place? Or shall I toast them for you?'

Lucky let out a sigh. He wasn't sure he could fight her with his head still spinning, and he also wasn't sure she wouldn't hit him again. 'I'll stay with you until we reach the next town. Then I'll see.' They'd understand soon enough.

'Good enough for now.' She let her hand drop and turned to call over her shoulder. 'Come on, Gabe. We're waiting here.'

Grumbling, he dropped down next to her, and handed her a waterskin. She took a drink and handed it to Lucky. Gabriel squeezed a second one, and a jet of water shot up.

He waved his hand and it coalesced into a ball, floating in mid-air. Another flick of his fingers and it started spinning. The paint on his nails was a deep green, Lucky noted, but chipped and worn as if he hadn't painted it in days.

'Is it wise to be dancing this close to a Beater stronghold?' Sienna asked.

'I think my secret's out already,' Gabriel replied. 'It helps me relax. Give me that at least.'

'How did you find me?' Lucky asked. 'The Beaters keep this place off the maps.'

Gabriel opened his mouth and directed the blob of water in. 'I followed your drawings.' He didn't meet Lucky's eyes.

'Huh.' The habit of sketching whenever he was still for a moment hadn't left him. As Yale had marched him away from Ciatheme, he'd doodled something on the rocks every time they paused to rest, eat, or sleep.

'They were clearly yours. I'd recognise your style anywhere.'

Lucky didn't know what to say, so he took another mouthful of water.

'We should get moving,' Sienna announced as she stood. 'I think the Beaters are going to be busy for a while, but we shouldn't take the chances after we kidnapped one of their own.'

'Lucky's not a Beater,' Gabriel protested. 'Uniforms and vows don't make a Beater.'

'That's up to Lucky, isn't it?' she replied as she set off down the path. Lucky followed without answering, leaving Gabriel to take up the rear. He wasn't a Beater, not officially, but he didn't want to bring that up, give Gabriel something to hold on to.

The path wound along the valley wall, far above the tumbling river below. Most of the time it was only wide enough for them to walk single file, which saved Lucky from any stilted conversations or awkward questions. Yale had explained that the hall was once a military post, and the valley kept enemies from successfully storming it on that side. But the need for the Beaters to be a martial force had ended hundreds and hundreds of years ago. Now it was just the place where the young acolytes went to have their spirits broken before they were passed off to be church enforcers.

Evening settled in by the time they reached the valley floor. Lucky glanced back up the path, but there was no sign of anyone coming after them.

'We should find somewhere to stop for the night,' Sienna said. 'Before it gets too hard to see.'

'Just over there.' Lucky pointed to where he and Yale had stopped on the last day before they reached The Fell. Before Lucky's life had changed all over again. He led them to a cleared area away from the river. 'We'll have to set a watch. There's no way to defend it.'

'You think the Beaters will come after us?' Gabriel asked and Sienna rolled her eyes.

'Two heretics and a runaway? We're lucky the earthshake did so much damage or we'd have never got away in the first place.'

He held up a hand. 'All right, all right. Just trying to think positive.'

She rolled them again. 'Yeah, that's always been your problem, Golden Boy.'

They shared a meagre meal of stale bread and jerked meat from Sienna's pack. Lucky picked at it, too troubled by roving memories and rampaging emotions to be hungry, whereas Gabriel devoured it and looked sadly at his empty hands.

'Get some sleep.' Lucky stood up and brushed down the black trousers of his Beater's uniform. 'I'll take the first watch.'

Sienna gave him a dismissive wave and lay down, wrapping her cloak around her. Lucky moved away from the clearing and found a place to sit where he could see the path up to the hall. Night brought out the insects, nipping and biting at any exposed skin, but it also brought out the swooping bats that preyed on them. They charged across the river surface, leathery wings flapping frantically.

He listened to the river, the chuckling, burbling sound so different to the rhythmic washing of the waves against the hull of the *Dreamer*. He wondered if he'd ever get to hear that again, then sighed. He had to let go, for everyone's sake. Curse Gabriel for not letting things be.

'Curse him,' he muttered out loud for good measure, smacking his hand against the rock he sat on.

'I'd rather we talked,' Gabriel said softly.

Lucky started, almost falling off his perch. He stood and turned to find Gabriel leaning up against a tree, watching him. He looked tired, the scratch stark against his pale cheek, his hair fraying from its braid. Lucky's stomach dropped, then he gritted his teeth. This was because of him. Gabriel had been hurt because he wouldn't leave Lucky alone.

'There's nothing to talk about, Gabriel.'

'Don't I get a say in that?' He left the tree and came to sit down on another rock, across from Lucky. 'I've had a really long journey. I think you could at least talk to me. I know why you left, and believe me, I'm grateful, but I came to help you and it's like you don't even want to be rescued.'

Lucky scowled. 'I don't. I'm not a pet or a helpless child. I can make my own decisions.' Of course Gabriel saw him like that. Had Lucky ever been anything but a project to him? At least Sienna appreciated he was his own person. *When are you going to start living as Lucky?*

Gabriel's cheeks flushed. 'I didn't mean it like that. There's nothing wrong with needing help, mate.'

'I don't need help.'

'So, you're happy being a Beater? You're going to spend your days harassing sailors, trying to find the water dancers so you can manipulate them into committing a crime and lock them up? Is that what you want?' His voice had gone cold, so unlike Gabriel's normal tone.

'I know who I am now!' The words burst out of him, and he glanced around guiltily, afraid he'd brought the Beaters down on them. In a softer voice, he added, 'This is what I deserve.'

Gabriel rubbed his temple. 'No, you don't. I won't believe it. I won't believe the friend who got me through the worst part of my life deserves this. We can fix this, Lucky. We can make it right again. You can go back to the *Dreamer*.'

Maybe Gabriel believed that, but Lucky didn't. 'It's done now. I've made my choice. Go home, Gabriel. The *Dreamer* is where you belong.'

'You could belong there too.' Gabriel stretched out a hand.

Fire smouldered in Lucky's guts, sending smoke through his veins. His skin itched with it. 'Why don't you get it? I'm a murderer! I killed my mother! I don't belong and I don't deserve to belong.'

Gabriel stood up. His eyes were filled with pity, and that only made Lucky's anger burn harder. 'I told you, I don't believe you're a bad person. I don't believe you killed her. I know you, Lucky.'

'You knew me,' he corrected. 'And maybe you didn't know me as well as you think.'

'I don't believe you're a killer,' he repeated.

Lucky threw up his hands. 'Then what? My memories are right and the ghost girl with the white hair did it? She's not real, Gabriel. She's just a figment of my imagination. I don't want to talk about her.' His mind had latched on to her, just as it had his nickname for Gabriel. Building a fantasy to save himself from having to deal with what he'd done.

'You don't want to talk about us,' Gabriel said sullenly.

'There is no us, Gabriel.' Saying it gave it power. Made it true. Lucky let his emotions leave with a long exhaled breath, and when he breathed in again, there was only a deep emptiness, like a still black pool in his heart. 'I'm not the boy you used to know.'

Gabriel put his head in his hands, his shoulders shaking. It was better this way, Lucky told himself. He hurt people. Better that he hurt Gabriel like this, than he hurt him like he'd hurt his mother.

When he raised his head again, Gabriel's eyes were red and tears streaked his cheeks. But his mouth was set in a firm line.

'Fine,' he said. 'I get it. You believe it, Lucky. I get that. But I don't. So we're going to sit down and talk through what happened that day. See if we can't figure something out. Figure out what's real.'

'It won't change anything,' Lucky said, but his resolve was weakening. The point was to stop Gabriel being hurt, and arguing was doing just that. He leaned back against the tree, watching the bats darting about above. He wondered what it would be like to be a bat, to live only for eating and flying, free of all the emotions and fears of being human. Gabriel waited, watching him, his braid bright in the moonlight.

Lucky gave up resisting and told Gabriel everything he could remember about that day, reliving the scent of sea salt on the air, the sound of the seabirds calling, the feel of the rock in his hands, slick with his mother's blood. The girl's smile. Despite what he now knew, he still saw her raise the rock in his mind's eye.

'What about before that?' Gabriel asked. 'What happened before you met her on the beach?'

Lucky paused. He'd buried much of his childhood, thrown it away as someone else, someone he could no longer be. 'I don't remember.' He shivered, the cold of the night creeping down his collar. 'Do you? If we were friends, maybe we were together before it happened?'

'I'm not sure.' Gabriel clasped his hands together, resting his chin on his fingers. He curled in on himself. Lucky fought the urge to rest a hand against his back, urge him to sit straighter. He had no right to touch that perfect form, not with hands stained with blood. 'That was around the time my father tried to kill me. It's not something I like to think about.'

'Then don't, Gabriel. You don't need to—'

Gabriel held up a hand, cutting him off. He closed his eyes. 'Before that moment . . . I'd been at home. I'd been waiting. For you, I think.'

I thought you'd gone, left without saying goodbye. Lucky felt guilt twisting at his insides.

'My father came back. He was angry with me for being out all night.' Gabriel rubbed at his neck. 'I don't know if he was angrier about me being out, or because I came back.'

'Where were you, the night before?' Lucky asked.

'I . . . I don't know.' Gabriel raised his head. 'I don't remember. Why can't I remember?'

'It's probably like you said,' Lucky said. 'You don't like thinking about it. You put it out of your mind and now you don't know how to pull it back.' That made sense. That day had changed them both.

'I don't know,' Gabriel said slowly. 'I remember everything else so clearly. I still feel his hands around my neck. Why can't I remember what happened the night before? Why don't either of us remember?'

Chapter Seventeen

Why don't either of us remember? The words echoed around Lucky's head as they walked. He'd been unable to give Gabriel a satisfactory answer the previous night, and eventually he'd left Lucky and gone to sleep. Lucky was grateful for the watch, because he'd have never been able to do the same.

He'd sat focusing on the river, forcing the sound of it to fill his mind and drive out the emotions and the memories. The hurt. The fear. Until Sienna had got up and told him to go to sleep or else she'd knock him out again.

They both let Gabriel sleep.

He slept like he did on the *Dreamer*, on his side, hands tucked under his chin. A picture of innocence. Lucky longed to find out if his back was as warm as it had been, and when he finally dropped off, it was with an ache of loneliness in his gut that invaded his dreams.

In the morning, they set off with barely a word. Sienna's face was clouded with simmering anger, while Gabriel looked sick and pale, his eyes still red and raw. Lucky just felt empty.

He couldn't let Gabriel's words drop, though. Even though both of them had good reason to have blocked memories around that day, it still felt off that there was a period neither of them could remember. It meant there was a connection between them that remained unresolved.

He couldn't have that. He'd hurt Gabriel enough and he hated to see him so hunched and miserable. He'd been good to Lucky. He deserved to be free of Lucky.

The day was dull, misty. The damp permeated clothes and hair, sticking both to skin. Gabriel started the day by dancing the water off himself in a great splash, but he was soaked again within a few paces and he quickly gave up on the idea.

'How far is it to the nearest town?' Gabriel called.

'Depends how much energy you waste whining on the way,' Sienna called back. 'We should get there by nightfall.'

'Hot coffee. I am going to drink so much hot coffee when we get there,' Gabriel muttered to himself. 'And have a hot bath. Wash my hair. Dry clothes. A bed.'

Lucky pulled his clothes around him and huddled on. The rain picked up as they walked. It dropped off his ears, splashed around his neck. Even the pewter feather felt heavier. He'd tried several times to get rid of it while living with the Beaters, but he could never quite bring himself to do so. Something that was his. He couldn't throw that away.

He passed a small fish, scratched into a stone by the road as he'd stopped to tie his laces. Yale hadn't noticed it, or any of the others, and he was a Beater, trained to observe and judge. Yet Gabriel had.

Gabriel had seen him.

He hunched deeper, bringing his collar up to his ears. He couldn't afford to think like that. As soon as they hit the town, he'd turn back. That was right.

'What was your plan, anyway?' he asked.

Gabriel mumbled something about coffee and looked up. 'Hmm?'

'Were you going to storm The Fell? Come in pistols cocked and ready for a fight?'

Gabriel chewed his lip and Lucky knew the answer. 'We were going to work something out when we got closer,' he admitted. 'But we got ambushed by a mountain cat.' He touched the scratch on his cheek.

'So you put Sienna in danger without even having a plan?'

The hurt on Gabriel's face echoed in Lucky's chest. He was punishing them both, and he hated it, but he needed to be sure Gabriel wouldn't come back.

'It wasn't like that!' Gabriel protested. 'It was important. Sometimes important things just need doing.'

Lucky snorted. 'That's where you're wrong. I'm not important.' He pushed down the path past Sienna. She spat something quietly at him, and he caught the word kidneys, but she didn't stop him. As he carried on, she spoke with Gabriel in a low voice. Planning something? Going to knock him out again? Let them try.

He wouldn't get caught out again.

By late afternoon, the rain had eased off and the clouds overhead broke up. The ground ahead was dry, and Lucky looked forward to not trudging through mud. The two water dancers dried themselves, leaving puddles at the side of the road, but Lucky refused to let either of them do the same for him. He'd borne the soggy boots and cold damp clothing all day and he wasn't going to give either of them power over him.

Up ahead, dark clouds smudged the sky. He sighed, hoping further rain would hold off until they found shelter, but the longer he looked at them, the more it became clear they were not rain clouds.

'Something's burning,' he said, holding up a hand for the others to stop.

'Shit.' Gabriel looked up at the sky. 'We should hurry, see if we can help.'

'Gabe,' Sienna said softly.

'Don't "Gabe" me, people could be in trouble.'

'And we'll be in trouble if the Beaters catch us dancing. You understand that, right?' She gave him a sad smile. 'We didn't come all this way and escape a Beater jail to end up in one again.'

He looked at her, then over to the smoke, and back again. 'I . . . I suppose.'

'I'm not saying we can't help. I'm just saying be careful. You're not very good at that.'

'You sound like my mothers.' He stuck his lip out in a pout.

'Because they, like me, know you well.'

'Let's just get on with it,' Lucky said, starting for the town. He was cold and damp and wanted nothing more than to rest a bit before heading back to The Fell. A fire wasn't his problem. Gabriel gave him an injured look and Lucky pushed down his shame.

It was better this way.

It wasn't hard to find the source of the fire as they entered the town. People rushed around like ants in a disturbed nest, some with buckets of water from the river, and others with their arms full of belongings. Gabriel led the way, his long legs leaving Lucky and Sienna struggling to keep up with him.

The burning building turned out to be the guildhall, a large timber-framed building in the centre of the town. By the time they got there, it was nothing more than smouldering ruins, the blackened timbers sticking up like the ribs of some vast creature. People poked through the remains, pulling out objects charred beyond recognition.

'Looks like we're too late to do much,' Sienna said, the relief shining in her voice.

'What happened here?' Gabriel asked a man sifting through the ruins.

The man looked up sharply, then his shoulders fell. 'No one quite knows. Something on the upper floor caught light. Maybe someone dropped a lantern? Impossible to say. Terrible business.' He drew two fingers across his chest.

'Was . . . was anyone hurt?'

'Five dead that we know of, at least another eight unaccounted for. There was no warning.' The man shook his head.

'There was no warning in the threads.' He moved to make the gesture again, but his hand trembled too much, and he let it fall.

Gabriel paled. 'I'm sorry.'

The man just shook his head again and Gabriel slunk back to Lucky and Sienna.

'Fire here, earthshakes up the valley. What's with all this?' he asked. 'The man said the church gave no warning. That's why the damage was so severe.'

'What's the point in having your life controlled by fate if disasters are going to happen without warning?' Sienna muttered.

Gabriel glanced at the smoking ruins. 'This isn't normal.'

'I hope they sort things out quickly. Because you know they're going to blame people like us otherwise.'

The inn on the main square was full of people talking about the fire, or just sitting and drinking, their expressions blank and their hands unsteady. There was one room left, and Gabriel claimed it in delight, along with a warm meal for all of them and the promise of a tub of hot water to be sent up later.

It was only when he entered the room that the situation seemed to dawn on him.

'Oh. One bed.'

'Mine.' Sienna pushed past him and leapt on to it, spreading herself out wide. 'Too slow, Golden Boy. You and Lucky can share the floor.'

'Works for me.' Lucky squeezed past Gabriel and settled himself on the floor in the far corner. He pulled off his boots and wrung out his socks. Sienna pinched her nose and waved a hand in front of her face as if warding off a bad smell.

'It's not that bad,' Lucky protested.

'It's pretty bad, mate,' Gabriel said, with a trace of his usual smile. Lucky looked away. 'Hang on. You're dripping on the floor.' He waved his fingers and the water that Lucky had wrung out coalesced into a ball. Gabriel moved his other hand, and the water in Lucky's clothes and hair pulled away from him.

'I told you, I don't need you to do that,' Lucky snapped.

There was a knock at the door and then it opened. In a panic, Gabriel swung the ball of water to the space behind the open door as one of the serving women from the inn walked in with a tray of food. She set it on the table and glanced at Lucky.

'Aren't you supposed to be with the other Beaters? They're all out in the square.'

'I'm coming. Just getting clean socks.'

She left the room without another word. As the door closed, Gabriel dropped the ball of water into the chamber pot.

'Idiot,' Lucky told him. Gabriel slumped, pulling in on himself, and Lucky felt a stab of guilt. 'I'm not angry, Gabriel. I'm not going to hit you.'

Gabriel slowly lowered his hands.

'You two eat. I'm going to check out what the Beaters know.' He pulled his socks and boots back on. They were much more pleasant now they were dry.

'You sure that's a good idea?' Sienna still lay on her back on the bed.

'Better than water dancing,' he replied with a pointed look at Gabriel. 'I'll be careful.'

He pushed through the throng of people in the common room and stepped out into the cool night air. The group of Beaters, despite their black clothes, was easy to find, standing in a huddle by the ravaged corpse of the guildhall. Lucky slipped into the back of the group, hoping not to be noticed. A woman turned to him. He tensed. Had news about the hall reached them? If it had, he could be in trouble.

'Who are you?' she asked.

'I'm . . . Robin. I've just come from the hall. Yale sent me,' he added. 'What have I missed?' He couldn't win people over like Gabriel did, with easy smiles and an open expression, so he tried to be more like Yale, using a tone that dripped with authority. He wasn't sure he'd quite pulled it off, but the woman tipped her head. Lucky smothered his relief. They didn't know. His uniform gave him another mask, another identity. Another shape he didn't quite fit into.

'No one can find any sign of heresy, but nothing showed up in the threads.'

There was that phrase again.

'Niall's going to send word to the church, get them to perform an augury,' she continued. 'We need answers at this point.'

Lucky nodded as if he knew what an augury was.

'First time in a hundred and fifty years,' the woman continued, sounding excited. 'At least we'll get to be part of history.'

'Will they do it here?' Lucky asked and she laughed.

'Hah. Good one. Minmouth. There's a good beach there. Probably in about a week. Takes time to prepare, of course.'

'Of course,' he said. Agree. Don't stand out. Follow orders. 'I'll let them know back at the hall.'

The other Beaters were drifting off now, and she gave him a nod. 'Keep your eyes out. Something's not right and we need to get to the bottom of it.'

Lucky raised his hand and turned back to the inn. When he reached the room, he paused with his hand on the handle. Gabriel and Sienna's voices carried through the door, but they were reduced to mumbles. Lucky put his ear against the wood.

'. . . Don't know how to help him,' Gabriel said.

'Maybe you can't, Gabe,' she replied. 'I know you want to, but you can't fix all the world's problems.'

'I don't want to fix the world. I want my friend back.'

Lucky's stomach clenched at the pain in Gabriel's voice. Perhaps it was better to go now and leave Gabriel alone. He'd get the message eventually. Or maybe he wouldn't and they'd spend their lives chasing each other across the country. Lucky didn't want that, for either of them. He'd tried being blunt, being honest, and that hadn't helped either. Perhaps the best thing would be to get Gabriel back to the *Dreamer*. Then he could leave things in the hands of Captain Haven. He could rely on her to make sure Gabriel stayed put, at least.

He sighed. None of this was what he wanted. But it was for the best.

He pushed open the door.

'Don't look!' Gabriel called. A splash of water told Lucky the bath had been delivered. He put a hand over his eyes and walked over to the table, peering under his fingers to find the uneaten bowl of stew.

'Don't worry, I'm not interested.'

'Now you're just being cruel,' Gabriel muttered.

Lucky picked up his dinner and turned towards the bed, away from the splashing. Sienna sat with her back to them on the far side, looking out the window.

'Make your mind up,' she said. 'Do you want him to look or not?'

'Not . . . I guess.'

Lucky tried, but he couldn't resist a quick glance over his shoulder. Gabriel sat in a tub barely big enough for him, his back to Lucky. His hair was free of the braid and hung down his back in a waterfall of dark gold as he manipulated water over his head. Lucky had only meant to take a quick glance, but he couldn't draw his eyes away. He wondered what it would be like to plunge his hands into that waterfall.

'You all right there, Lucky?' Sienna said. She hadn't turned around, but Lucky realised he must have been staring for several moments. Gabriel turned his head as Lucky looked away.

Their eyes only met for a moment, but it was enough for him to catch Gabriel's smirk.

He clenched his fist, almost spilling his food.

The corner he'd chosen before was no good, no way to fully avoid the tub, so he sat down on the bed next to Sienna. The stew was almost cold, but Lucky was hungry enough not to care.

Sienna waited until he had a mouthful before asking, 'What did you find out from the Beaters?'

Lucky rolled his eyes and ate another mouthful to spite her. 'Nothing much. They said there was no warning, and they're confused. They're planning something called an augury.'

Sienna paled and there was a rush of water as Gabriel stood up. Lucky fought the urge to turn around.

'What? When?' Gabriel demanded. 'We have to stop it.'

'Are you decent, Gabe?' Sienna asked.

'What? Hmm, one moment.' There was a smattering of falling droplets, then a rustle of fabric. 'You can look now.'

Lucky and Sienna moved to the other side of the bed as Gabriel sat cross-legged on the floor. His hair was dry but loose, and he played a strand of it around and around a finger.

'When's the augury? Where are they doing it?' Gabriel asked again.

'Tell me what one is, first,' Lucky replied. He hated that so much of the world still felt like a mystery. 'Why is it such a big deal?'

'The church uses it to predict things when they cannot read the threads clearly. It's a very rare occurrence,' Sienna said, which didn't explain why Gabriel was so panicked about the idea.

'And they do it with a leviathan,' Gabriel added, sounding sick. 'They kill a leviathan and read the future in its guts.'

Chapter Eighteen

Gabriel pulled his arms around his knees. 'We can't let them do it.'

'We won't,' Sienna said softly.

'How do you propose to stop them?' Lucky asked as they both turned on him with matched glares. 'I'm just asking the question. If the church has the power to kill a leviathan, then they're not going to respond well to a group of heretics saying no, are they?' He focused his attention on his food.

'It's . . . He has a point, Gabriel.' Sienna flopped back on the bed.

'We'll just have to be faster than them,' he replied. 'The church hasn't done this for over a century because it's a monumentally stupid and dangerous thing to do. Chasing a serpent the size of a ship and driving it to shore. And they're not dancers, either. Whereas we've worked with the leviathans for years. We can entice it, chase it away from their ships.' He slapped a hand against the floor. 'We can do it.'

'We'd have to draw it out to sea, get it away out of their reach. And avoid being eaten while doing so.' She pushed a hand through her hair as she sat up again. 'It's not going to be easy.'

'You don't have to,' he said. 'I couldn't force anyone to put themselves at risk. But I'm going to try.'

'Of course you are, Golden Boy.' She shook her head. 'Of course you are.'

Lucky fidgeted with his spoon. This wasn't the plan. He needed to get Gabriel back home to the ship. Get him somewhere where he couldn't follow Lucky.

Keep him safe.

'Wouldn't it be better to go back to the *Dreamer*,' he suggested, trying to keep his voice level. If Gabriel had any suspicions, he'd never go for it. 'We could help more if there was more than just you two.'

Gabriel divided his hair into three and started braiding it again. 'You're right, of course, apart from two small issues. One, we don't know where the *Dreamer* is right now. We slipped off as soon as she returned to Ciatheme. The other issue is Mum will absolutely murder me the moment I step back on board.'

Sienna rolled her eyes. 'She won't literally murder you.'

'Maybe you're right. But even if she doesn't, she'll lock me up for the rest of my life. And even if she doesn't do that, we don't know where the *Dreamer* is, so it doesn't matter.' He folded his arms.

'If they hear about an augury, they might turn up. Can't see either of your mothers being any happier about it than you,' Sienna said, and Lucky latched on to the hope.

'The augury is taking place in Minmouth. Maybe we could meet them there.'

'We're about half a day from the coast,' she said. 'We can get a ship to Minmouth, and someone might have news about the *Dreamer* while we're there.'

'Let's get some sleep,' Lucky suggested. Go to Minmouth, try to prevent Gabriel getting himself eaten by a leviathan, hope the *Dreamer* showed up. As plans went, it was less solid than water, but it was something. He could hold on to something.

Sienna rolled back on the bed and spread her arms, taking up as much space as she could. 'Still mine.'

Lucky went back to the corner and lay down facing the wall. At least the inn was warm and dry, which was more than could be said for his cell in the castle or the Beater dorms. He wrapped the black cloak up and used it as a pillow, breathing in the earthy scent of the wool. The room soon filled with the sound of Sienna snoring gently on the bed.

The back of Lucky's neck prickled.

'What, Gabriel?' he asked, refusing to roll over.

For a moment, there was silence. 'I saw you looking at me.'

Lucky sighed, not bothering to hide it. 'And?'

'No reason.' Even in the dark of the room, his grin was clear.

'Let it go, please.' He pushed his head down on the cloak, trying to smother any noise in the fabric.

'Why?' There was a rustle of movement and Lucky could picture him sitting up, staring at him while he fiddled with the end of his braid. Lucky didn't dare roll over in case his resolve broke. 'You're still attracted to me. You still have feelings for me.'

'Those are two different things.' Lucky sat up. If Gabriel wanted this, then they could do it properly. He met Gabriel's eye and crossed his arms. 'Yes, you're attractive. You can have that. But any feelings I had for you are gone, and that's the important thing.'

'But how can you have attraction without feelings?' Gabriel protested and Lucky shrugged. Gabriel's shoulders fell 'I . . . I just don't understand. You kiss me, you save my life, and now you want nothing to do with me?'

'It's just better this way. I'm a Beater, you're a water dancer. Not a good combination.' *Don't hurt him*, the captain's voice echoed in his mind. *He's been hurt enough in his life.*

'But you didn't even know anything about religion until we visited Sea Hall,' Gabriel pointed out. 'How can you suddenly devote your life to that?'

'I haven't. I don't care about the thread of fate, and I don't have any issue with dancers. But the Beaters told me what to do.' Punished him.

'That's pathetic,' Gabriel said, the closest Lucky had ever heard him come to angry.

'That's me.' He held out his hands. 'Pathetic.'

Silence moved between them, sinuous, enveloping. Lucky found himself caught in its coils, unable to breath. Gabriel folded his hands, resting his chin on them.

'I'm not giving up on you, Lucky. I'm not giving up on my friend.' His voice was soft, but firm. That calm, confident tone that meant so much to Lucky in the early days. Lucky closed his eyes, tears burning behind his eyelids. Lucky pictured Gabriel, bright smiles, outstretched hand, offering, never demanding. But then remembered him lying on the deck of the *Dreamer* in a pool of his own vomit, and his own resolve firmed. He wasn't going to let that happen again.

'Lucky isn't my name,' he said, words as bitter as bile. 'But of course, you know that.'

'Lucky wasn't a name,' Gabriel replied. 'It was a promise. It was a promise you gave me that things would get better. I clung to that. Through all the yelling and the beatings. Every time I thought he'd go too far and kill me. Because you were right. Things did get better. So now I'm giving it to you. And one day you'll believe me too.'

Lucky turned away, curling up and squeezing his eyes tight so Gabriel couldn't see any trace of the tears building. He couldn't believe him.

Sienna woke him in the morning by shouting in Lucky's ear. Lucky groaned, his back and shoulders stiff from sleeping on the hard floor. Gabriel pulled his cloak over his head.

'Come on, lazy lumps. We've got to get to Minmouth and save a leviathan.'

'How far is it?' Lucky asked, stretching. His body made an annoying series of clicks.

'Half a day to the coast, and then a couple of days by sea,' she replied. 'The Beaters said a week, right? We should get there in plenty of time. It will take them a while to organise the ships they need and find a leviathan. Come on, Gabe. Get up. It's rescue time.'

'I'm up. I'm up,' he mumbled. 'But first, coffee.'

They ate a quick breakfast in the common room and Sienna bought more supplies for the road. Lucky handed over some of his wages, taken that day in Ciatheme and left unspent on his person ever since.

Gabriel watched him over his coffee cup. 'You don't care about any of us, but you're contributing funds.'

'I care about the leviathan, not you.' It was a lie, of course. The leviathans terrified him, but so did his lingering feelings for Gabriel, the care he couldn't shake. He desperately hoped they'd catch up with the *Dreamer*, because the idea of walking away on his own was getting harder and harder to bear, no matter how hard he tried. Lucky finished his drink; it was still too hot for him to actually enjoy, but he welcomed the punishing burn as it slid down his throat. This was right.

Gabriel just gave him an obnoxious smile.

The landscape on the route to the coast was wide open farmland. Lucky could see for miles across the fields of crops and livestock, and it left him feeling open and exposed. The sky seemed endless, a vast savanna of deepening grey. He longed for something to hold on to, something solid he could ground himself with, but he could not go back to hanging on to Gabriel's braid.

Gabriel, fuelled by a hot coffee for the first time in days, was in a sickeningly cheerful mood. At first, Lucky had been afraid he'd turn that energy on him, but Gabriel seemed keener on plaguing Sienna. Every time they passed a field of animals, he'd lean over to her and say 'cows' or 'sheep', while she protested that she knew exactly what they were, her expression growing steadily darker and darker.

Lucky wondered if there would ever be a time where he could be like that. Free. Happy. If he would feel safe and comfortable enough to get close to people again. But every time Gabriel's cheerfulness started to affect him, he'd remind himself of Gabriel lying unconscious on the deck of the *Dreamer*, of Yale's callousness, of his mother, face down dead on the beach, her blood leaching into the sand. Of everything he'd caused. Of everything he'd lose if he let his guard down.

This was right.

The rain came down again, a sudden, thundery downpour that had them soaked to the skin in minutes. There was no shelter, only open fields, so there was no choice but to push on. The ground, already sodden from yesterday's rain, quickly became a quagmire of mud and surface run-off.

Lucky almost stepped into the river.

He'd been walking, head down, hood up, trying to keep the rain out of his face as much as possible. Sienna grabbed his arm, yanking him backwards. He turned to protest and she pointed ahead.

The river had burst its banks, spilling out over the grass, the water the same muddy brown as the run-off that had turned the paths into streams themselves. He'd almost put his foot in it and been washed away by the treacherous current.

Would that be so wrong?

Lucky stared at the river, twisting, changing, never the same pattern of water from one moment to the next. He wanted to lose himself to that, to lose any sense of Robin, of Lucky, of who he was.

He wanted to unravel.

The world was too big and he was too small and even still there didn't seem to be room for him. He didn't fit.

'Lucky?' Gabriel said softly. His hand lingered near Lucky's shoulder, not touching, just asking. Lucky longed to lean into it, to feel Gabriel's strength and warmth, but he'd be leeching off it. He didn't deserve it. He . . .

He lifted his head, peering into the misty grey of the pouring rain.

'Someone's shouting,' he said.

Gabriel followed his gaze. 'I don't hear anything.'

'No, he's right,' Sienna replied. She shaded her eyes, peering into the gloom. 'There's someone shouting for help.'

'Over there.' Lucky hurried along the side of the river and pointed towards the other bank. A tree had fallen over, lying across the water, and hanging on to one of its branches was a young boy, maybe eight or nine years old. 'Hey!'

The boy turned and his eyes widened. 'Help me!' he begged, gripping the branch for dear life.

'We've got to do something,' Lucky said, turning to the two water dancers.

'We have to, Sienna,' Gabriel said. 'There's no one else out here, and no way across to the other side.'

'I know, I know. I'm not going to let a child drown if I can help it. We'll have to try and hold the water back, make a path. Do you think we can?'

Gabriel gave her a tight smile. 'We can't just stand by.'

The two water dancers took up position on the bank, moving their hands in unison. At first, nothing seemed to be happening, but as he watched, Lucky realised they were holding back the river near the tree, letting it flow closer to their side of the bank. A wall of water built up, towering over the tree on one side while the river receded away from it on the other, giving the boy space to get to safety.

'Go on!' Lucky yelled. 'Quickly now!'

'I can't!' the boy wailed, clinging tightly to the branch. He stared at the wall of water in horror. 'I'm scared.'

'I can't hold this up forever,' Sienna said through gritted teeth. Her face was red with exertion.

'The moment we stop, that water is going to overwhelm him, sweep him right out to sea,' Gabriel replied. 'We'll never be able to catch up with him.'

'Please,' Lucky begged the boy. 'You have to move.'

But the boy just shut his eyes and clung on for dear life.

The wall of water wobbled, and Lucky knew the water dancers were nearing the end of their strength. He looked at the distance to the gap in the river, judging it against his physical abilities.

'Can you give me a bit more room?' he asked Gabriel. 'I think I can jump to him.'

'I'll try,' Gabriel said. The muscles in his arm and neck were taut, shuddering with effort.

The wall of water moved, spilling over at the far end, and pulling up closer to them. The damp space that was free from the rushing torrent moved closer to Lucky. He shifted back, readying himself for the jump.

'I promise I can do this,' he murmured to the rain, and then he ran, leaping out over the river. For a horrible moment, he thought he wasn't going to make it, that he'd land in the water and get swept away. But he threw himself forwards, grabbing at the long grass that had been buried underwater only minutes before. His feet and ankles landed in the water, which gripped him like fate, pulling him downriver.

Lucky held on for dear life.

'Come on, hurry!' Sienna yelled.

Lucky dragged himself to his feet and rushed to the boy.

'I'm Lucky,' he said, holding out a hand. 'I'm going to help you get to safety. Will you trust me?'

The boy stared at Lucky's hand, then over his shoulder at the water. 'Colin,' he said quietly, holding out a hand in return.

Lucky grabbed his hand and pulled him into his arms. Colin clung to him for dear life. They were caught in an empty bubble, the river flowing around them on both sides now. The boy shivered and whimpered in Lucky's ear.

It was a promise. It was a promise that things would get better. You gave it to me and now I'm giving it to you.

You better be right, Gabriel, Lucky thought, and turned back towards the bank.

Water crashed down behind him, but Lucky did his best to ignore it. He struggled towards Sienna and Gabriel, who shifted the gap in the water as he moved. The mud sucked at him, pulling his feet down, but Lucky couldn't give up.

When he was within reach of the bank, he held Colin up and Sienna reached down, pulling him on to solid ground. He collapsed, sobbing into her arms. Lucky gripped the bank, struggling to pull himself up. He couldn't get purchase on the slippery mud.

'Hurry!' Gabriel gasped.

The wall of water wobbled, spilling down around Lucky. Cold water gripped at him, tangling around him. Sienna struggled to pull the child off her, stretching a free hand towards Lucky. He reached for her, his fingers brushing against hers.

And then the water came down, spilling over his head.

Chapter Nineteen

The water crashed over him, forcing him under the surface. He couldn't see, couldn't breathe. All he could hear was the rush of river pounding in his ears. It gripped him, dragging him along, as if the river was rope tied around him.

This is right.

He let it carry him like a prize, clutched tightly like a precious toy. He didn't fight, didn't kick or scream. Just let the river hold him, the thread of his fate. Binding him.

Drowning him.

He'd done his penance, and he'd saved a life. It wouldn't bring his mother back, but maybe it went some way to redressing the balance of things. The water stroked at his cheek gently. Fondly.

He hoped Gabriel wouldn't miss him too much.

The current slammed him into something solid, knocking the breath he'd held out of him. Lucky gasped, water flooding into his mouth. Instincts he'd forgotten – instincts he didn't know he still had – kicked in and he floundered, struggling for air.

His head broke the surface and he gasped, sucking in a noisy breath as his body tried to expel the water at the same time.

'Lucky!'

Gabriel raced down the flowing river, but he couldn't run on the water fast enough to keep up with the current. Lucky knew he was lost, that he should give up. This was how it should be. But that breath had awakened something in him, reignited a spark he'd tried to smother. If he died here, he'd never see another leviathan. He'd never feel the sea spray on his face. He'd never sit, shoulders brushing with Gabriel, and stare up at the stars. He'd never fully understand what had happened on that beach ten years ago.

If he drowned, he'd hurt Gabriel worse than anything he'd done so far.

Lucky thrashed, trying to find something to grab on to. The river pushed him under again, smothering him. This is your fate, it whispered in his ears. This is what happens to you. This is what's written.

Fuck fate.

His hand smacked against something solid, and his fingers tightened around it, digging in. A young tree, the river water halfway up its trunk. Lucky gripped it with all his might.

'Lucky!' Gabriel called again. He was closer now, but if Lucky let go, he'd be swept away again.

The water receded, inching away from him, backing up around him.

'Go get him, Golden Boy,' Sienna called.

And then Gabriel's hands were on him, and then he was lying on the bank, and then the river was running again. Lucky lay back and closed his eyes.

'Hey,' Gabriel said, and the word wrapped itself around Lucky's heart, squeezing it tight. 'Hey, stay with me.'

I want to, Lucky wanted to say, but his body convulsed, and he retched up the foul, muddy river water. Gabriel eased him on to his side, rubbing his hand in circles on Lucky's back.

Gabriel's firm hand on his back was a comfort as he retched, long after his stomach was empty. Finally, the nausea eased and he sat up, shivering.

'Can I hold you?' Gabriel asked, and Lucky nodded, about all he felt he had the strength to do. Gabriel put an arm around him, and Lucky leaned into him, resting his head against Gabriel's shoulder. Solid. Safe.

'I thought I'd lost you,' Gabriel said and the pain in his voice made Lucky's chest ache.

'We shouldn't stay here,' Sienna said. 'We need to keep moving.'

'Give us a moment to catch our breath,' Gabriel protested. 'How are you doing, Lucky?'

'I'll live,' Lucky said. 'I'm . . . I'm not sure I should, though.'

'Of course you should.' Gabriel sounded horrified. 'Of course you should.' His grip tightened on Lucky, pulling them closer. Lucky could hear Gabriel's heart beating, the sound reliable.

'My mother deserved to live, too, and I took that from her.'

Gabriel rested his cheek against Lucky's head, his whole body enveloping Lucky's. 'I still don't believe you. I don't see how the boy who cleaned my split lips, and who saved his spare money to help me escape, could ever be a murderer. And I saw how you acted just now, how you put your own life at risk to save that boy.'

Lucky pressed his face against Gabriel, let his tears mix with the rain and the river water.

'You and Sienna should go, leave me,' he said because he had to. 'I don't want you to get hurt. The Beaters already tried it once. If you get in their way . . .' His voice choked off.

'Hey, that's not going to happen again. I'll be ready for them,' Gabriel said. 'I'm stronger than people think.'

He was. Strong enough to come all this way to find Lucky. Strong enough to hold back a river. Strong enough to survive an abusive father, witness a traumatising death, take on a whole new life. And strong enough to still remain kind and gentle after all that.

'You deserve better.' Lucky sniffed.

'Isn't that my choice? I mean, sure, if I had my way, I'd be living in the best cabin in the *Dreamer*, with all the coffee I can drink, and everyone would respect my amazing abilities.

But life doesn't work like that.' He leaned in closer. 'Please, Lucky? I'm not asking you to kiss me again. But please, stay with me. I miss my friend so much.'

Lucky's eyes burned with tears he couldn't fight back.

'I . . . I feel like we made a promise,' Gabriel continued. 'We made a promise to each other when we were younger. Something neither of us remember. Something important.'

Lucky thought about two boys, standing on a windswept beach while the tide was out. Holding hands tightly. Both afraid but determined.

'I think you're right,' he replied. He swallowed, preparing himself. 'And I miss my friend, too.'

This was wrong.

This was dangerous.

This was stupid.

Lucky knew all this and still he held out a hand. Gabriel took it, squeezed it. His palms, roughened by ropes and wind and seawater, pushed against Lucky's. Real.

'I'm scared,' Lucky said. 'I don't know what's going on, what the Beaters want. And I'm so scared you'll get caught in the middle of it.'

'Me too,' Gabriel admitted. 'But what fate could stand up against two Lucky men?'

Lucky shuddered, not wanting to consider it.

Chapter Twenty

It took Lucky three attempts to stand up, even with Gabriel's help. His vision swam, and his legs felt too wobbly to hold himself up. Gabriel had an arm around his waist, supporting him. Together, they staggered down the path alongside the river. Sienna followed behind, with the boy holding tightly on to her hand.

It felt like a lifetime before they reached the coastal path that wound down towards the town below. Gabriel kept a close grip on him, and Lucky didn't try to fight it.

'Just think how good that coffee's going to taste when we finally get it,' Gabriel said, his voice forced cheerful over the chattering of his teeth.

Lucky didn't have Gabriel's deep love of the drink, but he couldn't deny the appeal of something warm. He looked down, spotting several tall ships in the harbour.

'The *Dreamer*'s not there.'

'It was never very likely,' Gabriel pointed out. 'But as long as we can get a ship to Minmouth, then we'll be fine. We'll stop the augury, and we'll find the *Dreamer*, and everything will be all right again.'

'You miss your mums, huh?'

'I do. I miss everyone, and the ship. I haven't been away from home this long . . . well, ever.'

'I'm sorry,' Lucky mumbled. 'I'm sorry. I . . .'

'Shh.' Gabriel stopped and raised his hand, his thumb resting just in front of Lucky's lips. 'Sometimes things are important. People are important.'

'I'm not important,' Lucky protested.

'You're important to me,' Gabriel said firmly, and Lucky rested his head against Gabriel's shoulder.

'You're important to me, too.'

'Ugh. Could you two have this moment somewhere else?' Sienna grunted. 'Perhaps somewhere warm and dry? Would that be all right? Some of us are bloody cold out here.'

Gabriel laughed, and the sound was sunlight on water, the steam rising off fresh coffee, fingertips brushing together.

'Sorry, sorry. We're nearly there. Let's find out which one of these ships is going in the direction of Minmouth.'

The town was empty as they approached, which didn't surprise Lucky. The driving rain hadn't let up in hours, and the wind had whipped the waves to froth, which probably put off any smaller boats setting out. Colin left to find relatives in town and Sienna led the way down towards the waterfront. There was more chance of finding crew from one of the ships in an inn close to the harbour.

In the centre of the town stood a large square building, backed on to the town graveyard. The glass of the windows had threads of colour that twisted and wove in and out of each other, disappearing off one window and then reappearing on the other. They gripped Lucky's attention, holding him in place. As he watched, they seemed to move and change.

'Hey.' Gabriel tugged at his hand. 'This isn't a good place to hang around.'

'Just a moment.' He could almost see something, shapes in the threads. His head hurt but he couldn't look away.

'Move,' Sienna hissed.

Lucky dragged his gaze away from the windows to see three Beaters leaving the church. He blinked, trying to clear the fuzzy threads that still marred his vision. His head felt strangely hollow, and pain pulsed at his temples.

'They don't know anything about us, and Lucky's in uniform, which should give us some cover. But we shouldn't hang around,' she added pointedly.

Lucky forced his feet to move, to walk away from the threads. His body didn't quite feel like his own, as if something else was puppeteering it and he was merely an observer. Three more Beaters came around a corner and stood in front of them.

Sienna swore, not quite under her breath.

'Is there a problem?' Lucky asked, stepping forwards. He put that disdain in his voice that Yale had done so well, that tone that suggested even looking at his boots was an act of audacity.

'Two heretics and a deserter.' The Beater, a short man with dark, greasy hair, held up a hand. 'Surrender yourselves now.'

'None of that is true,' Lucky lied.

'We're just ordinary people,' Sienna agreed. 'You cannot pin any claims of heresy on us.'

A muffled shouting caught their attention. Two more Beaters, dragging Colin with them. Lucky's heart sank.

'Tell us what happened.'

'They helped me!' the boy protested. 'They saved my life.' He twisted in his captor's grip, but the Beater held him tightly.

'And how exactly did they do that?'

Colin hung his head. 'They moved the river.'

'How did you know?' Lucky asked. No one had been around; no one could have seen the rescue.

The Beater smirked. 'The tapestry informed the priest this morning that a boy would be rescued by two heretics and a deserter. It was only a matter of waiting for you all to arrive.'

'So you knew a boy was going to be in trouble, but you did nothing?' Gabriel sounded sick. 'You could have rescued him yourself.'

'You're monsters,' Sienna agreed.

'Fate said finding you three was more important. You're to come with us to Minmouth, and you will be dealt with after the augury.'

Lucky put his hand on Yale's dagger. There were too many Beaters for him to win. But maybe he could earn enough time for Gabriel and Sienna to get away.

'Don't,' Gabriel said softly. 'I'm not losing you again.'

'But . . .'

'We want to get to Minmouth, right?'

Lucky shook his head. This was a bad idea. It might bring them close to the leviathan, but they'd never be allowed near enough to save it. Gabriel was too optimistic.

But the Beaters had already surrounded them, and he knew he'd lost the opportunity. The knife was wrenched away from him, and his hands tied behind his back. The rough rope dug deep into his wrists.

Gabriel pressed against him on one side, and Sienna on the other. Lucky was bound, facing another prison, but this time, at least he wasn't alone.

'On your feet. We're here.'

Lucky pulled himself upright with a groan. For the last two days, they'd been locked away in a cell built into the hold of a Beater ship. It was barely tall enough for Sienna to stand up, let alone Gabriel, and with the three of them, there was little room to move around. He and Gabriel had spent most of the time resting in silence, while Sienna plotted ever more extravagant fates for her enemies.

The Beater with the greasy hair, a man Lucky learned was named Osborne, gestured with his pistol, driving them up out of the hold and on to the deck.

'Into the boat,' he ordered. 'You'll be taken to shore, where you can watch your precious monster die.'

'They're just creatures,' Gabriel said. 'How can you be so cruel? They deserve to live as much as you or I.'

The Beater just laughed.

Lucky brushed the back of his hand against Gabriel's, and after a moment, Gabriel locked fingers with him.

The town of Minmouth was a smear of houses around a wide, flat expanse of sand. All were single storey, as if anything taller might be blown away by the winds coming in off the sea. Around them, four other ships sat at anchor, bobbing up and down in the gentle swell. All were galleons, much larger than the *Dreamer*, heavily armed.

Ready to kill.

Lucky hadn't cared much for the fate of the leviathan, but now they were here, facing down its would-be killers, he felt rage and disgust. The leviathans were just animals – dangerous when threatened, but so was any creature. To hunt one down, not for safety or food, sickened him.

Three other Beaters climbed into the boat with them, each of them armed with pistols, and then another two to row. He and Gabriel sat side by side in the centre of the boat, with Sienna behind them. The boat hit the water with a splash and made for shore.

Lucky's back was to the town, and he kept his eye on the horizon, where the sea met the sky, trying to resist the urge to cling to the seat. More ships approached, the Beaters' flag flying off the top of their mainmasts. And something else, moving just below the surface.

'Shit, it's here!' Osborne yelled. He pointed out to sea, where the snout of the leviathan rose above the water. There was immediate panic amongst the other Beaters. 'Row faster! Row! We need to get out of the bloody sea before that thing swallows us all down.'

The two at the oars pulled harder, and the boat moved faster. Behind them, cannons fired, exploding into the water. Gabriel shuddered.

'Ready?' Sienna whispered.

Lucky didn't know what she was planning, didn't want to risk questions in case they were heard. The Beaters' attention was all focused on the leviathan, though, so it was now or never.

'Go,' she urged, and threw herself off the boat. Lucky shoved Gabriel and they tumbled into the water. A pistol shot went off, but it disappeared harmlessly into the sea.

'Gabe!' Sienna shouted. 'We gotta capsize it!'

Lucky struggled to keep his head above water as the two dancers manipulated the waves, tossing the boat on its side. The Beaters spilled into the water, floundering. Sienna flipped the boat back and threw herself in. Gabriel helped Lucky and the boat moved away from the Beaters, out towards the sea and the leviathan. Behind them, the Beaters screamed and shouted.

'Now they know how the leviathan feels,' Gabriel muttered.

'I hope they all get eaten,' Sienna replied.

Gabriel stood up in the bow of the boat, watching out over the water. His hands moved almost idly, guiding the water around them to drive them forwards. Ahead, the leviathan broke the surface again, yellow eye roving wildly. It let out a roar that made Lucky's bones shudder.

'Stay with Lucky,' Gabriel said.

'Don't be an idiot,' Sienna protested, but he leaned down and placed a kiss on the top of her head.

'Please?' he asked. 'Keep each other safe. I can do this.'

She opened her mouth and then shut it again, glaring at him. 'You better not get eaten, Gabe. I'm not explaining that to your mothers.'

'I promise. I just need to get it back out to deeper water. It's too shallow here for it to escape. That's why they use Minmouth as the killing ground.' His hand clenched and the boat rocked. Lucky reached out and rested his own hand over Gabriel's.

'You'll save it. I believe in you.'

'Don't let Sienna do anything stupid,' he said with a smile. He leaned in close, a question in his eyes. Lucky nodded, and Gabriel kissed him, quickly, gently, sea salt and hope on his lips.

'That's my line, Golden Boy,' Sienna growled.

The leviathan roared again, and more cannonballs hit the sea around it. It twisted, jaws snapping, the water pouring off its scales. Seven ships surrounded it, one directly behind, and three on each side, acting as a moving net. In the distance, another ship was racing towards the fray. Gabriel pressed his forehead against Lucky, just for a moment, then turned and dived into the water.

Chapter Twenty-One

Gabriel came up, surging out of the water like a dolphin leaping, then he was running across the surface, his long legs sprinting as easily as if he was on land, the sea spray foaming around his ankles.

The leviathan's head was fully out of the water now, swinging from side to side with a sinuous grace. It lunged for one of the ships that came closer but retracted when a cannonball impacted its neck. The creature let out a scream of pain that made Lucky clap his hands over his ears.

It ducked under the water, the shape still visible under the waves. This one was a mottled blue and green that reminded him of the paint Gabriel used on his nails. The head emerged again, still heading towards the shore. The water would get too shallow for it to swim soon and then it would be over. On the beach, people gathered to watch the spectacle.

To watch the slaughter.

Gabriel streaked across the water, and Lucky's chest fluttered at the sight of him. Gabriel's shirt clung to him, accentuating his muscles. Lucky wanted to be there with him, side by side. Being in the dinghy left him helpless.

'Hey!' Gabriel shouted, waving his arms. He brought up great sprays of water, and the leviathan turned its baleful gaze on him.

The ships spotted him too.

Men on the ships pointed at Gabriel. Lucky couldn't hear what they were saying from that distance, but it could be nothing good.

'Fuck,' Sienna muttered beside him.

'What can we do?' Lucky's voice came out in a trembling rush. 'We've got to help him.'

'Well, if you've got any bright ideas, I'm all ears. But I've got nothing.'

Lucky bit his lip. They couldn't face the galleons in a rowing boat and getting closer would only put them in the way of Gabriel and the leviathan. He didn't want to distract Gabriel, either.

'Fuck,' he said, and she gave an approving snort.

The leviathan turned towards Gabriel, and he gave a cheer, clapping his hands over his head. 'That's right. Here I am!'

With a snarl, the serpent bore down on him, slicing through the water. Gabriel stared at it for a moment, as if shocked by its speed, then spun on his heel and raced away. There was still a gap between the lead ship and the headland, and Gabriel made for it. The leviathan followed, snorting and snarling, its long whiskers quivering with rage, or hunger, or something completely alien.

On the ships, men ran around, tugging at ropes, changing sail direction. They'd registered the threat to their goal now, and they weren't going to let the leviathan go lightly. The eighth ship bore down on the carnage, travelling faster than any of the others. A Beater flag flew above her mainmast, and her sails were decorated with red threads. Lucky grabbed the oars, started rowing. Sienna raised her hands, moving the water to assist. Gabriel was behind them, the leviathan streaking rapidly towards him.

'Don't you dare get eaten, Gabe!' Sienna called, and there was no humour in her voice this time.

Cannonballs hit the water around the leviathan, sending up huge plumes of spray into the air. They struck the creature several times, and a greenish fluid oozed from wounds along its flank. But it still bore down after Gabriel, still going for that space and freedom. Lucky watched over his shoulder as he rowed, his neck aching as much as his shoulders now. But he couldn't stop.

Gabriel slowed.

Lucky remembered how exhausted the dancers had been that day with the leviathan, and that had been a shorter and much less energetic mission. If Gabriel's strength failed now, all would be lost. Lucky's heart hammered.

'It's right behind you!' he screamed out. 'Keep going! I believe in you!'

He couldn't see Gabriel's face, couldn't see if his words had even registered. Perhaps they'd been lost in the booms of the cannons and snarls of the beast. The air reeked of gunpowder and the strangely sickly scent of the leviathan's blood.

Then, Gabriel pushed on in a burst of speed, passing the ship and the headland, the seawater sparkling around him. He was going to make it. Lucky's heart leapt.

The leviathan lunged.

Gabriel dived underwater.

A galleon turned.

It swung around into the path of the leviathan. A mighty crack went up as the creature smashed into the bow and came down through the mizzenmast. It thrashed, tangled in rigging and sailcloth, spinning frantically in the water. The sea churned around it, like water boiling in a pot, as the thick coils of the leviathan rolled and rolled.

Men screamed, the leviathan screamed, and Lucky screamed in rage too. They'd sacrificed the ship. How many men had they thrown to their deaths? His stomach heaved. All that life.

'Where's Gabe?' Sienna shaded her eyes as she tried desperately to find him. But the sinking galleon and the enraged, entangled leviathan blocked their view.

'He'll be fine,' Lucky said, and it was a prayer more than a statement. A faith given to the wind and waves. 'He'll be fine.'

'Of course,' she said shakily. 'He's Golden Boy. You're right.'

The eighth ship had reached the fight, slowing now as it approached the thrashing, churning leviathan. The name *Providence* was written on her bow, the letters connected like a long white string. On her forecastle stood a quartet of Beaters, with red threads stitched into their uniforms. They stood in a square, facing each other, with red string twisted around their fingers. They moved their hands, and the pattern of the threads changed, shifting and twisting.

'What are they doing?' Sienna asked, but Lucky couldn't answer. His throat was dry and he couldn't keep his eyes off the threads. They bound his eyes, forcing him to watch as the patterns moved from abstract to something more solid. A leviathan, stretched out, empty eyes. Dead.

He tore his eyes away to scream at the leviathan, yell at it to flee, to get far away from this place. But it seemed held in place; its movements slowed to almost nothing. The other ships came in, surrounding the creature. They'd changed from cannonballs now, and instead, huge harpoons sunk into the creature's flesh. It flailed its huge head back, wailing, the sound turning Lucky's blood to ice. He'd feared the leviathan, but now it was an animal in pain, an animal dying, begging with its voice to be let free, to be allowed to live.

The thrashing slowed. The leviathan was almost gone, its huge flanks heaving, blood staining the surface of the water. Its shrieks had turned to moans, low moans that reverberated through bone and set every hair on Lucky's body on end.

They'd failed.

Lucky could only watch as the creature sank beneath the waves one last time, then bobbed back up, sinuous body now stretched out and lifeless, the yellow haunting eyes dull and blind.

Sienna let out a sob and buried her face in her hands.

The Beaters dragged the body back to the beach. One of the ships ran aground in the process. The price of the creature's death didn't seem to matter to them. Across the sea, the splintered remains of the sacrificed galleon floated, along with the bodies of countless sailors. Some still lived, calling for help, but they were secondary to the leviathan.

Sienna curled up weeping, her shaking sobs mixing with the calls of seabirds above. Lucky scanned the sea, searching for any sign of Gabriel beyond the wreckage. An icy hand gripped his heart as he leaned out, desperate to catch a glimpse of Gabriel's golden braid.

'Put your hands up!'

He turned, too overwrought to be surprised to see Yale with a pistol pointed at them from a larger boat, five more Beaters, all armed, sat with him. Lucky couldn't bring himself to feel anything at the sight of the man. They'd failed to save the leviathan and Gabriel was missing. Nothing Yale could do or say would be worse than that.

Gently, Lucky touched Sienna's shoulder. She flinched but turned around and gave Yale a death glare.

'Fuck off, would you?' she snapped.

'Hands up,' Yale repeated, cocking the pistol.

Lucky raised his hands. 'You can escape,' he hissed at Sienna. 'I'll hold him off.'

She glanced at the corpses floating in the water. 'I don't think I can.'

Lucky wanted to push her, shove her out of the boat, give her no choice but to try, but that wasn't fair on her. It was her choice.

'Up you get. Move over here. Nice and slowly.' Yale gestured with the pistol for them to come on to the larger dinghy.

With one last pleading look at Sienna, Lucky stood. The boat rocked precariously as he stepped over. After a moment,

Sienna did the same. They were forced to sit, their arms bound behind their backs.

'What are you going to do with us?' Sienna demanded. 'Gonna chase us to our deaths and murder us like you did the leviathan?'

Yale gave her a cold smile. 'Since you seem so interested in it, we'll give you front-row seats to the augury, how about that?'

Sienna threw herself at him. It was an awkward, clumsy manoeuvre that was never going to achieve anything, but Lucky couldn't blame her for wanting to do *something*. Yale grabbed her, pushing her face against the seat of the dinghy. Sienna winced, but bit her lip, refusing to cry out. The boat see-sawed and Lucky stumbled against the Beater next to him. He pushed Lucky back into his seat, his expression cold and filled with disdain.

Guard.

Uncaring, bored. Just like the guards in his cell. They were here for a job, and they didn't see him, Sienna, or the leviathan as anything more than that. Lucky hated them for that the most.

The boat reached the beach, and the guards manhandled them out and on to the sand.

'What happened to Gabriel?' Lucky asked Yale.

'Who?' he scoffed and Lucky clenched his fist.

'The water dancer. The one who almost saved the leviathan.' Gabriel would be devastated by the creature's death. If he was even still alive. 'He's been picked up. The church will see his heresy is suitably punished.'

Lucky's heart sank. Until this moment, he'd been harbouring the hope that Gabriel had made it to safety. But they'd failed at everything. The leviathan was dead and Gabriel was captured. The idea that Lucky might never see him again seized at him, and he couldn't breathe properly.

Yale gestured with his pistol. 'Come along, little bird.'

The hated nickname stung, one more insult to add to the string of injuries. Lucky thought about defying him, about taking that bullet and letting it end there. Let his blood bleed out on the sand. But the river had robbed him of the desire for death that used to rear like a leviathan in his heart. He'd almost drowned, and that taste of death had confirmed to him that he wanted to live. He wanted to live, and he wanted Gabriel, and he wasn't going to let these *guards* deprive him of that.

So instead, he followed them across the sand to the corpse of the leviathan.

It took up much of the beach, its long, muscular body laid out almost straight. That made it look unnatural, unreal. Leviathans were coiled, powerful. This thing was just meat.

It measured about thirty feet, smaller than the gold and green one with the mark on its neck. Its body stood about ten feet high, so blocked the view to the water beyond it. At this end, the great head lolled on the sand, seaweed tangled in its quills. Its mouth lay open, a forked tongue hanging out and dripping drool on the beach. The blank eyes were somehow more terrifying, and more tragic.

Sienna threw back her head and wailed.

'Silence,' Yale snapped, giving her a shove. She barely seemed to notice.

From the crowd on the beach, another man stepped forwards. He wasn't dressed like a Beater or a sailor – instead, he wore a long, deep red robe made of such thick wool that each stitch was clearly visible. Tassels hung from the sleeves and quivered as he walked.

Two Beaters walked behind him. As the trio reached the corpse of the leviathan, they stopped and bowed their heads. The man in the robe – a priest, Lucky assumed – began to speak. His voice was low and droning, like a vast bell tolling.

'The threads of fate have wrapped around this creature, and we give thanks for its sacrifice. The leviathans are creatures of fate themselves, woven into the tapestry of life. Their death is revelation.'

The word sacrifice rankled at Lucky. The leviathan hadn't chosen to die, hadn't offered anything of its own free will. The creature had been murdered.

As the priest finished speaking, one of the Beaters stepped forwards and drew a sword. The blade was thin and slightly curved. She pointed it at the leviathan, then flicked her wrist until the blade was perpendicular to her body. She ran along the length of the serpent, slicing into it. A greenish slit opened up, and then the grey guts poured out on to the sand with a wet slap.

The smell washed like a fog over the assembled crowd. A mix of rotting fish, blood, and something sickly sweet. Lucky doubled over, retching violently. From the sound of it, he wasn't the only one.

The priest walked around the mass of grey, twisted, tangled guts, apparently oblivious to the stench emanating from the corpse. He peered in from time to time, stroking his chin and mumbling to himself. He might have been a man at market, if it wasn't for the ghastly sight in front of him. Beside him, the second Beater frantically scribbled down notes.

Finally, he stopped his introspective walk and turned to the assembled crowd.

'The augury is done. The leviathan shows a battle between fate – the forces of order, strength, and protection – and the twisting chaos of the sea. It is this battle that is preventing the threads from being clear, and letting disasters go unforeseen.'

Behind him, Yale snorted. 'Unforeseen? They're completely new. We need action, not melodrama.'

The priest frowned, giving Yale a steely glare for a moment, then turned back to the assembled crowd. 'For the last ten years, the connection with fate has been fading, the proclamations in the tapestry less and less clear. And recently, we have been struck by disasters that have gone unnoticed in the threads altogether. It is time to change that. It is time to act. The leviathan's sacrifice has shown this to be true.'

Lucky and Sienna shared a look. There was no way this would be good.

'The trial of our new weapon has been a complete success,' the priest continued. 'For too long, we have had to tolerate the presence of heretics on the waves because of the leviathans. Now, we have a way to fight back against the creatures. To this end, we will destroy the shrine of Promise at Sea Hall. The shrine will be revealed in five days. Our forces will gather there, and the *Providence* will end the era of the water dancers once and for all.'

'You people are sick.' Lucky hadn't meant to say the words out loud, but in the silence left by the priest's last statement, they dominated.

The priest turned to him, and his face paled. 'It's you!' He pointed a shaky finger at Lucky, then slammed a hand against the Beater next to him. 'Bring him. Bring him here.'

The Beater shoved Lucky's shoulder and Lucky stumbled forwards. Sienna gave him a confused look and Lucky returned it. His mind whirled, leaving him sick and dizzy. He could feel every eye on him, digging into him, stripping down his essence and laying him bare with their gaze.

He dragged his feet as he walked, scuffing up the sand into a trail that marked his path. Marked him. He was no one. Yale had confirmed it. What had the priest seen? And did he actually want to find out?

But he wasn't given a choice.

The priest pointed at the mass of steaming leviathan guts on the beach and Lucky fought back the urge to retch again.

The slimy, purple-grey entrails were the last thing he wanted to look at.

'That's you,' the priest said, his voice a snarl, as if it was somehow Lucky's fault that the offal had landed this way. His curiosity was piqued. How could he possibly be in the leviathan guts?

And yet, he was.

It took a moment for the image to resolve, for the lines and the shadows, the meat and the sand to fall into place, but it *was* him. An image of Lucky, head and shoulders, formed on the beach. With a rope around his neck.

Except.

It wasn't a rope. As Lucky peered in horror at his own visage, he realised it wasn't a rope at all. It was a braid.

Chapter Twenty-Two

He staggered back, the sand writhing under his feet. Lucky stumbled and fell, staring in horror at the guts spewed on to the beach. He couldn't see the image anymore, but it didn't matter. It was burned into his mind. If he closed his eyes, it hung there, glistening.

Why?

His mind was a blur. Why? The augury was supposed to find out about the disasters. Why was it showing him? And why was he connected to Gabriel?

'. . . Feet!'

A high-pitched whine in his head blocked out most sound, but the voice came through, just before the kick to his back.

'Get on your feet.'

Lucky grunted at the pain, but with his hands bound behind his back, and his body shaking like a leaf in a storm, there was no way he could comply.

'I said, on your feet!' Yale hauled him up by his arm, and Lucky winced at the pain in his shoulder.

'He needs to be taken away,' the priest jabbered, staring between Lucky and the leviathan guts. His face had taken on an unhealthy pallor, sweat beading at his temples. 'There's something wrong with him. He's not right.'

Lucky knew that. He'd known that for a long time. What he wanted to know was why?

'What are you going to do with me?' he asked.

'Silence,' Yale barked.

'You're going to the mother church,' the priest said. 'They will decide what to do with you.' He peered again at Lucky, as if he were a specimen on display, or perhaps something scraped from the bottom of the priest's boot. 'Your threads are tangled. This must be fixed.'

'We could just kill him,' Yale suggested. 'If he's responsible for the disasters, then wouldn't it be better?'

The priest shook his head. 'Not until we understand more. It could tangle things further.' He leaned in close. 'Have you promised?'

Lucky shook his head, not quite understanding the question.

'You're not a dancer? You haven't promised at the shrine in Sea Hall?' the priest persisted.

Lucky shook his head again, this time more firmly.

'Get him on a ship. Get him out of here.'

Yale grabbed Lucky's shoulder and pushed him back towards Sienna and the dinghy.

'Back to sea already,' she said as they were forced into the seats. 'You could have just left us out there, saved us all the trouble.'

Yale ignored her.

They were taken to one of the ships still intact and floating. Lucky stared up at the immense vessel, at least twice the size of the *Dreamer*, if not more. It was heavily armed, with multiple gun ports pockmarking the flank. The leviathan screamed in his head again and he shuddered.

'What's going on?' Sienna whispered to him. 'Where are they taking us?'

He stared at her, unable to get the words out. His body shivered as if he'd taken a cold bath.

Once on deck, they were quickly marched below to a small cell in the bowels of the ship. It smelled of damp, in a way that reminded him of his old cell in Ciatheme. The scent made him strangely nostalgic.

Two narrow bunks were fixed to the walls, one on each side. Lucky lay down on the one on the right, and Yale closed and locked the door with a clunk. Sienna did not sit down.

'Be good, little bird,' Yale called.

'Tell me, now, what is going on,' Sienna said, leaning over Lucky. Her hands opened and closed as if she wanted to throttle him. He didn't blame her for that. 'What did the priest say? Did you find out anything more about Gabriel? What did you see there?'

Lucky laid a hand over his eyes. His head ached, his shoulder ached, his heart ached.

'Tell me,' she said again, and this time her voice was small and scared.

Lucky sat up slowly. 'I was in the augury. My face. It was my face.'

Her eyes widened. 'What can that mean?'

'I don't know. But it wasn't just me. Gabriel was there, too.' He rubbed at his temples. 'He rubbed at his temples. 'Think about it: the disasters started when I joined the *Dreamer*, then they stopped when I was in training, and began again when you and Gabriel came to The Fell. What if … what if it's me and Gabriel? What if us being together is causing this?'

She sat down on the bed next to him. 'How? I don't understand.'

'Do you think I do?' he snapped.

She looked shocked for a moment, then rolled her eyes. 'Duh. Course not. So what do we do?'

'What do you think we do? We're in a cell if you haven't noticed. Locked in. No escape.'

She rolled her eyes again. 'Fates, but you're miserable. I'd rather be stuck in a cell with Golden Boy.' As soon as the words left her mouth, her features fell. 'I hope he's safe.'

Lucky wished he could offer her comfort. Gabriel was a heretic in full view of the church. This couldn't end well for him. Lucky put his head down again, a crushing pressure around his heart.

I miss my friend.

Lucky missed him too, painfully. Hungrily. He stretched his hand out, imagining the pressure of Gabriel's fingertips meeting his. He closed his eyes again.

'Look. Let's get some rest, have a think about things. We'll come up with something,' Sienna said kindly. She gave his shoulder a pat and stood up. A moment later, the other bunk creaked as she sat down.

Lucky drew his knees up to his chest and wrapped his arms around them. A rat squeezed under the door and ran across the floor, sniffing around cautiously, seeming oblivious to the two humans. Sienna watched it closely, her body tense.

'It's all right. They don't care much about us,' Lucky told her. 'It's just looking for crumbs.'

His cell at Ciatheme had rats. Real ones, and ones sketched on to the walls. He'd liked watching them eat at the scraps of food he left, a connection between one living soul and another.

'Gabriel talked a bit about fate and promise, when we visited Sea Hall. Tell me more?'

Sienna didn't move for a moment. 'Fate is the force that shapes the world. Controls the world. It's like . . . the world is a tapestry, right? The things that are going to happen, happen, because they're there in the threads.'

'So you have no control?' he asked. The rat scuttled across the floor. Its little claws clicked on the floorboards, the sound enormous in the small room. 'That's it? It's written and it happens?'

'So the church says.' The shrug was audible in her voice. 'The priest reads the tapestry in the church and tells everyone what fate has proclaimed. When I was child, there was a big storm, and a lot of debris choked up the river. The church warned that the barrier was going to break, and the village evacuated. The next day it happened, and several houses were swept away. But all the people were saved.'

Lucky sat up slowly. 'So you think it's a good thing?'

'I . . . I don't know. They saved my family's life then. But they come down heavily on anyone who doesn't follow fate. Gabe and I chose to change ourselves, and we'll always be at risk because of that.'

'I don't like the idea of being controlled.' He leaned back against the wall, thinking about the words he'd said. Control was something he hadn't had until he met Gabriel. He'd always been controlled, ordered, pushed. In the cell, it had been life, and for a while, he thought he'd welcomed it. But now . . . now he didn't want to be anyone's prisoner. He wanted to make his own choices, his own mistakes.

'Gonna make your pledge at the shrine, become a dancer?' Sienna raised an eyebrow.

He shook his head. He found watching the water dancers beautiful, evocative, but he had no real urge to do it himself. 'I don't know about that. But I don't want to become a Beater. I don't want to do what the church says because it's written somewhere.' He looked down at his clothes, the black Beater uniform. It wasn't him, and he knew that now. He just wasn't sure what *was* him, yet.

'That will please Gabe,' she said softly.

'I don't get you two.' He stretched, massaging his shoulder. 'You fight and bicker all the time, but you obviously care about him.'

She rolled over, hiding her face from him. 'I do care about him. Very much. And I know he'll never feel the same way about me. Gabriel doesn't fall in love with bodies. He falls in love with souls. I think he's always been carrying a torch for the boy he grew up with in Ciatheme. That's you, right?'

'Yeah . . .'

'I'm happy for him. Honestly. Even though it hurts, I'm happy for him.' She sniffed quietly. 'So, I'll never get close to him that way, but needling him was a good way to spend time with him. He knows I don't mean harm, and I think he enjoys the banter most of the time.'

'I see.'

She sighed. 'See, this is why you shouldn't ask questions when you don't really want to know the answers. Gonna ask me what I promised at the shrine next?'

Not polite to ask, mate.

'No.' It wasn't any of his business. Neither was Gabriel's choice, but Lucky couldn't help wonder. Couldn't help worry.

Sienna didn't say anything more, so Lucky lay down on the bunk and closed his eyes. The day's events played over and over behind his eyes – the leviathan chasing Gabriel, the ship crashing into the serpent, his face in the guts. At some point he must have drifted off to sleep, because instead of an animal scream, the leviathan cried out for him to help it, and it cried out in Gabriel's voice.

The ship lurched, rolling to port. The motion tossed Lucky out of the bunk and on to the floor in a thump. Pain ricocheted up his arm, setting off a throb in his shoulder. The rat scurried under the door with a squeak. He sat up blinking, as Sienna did the same.

'What happened?' he asked. 'Is it a storm?'

'Pretty sudden storm,' she replied, rubbing her head. 'It was smooth sailing until that moment.'

Lucky stood up and moved to the door. 'Hey!' he called through it. 'Hey!'

'Yeah, that will work.'

'Well, have you got any better ideas?'

The ship lurched again. Lucky was thrown against the door, the impact knocking the wind out of him. Sienna slid along the floor with a shriek. The door creaked on its hinges.

Lucky pounded at it with his fists, which did nothing but send waves of pain from his hands to his shoulders. He kicked at it instead and made the door shudder.

'Come help me!' he yelled to Sienna.

She joined him, kicking at the wood around the lock. Lucky was impressed by both her agility and accuracy. The door groaned and the ship lurched again. Footsteps echoed down the passage, and Lucky held Sienna back from another kick.

'What are you doing?' a Beater demanded through the door.

'Drinking tea like civilised folk,' Sienna spat back. 'Only you seem to have forgotten to give us any tea.'

'Silence. Come with me.'

The Beater unlocked the door and gestured with his pistol for them to leave the cell. Lucky tensed, waiting for an opportunity. The odds of escape weren't exactly great right now – the ship could be anywhere on the sea, miles and miles from the coast. Even if Sienna could water dance her way to safety, he would be stuck. Still, the issue of the locked door was gone, and if one of them could get free, that was something.

He'd hold on to something.

Sienna went ahead, and Lucky walked behind her, the Beater's pistol firm against his back. The passage wasn't wide enough for them to walk more than single file. He'd been counting the time between the lurches, and when the next one came, he was ready. Sienna and the Beater were not.

She struck the wall with a grunt, and the Beater behind him did the same. Lucky planted his feet, pushing himself into the deck. As the pistol pressure disappeared from his back, he turned, using the momentum of the ship to spin around. The Beater looked up as Lucky bore down, raising the pistol, but Lucky was too quick. He kicked it away, then grabbed the

Beater's shoulders, dragging him down as he drove his knee up. The man hit the wall again and slumped down.

Lucky grabbed the pistol. 'Let's go.'

'Where did you learn to do that?' Sienna asked, a mixture of fear and awe on her face.

'From the Beaters,' he replied with a shrug. 'I was a good pupil.'

'Nice.'

They made their way in a cautious run to the stairs to the upper decks. Lucky paused at the entrance, peering into the deck. Beaters dashed about, but most were heading out to the open deck. Lucky pulled his hood down low. It wouldn't be much of a disguise, but hopefully they'd be too busy panicking to notice him. A row of thick cloaks hung on pegs and he threw one at Sienna.

'Let's find out what's going on.'

'I hope you have a plan. Gabe never has a plan.'

Lucky grinned. 'Absolutely none.'

'You two deserve each other,' she muttered.

They ran out on deck, ignoring anyone they saw. The sky was clear and blue, but the waves pounded the broadside of the galleon as if she were in the worst storm. At the helm, a sailor frantically turned the wheel, trying to get the ship's nose into the waves before she was capsized. Others frantically tugged at the sails.

Sienna let out a gasp and Lucky followed her gaze to a ship off the port side.

The *Dreamer.*

Chapter Twenty-Three

She sailed alongside the galleon, keeping pace with her. On the deck, the twin water dancers stood side by side with Poe and Captain Haven. All four moved their arms in unison, a slow, writhing movement that reminded Lucky of a serpent. The ship rolled again, and a wave sloshed over the rail.

'They're going to sink us!' someone yelled.

'Where are the prisoners?' someone else called.

Captain Haven raised a loudhailer to her mouth. 'What will it be? Your ship or my son?'

'We told you, he's not on board.' That was Yale, his voice terse and brittle.

'Prove it,' she snarled back. 'I'm happy to crack your entire ship open to check.'

Lucky ran to the rail and threw back his hood. 'Captain!'

She caught sight of him and paled. 'He's not with you?'

'Just me and Sienna.' He pointed as she came to join him.

Beaters moved towards them, and Lucky drew and cocked the pistol. He'd never fired one before – his training had only been hand-to-hand – but at this distance, he didn't think he could miss. Which meant neither could they.

'That will have to do,' Captain Haven said. She lowered her arms, and the other dancers did the same. Then she pointed a finger at Yale. 'Let them come aboard and turn back to shore. If you pursue us, I will sink your ship and drown everyone aboard.'

'You have the soul of a serpent,' Yale growled, and she grinned. It reminded Lucky of the girl, cold and empty.

Someone grabbed his shoulder. Lucky reacted on instinct, lashing out and smacking the Beater with a sharp blow. They let go, but more hands grabbed at him. He couldn't fight them all off, and he was lifted off his feet. Before he knew what was happening, the water was rushing up to meet him, and then it was flooding over his head and dragging him down, down into the depths.

Something touched his hand and he clung to it.

He broke the surface with Sienna, coughing and spluttering.

The galleon turned. It made a lazy arc in the water, heading back towards the shore. Lucky expected it to open fire, but she simply slipped away through the waves.

'Watch out below!'

A rope slapped the water near his hand, and he reached for it. He and Sienna were helped aboard, and he stood on the familiar deck, dripping wet, bruised and cold, but having a sense of comfort he hadn't felt in many months.

Captain Haven stepped towards him. With a flick of her hand, all the water clinging to him lifted off and drained back into the sea.

'Tha—' he started, but she cut him off.

'Someone get this man some *decent* clothes and then send him to my room.' She looked Lucky in the eye, rage burning in her expression. 'I want to know everything. Do you hear me? Absolutely everything.'

She stormed off, leaving Lucky dry but shivering on the deck. He waited for the captain to change her mind, to turn around and order him thrown back into the sea. She'd given her word to Yale, after all, over six months ago. Instead, someone – it might have been one of the twins – handed him a bundle of cloth. Poe put a hand on his shoulder.

'It's good to see you again, lad.'

He looked at the faces around him and found no anger, only concern.

'You better go,' Poe said. 'Captain Haven's not one to be kept waiting at the best of times.'

Lucky headed to his cell, ripping off the Beater uniform and throwing it in the corner. It and everything it represented disgusted him. He pulled on the sailor's clothing, comfortable, familiar, fighting back tears. Could he really wear this again? The image of Gabriel on the wall – blissful, happy, dancing Gabriel – made his heart twist.

'I'll find you again,' he promised, reaching a hand out to the wall. 'Just hold on, Gabriel. Wherever you are, I'll find you.'

The first mate met him at the door to the captain's cabin.

'It's good to see you again,' she said with a smile that added more curves to her face. 'Can I give you a hug?'

He looked up at her, searching for judgement but finding again only support. 'Please,' he said softly.

Her smile grew and she wrapped her arms around him. She was soft and warm, smelled of sea salt and something floral. She felt safe.

'Don't judge Mel,' she whispered in his ear. 'She's so scared about Gabe.'

He couldn't blame either of them for that. 'I am too.'

She held open the door and stepped in after him. Captain Haven paced across the room in front of her desk, but as Lucky entered, she crossed the room and stopped in front of him, her piercing gaze holding him in place.

'Where's Gabe? Where the fuck is my son?'

Lucky hung his head. 'I . . . I don't know. They caught him separately. I don't know where they took him.'

Her eyes flashed, and for a moment, he thought she was going to strike him. He deserved it. He'd let Gabriel down, let him be taken. Then her hand dropped, and she gestured to the chair at the desk. Her shoulders slumped and for the first time she looked small.

'We came as soon as we heard about the augury. I knew Gabe wouldn't stand by and let something like that happen. But we were too slow.' Her voice was flat, empty.

'What . . . what's going to happen to him?' Lucky asked as he sat, dreading the answer.

'He'll be tried as a heretic.' Amala's face was pale, her constellations of freckles standing out in sharp relief.

'Tried and found guilty,' the captain agreed. 'There's no disputing this.'

'Idiot child,' her wife said, but the words were swallowed up by a sob. The captain squeezed her hand.

'What does that mean for him?' Lucky asked. He felt shut out again, ignorant of how the world worked. It made him itchy.

'He'll be executed,' the captain said. She put her arm around her wife, who sobbed into her shoulder. 'Sea Hall council control the sea. Dancing is permitted away from shore, in the defence of ships, and to harvest from leviathans. But that close to the beach, and you're under church rules, where it's illegal. And that's before you get into directly trying to interfere with church business. So there will be a trial out of principle, but they'll find him guilty and then they'll hang him.'

Lucky stood up. The chair clattered behind him. 'We can't let that happen.' Cold hands clenched around his stomach, threatening to squeeze back out his last meal. 'We can't let them kill Gabriel.'

The captain gave him a cold smile. 'No, we can't. It's not exactly going to be easy though.'

'But we have to try!' He thought of Gabriel's earnest anxiety to save the leviathan. He'd thrown his life away because it was the right thing to do. *Idiot.* Lucky's heart ached. *Stupid, beautiful idiot.*

Captain Haven straightened her back, fire kindling in her eyes. 'Amala, bring the ship around, back to the bay to the west of the town. Take it wide, we don't want to attract any Beater attention. Inform the crew the rescue mission is strictly voluntary. I can't force any of them to go through it with me.'

'Aye, Captain.' She moved towards the door, then stopped and turned back. 'We'll save him, Mel. Even if it's just the two of us.'

'And me,' Lucky said firmly. Amala held out her arms and he allowed her to wrap her arms around him, hold him tight.

'You're a good person, Lucky,' she murmured. 'I'm so glad Gabe found you again.'

Lucky didn't know if he believed it, not yet. But he could *do* good. He could try to make things right. Amala let him go and left, shouting orders the moment she passed through the door. Lucky turned back to the captain.

'There's more.' He sat down at the desk, and she did the same. 'They're planning to attack the shrine of Promise. They've got a new weapon, one they can use on the leviathans. They think they don't need the dancers anymore.' He told her everything that had happened with the leviathan and the *Providence*. She listened without interruption, her eyes wide and her hands curled around the edge of the desk.

As he was finishing, Amala came in with a tray, three cups of coffee, and several rounds of fresh bread sliced up and served with a spicy sauce to dip in. He paused, his hand over the bread.

'Let him have a moment, Mel,' Amala said. 'Poor boy looks famished.'

The captain gave Lucky a nod. The taste of Poe's cooking was painfully nostalgic and he wiped his hand over his eyes. Captain Haven let him eat for a couple of moments, and the first mate sat down next to her, wrapping her hand in her wife's. Lucky envied them their closeness.

'Time to continue,' the captain said as Lucky finished his piece of bread. The first mate squeezed her hand, but she shook her head. 'I need to know more.'

The first mate wiped away a tear as Lucky finished describing how the ship had crashed into the leviathan, and Gabriel had been lost from sight. 'That's our Gabe.'

The captain's expression softened, just slightly.

'I wanted to go after him,' Lucky said. 'I wanted to find him, make sure he was safe, but there was a boat of armed Beaters in the way. I didn't think getting shot would help him.'

'You're right,' she admitted, though pain laced her words. 'What then? They put you on the ship? Did they tell you where you were going?'

'Not quite. They made us watch the augury. Which was horrible. They murdered that creature and then they butchered it.' He shuddered, wrapping his hands around the coffee cup to keep them from shaking. 'But . . . but when the priest looked, my image was there. My face. And I think Gabriel too, but he was less clear.'

The first mate gasped, and the captain's eyes narrowed. 'You're sure?'

'I am.'

'What does it mean?' Amala asked.

'I don't know. I know that Gabriel and I knew each other as children. And it looks like when we're together, there are disasters across the country. Floods, fires, earthshakes. But I don't understand why, and neither did the priest. He was sending me to the mother church to be examined.' The thought sent shivers down his spine. 'I don't think they recognised Gabriel – it was only really his braid – so I don't think they had the same fate in store for him.'

The captain stood. 'We get Gabe, then we put sail to Sea Hall. Stop this ship and their new weapon before they can destroy the shrine.'

'I thought you hated the shrine,' Lucky said. 'You didn't want Gabriel to make the sacrifice.'

Captain Haven glanced at her wife and then sighed. 'I don't hate the shrine. I wanted Gabriel to wait until he was older, to have enough time to fully understand the implications of the sacrifice. But I don't hate it, or what it represents. And the church, they . . . they don't know how to think for themselves, how to approach things with nuance. They'll just murder every leviathan they can get their hands on.'

'Gabriel would hate that,' Lucky said quietly.

'He would. You ready?' she asked and Lucky nodded.

'Then let's get my son back.'

Chapter Twenty-Four

The *Dreamer* dropped anchor just around the headland from Minmouth. After their attack on the church vessel, Captain Haven didn't feel comfortable putting into port. She explained that she suspected the crew would be made to keep quiet – the idea of a church galleon losing to a smaller vessel controlled by heretics wouldn't sit easily with them – but she couldn't be certain.

So Lucky found himself seated in a dinghy with Sienna, the captain, and the twins, Cass and Erin. First Mate Haven waved them off from the rail, her eyes wet but her mouth set.

'Bring him back, Mel!' she called. 'Bring back our boy.'

'What's the plan, Captain?' Sienna asked as they drew away from the ship.

'We need to break him out of jail tonight, get out of there under cover of darkness. If we let things get too close to the execution, we'll never have the chance.'

Lucky glanced up at the sky. A clear, moonless night. The sea was as black as the sky, only the crests of the waves showing any differentiation. They carried no oars – the four water dancers moved the boat across the water easily, and much more quickly and quietly than could be done by rowing.

They beached the dinghy on a shingled bay, littered with bladderwrack and driftwood. Much of it came from the wreckage of the galleon. Lucky kicked at a piece, knocking it over and revealing part of a word painted on the plank. Part of the ship's name, no doubt.

It took almost an hour to reach the town from the bay, taking a route away from the main road and through the scrubby countryside. The ground was uneven, covered in spiky gorse bushes, and riddled with rabbit holes, making the journey slow and awkward. Captain Haven led the way, and everyone followed without question.

No one spoke.

There was no castle in Minmouth, unlike Ciatheme, so Lucky was initially unsure where the jail might be. But Captain Haven strode straight towards a large building in the centre of the town. It was built of grey stone, unlike the whitewashed houses, single storey but still taller than the rest. The windows had the same coloured threads that mesmerised Lucky.

At the front were two heavy oak doors, closed tight shut. They were decorated with the same swirling patterns of threads, meant to represent the threads of fate.

'How do we get in?' he asked, and the captain fixed him with a cool stare.

'Not through the front doors, certainly.'

'The jail cells will be underneath the back of the building,' Sienna said.

The captain glanced around her. She moved like a predator, slow, deliberate, constantly checking and listening. While the town appeared quiet and slumbering, there was no way of knowing how many Beaters lurked about. None of the ships remained, but that didn't mean luck was on their side.

He'd always been misnamed.

Haven made a sharp gesture and set off down the side of the church. The windows were small and high up on the wall, giving them cover as they pressed against the stones. Lucky's heart echoed his footsteps, rapid and heavy. Beside him, Sienna focused on a patch of ground in front of her, her eyes narrow, a frown etched deep into her brow.

'We'll save him,' he whispered.

'Yeah, we will.'

At the rear of the church was the graveyard. Rows of stone markers stood to attention, each one carved in the shape of a knotted thread. Over to the far side, the markers were a similar shape, but made of wood. Many looked worn and chipped by the elements. He wondered if his mother had a marker like that in Ciatheme.

Haven held up a hand and the group stopped. She pointed to a pair of doors, set in the ground.

'That will be the coffin door,' she said, her voice a whisper. 'We'll get in that way.'

The rest of the group muttered in assent and the captain folded her arms.

'You don't have to do this. This is my son, and my fight. I can't ask any of you to risk yourself for this if you want to change your minds.'

She was met with four stares.

'Not going to dignify that with an answer, Captain,' Sienna said.

'We don't leave one of our own to the Beaters,' agreed Cass.

'I'm not leaving Gabriel,' Lucky said.

Captain Haven gave them a tired smile. 'Thank you, all of you. Right, let me see if I can get the doors open. Watch my back.'

The water dancers drew out pistols, and Lucky fingered the hilt of his knife. A pistol rested in his belt – no sense in being unprepared – but he much preferred the familiar, close combat of the blade.

Captain Haven opened a waterskin and waved her fingers, drawing out the water. She formed it into a ball and smashed it into the space between the two doors. The smack of water on wood echoed eerily over the graveyard, but it wasn't as loud as a hammer or similar tool would have been.

Again and again, the water hit the wood, and the rest of the group looked out, each watching in a different direction, ready to raise the alarm in case anyone came. The walls and doors of the church must have been made thick and strong, as no one did. After a while, the noise changed. The captain raised a foot and stamped down, and the doors swung inwards. She waved at them, and they hurried to the stone steps leading down into darkness.

Captain Haven lit a torch and handed it to one of the twins. She led the way, a pistol in one hand, the other trailing the damp wall of the crypt entrance. Lucky followed and, after a moment, Sienna gave an audible swallow and hurried after them.

'You owe me big time, Gabe Haven,' she muttered to herself.

The steps led to a narrow room with small sections walled off at regular intervals. Each section had a simple wood table built into the wall.

'That's where they leave the coffins,' Erin said to Sienna, nudging her in the ribs.

'Yes, thank you, I was well aware, Erin,' she snapped back. Captain Haven looked round and gave them a stern shush.

At the end of the coffin room, another door awaited. Captain Haven pressed her ear to the wood, and then gave the handle an experimental turn. It rattled, and the door moved a little.

'Now it gets difficult,' she said. 'Keep the pistol shots to a minimum – threaten only, unless you absolutely have to escalate. Noise will only bring down more on us.'

She opened the door slowly, wincing at the creak that welled out of the hinges, setting Lucky's hair on end. Immediately she closed it again.

'Someone's coming.'

Lucky pushed to the front of the group as the others scrambled to hide behind a wall. He settled himself behind the door, the knife in his hands. It opened again, and someone entered.

'Who's in here?' The voice was rough, a slight tremor afflicting it. Scared of walking where the coffins lay? Lucky smothered a scoff. Wasn't like the dead could hurt you. Dead was dead. The man paused, and Lucky mentally urged him to leave. His heartbeat echoed the sentiment: *Go. Go. Go.*

The man stepped into the room. He glanced around, his eyes wide, hands raised as if to ward off an attack. Every shadow grabbed his focus, every slight sound. Lucky suspected they were both thinking the same thing: had he seen a person, was that a breath he heard?

'Who's there?'

He didn't move, didn't make any indication that he'd seen any of the dancers, but Lucky's nerves had had enough. He stepped out of his hiding position, and slipped next to the man, standing side-on so one foot was behind his left leg and the other in front of his right.

The Beaters' training took control of Lucky's muscles, guiding them into place with flawless accuracy. With his left hand, he covered the man's mouth, forcing his jaws together. The right hand brought the dagger to his neck.

Lucky pinned the Beater before either of them had truly registered what had happened.

He dragged the man back, out of the doorway. The Beater whimpered in his grip, but he didn't fight back, probably due to the sharp steel resting on the skin above his jugular.

Kill him, Yale's voice echoed in his head. *A prisoner will only slow you down. If they have no value to you alive, kill them and move on.*

Lucky's hand tightened around the knife. One swift movement and the Beater would be dead. One fewer Beater. One fewer enforcer to come after the crew of the *Dreamer*. One fewer problem in rescuing Gabriel.

One more life taken by a killer.

With a grunt he drove the hilt of the dagger into the man's temple. The Beater's eyes rolled back in his head, and he slumped in Lucky's arms. Lucky wasn't Yale. He wasn't a Beater. He wasn't a cold-blooded killer.

They moved the unconscious Beater into one of the furthest coffin holds, bound his hands and stuffed his own sock in his mouth.

'Nice work,' Captain Haven said, glancing down at the man, undisguised disgust on her lips.

'Let's go,' he replied, pushing down the shakiness that threatened to take over his hands.

Lucky took the lead, peering through the door. A corridor stretched to the left, ending with a door that he guessed must lead up to the main body of the church. To the right, it ended in a set of steps that went further down into the darkness.

No sounds came from either direction, so Lucky raised a hand and led the group down into the depths.

'Do you know how many Beaters could be down here?' he asked the captain.

'Normally, not many. The Beaters and church jails only deal with heresy, and most dancers are careful. But with the numbers around for the augury, who can say?'

'Who indeed.'

The smell hit him halfway down the stairs. Damp. Excrement. Misery. Even his cell back at the castle hadn't been as bad as this. Or maybe it had, and he'd simply blocked it out over time. Perhaps freedom had reawakened his senses.

Either way, he wasn't leaving sweet, kind, brave Gabriel down here a moment longer than necessary.

There was no door at the end of the steps, so he paused, peering into the gloom. The corridor continued on straight ahead, unlit and shrouded in darkness. To the left, an open room, warm with lantern light. Voices floated out and Lucky counted at least three. Three against five – even if the three were armed and trained Beaters, it felt like good odds to him.

He retreated a little way back up the stairs and spoke to the captain.

'There's three, I think, in a room to the left. We can take them if we surprise them. The rest of the place seems dark.'

She gave him a grim smile. 'Let's make them pay.'

Captain Haven and the other dancers took out their water-skins, each manipulating a ball of water between their hands. In the almost darkness, the water shimmered in an ethereal manner, almost glowing. Lucky drew his knife.

They charged down the steps and into the room. Two Beaters, a man and a woman, were in the process of standing up from a game of dice at a table, while a third struggled to get up from where he'd been sprawled on a bench. Captain Haven went for the man on the bench, knocking him back with a flying ball of water. As he opened his mouth to cry out, she directed the water into his mouth. The guard's eyes bulged, and his throat worked to try and expel the liquid, but he could only utter a wet, gargling sound.

'That's for my son,' she hissed, as his eyes rolled back in his head.

The other three dancers went for the two at the table, sending out water like punches. The Beaters couldn't reach for their weapons, could barely raise their hands to try and ward off the blows. Lucky watched, feeling somewhat inadequate as the other two Beaters went down and all three were quickly bound and gagged like their colleague upstairs.

'Check them for keys,' Captain Haven called.

As Lucky glanced around the room, a movement caught his eye. From across the room, a pistol pointed at Captain Haven. A fourth Beater emerged from hiding, gun aimed at her heart. Lucky reacted as the gun went off, the sound a blow to his ears, diving for the captain. They both hit the floor and rolled.

Lucky reacted first, propelling himself up and dashing across the room to the man. He'd dropped his spent pistol and drawn a knife, and Lucky met him with his own. The Beater parried his blow, but Lucky didn't stop, couldn't stop. He ploughed into the man, sending them both sprawling.

The man ended up on top, pinning Lucky down. He grabbed Lucky's wrist, smacking it into the cold hard floor. The knife fell from Lucky's grip, clattering on to the floor.

'You've made a big mistake coming here,' the man said, his face contorted in a cruel grin.

'I don't think so,' Lucky replied. Saving Gabriel would never be a mistake.

He drew his knees back and drove his legs up into the man's gut. The Beater gave a soft oof and released his grip. Lucky rolled away and got to his feet. The Beater lashed out at him with his knife, the blade barely missing Lucky by a hair's width. Lucky ducked under the man's arm, coming up on the side of him. He grabbed the man's wrist and twisted, pulling back, and the man cried out.

He twisted further, forcing the man to drop the knife, then kicked at the back of his knee, dropping him to the floor. The man groaned as Lucky held his arm back until Sienna could bind his hands and gag him.

'Captain?' he called over his shoulder.

She got to her feet. 'I'm fine. Thank you, Lucky.'

He grunted and turned back to the Beater. A ring of keys gleamed on the Beater's belt. Lucky slipped them off.

'Let's go.' He held them up.

They hurried from the room, but before they could move further down the dark corridor, the captain paused. She turned back to the steps and Lucky heard it too – voices from up above.

Chapter Twenty-Five

'They must have heard the gunshot,' the captain said.

'What do we do?' Sienna tugged at her hair.

'We carry on. We get Gabe. And we fight our way back out if we have to.'

There was no other option at this stage. Even if the others wanted to flee, they'd be unlikely to get out of the building without being spotted. And he wasn't leaving Gabriel here. Gabriel belonged with the sun in his hair and the waves at his feet. Not down here in the foul dark.

There were six cells, three on one side and three on the other, each closed off with a heavy door with a grill at the top.

'Gabriel?' Lucky called into the gloom. They'd already been detected, staying quiet now seemed pointless.

There was no answer. Was he sleeping? Or had they hurt him badly enough that he was unconscious? Anger flared through Lucky's veins. How dare they? He stalked down between the cells, peering in each one in turn. How dare they? He'd rip them and this place apart if they'd hurt Gabriel.

He found him in the second to last cell, lying with his back to the door on the narrow bunk. The end of his braid brushed against the dirty floor. Lucky put a key in the lock and tried to turn it, but it refused to budge, and so did the next one. His hands shook as he fumbled for the next one, spilling the ring of keys on to the floor with a clang.

He cursed himself and bent down to pick it up again, but Captain Haven was quicker.

'Let me,' she said softly.

She worked through several more keys, until one turned with a heavy clunk that lifted Lucky's heart. He rushed past her into the cell and crouched down in front of the bunk.

'Gabriel?' His hand hovered uncertainly. Though he longed to touch Gabriel for his own sake, he didn't want to risk startling him or setting anything off. 'Please, wake up. It's me. It's Lucky.'

Gabriel shifted, mumbled something, then sat up slowly. He peered at Lucky, as if his vision was blurred.

'Who . . . who are you?' he asked, his voice weak and scratchy.

Lucky's heart sank. 'It's me. It's Lucky. You remember me, right? You're the only person who does remember me.'

Captain Haven stepped into the room, holding the torch. Gabriel shied away, holding his hand over his face. The captain handed the torch back, but the brief burst of light was enough for Lucky to see the black eye, the split lip, the bruise on his cheek.

'Gabe?' the captain said. Lucky recognised the low, gentle tone Gabriel had used with him when he'd first come to the *Dreamer*. 'Gabe? It's Mum. I'm here now. Talk to me. Tell me what's real.'

He blinked at her, and then his eyes widened. 'Mum! And Lucky. You came back for me.'

'Come to get you out,' she said with a grim smile. 'I won't let the Beaters take my family. Are you hurt? Can you stand?'

Gabriel put his feet down on the floor and tried. He wobbled for a moment but waved away Captain Haven's hand and stood steady. 'I'm good. But . . . what about the Beaters?'

The smile grew grimmer. 'They haven't been a problem so far.'

The approaching footsteps grew louder. They must be coming down the stairs by now.

'Let's go,' he called, and Haven hurried from the cell.

'Thank you,' Gabriel said softly, turning to Lucky. 'For coming back for me. You didn't have to do that.'

Lucky shook his head. 'You're wrong. I absolutely had to. Come on, let's get you out of here.' He offered Gabriel a hand, but Gabriel shied back.

'I'm fine,' he said, rubbing his neck.

They emerged from the cell to find six Beaters coming down the stairs towards them. There was nowhere to go but back in the cell, no cover to take from the pistols. Lucky stepped in front of Gabriel and drew his knife. Their chances were slim – even the skill and speed of the water dancers couldn't save them from that many firearms.

'Stay back,' he hissed to Gabriel.

'I've got him,' Sienna called back, taking up position in front of Gabriel. 'Stay behind me, Golden Boy. We'll get you out of here.'

Lucky squared his shoulders and waited to move.

The corridor convulsed.

The whole floor twisted like a leviathan beneath his feet. He hit the wall with a thud, and behind him, Gabriel gave a yelp of surprise. The Beaters spilled down the steps, some dropping their weapons, some falling completely. A loud groaning, grinding sound filled the area, and a crack opened up, running right down the length of the cells in a ragged zigzag.

Captain Haven recovered her balance first.

'We can kill each other down here, or we can all try to leave and survive,' she suggested as the floor twisted again. Dust and debris rained down from the ceiling, compounding the darkness.

The Beaters hesitated.

Lucky suspected they would. Beaters are taught to be arrogant, to believe they're right, that fate is always on their side, and they act in the interests of preserving the world. As the ground shook, the stone slabs fracturing under his feet, Lucky wondered for a moment if they had a point.

But if this was the fate of the world – to die down here in the church cells or with a noose around his neck – then Lucky wasn't interested.

Fuck fate.

A pistol shot rang out, a sudden, violent sound, and Lucky fought the urge to clap his hands over his ears. He tensed, waiting to see who cried out, who fell, one of his or one of theirs.

Captain Haven drew a second pistol from her belt, and the Beaters bolted.

'Let's go,' she said firmly, glancing over her shoulder at her son. 'Let's get you home.'

As they moved towards the steps, staggering over the rolling ground, Lucky felt torn. Part of him wanted to rush ahead, meet the Beaters he knew must be waiting. They wouldn't give up that easily, and he owed them for the bruises on Gabriel's face. But he didn't want to leave Gabriel's side, either.

Gabriel looked pale and dazed, and Lucky wasn't sure how much of that was the current events, and how much was what the Beaters had done to him. He remembered the comfort of having Gabriel close when the world felt new and strange, and he didn't want to deprive Gabriel of that if he needed it, too.

As Cass reached the top of the stairs, another shot rang back, and they pushed back against the wall.

'Fuck,' Haven said under her breath.

Lucky turned to Gabriel. 'Stay close to your mother,' he said. 'I'm going to get us out of here.'

Gabriel shook his head. 'Don't – don't get hurt.' He pulled his arms around himself.

Lucky gave him a smile that he hoped was reassuring. 'I'll be fine. Lucky, remember?'

Before Gabriel could say anything else and change his mind, Lucky pushed up the steps. The twins stood pressed to the wall on each side. He slunk in next to Erin.

'There's four this side,' they said.

'And two that way,' Cass confirmed, pointing towards the main body of the church. 'Hope you've got some sort of secret weapon on you.'

Lucky wished he did. The water dancers could hold the Beaters back, but they couldn't push through without the other group of Beaters taking them out from the rear. The earthshakes were easing, which would give the Beaters further impetus to come after them.

The iron band tightened around Lucky's chest.

'We need to take out the two behind us.'

'Would love to,' Erin said between gritted teeth, 'but I can barely see as it is, and they're covered by furniture.'

'Maybe I can change that,' Lucky replied. Before the twins could respond, he stepped out from the stairs.

Immediately all the pistols were trained on him. Lucky held up his hands. 'I want to talk. I have some information that might be useful.' He took a step towards the group of four, hoping that both the Beaters and the twins would act the way he wanted.

The room had a heavy, oppressive atmosphere, an emotional storm brewing. Any moment now, lightning would strike. Lucky took another step forwards.

A pair of sounds behind him, a whoosh of water and a dull thump, told him the twins had taken the initiative. He didn't have the time to check if they'd been successful. Lucky threw himself at the floor as pistols went off around him, filling the air with thundercracks and flashes. Dust and gunpowder smoke tickled his nose as he lay there, waiting to feel the burst of pain that would tell him he'd been shot.

Footsteps raced up the stairs and more splashes and thuds told him the other water dancers had mobilised. Now the Beaters' pistols were expended, they had the advantage. Lucky struggled to his feet, the action setting off a burning pain in his hip. Blood ran down his leg, staining his slacks, but he could put most of his weight on the limb, so the damage didn't seem too terrible.

Gabriel rushed up to his side. 'You moon-touched idiot! What were you thinking?' He stood close enough to touch, but neither of them reached out. Their presence was enough.

'I'm Lucky, remember?' he said with a tired smile.

'Let's not hang around and test that theory,' Captain Haven suggested.

Lucky grabbed a cloak from a fallen Beater and tossed it at Gabriel. 'Cover your head.' The rest of them might be able to slip out in the chaos, but Gabriel's long golden braid was distinctive.

The group headed up the steps and out into the graveyard. Voices all around them, raised in fear, concern, and confusion, told them the town had been awoken by the shakes. People milled about the church, frustration and anxiety written in both their voices and actions. Given what Sienna had said about the church providing a warning system for disasters, he could understand their aggravation.

Lucky wished it wasn't his problem, but he had little doubt on the matter. The earthshake had started within moments of reuniting with Gabriel. How long before the next one? Would some disaster occur on the *Dreamer*?

Most of the crew stood on the deck, lining the rail, watching as they approached. Poe and First Mate Haven waited at the centre of the group. Captain Haven stepped on board first to applause and cheers, followed by the other three dancers. Lucky offered a hand to Gabriel, but he shook his head.

He climbed on to the ship and approached his mother, shoulders hunched, head down.

'Permission to come aboard?' he asked softly.

Captain Haven wiped the corner of her eye. 'You never have to ask permission to come home, Gabe.' She looked over his shoulder at Lucky. 'And neither do you.'

Conflicting emotions tore at Lucky – the warmth and comfort of family, and the cold fear of all they'd be facing soon. Still, he managed to fix a smile in place and hoped that covered the tremors in his heart.

'How about permission for a hug?' the first mate asked. Gabriel nodded, but as she opened her arms and took a step towards him, he backed away, throwing up his hands in front of his face. His whole body tensed and shook.

The first mate lowered her hands. 'It's all right. It's all right, sweet boy. I'm not going to touch you.'

'I'm sorry, Ma,' he mumbled. 'I'm sorry.'

'Hush, none of that. Let's get you somewhere quiet and you'll feel better soon.' She stood on one side of Gabriel, and the captain took the other side. Without any contact, they guided him across the deck and into the captain's cabin.

Lucky watched him go, feeling a little lost.

'Let's get that leg looked at.'

He turned to see Poe leaning on the rail next to him. The old cook glanced down at Lucky's leg, to where the blood stuck the fabric to his skin. With a shrug, he followed Poe down to his old cell. The picture of Gabriel was uncovered on the wall.

'You do that?' Poe asked, as Lucky settled down on the blanket.

'Mmm.' Lucky didn't meet his eyes.

'You're pretty talented. We should get you to decorate more of the ship.'

'Mmm,' Lucky said again. He wasn't sure he wanted people perceiving him in that way.

Poe helped him out of the slacks and cleaned and stitched the wound. A bullet had grazed his thigh, leaving a red trail across the skin. Poe applied the leviathan slime and wrapped it with a clean white bandage.

'You're back then?' he asked as he finished.

'If the captain will let me.'

'She'll have me to answer to if she doesn't,' Poe said with a laugh. 'And Amala. Mel said you belong, lad. You should believe her.'

Lucky ran a hand over the bandage. Already the pain had receded. 'When . . . when do you start accepting it? That you belong somewhere? When do you stop paying attention to the voices that say you don't, all the fears that you'll cause trouble, hurt people?' There was an empty space in his chest, now all the fear of the rescue had faded away. He felt as if it could swallow him up, turn him inside out.

Poe settled down next to him, his legs stretched out. 'Well now, there's a question. I think, for some people, those feelings never quite go away. And that's not necessarily a bad thing.' He held up his hand as Lucky opened his mouth. 'People like that care, deeply. But they're always looking at their faults, rather than their strengths. Their mistakes rather than their achievements, wouldn't you agree?'

Lucky looked away, feeling his face flush.

'You can't always change that, and you shouldn't beat yourself up over it. But you can start learning how to deal with it better.'

'How?' Lucky looked back at Poe.

'Start by talking to us.' Poe put a hand on his shoulder. 'Those voices get too loud, those doubts start eating at you, talk them through with us, rather than taking them at face value. Maybe you'll find they ain't so true after all. Can you do that?'

'I can try.'

'Good lad.' Poe squeezed his shoulder, then stood up. 'Get some rest. Tomorrow, I'll show you how to make pancakes. Reckon we could all use a treat.'

Poe left, but it wasn't long before Captain Haven knocked on the door. Lucky leapt to his feet.

'Captain. How's Gabriel?'

'Physically? A bit battered and bruised, but nothing serious. But he's hurt and scared, and there's something troubling him, and he won't admit it to me. Will you talk to him?'

'Of course.'

'Thank you. And thank you for your help earlier.'

'Captain . . .' He swallowed, and she raised an eyebrow. 'When I left with the Beater, you . . . you promised Yale that you wouldn't let me back on the ship.'

She frowned, pursing her lips, then a look of understanding crossed her face. 'You're misremembering. I said I wouldn't come looking for you, and I haven't. I thought it was Gabe on that ship, not you. But I never promised anything about not letting you back on board. The Beater just heard what he wanted to hear. You belong here, Lucky.'

'Thank you.'

She brushed a hand over his shoulder but said nothing more.

Lucky moved past her, feeling self-conscious. She didn't make any attempt to further the conversation, and Lucky made his way to the cabin. The first mate was in the office sipping coffee as he entered.

'He's in there,' she said, pointing to a door.

Lucky knocked and Gabriel responded from inside. The room was clearly the captain's bedroom, but a piece of sailcloth had been hung up, dividing it in two. On this side of the cloth was a low bunk and a bedside desk. A tub of water, soap suds floating on the surface, stood in one corner. Gabriel paced beside the bed.

'How many of those have you had?' Lucky asked, pointing at the coffee cup on the table.

Gabriel turned and gave him a grin. 'Just the one, and it had a big old slug of rum in it. Supposed to calm me down. It's not really helping.'

'I'm not surprised,' Lucky replied. 'How are you feeling?'

Gabriel sat down on the bed, rubbing his neck. 'I'm scared. I hate this. I hate reacting like this. I want to hug my mums. I want to hug you.' He looked up at Lucky with a pleading expression.

Lucky knelt down in front of him. 'It's all right to take your time.'

Gabriel looked away. 'What . . . what if it's not, though?'

Lucky froze, a shiver running down his spine. 'What do you mean?'

'I . . . I think the sacrifice is happening.'

'The water dancer sacrifice?' The icy sensation intensified, spreading through his veins and settling around his heart. 'Gabriel, what did you promise?'

'I didn't recognise you, or Mum, when you first came into the cell. And I've been struggling to remember some things.' His hands closed and opened on the edge on the bed. 'I offered my memories. I thought . . . I thought that would be safe. After all, I'd be losing memories of an abusive father, a best friend who disappeared. I didn't think I needed them.' He raised his head, eyes wide, lips trembling. 'But what . . . what if it takes them all?'

Chapter Twenty-Six

'I don't want to forget,' he said, the last word buried in a sob. He put his head in his hands, his shoulders shaking. Lucky's heart ached for him, and he longed to wrap him up in his arms, enveloping him in a protective embrace that would separate him from the cruel world.

But the cruel world had already twisted that, turned it into something bitter and painful.

He sat down on the bed, close, but not too close. Gabriel turned towards him, tears running down his cheeks.

'You don't know it's the sacrifice,' Lucky said softly. 'It might be a consequence of everything you've been through in the last couple of days. You exhausted yourself trying to save that leviathan, and then the Beaters . . .' He glanced at Gabriel's face, one eye still half closed under the swelling. 'The Beaters hurt you.'

Gabriel touched his neck again. 'Like my father. Only, only it wasn't like him. He was angry and frustrated, lashing out at an easy target. The Beaters hit me because they were cruel. They knew it hurt and that's why they did it.'

'That's the Beaters,' Lucky muttered.

'Please don't join them.' Gabriel's voice trembled. He lowered his head. 'I know you don't think you belong anywhere. I know you want stability. But you're not like them, Lucky. I don't want to see them break you down into something cruel and callous. Please, Lucky, I couldn't bear it.' The words tumbled out of him like a waterfall, wrapping around Lucky, filling him with Gabriel's emotions.

'I know where I belong.' Something was coming. Something that would forever change things between them. A good change, he hoped, because he couldn't hold the words back. Gabriel turned to him, one eye wide, hopeful. Lucky met his gaze. 'I love you, Gabriel Haven.'

Gabriel let out that same happy squeak he'd made when Lucky kissed him in his cell, all those months ago, and his hand flew to his mouth. It was such a sweet, innocent reaction, and it only made Lucky's heart swell. He reached a hand up, slowly, carefully, but Gabriel flinched, and Lucky lowered it again. Gabriel put his head in his hands and wept, sobs shaking his body.

'Gabriel? What's wrong?'

Gabriel could only shake his head. The sobs consumed him, locking his muscles, eating his breath, until Lucky was afraid they'd destroy him completely.

'Gabriel?' He leaned closer, his shoulder brushing against Gabriel's, ever so slightly. 'Please, talk to me.'

Gabriel took a breath, deeper than the last. It took a while, but eventually he smothered the sobs into shuddering sighs. Lucky glanced around the room, but he couldn't find anything resembling a handkerchief. He rooted around until he found an old shirt, far too small now, in a sea chest, and handed it over.

'Best I can do,' he said with an apologetic smile.

Gabriel took it without a word, wiping the tears away from his face and blowing his nose. He lay down on the bed, one hand gripping the pillow. His nails were almost entirely free from paint, just little flecks of green here and there.

'Talk to me,' Lucky pressed. 'If you don't feel the same way, that's all right. You don't owe me your heart.'

'No, I do. I do. I love you, too, and hearing you say it . . . that was the most amazing feeling I've ever had. Another sob threatened to overwhelm him. 'But I'm going to forget it someday. I'm going to forget you saying it. I'm going to forget all the moments we've shared. I'm going to forget you. Even if this isn't the sacrifice now, it's going to happen sooner or later.' He buried his face in the pillow.

'I won't let you forget me, Gabriel. I promise. Your mothers won't let you forget them, either. When it happens, we'll all be here to remind you.' Lucky reached up and undid the clasp on his necklace. 'Here.'

Gabriel raised his head and Lucky placed the necklace on the pillow next to him.

'You gave me a name. I'm giving you this. As a promise. That whatever happens in the future, wherever I am, I love you and I'm thinking about you. You touch that, and you'll remember.'

Gabriel slipped the necklace around his neck, fingering the pewter feather. 'You're not going away, are you?'

'I'm staying right here, if you want me to.' He wiped a tear away from his own eye, hot and burning as it tracked down his cheek. But real.

This was real.

Gabriel lay down, curling into a foetal position. 'Please.'

'Where do you want me?' Lucky asked.

Gabriel's face flushed and he coughed. Lucky grinned.

'If you want to,' he said softly.

'I ... er ... I don't think I'm up for that. Not tonight. I want to touch you so badly. But I don't want to panic. I don't want to taint this.' He sniffed. 'I hate being me.'

'Don't. There's nothing to hate about you. You're kind, and you're brave, and you're funny. You put your whole heart into everything you do. I love to watch you dance, the way you move, like you're part of the sea itself.' He held out a hand. 'You're so strong. You can do this, Gabriel.'

Gabriel sat up slowly. He reached his own hand out, fingers outstretched, then pulled it back.

'You can do this,' Lucky said again.

The pewter feather rose and fell with his chest as Gabriel took in a deep breath. He spread his fingers again, this time bringing them close enough to brush against the tips of Lucky's.

'See,' Lucky told him. He let the touch linger, enjoying the rough sensation, the warmth that emanated, then pushed his fingers past, closing his hand around Gabriel's. 'Safe.'

Gabriel made a soft sound in his throat, like a hiccup. 'Safe.'

Lucky drew their hands towards him. 'Can I kiss you, here?' He inclined his head towards Gabriel's fingers. Gabriel nodded quickly. Lucky brought Gabriel's hand to his lips, kissing his knuckles. A fleeting brush, soft and subtle, but enough to breathe him in, and Lucky's heart quickened. He'd washed before Lucky arrived, and his skin smelled of soap infused with rose oil. Behind that, sea salt, the trace of coffee. And behind even that, the scent of Gabriel himself.

Lucky was hungry for it.

He turned their hands and indicated Gabriel's wrist. 'What about here?'

Gabriel moaned as Lucky's lips brushed his skin.

'Good?' Lucky asked.

'Good,' Gabriel breathed.

Lucky moved his way slowly up Gabriel's arm, bringing his whole body closer each time, so by the time he'd reached Gabriel's shoulder, they were sitting side by side on the bed. He was aware of Gabriel's body, ready to pull back the moment he seemed in any way uncomfortable. But he was also very aware of his own, too. His heart, untethered, floating loose and free in his chest. His skin, alive to every sensation, every shift of Gabriel against him. His lips, hungry to taste more.

'How about here?' He pointed to Gabriel's cheek.

The corner of Gabriel's mouth turned up, a faded version of the bright teasing grin Lucky adored him for.

'It's still a bit sore, there,' Gabriel said. 'How about here?' He touched a finger to his lips, parting them slightly.

'Yeah?' Lucky asked, raising an eyebrow.

'Yeah,' Gabriel whispered in return.

Lucky poured himself into the kiss, pushed his very essence into the moment. Every feeling, every emotion, every flutter of his heart. All the hunger and the love. For the first time he could remember, he felt free. Felt whole.

Felt Lucky.

Gabriel's hand caressed his cheek; the other buried in Lucky's hair. The Beaters had shaved out the style Gabriel had given it, and he'd let it grow back shaggy again. Appearance hadn't mattered much then, and he wasn't sure it mattered much now. Only Gabriel. Only Gabriel's hands, his arms, his lips.

They broke away from the embrace, and Lucky looked up at Gabriel. His brown eyes shone with happiness, and Lucky never wanted that to change. They'd find a way to save the leviathans, the dancers. To keep Gabriel happy.

'What would you like to do now?'

'I'm not sure.' Gabriel leaned his head against Lucky's. 'I want more, but I'm still scared I'll panic or lash out. Spoil everything.'

Lucky squeezed his hands. 'This is fine. We'll have time. I know we will. Everything's going to work out, Gabriel.'

'There you go, making me believe that again.' Gabriel kissed his cheek. 'How . . . how about you?'

Lucky's face warmed. 'Could you . . .' He ducked his gaze, focusing on the blanket. 'Could you show me how to do that?' He pointed at Gabriel's braid. 'I really want to do it myself once.'

Gabriel's eyes widened, then he threw back his head and roared with laughter. Lucky blushed harder.

'You're adorable,' Gabriel said, pressing a kiss on Lucky's forehead. He undid the leather band, working his fingers through the tendrils of the braid until his hair hung loose down his back. He twisted, so his back was turned towards Lucky. 'First, divide it into three sections.'

Lucky reached out, feeling more awkward and self-conscious about this than anything they'd done before. His fingers caressed the long strands of Gabriel's hair, releasing more of the floral scent of the soap. He took a deep breath and plunged his hands into the golden waterfall.

'When you've done that,' Gabriel continued, 'you alternate passing the outside sections over the central one. So left over centre, and then right over centre, and so on.'

'Like this?' He used a finger to divide up Gabriel's hair, and slowly weaved the sections one over the other. 'Let me know if I'm being too rough.'

'It's fine,' Gabriel replied. 'It's relaxing actually.' He smothered, not quite successfully, a yawn.

Lucky finished up and tied the end of the braid. It wasn't as neat or smooth as Gabriel did it, but there would be time in the future to practise. And if Gabriel did ever forget, then Lucky could do this for him.

Gabriel turned back to him, and Lucky held out his arms, asking with a gesture this time. Gabriel wrapped himself around him, nuzzling Lucky's cheek.

'Tired?' Lucky asked.

'Sorry.'

'Don't be. You've been through a lot. Do you want me to stay here, tonight?'

'Please,' Gabriel whispered.

There wasn't much room on the bunk for one, let alone two, so Lucky found himself lying almost on top of Gabriel. He laid his head on Gabriel's shoulder, one arm wrapped around his waist. Gabriel's hand rested on the back of Lucky's head, his fingers idly playing with his hair.

The fatigue hit Lucky suddenly. All the tension of the jail-break, all his fears for Gabriel – and then the emotions of touching him – washed out, leaving him warm, content, and exhausted. The ship was on its way to Sea Hall to save the shrine, and in doing so, save the dancers and the leviathans.

'You comfortable?' he asked as his eyes flickered.

Gabriel kissed his head. 'Very. Goodnight, Lucky.'

'Goodnight, my Gabriel.'

PART THREE

Chapter Twenty-Seven

The wind had their back, and the *Dreamer*'s sails were full and billowing as she ploughed through the sea. Unfortunately, the same wind also benefitted their enemy: somewhere ahead of them, the *Providence* bore down on Sea Hall.

Lucky turned his attention back to the group in front of him. He'd been drilling them in hand-to-hand combat for the last hour, and it was clear many were starting to flag. The Beaters would have made them train until one fell, but Lucky wasn't a Beater.

And he never would be.

'Take a break,' he called. 'We'll pair off and practise sparring in half an hour.'

There was a collective sigh of relief and several of the sailors sank to the deck. Lucky tried to keep the concern from his face. It was only a few days to Sea Hall – not enough time to train them well enough to be confident in fighting a ship of Beaters.

'You're a good teacher,' Amala said, startling him. 'Patient.'

'I'm not sure I've got time to be patient,' he said, taking the cup of water she offered him. 'If I don't do a good job, if I can't do enough to . . .' The words died in his throat, buried under visions of leviathan guts, of blood on the sand.

'You're doing the best you can. No one can ask more of you, or anyone else, than that.'

'I'm so tired of being around death, loss,' he admitted, and she wrapped an arm around him as he rested his head against her shoulder.

'We'll stop them,' she said firmly. 'We'll save the shrine.'

'But what if we don't?' he protested. 'Or we do, but they come back next year. What if the earthshakes keep happening and the Beaters keep coming, year after year? What if—'

'Lucky.'

He looked up into her dark eyes and she gave him a smile.

'Let's focus on one fight at a time, all right?'

'Right, yeah.' He handed back the cup. 'How's Gabriel?'

'Mel's got him cataloguing the ship, deciding what we can throw overboard if we need to lose weight and go faster. She's keeping him busy,' she added with a wink.

'That's good.' He knew Gabriel felt guilty at not being able to take part in the combat training, and also that it wasn't enough to point out no one judged him for the matter. He wished he could do more to make him understand.

'You're good for him,' she said. 'Some seas just take a long time to navigate, that's all. Here. I came to give you something.' She pushed a woollen bundle into his hands. Lucky turned it over, unfolding a scarf made of crimson, orange, and gold wool. Like a fire.

'It's beautiful.'

'It's getting colder in the evening. Thought you could use it.' She gave him another wink, patted his shoulder, and walked off, waving a hand over her shoulder as she went. Lucky turned the scarf over and over in his hands. It smelled of citrus oil and cinnamon, and he pulled it to his face, pressing it against his skin to push back the tears that threatened to spill out of him.

He sat there for a while, wool on his cheek, salt and spice in his nostrils; he focused his entire being into those sensations, the rest of his body floating free, untethered. Gradually, the feeling came back to his limbs, along with an awareness of people gathering.

Lucky ordered everyone into a circle, pulled out two at random, and gave each one a knife wrapped in leather. Then he watched, judged, critiqued as they went against each other. Sometimes the matches went on several minutes, other times they were over in seconds. By the end of it all, he was more nervous.

When each person had fought twice, Lucky dismissed the group and went to find Gabriel. He had time before he had to start training the next group of sailors. Lucky found him in the hold with a clipboard, chewing on the end of a pencil.

'Want to see if Poe's ready with lunch?' Lucky called and Gabriel jumped. The pencil skittered off into the shadows. 'Sorry, I didn't mean to startle you.'

Gabriel shook his head. 'It's fine. I just got caught up counting the . . . the . . .' He gestured in front of himself in frustration, biting his lip.

'Sacks?' Lucky suggested and Gabriel smacked his fist into his palm.

'Sacks! Sacks of flour. So stupid. I couldn't remember the word. I couldn't . . .' His voice choked up. Lucky held out a hand, and after a moment, Gabriel reached out and took it, moving in close.

'It's not stupid, Gabriel. It's not,' he said softly. Gabriel trembled against him. 'Come on, let's go and get some food.'

Gabriel made no attempt to move, pressed against Lucky, his breath tickling Lucky's ear. Lucky moved his hands, slowly at first, until they were wrapped around Gabriel, holding him tight.

'I'm tired of being broken,' Gabriel whispered. 'Of being wrong.'

'You're not broken. You're not wrong.' Lucky moved his hand to the side of Gabriel's face, gently urging him to meet Lucky's gaze. 'You're you and I love every part of you. Remember the day with the leviathan? You told me you didn't know if you wanted things to be different, because then you wouldn't be where you are now, wouldn't be who you are now.

It's not been an easy road, for either of us. But it has brought us together, right?'

Gabriel closed his eyes. His face was still swollen on one side, but not as badly as it had been the night before. He leaned in, his kiss lingering, slow. 'Together.'

Lucky put his hand on Gabriel's chest, over the pewter feather. It felt warm to his touch, almost alive. *I . . . I feel like we made a promise. We made a promise to each other when we were younger.* He wished he could remember more of the boy who lived in Ciatheme, who carved his initials in the rocks above the tideline.

'Together.' He let Gabriel set the pace, not moving until he did. They were halfway to the galley before Gabriel stopped.

'I forgot my pencil.'

'It's fine.' Lucky held up a hand. 'I'll fetch it. You go and find lunch.'

The hold was dark, the lantern light casting flickering shadows. Lucky hung the lamp up and rooted around amongst the stores of provisions, sacks and boxes and barrels. The idea that the captain was considering throwing away food told him how seriously she was taking the matter. Which only added to the weight of his concerns.

'Gabe?' Captain Haven called.

'He's in the galley,' Lucky called back. He spotted the pencil caught between two boxes and picked it up. There was a moment of silence, and then footsteps as Captain Haven came down into the hold.

'How is it going?' She folded her arms, and then unfolded them again.

'Everyone's trying really hard,' he said. 'Some of them have good reactions, good instincts, but . . .'

'They're not fighters,' she finished for him.

'It's not their fault.' He leaned against the box, tucking the pencil into his pocket. 'But the Beaters, they've been training since childhood in many cases. Not just how to fight. How to think. How they're part of this great tapestry and nothing matters except fulfilling it. They wash the individuality out of their acolytes, and then they are no longer able to care. Not about each other, not about anything except following the threads.' He rubbed at his temple. 'I just don't think we'll be ready to stand against that. Even if we had a year to train.'

She said nothing and Lucky fiddled with the pencil, not wanting to see the fear or anger in her eyes. He'd let her down, let the crew down. Yale might have whipped them into enough shape with his cruelty, but Lucky couldn't do that, even if it ended up costing them their lives.

'I think you're underestimating us,' she said.

He lifted his eyes to her and found she'd settled on the steps, resting her arms on her knees. The silver in her hair flashed in the lamplight.

'You're right, we'll never be a fighting force like the Beaters. But we care, and that's a strength. We care about each other, protect each other. We care about the shrine, about what it means to us. That's a strength, Lucky, one the Beaters will never be able to draw on. And we have the sea on our side.' She twisted her hand, fingers splayed. Lucky recognised it as a water dancer gesture.

'Will it be enough?' he asked quietly.

'It will have to be,' she said grimly. 'We've all lost enough. No more. Keep training the crew. Give them as much of an edge as you can. In the evening, I'll convene the other dancers and we'll discuss tactics then. We almost sank a Beater ship once already.' She gave him a hungry grin.

'Yes, Captain.' He shared her determination, but he couldn't bring himself to share her optimism.

'I don't suppose you can summon a leviathan?' she asked as she rose. 'Help us out like it helped you escape?'

He shook his head. 'No, sadly, I think that was just luck. And I don't think Gabriel would approve.'

Her smile faltered. 'No, he would not.'

'What's going to happen to him?' A knot tightened in his stomach.

'I . . . I don't know, Lucky.' Her voice trembled. 'I don't know what words he used to promise at the shrine, and I don't know if he even remembers them anymore. It's different for every person – sometimes it's a sudden thing, other times it's more gradual. I don't know why it's happening so soon, though. Normally people can go decades before the sacrifice takes place.'

'There's so much we don't understand.' The sudden sacrifice. The earthshakes. The reason for his mother's death. It felt like a web around him, pulling tight. Choking him.

'Let's focus on stopping them laying a finger on the shrine first,' she said, giving his shoulder a rough squeeze.

'One fight at a time, right?'

'Right.' She gave him a tight smile, then turned to the steps, sighing. 'My wife is a smart woman, but I should probably check in on her. She knits when she's worried and if I leave her to it, everyone – including the figurehead – is going to be sporting gloves, scarfs, and hats.'

Lucky held out his new scarf and the captain barked a laugh that sounded genuine.

'So it's begun. I better get on. Go find something to eat. I'll join you for training later.'

She walked away, leaving Lucky alone in the hold. Shadows. Walls. No matter where he wanted to be, somehow he always ended back in places like that. He could walk out this time, but how long before he found himself in another prison? He climbed out of the gloom, and the damp of the hold gave way to something warm and spicy from the galley ahead.

One fight at a time.

Amala was right, there was no other way to do it. One fight. One mystery. One connection. Sometimes threads were a web that tightened, binding you. But sometimes they were rigging that you could climb to a better place, away from the walls.

Lucky found Gabriel sitting in the galley, two bowls of soup in front of him. Lucky slid into the seat opposite and Gabriel pushed a bowl across to him.

'Poe says this is my favourite,' Gabriel said. His hand hovered above his own spoon. 'I didn't remember what it tasted like.'

Lucky reached out a hand, and Gabriel rested his fingertips against it.

'So many things are disappearing already. When they all go, what happens to me then?' His voice crumbled like stale bread.

'Nothing will change.' Lucky pushed his fingers against Gabriel's, looking up into his dark eyes. 'Nothing, I promise. The leviathans will swim the seas and your home will be the *Dreamer* and I will love you. Always. You're not your past. Even if you lose all your memories, you will always be so much more than that, Gabriel.'

Gabriel choked back a sob, his hand tightening around Lucky's. Before he could say anything else, there were two short whistle blasts, a pause, followed by two more short ones.

'What does that mean?' he asked.

Gabriel frowned. 'It's . . . It's . . .'

'It's a storm,' Poe said, coming out of the galley. 'We better get up on deck.'

Chapter Twenty-Eight

Lucky dashed up on deck, Gabriel on his heels. Behind them, Poe followed, his wooden leg thumping against the steps. The wind hit Lucky the moment he stepped out on to the deck, almost blowing him back into Gabriel. The sky had darkened, thick iron-grey clouds swallowing up the sun.

The *Dreamer* dipped down, making him stagger. Gabriel pushed a hand against his back, steadying him. The air crackled, heavy with tension, and Lucky pressed himself against Gabriel.

'Strike the topsails!' Captain Haven yelled over the rising howl of the wind. 'Batten the hatches and get everything on deck secure.'

Gabriel and Poe turned to lock down the hatch to the lower decks.

'What happened?' Lucky asked the cook. 'The weather was clear before I went below. There was barely a cloud in the sky.'

The ship dipped again, her bow plunging down as she rode the waves. A tin water cup, left out from the training earlier, rattled across the deck and skidded off into the surging sea. Sailors scurried over the rigging, bringing down the upper sails, fighting against the wind.

If they couldn't get the ship prepared quickly, if the wind and waves took too much out of the *Dreamer*, it could be a disaster.

Lucky was in the centre of yet another one.

'Reef the mainsail!' Captain Haven yelled. 'Cass, Erin, to the stern. The rest of the dancers to the bow.' She gave Gabriel a look, and he hurried to position.

'What do I do?' Lucky asked. He'd learned a bit during his time on the *Dreamer*, but mostly he'd been working in the galley.

'Help Amala with the wheel,' she said, gesturing towards her wife.

Lucky gave Gabriel's hand a squeeze, and then they parted and headed to the opposite ends of the ship. Lucky climbed up to the quarterdeck, where Amala was battling to hold the wheel steady. She gave him a grim smile as he took hold of the other side, bracing himself. The rain lashed against him, mixing with the waves that battered at the ship. Amala was already soaked through, her black curls clinging limply to her face.

'Welcome to your first storm!' She was standing only feet away, but she had to shout over the noise.

Is this my fault, he wanted to ask, but it wouldn't have made any difference to the situation. 'How bad is it?' he called instead as he fixed the scarf she'd given him around his neck. She gave him a warm smile at the sight of it, but it faded away quickly.

'Never seen a storm brew up so quickly,' she said grimly. 'But it's here now, so all we can do is ride it out, hope it doesn't send us too far off course.'

'So we can't continue directly to Sea Hall during this?'

She shook her head. 'Leaving the sails up would be madness, risk capsizing us. If we tried to maintain course, we risk being swamped. Better to point her at the wind and let her run. The dancers will do their best to manage the worst of the waves, but we don't know how long this storm will last.'

Lucky gripped the wheel, feeling the mighty structure fighting against him. No time for more training, pushed off course. He thought of the leviathan, caught in the Beaters' trap, helpless against the harpoons. If they couldn't get there in time . . .

A bright flash forked across the sky, white and purple against the dark storm clouds. A moment later thunder rumbled overhead, so loud he wanted to clap his hands over his ears. But he couldn't let go of the wheel.

If the storm sprang up suddenly, it refused to die with any speed or grace. Rain fell relentlessly, soaking him to the skin. The wind howled around the mast, threatening the last bit of sailcloth still unfurled. Waves towered, higher than the rail, whipped into sharp peaks.

At either end of the ship, the dancers worked to keep the worst of them away from the ship, preventing her getting swamped. Gabriel worked with his mother, while Poe and Sienna took the other side. The twins had the stern, preventing the waves from pushing against the *Dreamer*'s rear.

On deck, the rest of the crew fought to deal with the consequences of the rain, and any waves the dancers couldn't handle. Two worked the ship's bilge pumps, while others used buckets to clear the water.

Lucky's hands had become welded to the wheel, the wood now as much a part of him as his jagged fingernails. Beside him, Amala grunted with effort, the rain running down her face, bouncing off her nose. Her eyes were half closed, a frown creasing her brow. Every now and then she'd raise her head towards her wife and son, and the frown would deepen.

Time blurred. Lucky couldn't feel his feet in his sodden boots. The *Dreamer* rode the waves, every new dip making her planks and joints creak and moan. The twins held back the worst of them, but more and more were breaking over the top of the rail. Erin turned away from the sea, raising their arms above their head. The pool of water on the quarterdeck lifted, hovering several inches above the deck, before they flung their hands forwards, and it shot back to the sea.

Erin caught Lucky watching and gave him a grin. 'Takes more than a storm to put us down.'

'Erin!' Cass called.

They both turned to see a monster wave towering six feet over the rail, ready to break down on the *Dreamer*. Cass's hands were up, but they couldn't hold back all that water on their own.

Erin rushed forwards just as the wave broke and cascaded over the deck. It slammed into Erin, knocking them to the deck, dragging them towards the side of the ship like a prize. Cass hung desperately to the rail, fighting to stay upright.

Lucky let go of the wheel and rushed across the deck. Wading through two-feet-deep water was difficult, slow, painfully slow. He focused on the dark red of Erin's hair, the blue fabric around their waist. Their pale hand, reaching frantically for something, anything, to hold on to.

The wave smacked Erin against the rail, dragging them over towards the churning sea. Even a dancer couldn't survive in that. Lucky threw himself forwards, grabbing at Erin's hand. He caught them, but the water pulled at him too, sucking hungrily. He staggered forwards, the rail catching him in the gut, knocking his breath away.

'Not today.' Cass grabbed Erin's other hand. Between the two of them, they managed to pull Erin to the deck, and all three collapsed in a heap.

Erin coughed, spitting out seawater. 'Not today.' They raised their head and gave Lucky another grin. 'Thanks for the save. I'm glad you decide to come back home.'

Lucky looked away, his face warming despite the icy rain. He touched the scarf, fingering the sodden wool. Home.

'No time for getting maudlin,' Erin said, getting to their feet. 'Got a storm to ride first.' The twins hurried back to the stern and stood, hands raised, feet planted firmly, facing down the sea. Lucky watched, a little bemused at their nonchalance in the face of something that could have killed them only moments before. It reminded him of Gabriel and the leviathans.

'Crew will get you through,' Amala said as he took his place at the wheel again. 'We've got your back, and we know you've got ours too.'

It took another few hours – time had been diluted by the rain and waves – for the wind to drop and the clouds to break enough for the stars to shine through. Lucky stared up at them, remembering that first night when Gabriel had encouraged him outside. They'd looked magical that night, and they carried that same sense of wonder with them now. A glittering promise that things would work out. That home was out there.

That crew would get you through.

Amala touched his shoulder and he rubbed his eyes. 'I've got this now,' she said, patting the wheel. 'Why don't you give Poe a hand?'

The cook stomped across the deck towards the hatch. Lucky took the steps from the quarterdeck two at a time and skidded to a stop beside him.

'Feels good to be alive, doesn't it?' Poe reached a hand towards him and flicked the water away from Lucky's clothes and hair.

Lucky felt the tug of a smile. His limbs were leaden, his body like a lump of wood: a lifeless thing. But his heart raced with a heady mixture of emotions: twin ribbons of hope and fear wrapped around each other in a complex dance. Words like crew and home sparkled like stars, but there was a dark cloud too – how long could a home be sustained if Lucky only brought disaster?

'You look like you need soup,' Poe said, clapping a hand on his shoulder.

They headed below deck as Captain Haven shouted orders to get the ship back on course. Lucky wondered how far they'd been blown from their destination. How much time had been lost.

In the galley, the warmth gradually brought life and feeling back to his fingers. Poe passed him things to chop while he made bread, and Lucky let himself focus on the repetitive motion of the knife.

'Want to talk about it?' Poe asked. His back was to Lucky, his hands shaping the dough.

'Just tired.' How could he find the words to vocalise his fears? That he might have found a home, a family, and yet be the thing that destroyed them all? If the disasters were focused on him, if the world had rejected him so much that it stormed and shook around him, what could he possibly do to fight that?

'So be it. Get that bread cooking then.' The words came with no judgement, no pressure.

He swapped places with Poe, letting the cook season and taste the big pot of soup while Lucky shaped the bread into flat rounds and set them on the pan. Poe shuffled about, adding this and that, and soon a warm and hearty scent joined the mouth-watering smell of fresh bread.

'Don't suppose that's ready for a hungry sailor?'

Lucky turned to find Gabriel leaning against the door frame, arms folded across his chest, a tired smile on his face. Lucky's hunger for food was eclipsed by a desperate, visceral need to hold him, to lose himself in those arms, in the scent of sea salt and coffee.

'Can I . . .' he asked softly, and Gabriel held out a hand.

'Please. It's been a long night.'

Lucky entwined his fingers in Gabriel's, pulling them up to his lips. Gabriel wrapped his other arm around Lucky, pulling him close, so Lucky's ear rested against his chest. The steady thump of Gabriel's heart was a lullaby.

Poe gave them a moment, then cleared his throat. 'Right, let's get this out on deck.' He ladled out cups of soup and gave them each a tray to carry out to the crew.

Up on deck, the sails were back, fluttering in the wind, stark and white in the light of the two moons. Everything was dry, both the ship and the sailors. The only remnant of the storm was the fatigue that lingered over everyone's faces.

'Your first storm!' Sienna said cheerfully, snatching a cup from his tray. She took a long drink and let out a contented sigh. 'You're a proper sailor now you've been through that.'

'Do you know how far off course we are?' he asked.

She held up a finger while she drank the rest of the soup, then wiped her mouth with the back of her hand. 'Could be worse. Storm drove us east a bit, but Captain Haven thinks we should be able to get to Sea Hall before the shrine is revealed. Gonna be a tough thing. Hope you don't like sleep.'

Lucky had just finished handing out the cups and was about to head down to the galley for more, when the lookout let out a long whistle from the crow's nest.

'Captain! Sail. Thirty degrees east.'

Captain Haven strode to the rail and pulled out a spyglass. 'Take us closer,' she called to the sailor at the wheel. 'I want all hands on deck.'

Lucky stood at the rail, his hand curled around Gabriel's, watching the dark shape grow closer. A tension arced across the crew as they worked their tasks. The storm had been new and frightening to Lucky, but to the crew it was just something that happened. This, however, was different. The ship ahead could be anyone, friend or foe, and there was a risk that they wouldn't find out which before they got too close.

Whoever she was, the ship was in a bad way, that was clear. Her mainmast had broken, and now hung limply over the water. The ship listed to one side, clearly taking on water. Lucky didn't need to read the name on her flank – he recognised her instantly.

The *Providence*.

Chapter Twenty-Nine

The sight of the ship sent memories of the leviathan flooding through Lucky. The scent of its sickly sweet blood filled his nostrils. The thrashing, churning coils. The sound of its screams; the light fading from its eyes. His chest tightened, and he couldn't draw in a breath.

'Lucky.'

He started as Gabriel squeezed his hand. The memories pushed at him, shoving him out of his present and back to that moment. Back to the failure.

'Lucky,' Gabriel said again. 'Tell me what's real.'

'You.' He hadn't lost Gabriel. They'd found him again. He was here. Home. Safe. He tightened his grip on Gabriel's hand and Gabriel pulled him in close, his hand working circles on Lucky's back. 'You. You're real. You're real.'

'I am.' He kissed the top of Lucky's head. 'What happened?'

'I was thinking about the leviathan.'

'The one with the mark?' Gabriel asked and Lucky shook his head.

'No, the one at Minmouth. The one that we couldn't save.'

Gabriel looked at him blankly. 'I don't think I've ever been to Minmouth. You must be mistaken.'

'Don't you . . .' Lucky started, but there was no point. Of course Gabriel didn't remember. How quickly would his memories fade? How long before Lucky was just a stranger to him? Lucky looked up into Gabriel's eyes, his expression quizzical, fond, a hint of concern in the set of his eyebrows.

'You're staring, mate,' Gabriel teased. 'I know I'm pretty, but we should probably focus on that.' He pointed over at the

Providence. 'She must have been caught in the storm like us. I wonder what she's doing out here?'

Lucky bit down his rage at the unfairness of it all. He couldn't change anything, and Gabriel was right, the *Providence* was the important thing at the moment. He gazed over at her, searching for movement, but there was nothing.

'No sign of life,' Captain Haven said, setting aside her spyglass.

'Looks like she's missing her boats as well,' Sienna commented. 'Crew probably decided they couldn't bail her out and fled. Which is a nice bonus for us.'

'We should check it out, still,' Lucky said. He didn't trust luck to be on their side. Not when he was around. The church's weapon could still be on board, or the crew could be hiding, waiting for the *Dreamer* to pass so they could fill her stern with cannonballs.

Captain Haven frowned. Lucky could see her calculating the time they'd already lost against the risk that the ship presented some sort of unseen danger. 'Fine. Take Sienna, Cass, and Erin. Ten minutes. Don't take any risks. If you do find anyone, don't engage.'

'What about me?' Gabriel protested.

'I need you on the *Dreamer*. We're going to need to travel hard, use all dancers and the wind to get the most speed. I need you to help me organise the crew to make sure we have the most hands available without working anyone to exhaustion.'

'We won't be long,' Lucky said. He brought Gabriel's hand to his lips, kissing the knuckles. 'We'll be fine, I promise.'

'I'll look after him, Golden Boy,' Sienna agreed cheerfully, putting her arm around Lucky's shoulder. 'Don't you worry.'

Gabriel heaved a sigh, but didn't protest any further.

The deck of the *Providence* was eerily still. The broken mast creaked, and the sailcloth shuffled in the breeze, as if uncomfortable at being perceived. Sienna walked up to the mast and gave it the finger.

'That's for the leviathan,' she spat.

Lucky crossed the deck, kicking aside a stray length of sodden rope. He caught a glimpse of something red and found a length of thin red wool caught around the rail. He caressed a finger against it and voices whispered in his ear, hundreds of voices, all talking at once. Flashes of bright colour went off behind his eyes, so rapidly they were almost pictures, visions. He could see Sea Hall. He could see the castle at Ciatheme. He could see . . .

'Lucky?'

Someone touched his shoulder. He flinched, losing his connection to the thread, and suddenly the voices were gone and he was standing on the deck of the *Providence*. Cass stood in front of him, a look of concern on their face.

'I'm fine.'

'You don't look fine,' they said, and Lucky suspected they had a point. He rubbed at his head. It felt as if someone had clamped a vice around it and was squeezing tight.

'Just a headache. It will pass. Don't touch that,' he added, pointing to the thread. Cass pulled out a handkerchief and gingerly collected the thread up in it. They bundled the handkerchief into their pocket. Lucky took several deep breaths, counting to five each time, grounding himself on the solid deck beneath his feet, the sound of the waves. He paused, another sound coming to his attention. 'Someone's knocking.'

Cass frowned, their head cocked to one side. 'You're right. Hey!' they called over to Erin and Sienna on the other side of the deck. 'I think there's someone below deck.'

'Should we go back?' Erin asked. 'Captain said not to engage.'

'We should at least take a look,' Cass said and Lucky nodded. They crossed the deck and headed down into the ship.

'Is it true?' Erin asked as they stepped down into the bowels of the ship. It smelled of damp and rot down here, of sweat and fear. 'Gabriel's sacrifice is setting in?'

'It looks like it. I don't understand. If you know there's a sacrifice, why did you all go through with it? Is the power to control water that important?'

'It's not about power,' Sienna replied. 'At least, not like that. It's about making a choice, about taking something for our own. For people like us –' she glanced at Cass and Erin – 'for people like us, there is always going to be a cost. At least this is on our terms. Whatever the threads say, whatever we're supposed to be, we can turn around and say, "No, this is what we *are*."' She thumped a hand into her fist. 'Gabe's the same. Whatever happens, Lucky, this was his choice.'

Lucky closed his eyes, picturing Gabriel racing across the waves, the wind in his hair, the spray dancing with him. He thought of the picture he'd sketched, of the bliss on Gabriel's face. He'd drawn him like that because it was the moment that felt the most quintessentially Gabriel. The moment he was completely himself.

'I . . . I see.'

Sienna squeezed his shoulder. 'Come on, let's see who's still lurking on board.' She held out a middle finger and gave Lucky a wink. 'Got a few more of these to hand out.'

There was no sign of anyone in the galley, or the mess, or on the deck below, where the bunk room lay. It reminded him of the acolyte dorms – neat, tidy, inhuman. A place where people were as they were dictated to be.

The ship shifted suddenly, knocking him into Sienna. Timber creaked and groaned.

'Maybe we should go back,' he suggested. 'She might not have much longer.'

'We've come this far,' Sienna protested.

Cass lifted the lantern, peering down the steps. 'Exactly. If there is someone down there, maybe we can get more information about what the church plans to do at the shrine?'

Lucky couldn't argue with that, so he led the way down the next flight of steps, the lantern sending swinging shadows ahead of him. Somewhere ahead, water gurgled, sounding like a voice speaking a strange language. Something rushed over his boot, making him flinch, but it was only a rat, one that had not yet managed to flee the ship.

The banging was louder now – a thud-thud-thud, followed by a pause, then another thud-thud-thud. Lucky took a breath, trying to ignore the damp and decay that lingered in his nostrils.

'Hello?'

The banging stopped. 'Get me out of here!' a voice called out from ahead. 'Get me out of here, you cowards.'

Slowly. Lucky crept forwards. The voice set him on edge, and his fingers itched for a knife.

Blinking through the gloom, he could make out a dishevelled stack of boxes and barrels, half come away from their bindings in the storm. Beyond them was a heavy-looking door with a grill set at eye-height. Fingers clutched at the bars.

'Come on,' called the voice. 'Get your arses over here and let me out. I'll see you all hanged for treason.'

'Yale,' Lucky said, and there was a sharp intake of breath.

'Well, well, well, little bird. Everything's fucked, so I shouldn't be surprised that you're in the middle of it again. Come to gloat, have you?' He peered through the bars at Lucky, his lip curled in disgust.

'Came to find out what happened,' Lucky replied calmly.

Yale's knuckles tightened around the bars. 'You happened. This is your doing. He'll bring you down, bring you all down.' His eyes rolled wildly. 'You're bad luck, little bird.'

'Friend of yours, Lucky?' Cass asked, leaning back against the wall.

'He was my mentor, when I was an acolyte,' Lucky admitted.

'He's an arsehole,' Sienna said. 'I owe him for the leviathan.'

Lucky put a hand on her arm before she could do anything thoughtless. 'What happened?' he asked Yale.

Yale let go of the bars, and there was a shuffling sound on the other side of the doors. 'After you escaped, I transferred to the *Providence*. I knew you and your ilk wouldn't sit back and let fate play out. I wanted to make sure nothing could stop us getting to Sea Hall before the shrine uncovered. But that storm . . . That was your fault, wasn't it?'

'How can a storm be anyone's fault?' Erin protested. 'You're clearly not a sailor. You've never seen the weather change on a whim.'

'Do you really believe that?' Yale spat back. 'After everything that has happened? All the earthshakes and fires and floods and storms, always with *him* at the centre.'

'I think you're just bitter your acolyte grew a conscience,' Cass retorted.

'What happened during the storm?' Lucky pressed. Yale's talk of disasters made him uncomfortable, because Lucky knew he wasn't wrong. Somehow these things *were* all happening around him. 'Why did they lock you up?'

'Because I'm the only one on this ship that isn't a coward. I tried to keep us on our course, and the crew fought back. When the mast was damaged, they wanted to abandon ship, abandon duty. Bastards.' He spat on the floor. 'They locked me up in here and I assume fled. I hope they all drown.'

Erin gasped. 'What's wrong with you?'

'What's wrong with me?' He gripped the bars again, making the door rattle and forcing Erin to take a step back. 'There's nothing wrong with me. There's something wrong with the world, with him.'

'Careful there.' Cass raised a hand, examining their nails. 'That's our friend you're talking about. You're a bit too out-numbered to be talking so carelessly.'

Yale held up his hands. 'Fine, fine. You want to defend him, be my guest. But mark my words, there is something off about him. And I fully intend to get to the bottom of it.'

Chapter Thirty

Yale's words itched at Lucky, an irritation at the base of his neck, needling at him. Part of him wanted to go and confront the man. Part of him wanted to throw him overboard so he never had to deal with him again.

In the end, though, he worked. It was easier to throw himself into whatever needed doing, and to leave Yale in his makeshift cell in the *Dreamer*'s hold. And there was plenty that needed doing. Captain Haven had the ship racing to Sea Hall as fast as it could, which meant constantly adjusting the sails to catch the most wind. Teams of dancers helped move the water around the ship.

So Lucky bounced from job to job, doing what jobs were going above and below deck. There was no time to deal with Yale, and little opportunity to speak with Gabriel. It was easier to put his worries out of his mind, to leave them in that little itchy patch at the top of his spine, than confront them.

The day after the discovery of the wreck of the *Providence*, Captain Haven summoned Lucky to speak with Yale.

'You know him better than anyone else,' she told him. 'If you suspect he's lying about anything, I need to know.'

There was nowhere on the *Dreamer* to hold a prisoner, so he'd been bound and left in the hold. The sailor guarding the hatch gave Captain Haven a nod as she approached.

'How's the prisoner behaving?' she asked.

'Behaving himself so far,' came the reply. 'Do you want me to come down with you?'

She shook her head. 'He won't give me any trouble.'

The sailor gave her a salute and lifted the hatch. Lucky followed Captain Haven down into the gloom.

'Captain Haven, this is a pleasant surprise,' Yale said. 'I must say this is a delightful little ship. Fantastic views.' He indicated the dark walls of the hull. 'Excellent food, and I do mean that part genuinely.'

'Shut up,' she said, though there was little venom in it. Her tone was dismissive, as if Yale was barely worth even those two meagre syllables. 'You'll tell me everything you know about the attack on the shrine.'

He met her gaze calmly. 'And if I don't? What will you do, Captain? Torture me? Kill me?'

'Of course not. You're so lacking in imagination that you cannot perceive anyone acting in a way different to you. But I don't expect you to do this out of the goodness of your heart. We'll be entering conflict with your forces, and they don't know you're on board. And even if they did, I'm not sure they'd care.'

Yale scowled as the captain's words sank in.

'So, if you'd like to have a chance of surviving, I suggest you tell me everything you know,' she finished, crossing her arms.

'You think you can win? You're fighting against fate.'

'I think if fate was genuinely set in stone,' she replied, 'we wouldn't be able to fight at all. Yet here we are.'

He turned to Lucky. 'What about you, little bird? Do you think this is the right path? You want to stand there with the world crumbling around you, and say this is fine?'

'This is what I choose,' Lucky said. 'This is what I am.'

'Fine.' Yale gave a disgusted snort. 'The *Providence* was supposed to lead the attack, but she's hardly the only ship. Do you think you can stand up against us? Do you think you can protect the shrine with one little ship?'

'It won't be just us,' Captain Haven replied. 'There will be ships at Sea Hall, and others will have heard about the events of Minmouth.'

'Well.' Yale settled back against the wall. 'I hope you're right, for all our sakes.'

Captain Haven tried to get more information – about numbers of ships, guns, any plans they had – but either Yale didn't know, or he'd accepted his situation with all that came with it.

'I don't think he knows anything more,' Lucky said quietly as they headed back up the steps. 'Yale likes to consider himself a big deal, but I doubt he was involved in the planning.'

'Sadly, I think you're right. Which means we're rushing headlong with no idea of what we will be facing.'

'No different than yesterday, then,' Lucky pointed out.

She gave him a tired smile. 'I suppose.'

'How long before we get to Sea Hall?'

'We should get there early tomorrow morning if the winds hold like this.' She did a good job keeping the tension out of her voice, off her face, but it lingered in the way her hand tightened around the butt of her pistol, in the way her gaze never quite settled, as if she expected an attack at any time. Lucky wished there was something he could do to help the situation, but if Yale knew nothing useful, they were just as blind as before.

He left the captain and headed into the galley. Poe was taking shifts with the other dancers, so much of the cooking had fallen to him. He was nowhere near as skilled as Poe, but no one had complained about anything yet. Before he set to work on the main meal, he pulled together a couple of bowls of porridge, smoked fish, and sweetened stewed apple for the two dancers who'd just come off shift.

In the bunk room he found Cass and Sienna collapsed in their hammocks. Cass lay on their back, while Sienna was on her stomach, her face buried in a pillow.

'Grub's up,' he called. Sienna gave him a grunt, and Cass held out their hand, shovelling porridge into their mouth as soon as their hand closed around the spoon. He set the other tray down for Sienna. 'I'll leave you to rest.'

It would mean nothing if they couldn't get there in time, but he worried that Captain Haven was pushing the crew too hard, and they'd be exhausted by the time they reached Sea Hall.

'Mmph, Lucky, wait,' Cass called around a mouthful. They held up a little bundle of cloth. 'Take your bit of thread or throw it overboard. I don't want it.'

'Sure.' He held up his hand and Cass tossed the handkerchief at him. Lucky closed his hand around it and the room went black. Gun smoke filled his nose. Cannon fire. Shouts. A dark cave deep inside the cliffs. He couldn't breathe. The air was gone and there was only fire and salt water in his nose and mouth, filling his lungs, drowning him—

'Lucky!'

He opened his eyes. He wasn't drowning. He wasn't drowning; he was lying on the floor of the bunk room, staring up at Cass and Sienna. Sienna lowered her hand and Lucky touched the stinging patch in his cheek.

'Sorry,' Sienna muttered. 'But you wouldn't stop yelling and you wouldn't let go.'

Lucky glanced over at Cass, holding the thread, now half out of its handkerchief shield. 'It doesn't do anything to you?'

'Sorry, mate.' They scratched at their jaw. 'I guess I should throw it overboard myself.'

Lucky rubbed the back of his head. He felt caught, half in and out of a dream, a place he didn't recognise, a fight he wasn't part of. 'Wait! Don't throw it. Hang on.' He ran from the room and came back with his piece of chalk. He sketched the cave he'd seen in his visions. 'Is that it? Is that the shrine?'

Sienna peered over his shoulder. 'Yeah, that's it. How do you know? You've never been there, right?'

'I saw it.' Lucky sat back on his heels. 'I saw it. There was a big fight going on. Lots of ships. How is this possible?'

Cass pulled out the thread, running it through their fingers. Lucky cringed, but it seemed nothing more than a length of spun wool in their hands. It was a dark reddish-brown, like old blood.

'The tapestries foretell, right? Maybe you can read it too?'

Mark my words, there is something off about him, Yale had said. Lucky shivered.

'How does it work, with the tapestries?' he asked.

Sienna shrugged. 'There's one in every church. They change, show images, sometimes words, and the priest makes a judgement about what each one means. Sometimes the priest will ask a question – for example, after a marriage request – and then the answer will appear later on. But how it works, no one knows. That's why it's called faith.'

Lucky tightened his grip on the chalk, rubbing his thumb over the smooth surface, grounding himself on the familiar sensation. 'What if . . . what if I could use it, to try and see the battle at the shrine? Maybe I could see something useful, something that could help us.'

'Is that wise?' Cass asked.

'No, it's not,' Sienna retorted. 'Lucky, just touching that thing knocked you on your arse. I don't think using it is a very good idea at all.'

'But what if I can help?' he protested. 'I can't just sit and do nothing if there's a chance I can do something to change the situation. Like you said, there's always a cost, but at least this is on my terms.'

'Ooh, using my words against me is a low blow.' She scowled.

'I'll be careful, I promise. But everyone's working so hard, and I want to help too.'

She gripped his hand, her face close to his. 'Lucky, I love you dearly, but you are a melodramatic fool at times, you know that? You are helping. You're doing as much as anyone else on board.' She pressed her forehead again his. 'You first came on board and you couldn't even speak. Now you're pretty much running the galley. You're doing fine. If you get yourself knocked out by magic, who's going to feed me, huh?'

He laughed and pushed her away. 'I'm glad you've got your priorities straight.'

'Damn straight.' She rubbed her stomach. 'Just be careful, all right?'

So later he stood in the captain's cabin, the thread lying carefully coiled on Cass's handkerchief. Gabriel stood at his side, his presence solid and comforting. Captain Haven stared back at him, one incredulous eyebrow raised.

'You're telling me you can see the future?'

'I . . . I don't know,' he admitted. 'Maybe. I can see something, definitely. I saw the shrine. Whether it's a vision of the future, I can't be certain.'

'And you're asking me to act on this 'something'? To risk the ship for something you can't be certain about?'

Lucky shook his head. 'We're risking the ship whatever happens. I'm asking you to let me help, if I can.'

She stared at him, eyes narrowed, and he could feel it eating through his layers, leaving him unravelled. 'Fine. If you're sure you're happy to do this, then let's try.'

Lucky reached for the thread, and she shook her head.

'Sit down somewhere comfortable first.'

Gabriel closed his hand around Lucky's and led him to an easy chair on the far side of the room. He sat down on the chair and gestured for Lucky to join him. Carefully, Lucky eased himself on to Gabriel's lap, feeling self-conscious under the gaze of Captain Haven.

'I'll keep you safe,' Gabriel whispered, wrapping an arm around Lucky.

Lucky rested his head against Gabriel's chest, closed his eyes for a moment. 'I'm ready.'

Captain Haven brought over the thread. Lucky reached for it, and no sooner had his finger caressed the surface than everything went black.

He looked for the shrine, for the island, for cannon fire and galleons dashing across the waves, but there was only darkness.

Come to us.

Lucky looked around for the source, but he could see nothing. 'Who are you?'

Come to us.

'Show me the shrine!' He clenched his fists. Why wasn't it working now? He tried to focus on the dark cave he'd seen last time, tried to force himself to see it again.

Come to us. Promise.

Now he saw something, a large building, windows decorated with colourful threads. It reminded him of the church building, but this was bigger than any he'd seen before.

'That's not the shrine.'

Promise. Promise and we'll show you.

The voices surrounded him, each different and yet similar, so he couldn't possibly tell how many there were. Or who they were. They sounded cold, hungry, and he wanted nothing to do with them, but he needed to see the shrine, needed to see the battle.

'I promise,' he said and with a snap, the image changed and he found himself floating over the island. The water dancer shrine lay below him, and a fleet of ships bore down on it. The midday sun made the sea glitter as they ploughed towards the cave. Other ships moved towards them, from the island, and cannon fire filled the air. The ships that surrounded Sea Hall wouldn't be enough, he could see it from here. They were too small, too few weapons. The only thing that had saved the shrine so far had been the need for the water dancers, and the sea itself that kept it underwater for a year at a time.

Do you see it? Your answer?

Lucky's eyes snapped open. 'We need waves!'

Chapter Thirty-One

The sun crept over the horizon and the *Dreamer* reached Sea Hall at last. The island was dark in the early morning, the heavy doors closed over the harbour. The statue of the goddess stood proud, her hand raised in benediction to the sea.

There was no sign of damage or distraction. Yet. The fleet had arrived around midday, according to his vision, but he still wasn't sure how much he could trust it.

'We'll save her,' Gabriel said in his ear. Lucky turned to find him standing on the deck behind him.

'Couldn't sleep either?'

'No, not today.' He held out a hand and Lucky took it, allowing himself to be pulled close. The swelling around Gabriel's eye had gone down almost entirely, leaving just the remains of a bruise marring his face. Blond stubble covered his jaw, and there was no scent of coffee on his lips, either. He'd clearly come straight on deck from waking.

'May I?' Lucky asked, and Gabriel smiled, warm as the rising sun. He leaned into Lucky's kiss, his hand moving to the back of Lucky's head, fingers playing through his hair. 'For luck,' he added as they broke away.

Gabriel touched the pewter feather around his neck. 'Two Lucky men and a ship of dreamers,' he said softly. 'What possible force could stand against us?'

'Indeed.' Lucky stood for a moment, his head against Gabriel's chest, enjoying a moment of warmth and comfort. If his idea worked, they'd have a way of protecting the shrine, but he didn't want to rely on luck.

'Open the gates!' Captain Haven called out through a loudhailer. Over her shoulder, she called out, 'Reef the sails, weigh anchor.'

A grating, grinding sound filled the air as the capstan turned and the anchor chain paid out into the water. The heavy gates swung open, revealing the harbour and a dozen ships at rest. Would it be enough? Lucky pushed the fear aside. It would have to be.

'Ready?' Captain Haven asked her son. Gabriel gave Lucky a quick kiss and turned to follow the captain to the rail where the other dancers waited. Lucky took up position on the quarterdeck, watching out across the harbour.

'This is it,' Amala said as she joined him. 'Last battle. It all changes here.'

Lucky nodded, though he didn't believe it. Even if they stopped the attack today, another one would happen next year. *Do you see it? Your answer?* Victory wouldn't happen here, not for him. He'd made a promise and he had to follow through with it. But he didn't want to bring that up here and now.

'It's getting worse,' she said, so quietly he barely heard her. 'He didn't recognise either of us when he woke up this morning. I'm sorry, Lucky.'

'It was his choice,' Lucky said, but it didn't make it any easier to deal with.

'All he ever wanted was to make the world a better place. He thought the shrine would help with that.'

'Let's make sure we save the shrine for him, then, to keep that better world.'

She pulled him into a tight hug. 'For Gabe.'

A huge plume of water went up in the middle of the harbour, and the air was full of shouts and cries. On deck, Captain Haven lowered her hands. That had got everyone's attention. Now they just had to detail their plan, and hope that everyone would follow it.

The six dancers used the water in the harbour to spell out a message in glittering letters that hung in the air. They left each sentence hovering for several moments, before dropping it back down into the harbour, and went through the whole thing three times. Then they waited.

The last part of the message had instructed each ship that agreed to sound a whistle three times. Lucky leaned against the rail, waiting, hoping, urging each ship to respond. They might not. They might prefer not to risk themselves, and stay behind the sturdy harbour doors that had kept out intruders all these years. But if they did, then the shrine was doomed.

Three loud whistles pierced the air. Followed by another three. And again and again. A shout of triumph rang out from the decks of the *Dreamer*. They'd been heard. And the other crews stood with them.

'Get us moving,' Captain Haven shouted. 'Around to the shrine. We'll be the anchor for the chain.'

Sailors turned the capstan and unfurled the sails, and the *Dreamer* carried on again, past the harbour and around the island towards the shrine on the other side. From the stern, Lucky could see the ships in the harbour making their own preparations to make sail.

The shrine was just as he'd seen it in his mind. A cave, set deep back in the hillside, the cliffs around it dripping with water as the tides pulled back the sea. There was a small beach in front of it, and a winding path that led from the cliffs above down to the sand. Little statues dotted the path and the beach, covered in barnacles and seaweed. There was a magic in the air that gripped at Lucky's attention.

'What's the shrine like?' Lucky asked Gabriel. 'Inside.'

'It's . . .' He rubbed at his temple. 'It's . . . there's a big . . . there's a big statue, I think . . . I . . . I . . .'

Lucky put a hand on his wrist. 'It's all right. I'm sorry, I shouldn't have asked. It's all right, Gabriel.'

'It was beautiful,' Gabriel said softly. 'I remember that much, but I can't remember what that means. I can't remember any of the details.'

'We'll go back there,' Lucky told him. 'After we've driven away the church ships. So you can see it again for yourself.'

'Right. Yeah, sure.' He didn't sound confident, and Lucky hated himself for making the mistake of putting another reminder of what Gabriel was going through in front of them.

The wait was worse than the frantic voyage down. Then, he could lose himself in work, drive himself to exhaustion and fall asleep. Now, there was only the waiting, scanning the horizon for the inevitable. He had time to focus on Gabriel, and what he was losing. He had time to think about the visions from the thread, and the voices.

Promise.

The other ships were moving into position, setting up a chain around the island. It would be enough. It had to be enough. The shrine was a choice for people who'd had their freedom taken from them one way or another. Maybe it was a bad choice, but it was their choice and Lucky would see it stand for the next cohort who travelled to that cave.

A long whistle shrieked across the still morning sky. It was quickly followed by three short ones. Church vessels. Lucky rushed to the rail, peering out across the sea. A dark smudge on the horizon, drifting towards them.

'All hands on deck!' Captain Haven yelled. 'Places, everyone. Prepare for battle.'

The crew moved like a well-oiled machine, as if they'd been born for this role, instead of falling through fate to find themselves there. The sails were furled, the anchor weighed. The *Dreamer*'s bow faced the oncoming threat, her stern towards the shrine. The dancers had split into two groups: Cass, Erin, and Poe on one side, and Gabriel, Sienna, and the captain on the other.

Around them, other sailors stood ready by the *Dreamer*'s cannons, or waited with medical supplies for the inevitable injuries. Others prepared to patch and repair any damage from cannon fire. In the middle of them all, Lucky felt lost. As if he'd pushed them into this, as if this was his fault and now, suddenly, he didn't know what to do.

The fleet sailed closer, six galleons, tall and bristling with sails and guns. Fast and deadly. Bearing down on them. The *Dreamer* would be a smaller target as she was, but she also stood less chance of hitting them with her own weapons.

Captain Haven raised a question in the sea to the vessel on their right, and Poe did the same on the other side. The answer came from both ships in clear letters of seawater.

READY.

'It's been an honour to sail with all of you,' Captain Haven called to her crew. 'And it will be an honour to sail with you again tomorrow. We'll save the shrine, not because it's fate, not because it's promised, but because we commit ourselves to this fight, heart and soul. And we'll win, not because we're physically stronger, not because we can dance, but because each and every one of us can look the person next to us in the eye and see friend, see family.' She raised her pistol into the air and fired off a shot at the sky. 'For the *Dreamer*!'

'For the *Dreamer*!' The cry echoed off the ship, reflected back across the souls of her crew.

The first cannonball hit the water in front of them sooner than anyone expected. It shot up a plume of water, spraying the deck.

'Get the waves up,' Captain Haven called. On each side, the two teams of dancers worked with the other ships to raise a wall of water that stood the height of each ship's deck. Lucky watched and saw similar waves come up between the next ships and the ones beyond them.

'Forward!'

The anchor raised and the *Dreamer* drifted forwards, bringing the sea with her.

The six church ships had split out from one another. Lucky sensed that they were puzzled by how to approach the encroaching wave, but it didn't take them long to decide that 'blow the shit out of it' was a good strategy. Gun smoke filled the air as they attacked and the *Dreamer* and her companions returned fire.

A cannonball struck the deck, eating a hole in the wood and sending a sailor flying backwards. She hit the ground awkwardly, and there was a snap from her arm, followed by a scream. Lucky hurried over to her side.

'It's all right. You're going to be all right,' he murmured.

She pulled her arm close to her, her face pale. 'Right. Sure. Just a minor cannonball, right?'

'Let's get you below deck. Can I help you up?'

'Thanks.'

He eased her to her feet, and guided her down to the bunk room, where he was joined by another crewman with medical supplies.

'I've got it from here,' he told Lucky.

Lucky scrambled back up on deck, just as a cheer went up. The *Dreamer* had struck a return blow to the lead galleon. It wasn't a fight they could win with cannons, though. He glanced around him, looking at the other ships. They were coming, emerging from around the island, each one bringing with them a wave of water.

'Change the flag!' Captain Haven ordered. She moved away from Gabriel and Sienna, thrusting her arms out and generating a plume of water ahead of the ship. A flying cannonball hit the water, losing much of its power and dropping harmlessly into the water ahead of the ship.

On the top of the mainmast, sailors ran up a green triangular flag. Around them, ships adjusted their sails, moving faster on the group of church vessels, bringing with them the sea. It rose and undulated between the ships, like a great leviathan of water. They circled around, trapping the enemy in a closing net.

The church vessels fired back harder, as the realisation that they were trapped dawned on them. They hit a small ship with lateen rigging, blowing her figurehead to smithereens and opening a great hole in her bow. The waves dropped on each side of her, but the other ships kept coming, and when they were close enough, they raised the waves back up between them.

The *Dreamer* and the eleven remaining ships from Sea Hall closed around their target. They dropped anchor, and the dancers pushed the wall of water forwards so it stood proud of the ships, moving closer and closer to the church vessels. As the net drew tighter, the wall of water grew taller and taller.

'Ready the red flag!' Captain Haven called. 'On my mark.'

The green flag was run down and the red one prepared. The last signal. On that sign, it would all end.

The wall of water hid the ships, but it didn't block out the sound of the cannon fire. A loud boom, a rush of water and air. Lucky threw himself to the side on pure instinct, and a cannonball smashed into the *Dreamer*'s mainmast. It came down with a sickening crunch, drenching the deck in sailcloth.

'Don't let it fall!' Captain Haven screamed. 'Don't let the waves fall.'

Lucky pulled himself to his feet and skidded across the deck, dodging the fallen yardarm and the spilled sailcloth. He rummaged around where he'd seen the red flag last, and pulled it out of an unconscious sailor's hands.

'Captain!' he called, waving it at her. 'Give me the signal.'

He raced for the mizzenmast rigging, climbing above the carnage, until he was as high as he could go. He peered down at the captain, one hand clutching the rigging for dear life, the other with a death grip on the flag.

'Mark!' Captain Haven called.

'Red flag!' Lucky shouted, waving it above his head. 'Red flag! Red flag! Let them have it!'

The dancers sent the wall of water cascading down over the church ships. It hid the carnage for a moment under a dome of blue-green destruction, but the sounds painted a picture as clear as if it'd been drawn in chalk. Wood snapped, buckled, cracked. People screamed. A cannon in the process of firing dropped its load in the sea with a dull plop that sounded comically sad.

High above it all, Lucky watched as the water fell away, leaving a wreck of broken hulls and splintered masts. None of the vessels were anywhere near intact enough to limp away, let alone cause any more damage. And by the time they raised reinforcements, the shrine would be back underwater.

They'd done it.

And now Lucky would have to face what came next.

Chapter Thirty-Two

The *Dreamer* limped back to the harbour, her mast broken down and as much of the sails salvaged as they could. It was only superficial damage, but it still hurt to see the ship in such a state. She was home and home was supposed to be safe, unassailable.

The crew had suffered worse. Multiple broken limbs, concussions, lacerations. Lucky spent the short journey back to Sea Hall fetching bandages and salves, holding hands while limbs were reset. But despite the injuries, the crew were in good spirits. The shrine was safe and everything else could be fixed or healed with time.

Everything except him.

'You don't look very happy.'

Lucky turned to find Gabriel walking towards him. His upper arm was bandaged, and he sported three stitches on his cheek, but other than that, he appeared uninjured. The sight of him made Lucky's heart rise and fall in quick succession.

'Come on, Lucky, we won.' Gabriel held out his arms and Lucky pressed himself against him. 'The medical facilities at Sea Hall will fix everyone up, and we can't go anywhere until the mast is fixed, so we can just relax for a few days. It will be fun. It will be just what we need.'

'I need to leave.'

The words tumbled out of him before he could stop them, before he could dress them up and make them into something presentable. Gabriel's face fell.

'No. No, no, you can't. We won, Lucky. We get to celebrate, to be happy. You can't leave me again.' His voice hitched.

'I . . . I don't know how long I have. I don't know how long I'll . . .' He tightened his grip on Lucky, as if he could hold him fast in that moment. Lucky wished he could, wished they could build a bubble that time would leave undisturbed, a sanctuary against the ravages of the world.

'You can beat this, Gabriel. If anyone can, it's you. And we saved the shrine. Surely that must mean something, right?' He reached up, resting his hand against Gabriel's cheek.

'Maybe, I guess. But I don't understand. Why do you have to go? I want to show you around the town again. I want to eat crab on the harbour wall with you. I want to drink and watch the stars. I want to . . .' He broke off, his face flushing.

'I want that too,' Lucky said softly. 'But this isn't the end, Gabriel. They'll keep coming after the shrine, year after year. And there's the disasters – they follow me. And the thread, how it affects me. I need to get to the bottom of all of this, and I won't find the answers in Sea Hall.'

There is something off about him.

Promise.

'Then let me come with you,' Gabriel begged.

'I don't think that's wise. You're still the dancer who tried to save the leviathan. If someone recognises you . . .' He pressed a kiss against Gabriel's lips. 'I'll come back. I'll come back as soon as I can. And then we can be together. For the rest of our lives, my Gabriel.'

Gabriel choked back a sob. 'You better. You better or I'm hunting you down and dragging you back to the ship. Just you wait.'

Lucky gripped his hand, leading him across the ship and back to Lucky's little room. Around them, the crew were sorting through the wreckage, or helping the wounded off to receive care at the hospital. No one paid them much attention.

He closed the door behind them, taking in the little room, marvelling at how much he'd managed to transform it into a

space that was his. Four walls, but no longer his closest companions. Now he had friends, family. Gabriel.

'I love you,' he said, turning back to Gabriel. 'I love you
so much. I made my home in your heart, and whatever happens, it will always be the most precious place in the world.
The place where I am completely myself. The place where
I'm free.'

'I love you, too.' Gabriel put his hands on Lucky's shoulders, pressed his forehead against Lucky's. 'From the moment
I first saw you in the water, something about you shone. I'm
glad you can see it too, now.'

'We've come so far, both of us.' He kissed away a tear that
trickled down Gabriel's cheek. It tasted of the sea. 'And there's
still a whole world out there for you to show me. Gabriel?'

'Yes?'

'May I undress you?'

Gabriel's smile was as bright as the sunlight reflecting off
the crest of a wave. 'Please.'

Gently, Lucky lifted the shirt over Gabriel's head, conscious of his injuries. He let the fabric fall to the floor and
turned his attention to the man in front of him. To his broad
shoulders and the swell of his biceps, the lines of his abs and
the curve of his hips. Lucky wondered what it would be like
to nibble just there.

'Can I do the same?' Gabriel asked, and Lucky nodded
slowly. Gabriel pulled his shirt off and set it aside, and Lucky
felt the urge to snatch it up again, cover himself. Cover the
scars and the way his ribs still showed prominently, the way
his name was carved into his arm.

But when he raised his head, Gabriel was staring at him
with a mixture of awe and hunger, and Lucky felt himself
seen in the best possible way. His skin tingled, sensations
heightened, until the need to touch, to be touched, was
almost unbearable.

'Can I kiss you there?' He pointed at the side of Gabriel's neck, just below the jaw. 'Can I keep going?'

Gabriel's assent was barely out of his lips and then Lucky was kissing him hungrily, tenderly, moving from his neck, over his chest, down towards his hips. Gabriel moaned, pushing himself into Lucky's kisses.

'We can stop at any time,' Lucky said. 'Just shake your head, and I'll stop.'

'Same goes for you,' Gabriel replied, his voice husky, breathless.

But neither of them did.

Later, they dozed beneath the blankets, warm and content. Lucky lay with his head on Gabriel's chest, one hand fiddling idly with the end of his braid. He didn't want to get up. He didn't want to leave Gabriel, his warm body, his soft, sleepy breathing. He wanted more than anything to wrap the moment in his fist, squeeze it down into something solid he could carry with him.

'Is it time?' Gabriel asked. The hurt, the fear in his voice made Lucky cringe with regret.

'I don't want to go. I don't want to, but I can't risk anything happening here. The *Dreamer*'s been through so much. If another storm came, or an earthshake, or . . .'

Gabriel rested his thumb on Lucky's lips. 'Shh. I understand. I do. But promise you'll come back to me.'

'I promise.' Lucky kissed the pad of his thumb. 'Wish me luck. I think the first task is going to be the hardest.'

'Oh?' Gabriel raised an eyebrow.

'I have to convince your mother to let me leave with her prisoner.'

'The Beater? Is that a good idea?' Gabriel asked.

'Probably not, but he knows where I need to go, and he's told me I need to go there, so I don't think he'll give me any trouble getting to the mother church. Leaving again might be a different story, but I'll find a way. I'll always find a way back to you.' He touched the pewter feather around Gabriel's neck.

'Let me give you something in return.' Gabriel untied the leather thong from the end of his braid and looped it around Lucky's wrist. 'There.'

Lucky brushed his thumb over the leather, remembering the sensation of holding it that first time, how solid it had felt against his skin. He picked up the scarf Amala had made for him, and wrapped it around his neck. It wasn't cold, but that didn't matter.

Gabriel closed his hand around Lucky's and they walked out on deck together. As Lucky approached the captain's cabin, Gabriel kissed Lucky's cheek.

'I'll be back shortly.'

Lucky watched him head back below deck, his braid steadily unravelling as he moved, then he turned and knocked on the captain's door. She was at the table, several pieces of paper in front of her. Amala sat opposite her, pouring tea into little teacups decorated with leviathans.

'I need to leave,' he said. 'I intend to come back, as soon as I can.'

'Gabe know?' she asked without raising her head.

'Of course.'

She pushed aside the papers and stood up. 'Then make sure you come back soon. After the ship's repaired, I'm planning to sail to Ciatheme. Does that suit you as a meeting place once you're done?'

'That . . . that sounds good.' Maybe he'd understand more about what he did that day. Maybe he could finally apologise to his mother.

'Good,' she said brusquely, then flicked her dagger out and held it towards him, hilt first. 'I see you've been collecting gifts from my family. Let me give you one too.'

Lucky took it, fingering the smooth rosewood hilt. It fitted comfortably in his palm, the steel blade bright and sharp. 'Thank you. There was one other thing . . .'

She raised an eyebrow.

'I want to take Yale, the Beater, with me.'

The eyebrow rose higher. 'What makes you think you can trust him not to stab you in the back at the first opportunity?'

'Oh, I'm fully expecting him to try,' Lucky said with a humourless smile. 'But he wants to take me to the mother church, and I want to go there, so I have a bit of time before he tries to betray me. And I'll be ready for it.'

'Well, if you're sure,' she said. 'I'll go and fetch him. Say goodbye to Amala properly, or she'll never forgive you, and then I'll never forgive you.'

She squeezed his shoulder as she passed. Lucky turned to Amala, who enveloped him in a hug. The smoky scent of the tea lingered around her, warm and homely.

'You make sure you look after yourself,' she said, fussing with the scarf around his neck. 'Eat properly, you hear. Don't let that Beater get in your head.'

'I'll be fine,' he mumbled, his voice crumbly with the weight of the emotions behind it.

'Sorry, I know you don't like the fuss. But the health and well-being of the crew is the first mate's responsibility, so you'll have to put up with it for a bit.'

She walked out with him to the main deck, where Poe and Gabriel were waiting. Gabriel thrust a knapsack at him.

'We made you some food for the road,' Gabriel said. 'I helped.'

'He did,' Poe said as Gabriel gave him a pointed look.

Lucky accepted the bag, his fingers lingering on Gabriel's.

'I hope there's some of that for me,' Yale said dryly. Lucky pulled the knapsack close to him. The Beater's voice made him itchy, uncomfortable. Ready to lash out. The idea of spending days in his company chafed, but if Lucky caused the disasters by being around Gabriel, then he needed to find a way to stop them. They'd spent so long apart, and Lucky wasn't going to let that continue any longer.

He kissed Gabriel one more time, trying not to think about it maybe being the last time, shouldered the knapsack, and set out to find some answers from fate.

Chapter Thirty-Three

Yale said nothing as they stepped off the *Dreamer*. Nor when Lucky negotiated passage on a ship heading back to the mainland. His silence bothered Lucky more than any needling. It felt as if Yale was planning something, but he couldn't work out what.

They stepped back on to dry land at a small coastal town, famed for its lobster fishing. One day he'd come back here with Gabriel and they'd sit on the sea wall, watching the waves and drinking lobster bisque. He shouldered his pack and set off.

'That way, is it, little bird?' Yale asked. He had his hands in his pockets, kicking at pebbles scattered on the path.

Lucky paused, tensed.

'Only, I thought we were heading to the mother church. And, well, she's that way.' Yale jerked his thumb over to the left.

Lucky stopped and swore under his breath. He'd brought Yale along for this reason, but it rattled him to make a mistake this early, give him power this quickly.

With a sigh, Lucky set off away from the town.

'So, truant from the Beaters on the day of your oath, breaking a heretic out of jail, followed by a full-on assault on church vessels. You're building up quite the list of crimes, little bird.'

'Stop calling me that.' Lucky put his head down, kept walking, trying to drown out the sound of Yale's oil-smooth voice by focusing on his footsteps. Whatever force had kept him quiet until now was well and truly broken.

'Make me.' Yale flashed him a sneer.

'I've bested you before. Do you really want me to knock you on your arse here in the middle of the road?'

Yale's sneer grew, testing him, and Lucky rolled his eyes.

'This isn't the end, you know that, right?' Yale continued. He'd been patronising and callous when Lucky knew him before, but it appeared that since Lucky had left The Fell, he'd got patronising, callous, and *chatty* as well. 'We'll keep coming, year after year. You can't stop us.'

'Why?' Lucky asked, before he could stop himself. 'What does it matter to you?'

'Fate hates the promises, what they stand for,' Yale replied. 'The only reason that shrine has been allowed to remain is because of the leviathans.'

They walked through similar farmland to the sort he'd crossed with Gabriel and Sienna recently, only this time there was no playful banter, or Gabriel shouting 'cows' every time they passed a field. Just Lucky and the detestable Beater.

'What's your interest in me?'

Yale raised an eyebrow. 'Interest? I had no interest in you. Merely a job to do, and yet you managed to get in the way, every single time. Disaster dogs your footsteps, but this is going to be the end of it, little bird. I'll see to it myself.'

Lucky didn't doubt he'd try.

'My turn,' Yale said. 'What made you change your mind? You broke your oath; ran away from everything I taught you. Why come back now?'

Not everything, Lucky thought, fingering the hilt of the knife in his belt. 'Because, like you say, it won't stop, and I am dogged by disaster. If I'm ever to be free, I need to know how to stop it.'

'There's no such thing as free,' Yale scoffed. 'Even the dancers know that.'

'Free enough then.' Lucky shrugged. 'I can live with that.'

They took the road along the coast for most of the day, and then Yale turned north, cutting across country through thick woodland.

'Is this really the best way?' Lucky protested.

'No, little bird, I just thought we'd take a little constitutional amongst the trees and build our spirits up. What do you say?'

'I say you're an insufferable arsehole and I should have put my knife through your guts in the training yard,' Lucky hissed, and Yale laughed.

'You're adorable when you're angry, you know that?'

'It's a shame you didn't get flattened by the earthshake that took out The Fell,' Lucky snapped back.

Yale stopped. His arm shot out like a striking snake, and he grabbed the front of Lucky's shirt.

'You killed a lot of Beaters that day.' His voice was cold, empty.

Lucky struggled in his grip. 'I didn't . . . I didn't choose to do that.'

'Pity.' Yale released his grip, letting Lucky fall back. 'Couldn't stand most of them. It would be a useful skill if you could control it.'

Lucky flushed, anger and frustration boiling his blood. How far was it to the mother church? If they weren't there by tomorrow, he was pretty sure he was going to lose his temper and try to kill Yale. And then it would depend on which one of them really was the better fighter. Lucky rolled his eyes again and kept walking.

This is right.

'Why don't we take a break for the night?' Yale suggested. They'd reached a wide clearing that clearly got regular use. A scrape had been made in the centre, filled with cold ashes and half-burned sticks, surrounded by stones. Around it, fallen logs had been arranged for seating.

'Well? What are you waiting for? Go fetch some firewood.' Yale made shooing motions with his hands. Lucky sighed, then turned to comply.

'There . . . there aren't any snakes in the woods, are there?' he asked quietly, but Yale just laughed.

Lucky busied himself picking up wood for the fire, keeping a nervous eye out for anything that might be fanged and reptilian. When he returned, Yale was setting up snares in the bushes around the clearing.

'No good for dinner, but might catch us some breakfast,' he said as Lucky dumped the wood down by the scrape. 'Are you just going to leave it there?'

'I don't know how to start a fire,' Lucky admitted.

'Typical.' Yale set the last snare and strode over to the scrape. 'You're going to fix what's wrong with the world, and you can't even start a fire. Did you ever consider that what might be wrong is you?'

'Yes.' He hadn't meant to answer, hadn't meant to rise to it. But the word spilled out of him. Yale raised an eyebrow. 'Yes, I have considered it's me. I've thought I don't belong so many times. I've felt like I should just die. But . . . but why should I? Even if I'm wrong, even if there's something broken about me, don't I deserve a chance?' His voice rose, wild with rage. 'I didn't ask for this. I didn't ask for any of this. Why should I have to lie down and accept fate, accept being wiped out? I want to live.'

'Well said, little bird.' Yale gave him a mocking round of applause. 'That's right. Spit in the face of god, defy the strings of fate. Who cares if you bring the whole world down on top of you, right?'

Lucky shrank back in on himself. 'I'm not trying to break anything. I just want to live. I just want to go back to the *Dreamer*, back to Gabriel . . .' He stopped, a chill spreading through him.

'So, Haven's boy is special to you, is he?'

'I didn't say that,' Lucky mumbled, scuffing his feet. The last thing he wanted was for Yale's attention to fall on Gabriel.

'You didn't have to, little bird. I saw your goodbyes.'

Lucky retreated to one of the logs, wrapping his arms around himself. The idea of killing Yale and fleeing grew louder and louder. Wait until he was sleeping, stick a knife in his jugular. Clean and easy.

Detestable as Yale was, Lucky didn't think he could actually murder him in cold blood. But it would be easy enough to flee into the night, going ahead to the mother church without him. Already the darkness spread around them, and it was almost impossible to see beyond the trees at the edge of the clearing.

That was assuming he didn't find himself devoured by wild animals, of course.

As if reading his thoughts, a wolf howled in the distance. Lucky shuddered.

Yale set the fire going, a rush of dancing red and orange flames, sending little sparks swirling into the air. Lucky moved a little closer to it as the wolf howled again.

'Don't look so panicked,' Yale said. 'The animals won't come close to the fire. Don't worry, little bird. I won't let you get eaten. Not when you're going to save the world.' He roared with laughter, the sound echoing off the trees. 'I'm sorry. It's just too funny.'

Lucky met his gaze. 'Is it? Why are you here then, Yale? If I'm such a joke, why are you following me so willingly?' He'd half expected the man to knock him out or tie him up by now.

Yale's sneer faded, and a frown appeared in its place. Lucky expected him to yell, or insult, but instead he tapped his chin thoughtfully.

'You've got me there, I think. There is something about you.'

'What?' Lucky held out his hands. 'What is it about me that you think is worth traipsing across country, risking wild animals?'

'It's certainly not your sense of humour or quality of conversation,' he replied. 'No, there's something in the air about you. You feel like standing in a lightning storm, next to the tallest tree.'

'So I'm a tree now, not a bird?'

Yale sniffed. 'You're definitely a bird. Chirping away.'

Lucky crossed his arms. Yale offered him some food, but Lucky shook his head, preferring to raid the pack Gabriel had given him before leaving. He pulled out a round of seaweed bread and the rush of memories brought on by the scent raised tears in his eyes. He turned away so Yale couldn't see.

'Get some rest, little bird,' Yale called as he finished his meal. 'I'll make sure the wild beasties stay away. I'll wake you in a few hours.'

Lucky gave him a dismissive wave and wrapped himself up in his cloak. He lay with his back to the fire, the cold night air chilling his face. At first, he closed his eyes, listening to the sounds of the forest. The fire crackled behind him, and occasionally a knot would pop, a sound like a pistol crack that made him flinch each time no matter how hard he tried to suppress it.

As the fire became familiar, it settled into the background and Lucky became aware of more. The rustle of leaves above him, stirred by an exploratory breeze. An owl, hooting softly in the canopy. One would call, and then a moment later, another would answer from a distance. What did owls say to each other? It sounded like they were reassuring each other that they were still there, and Lucky could understand that.

He touched the leather band around his wrist.

The wolf howled, sounding reassuringly further away now. Another picked up the call and then a third and fourth. Now that he felt less concerned about being devoured in his sleep, the sound was hauntingly beautiful. It still raised goosebumps on his arms, but the howl was like a song, rising and falling, various choir members joining in and dropping out again. Like the owls, it reminded him of community, of the shared bond of family, and it resonated in the empty part of his heart.

He wondered what Gabriel was doing right now. Drinking in one of the port-side inns? Or perhaps sharing a meal with his mothers. Lucky was glad Gabriel wasn't alone, that he had his mothers, and the other dancers, to confide in.

Yale shook his shoulder what felt like seconds later, but as Lucky opened his eyes and peered blearily around, he found it was morning.

'Sunrise, little bird. Time to go.'

He thought about Gabriel again, hoped he was enjoying his morning coffee, and wondered if he was thinking about Lucky too. The ache in his chest swelled, threatening to consume him. He wanted nothing more than to feel that butterfly-light touch of Gabriel's shoulder against his own.

'Don't cry,' Yale teased. 'You can eat breakfast while you walk.'

Lucky grabbed the front of his shirt. 'Don't try my patience.'

'My, my, you're very forward this morning, little bird.' Yale's face had paled but he hadn't lost his sneer. 'Aren't you going to make Haven's son jealous?'

Lucky launched himself at Yale, his body moving almost before he'd made the decision. Yale's eyes widened in surprise, but he couldn't react in time and Lucky was on top of him, knife in hand, raised above Yale's eye.

'His name is Gabriel,' Lucky snapped, then shook his head. That wasn't the point he was trying to make. 'Give me one good reason why I shouldn't kill you, right here.' He could find his own way to the church, even if it took him much longer.

'You haven't killed me yet.' Yale raised an eyebrow. Lucky frowned and he sighed. 'It's not like you haven't had the chance. If you really wanted me dead, you'd have done it by now. You're not a killer.'

'I killed my mother,' Lucky replied, though he knew Yale was right. Maybe he had been a killer at fourteen. He wasn't now.

'So you did. Very well.' He went limp under Lucky. 'Do your worst.'

Lucky sheathed his knife and stood up. He didn't have time for Yale and his mind games.

'That's what I thought,' Yale replied smugly.

'What did you mean, yesterday?' Lucky sheathed his knife. 'You said there's something about me. Who am I?'

Yale got to his feet and dusted himself down. 'I told you. Your name is Robin Tress. Your mother was a poor woman. You were promised to the church, probably for money. We get many Beater recruits that way. We know that much, at least. Unfortunately, the Beater who made the deal with her was mugged and killed around the same time. We found the contract, drenched in his blood, with only her name and yours visible. Then, after your mother was killed, you were already promised to the church, so they couldn't execute you for her death, so they kept you locked up. You would have been released about three days after the leviathan managed to set you free.'

Lucky shivered. A coincidence? He wasn't sure he could believe that. But who could control a leviathan, and why would they set him free? He rubbed his temple. It made no sense to him.

'Death seems to follow you around, doesn't it?' Yale continued. 'Don't think I haven't noticed that the disasters started happening when you escaped, stopped when you joined the Beaters, and then started again when you left. The messages from the fates have been fainter these last ten years, and worse still over the last year.'

'So you're all full of altruism, wanting to prevent any further disasters?' Lucky asked, and Yale laughed.

'My own mother wouldn't accuse me of altruism. But you are a threat to the order of things. You stand against fate, and the world knows it. I intend to see you delivered to the church, and if they decide that the best thing to do is kill you, then I'll happily do it myself.'

'I don't think so.'

Yale raised an eyebrow. 'What do you think the alternative is? You going to give me the slip, walk straight into the church by yourself? You gonna wave that little blade around until someone gives you the answers you're looking for? How far do you think you're going to get?'

Lucky glared at him, but he couldn't refute any of that. 'I'll find a way.'

Yale gave him an elaborate bow. 'Well, you best be on your way then, little bird. I'd hate to delay you further.'

Lucky glanced around. The hollow they'd slept in had several paths leading to it, and they all looked similar. He couldn't remember which direction they'd come from, and no idea which direction he had to go. His shoulders slumped.

'That's what I thought,' said Yale with a smug grin.

Chapter Thirty-Four

Lucky pushed down his anger and followed Yale as he headed out of the hollow and back on to the path. Out in the daylight, the forest didn't feel nearly as intimidating. The sun created dappled patterns on the fallen leaves that scattered with the breeze. It reminded him of the shifting white spray that rose and fell on the waves. Birds called from the trees, sometimes harsh alarm cries, but often trilling songs that echoed from bird to bird around him. Once, he caught sight of a squirrel, racing around the monumental trunk of an oak tree.

'Good eating on that,' Yale commented, eyeing the creature as it scampered across a branch. His stomach rumbled. Lucky turned away in disgust.

He nibbled on seaweed bread as he walked, savouring the flavour, the idea that Gabriel's fingers had touched this only a couple of days ago. It helped push back against the distance between them. Yale cast frequent glances at the food, but he didn't ask, and Lucky didn't offer.

It was late in the afternoon when they emerged from the forest and stood staring down at the land below. It was mostly scrubby grassland, no sign of any farmland. In the centre of it all was a huge dip, as if someone had fired an immense cannonball at the land. And nestled down at the bottom was a series of buildings.

'That's our destination, little bird,' Yale said, somewhat unnecessarily. It was the only sign of life for miles around.

Lucky stared down at the buildings. They seemed small, insignificant. They didn't seem important enough to hold the answers he'd been seeking for so long.

'This is where you and I stop being friends,' Yale said and pushed a hand against Lucky's back. Before Lucky could react, he'd tumbled over the lip of the hill and was rolling down the steep slope. The sky spun around him as he bounced off rocks and snagged on sharp, spiky plants.

Lucky finally came to a stop and lay dazed, his vision still turning cartwheels. Yale stepped into view, his expression cold.

'That's for yesterday,' he said.

'Coward,' Lucky spat back. 'You know you couldn't beat me in a fair fight.'

'Then what's the point of a fair fight?' Yale retorted. He rolled Lucky on to his side, pushing him into the ground with his whole weight while he tied Lucky's hands behind his back. Lucky bucked and shook, trying to dislodge him, but Yale had him pinned completely.

Yale tested the knots one more time, then yanked Lucky to his feet. 'Come along, little bird. You're almost back where you belong.'

But that wasn't true. Lucky touched the leather band around his wrist. It wasn't true. Whatever it cost him, he'd find a way back to the *Dreamer*. Back to Gabriel.

The buildings he'd seen from above were surrounded by a thick wall of rust-coloured stone, around nine feet high, blocking off any view of the interior. Yale shoved his shoulder, forcing him to march around the wall to a rough path and a pair of heavy gates. A pattern of threads had been worked into the iron, and the design twisted in Lucky's eyes like snakes.

For a church, it seemed strangely fortified locked away behind the high walls and set well away from civilisation.

'Oi!' Yale called. 'Open up. I've brought something for the head priest.'

There was a pause and a head appeared over the wall, staring down at them. After a moment, the gates swung open with a throaty screech. They walked through into a hexagonal courtyard. In the centre was a fish pond, with a statue of a man holding a tapestry in the middle of it. The marble was stained green with moss and lichen, as if it had been there since the dawn of time, and nature treated it as just another cliff or tree. Yale tipped it a salute as he passed.

Ahead, two people faced them. They wore a uniform similar to that of the Beaters, but burgundy instead of black.

'Who is this? Why have you brought them here?'

'I'm not speaking to anyone except the high priest.' Yale folded his arms. The two eyed each other, neither giving anything away in their body language. Then the man stepped aside.

'Follow me,' he said to Yale. 'Oliver will deal with your prisoner.'

The other man grabbed Lucky's arm, dragging him away. Lucky thought about putting up a fight, about protesting his innocence, but he'd have little chance against one of them, bound as he was, and he didn't trust Yale not to put a knife in his ribs now he was here, just to end everything. So he allowed Oliver to lead him to a low stone building which appeared to contain a single corridor with doors on either side.

Oliver pulled a key out of his pocket.

'Why does this church have prison cells?' Lucky asked. This wasn't Minmouth or Ciatheme. There were no towns here, no people except those living as part of the church.

'Not everyone accepts their purpose immediately,' he replied with a shrug. 'Sometimes they need time to come to terms with everything. In you go.'

Now Lucky fought back. He was not ready to go back to being locked up. Whatever his crimes in the past, he'd served his time, and now he had a new life, a new future.

He twisted, ducking under Oliver's grip, shoving the man aside with his shoulder and barging back out into the courtyard. There was no sign of Yale or the other man, so Lucky ran on, through a smaller gate, and into a wide open space.

Buildings lined the walls, and people moved amongst them. They gave him a look, but not a second one, as if bound men running around was not an unusual sight. Perhaps it wasn't. The whole place had a strange, deeply unsettling feeling.

In the centre lay the church. There was no sign, the doors were open, and he couldn't see any windows, yet he knew it had to be the church building.

Come to us.

You promised.

Come. Come.

Lucky tried to push the voices out of his head. There was no thread in his hands. It was just his imagination. But the church building seemed much quieter than the ones around it, and Oliver had to be right behind him.

He had to get his answers. Survive. Get back to Gabriel.

Lucky dashed through the doors and into the church. He slammed them behind him using his elbow and looked around for something to block them with, but the huge wooden seats were fixed to the floor, and there was no convenient pole to slip between the handles. He only needed to stay hidden long enough . . .

He gave up and carried on into the building. His feet made no noise here, as he ran down a thick red carpet. Up ahead, past the rows of pews three steps led to the altar. A great woven tapestry hung down from the centre, easily twenty foot long and maybe eight foot wide. It had no image, but as he stared at it, pictures emerged, rising and fading in the threads like dolphins leaping from the sea and disappearing underwater again.

He saw the leviathans, long sinuous bodies twisting through the waves. He saw Gabriel, sitting with arms around his knees, his head bowed. He saw himself, caught in a knot of multi-coloured threads wrapped around his arms and legs, pulling him apart. The images came faster and faster – people he knew; people who were strangers. Places he'd never been.

Lucky screamed. His skull felt as if it were rupturing. Closing his eyes made no difference. The images continued to come thick and fast. His mother, face down in a rock pool, blood staining the sands. The *Dreamer*, tossed on a storm. He saw Yale, arms bound behind his back.

'So, that's it.'

Lucky turned around, staggering back. Flashes of the past mixed with the real view of the church. There was – a ship, a crab, a lobster pot, Gabriel – a man in front of him, watching him with a mixture of curiosity and compassion.

'What's happening to me?' Lucky couldn't see straight. Couldn't tell what was real. His head felt as if it was swelling, filling up with all the sights and sounds of things that had happened, had yet to happen. He fell to his knees and retched up the seaweed bread on to the red carpet. The man approached and rubbed his back gently. 'What's wrong with me?'

'Nothing's wrong with you,' the man said. His voice was soft and calm, reassuring. 'You're very special. Come with me, and I'll get you where you need to be.' He took Lucky's hand, helped him to his feet. 'We've been waiting a very long time for you.'

With his back to the tapestry, the visions started to fade. He looked down the church and saw a pair of Beaters struggling to hold back Yale, even though his hands were bound behind his back. The sudden sensation of seeing the same thing all over again was a punch to the gut that made him retch, but there was nothing left to come up.

The man put a hand on his shoulder, guiding him. Yale glared at him, nothing but hatred in his eyes.

'Let me go!' Yale demanded. 'You can't keep me here. What do you mean, I can't leave? Hey!' He kicked out at one of his captors, catching them in the knee. 'Tell me what's going on here.'

The priest gave Yale a quick bow. 'We thank you for bringing back our lost Weaver. You have done a very valuable thing

for us. Unfortunately, no one who has entered the inner sanc-
tum is ever permitted to leave. The understanding you will
gain here cannot be shared.'

'Fuck you,' Yale snarled.

'This way.' The man's voice was a guiding light in the storm
of Lucky's mind. He lost himself, reverting back to his prisoner state. Letting the world form around him. Lucky couldn't
feel his hands, couldn't feel his feet. His body had evaporated,
leaving him floating and untethered. If he let go, he'd disappear altogether.

Would that be so bad?

This is right.

Come to us.

Gabriel.

'You're where you belong now. It has been tough, but it was
inevitable you'd find your way back here,' the priest said. 'It
will be good to be back up to full strength.'

'I don't understand,' Lucky murmured. His voice sounded
odd, wrong. Too empty on its own.

'I don't know how you managed to evade us for ten years.
Your abilities would have been noted as soon as they mani-
fested. Someone should have brought you here long ago.'

A memory – was it real or lies – floated through his mind.
A contract, almost illegible from blood, taken from the body
of a dead Beater. He could picture the document in his mind,
so clearly it might have been in his hands. He cried out and
curled up, pressing his knees against his chest.

Was it real?

Was it lies?

'Hush, now. Your journey is almost over. You can rest soon.'

Rest. Lucky wanted rest. He was so tired. Tired of being
pulled around. Tired of being used. Of being hurt. Rest
sounded so good.

Can't rest.

The thought tugged at his mind. He was forgetting something. Someone. Important. His head pounded, the pain coming in huge storm waves, washing over him, each one trying to knock him down. You couldn't fight water. Couldn't resist that kind of power.

Unless.

Unless you danced.

Another image. A picture on a wooden wall, done in white chalk. A figure, standing on the sea, hand held out. Dancing.

Gabriel.

Lucky tensed, his senses coming back to him. Gabriel. His Gabriel. He had to get back to Gabriel. Suddenly the man's gentle tone was sickly, not kind. His touch controlling, not safe. Lucky shoved away from him, staggering slightly. He turned to run, and two more hands grabbed his arms. A Beater on each side of him. They frog-marched him back to the man. Priest? What did it matter what his title was? Lucky struggled in their grip, lashing, trying to bite, doing anything he could to break free.

It wasn't enough.

They took him through a locked door at the back of the church, and down a series of long steps. Lucky tried to throw himself down them, but the Beaters' grip was too strong. The priest unlocked another door.

He held open the door and the Beaters took Lucky into a room. Six flat beds sat in a circle, each with a figure lying on them, apart from one. Beside each figure was a Beater, noting down all that they said. The figures were pale, and their muscles wasted. How long had they each been lying there? They spoke constantly, babbling a stream of words, their eyes open but blank and unseeing. In the centre of the room hung another tapestry, this one glowing with a strange and ethereal light.

'Our missing Weaver has returned at last,' the priest said with a smile. He turned to Lucky, and cut the bonds around

Lucky's wrists. 'There are always six, you see. Always have been. When one dies, another awakens in the population. The Beaters, the priests out in the other churches, they don't understand the full story, but they know to send anyone with visions here. We were missing one for ten years, but now you're here, and the threads will be back to full force.'

Lucky slammed his eyes shut, fighting with every ounce of strength he had.

'Gabriel!' he screamed, and the name was a prayer, a hope, a promise. 'Gabriel!'

But Gabriel wasn't there.

The Beater shoved Lucky on to the empty bed and everything went black.

Chapter Thirty-Five

Lucky floated. Darkness all around him. Quiet. He couldn't hear his heart. Wasn't even sure he was breathing. Was he dead?

A light flashed, blinding him. He raised his hands, but it did nothing. Images flooded his mind. A barn, the straw set alight by a carelessly knocked lantern. A river, healthy, full of fish. A storm coming in, lightning striking the surface of a lake over and over again.

Lucky spoke. He didn't mean to, but he couldn't stop it. He found himself describing the images as they came to him. Flash. A new scene. Flash. A new disaster. Flash. Weather. Flash. A birth. Flash. A death.

The words spewed out of his mouth, a string of them. It was as if something had a hand in his throat, reaching down and pulling them out, hand over hand, a rope of knowledge, a thread of prescience. Lucky vomited the words over and over and over again with no relief.

No!

Yes, the threads answered. They wrapped themselves around him, tying him down, smothering him. Destroying everything that made him who he was. He lost his appearance. He lost his name.

No!

His name was Lucky.

It was a promise. That things would get better, Gabriel's voice echoed in his mind. *I'm giving it to you.*

The air shuddered. The threads bit tight into his flesh.

What flesh? There was no flesh here. Only the threads.

And the promise.

You were promised here.

Lucky flexed his arms. Threads snapped with a scream. That may have been true. He had been promised here. But he'd promised Gabriel, too. And Gabriel said promises were powerful.

A mocking sound. *Promises between lovers mean nothing.*

Lies, he told them.

Only promises *matter.* He saw a shrine, decorated with seashells and bones of fish. Old. So old. Set in the cliffs. A statue of a woman had been carved into the rock. She held her hand out, and carved waves hung in a frozen tableau around her.

The water dancer shrine.

That's a Promise. Last one. All gone, bar her.

More images flashed in his mind. Beaters, fighting. Somehow, he knew this was long ago. They fought in great armies, crossing the land, burning, destroying. He saw more shrines, desecrated, destroyed. And then . . . a leviathan, smaller than he'd ever seen before, disappearing into the sea.

The leviathans . . . were they what became of the Promises?

All gone now. The words – there was no voice, only words – were smug. *Their bodies belong to the sea. Their minds are part of us. Part of the greater sum. No individuals. Only us. Only fate.*

Not all gone now. The dancers remain.

No matter. They won't last.

Fate and the Promises were the same. Lucky floated, letting the revelations sink in. Fate had used the Beaters to break down the shrines of the other Promises, one by one, until their power had become part of the collective, and their bodies were now monsters. The one at Sea Hall was the last surviving one. It had only survived because the dancers gave an advantage against the leviathans, creatures created from the destruction.

No wonder an augury needed a leviathan.

And then time had passed, and knowledge had come and gone. The war faded from both memory and paper. The Beaters were now merely enforcers, no longer a rampaging army. Lucky thought of Yale leading such a force and shuddered.

Focus. The words sounded uncertain. *Focus.*

The images pushed into his mind. Landscape, people, situations. The hand reached down his throat and he choked against it.

NO!

He ripped it out, gasping.

No. I'm not your puppet. I'm not your prisoner. I'm going to live.

You are living. This is life.

This is a cell.

Lucky had spent ten years in a cell. He'd done his penance. No more.

He took a deep breath, feeling it in his chest. There was his heart, beating a steady rhythm. He turned over his hands, seeing his palms, then clenched them into fists.

How?

The uncertainty turned to panic and Lucky smiled. A cold smile. A hungry smile.

You can't keep me here.

You can't leave.

You can't keep me here, he repeated, and the fates didn't respond. He turned around, floating in the blackness. There had to be a way out. Had to be an exit. If he had come in here, he could come out.

He reached out, his fingers clutching around the blackness. Prodding. Pulling. Poking.

You'll break it.

A vision filled his mind. People trapped in a burning building. A flash flood racing down a valley to an unsuspecting village. A heavy storm capsizing a vessel, men and women drowning in the sea.

You'll break it and they'll never know.

Maybe it's better that way.

How? The words showed him more death. More destruction. More chaos.

They'll learn, Lucky said. They'll learn to understand, to make their own predictions. Maybe it will take time, maybe they won't ever be as accurate, but they'll be free to make their own choices. Not controlled. Not manipulated. Everything had acted to bring him here. He'd escaped his cell, but he'd simply been in a bigger one this whole time.

I'm no one's prisoner.

Not your choice to make, the fates begged, and Lucky ignored them.

He reached out again, clutching at the darkness. The threads wrapped themselves around his fingers, and Lucky spread his hands, pulling them apart. Ripping. Tearing. Destroying.

How? they asked again. *Did you promise?*

Lucky didn't know. The words said Gabriel didn't count. He hadn't made a promise at the water dancer shrine. It didn't matter. What mattered was getting out. He pulled again and the words screamed, no longer words, just sound. Emotion.

Hatred.

They bombarded him with images, so much death and destruction, so much pain and misery. They raged and shrieked and snarled in his head. Lucky tugged, twisted, pulled. He used his hands, his fingernails, his teeth. The threads screamed and yelled, pleaded and wailed.

A crack.

Lucky pushed his fingers into it, grabbing the edges, frayed and tatty. He grabbed the pieces, fixed his thoughts on Gabriel, and he tore.

Chapter Thirty-Six

A blinding flash.

Lucky covered his eyes.

Silence.

He lay back, breathing heavily, his heart pounding in his ears. Normal sounds. Natural sounds. He opened his eyes.

He lay on the bed, staring up at the wooden beams of the ceiling. For a moment, the silence continued, and then it was broken by screaming.

The five other figures on the beds were awake too. For the first time in possibly decades. Their panicked voices rose, higher and higher, laced with pain. They hadn't moved from their beds since they arrived, Lucky knew. No one ever gave them a walk around a courtyard. Their prison had been both body and mind, and even if their mind had been freed, their bodies were wasted and useless.

The Beaters were panicking too. They looked around at each other wildly, sharing frantic gestures. One pushed a hand over the eyes of one of the Weavers, and begged them to go back under, to go back to the threads.

But the threads were gone.

Lucky stared at the tapestry, and it was just cloth. No images assaulted his mind as he looked at it. The swirls of colour meant nothing to him anymore. A great rent ran down the centre, leaving it in two frayed halves.

He stood up.

'Hey. Where are you going?' A Beater took a step towards him.

'I'm going home,' Lucky said, and left.

Chapter Thirty-Seven

The Beaters didn't follow him. Lucky wasn't surprised. He'd broken the very essence of their order. It would take them a while to process that.

He felt light, his head free from pain for the first time in far too long. Behind him, the screams continued unabated. Those poor people. He wished he had something to help them, but it was far outside of any skill he had. He made his way up the stairs, out into the main church. The tapestry hung in shreds here, too.

Lucky stepped out into the sunshine. The screams and shouts had drawn attention, and Beaters came running. He forced himself to put on a panicked expression.

'Fire,' he called, pointing to the main church. 'Underground. I'm going to get the healers.'

The Beaters nodded and let him pass. Lucky ran.

It was hard to remember not to grin.

I'm coming home, Gabriel, he thought. He'd lost track of the days, didn't know if he had time to get to Ciatheme before the *Dreamer* or not. It didn't matter. Gabriel would wait for him. The thought of seeing him again made Lucky's heart leap. He anticipated tasting his lips, running his hands through Gabriel's long hair. Sitting on the deck, watching the sunset, leaning into each other.

Home.

'You!'

Lucky turned, the voice sending an icy shiver down his spine. Yale stormed across the courtyard towards him. His hands were unbound and he'd lost his Beater escort, though not without a fight, given the oozing gash on his forehead.

Lucky drew his knife, ready to fight. Yale was just a man. He'd taken him in fights before, and he wouldn't let Yale stop him getting to Gabriel.

But Yale didn't draw his own weapon.

'What is going on here?' Yale demanded. 'What are you?'

Lucky shrugged. 'Nothing now.'

He tried to push past Yale, but the other man grabbed his arm.

'Not good enough. They want to keep me here. Forever. Locked up like some common criminal. All because of you.' He was breathing heavily, each clipped sentence delivered like a stab. 'What are they doing in there?'

'Fate and Promise, they're the same thing. At least Promise took a sacrifice willingly offered. Fate decided for them. Stole their lives. Locked them up in secret.' Each revelation was an answering blow, and he saw them hit home on Yale's face.

'I don't believe you,' Yale snapped, but there was a tremor in his voice.

'Then see for yourself.' Lucky shrugged again. He felt as if a storm had blown through him, and now the sun was breaking through the dark clouds. The exhaustion that pulled at his bones was comfortable, satisfying. 'The reason they won't let you leave is down the steps in the church. But it's over now. There's nothing left. No fate. No Weavers. People will need to make their own choices.'

'How?' Yale froze. His mouth worked, as if he was trying to swallow something. The priest emerged from the church, screaming wordlessly. 'How?'

'Maybe because I know what it's like to be a prisoner. Maybe because I had someone important to go back to. Maybe the other Weavers never had enough of a life to learn how wrong this is.' He should have been forced on that bed aged fourteen, if it wasn't for his mother's murder. In that limbo between child and adult, he'd have never had the strength to break free. Lucky turned away. It didn't matter anymore. Time to go home.

Yale grabbed his shoulder, his fingers digging into Lucky's flesh.

'You're not going anywhere. I brought you here to fix things, little bird, and that's what we're doing. This isn't over.'

'No.' The word tasted delicious. It tasted free. Lucky was done with walls and cells and guards and being controlled. His whole body felt light, as if he could leap and fly away. He wondered if this was what being drunk felt like. 'It is over.'

He grabbed Yale's hand, twisted, freeing himself. Part of him felt a little sorry for the man. Lucky had destroyed everything he'd believed in. But another part remembered the scream of the leviathan, the bruises on Gabriel's face. Even if Yale hadn't known the whole truth, he'd known how ugly and cruel the system was.

'Not your choice,' Yale growled. He drew his knife and attacked, hard and fast, forcing Lucky to dance back.

Lucky parried his blows, catching a scrape along the back of his hand. He barely felt it. 'It is my choice,' he replied. 'It is always my choice from now on. And I choose to walk away.'

More and more people were aware of the growing sense of wrong. The area had the feeling of a kicked anthill, insects scuttling around in horror at the sudden appearance of the sun. No one seemed particularly inclined to step in between two Beaters fighting.

Yale had nearly always had the upper hand on him. He was taller, faster, more experienced. More than that, he was cruel. That had given him the edge when they'd trained in The Fell. But Lucky was different now. Lucky was a free man, and that gave him something worth fighting for.

Again and again Yale came for him, and Lucky blocked, parried, and turned the blade. They clashed and parted, Yale breathing heavily. The sweat dripped down his face, which was contorted in a scowl.

'Go away, Yale,' Lucky told him. 'Make a new life for yourself. Make your own choices. If you're lost, you can find yourself at sea. If you want power, you can make a promise at the shrine. Just know it comes at a cost, one you might not fully understand.'

'Never! I'll never!' Yale pushed into an attack, his blade held out in front of him. He moved with a speed Lucky could never hope to match, but Lucky was prepared. At the last moment, just before the dagger hit his chest, Lucky pivoted, one leg out, just as he had in their last sparring match. Yale crashed into it, stumbling forwards. Lucky swept his leg back, knocking Yale to the ground. He drove the dagger down to the back of Yale's neck.

'It's over, Yale. It's all over. Just our own lives to live as we choose. And I choose to go home.'

Yale didn't rise, didn't move, his face pale and wan. The knife fell from his fingers. Lucky felt another pang of sympathy.

'You can choose now,' he said kindly. 'You don't have to be a Beater. You can be anything you want to be.'

'But . . .' Yale's voice trembled. 'How will I know what that's supposed to be?'

Lucky shook his head and turned away. It took time, he knew that. It took time to understand that the walls were gone, that the cell they'd built in your mind was open. It took time to work out that you deserved to be outside. Being able to choose for yourself was occasionally terrifying, knowing that the repercussions were all on you. He understood all of that, and Yale would come to understand it too. Lucky had one thing left to offer him.

'I know what it's like, to not know who you are, to be caught between all the forces telling you what you should be. And I know it gets better,' he called over his shoulder.

'Come back, little bird,' Yale called. 'Robin! Robin, come back!'

But that wasn't his name, so Lucky didn't respond.

He walked away from the church complex, from the priests and Beaters and other staff who yelled and wept and fought with each other. He walked away with his heart light and his head held high.

He walked towards home, and Gabriel.

Lucky walked.

He stuck to the main roads and the directions people gave him when he stopped, so it might not have been the quickest route, but Lucky didn't want to risk getting lost. He had no money, but most of the inns were willing to let him work a few hours for a meal and a space in the stable.

He enjoyed the solitude. For the first time in his life, he was truly alone. There had always been people around – the guards, the crew of the *Dreamer*, the other acolytes, Yale. Now, the roads were almost entirely empty, and he could walk all day without seeing another soul. It gave him time to come to terms with what he'd learned, what he'd done.

In each town he passed through, the atmosphere was the same – one of shock and confusion. In each church, the tapestry had torn. The people outside the mother church knew nothing of the Weavers, but the effect of their waking was clear – the threads were broken. Whole swathes of people had suddenly learned that there was no magical set of instructions, and the future was an empty page. They, like Yale, panicked, and they, like Yale, would come around to it in time.

Every day, he woke up thinking of Gabriel, and every day he grew more excited with the knowledge that he was getting closer and closer to seeing him again. Even on the day when it poured with rain and soaked him to the skin, or the time he had to sell his old knife to afford to eat, his good mood couldn't be quashed.

Would Gabriel be in town, perhaps waiting on the beach? Or perhaps he'd stay on the ship until Lucky approached the harbour and come running across the waves towards him. A hundred scenarios passed through his mind. A hundred sweet kisses. A hundred gentle caresses. A hundred times, he heard Gabriel say, 'Hey,' in his ear.

As evening approached on the fifth day, he knew he was close. He could feel it in his bones. Lucky picked up his pace, the taste of Gabriel's lips heavy in his mind. The air smelled different this close, and even though he knew that it was all in his mind, the thought was strong enough to cause a physical effect.

With every step, the smell grew in intensity, and then he crested a hill, looked down on the city, and understood why. It wasn't in his head.

Ciatheme was burning.

Chapter Thirty-Eight

Smoke rose up from dozens of locations. Lucky stopped at the top of the hill, unable to move. Below him, the city looked as if an army had run through it. The church roof burned, the flames visible even from his vantage point. The castle, already damaged from the leviathan attack, emitted smoke from multiple locations.

The iron band tightened around Lucky's chest. It pushed against his lungs, forcing his breath out of his body. His vision swam, and for a moment he thought he might fall. He closed his eyes waiting for the world to stop spinning.

Lucky scanned the harbour. Was the *Dreamer* there? Was she in trouble? The rising smoke obscured his view, and he couldn't be certain.

That was enough to break him out of his thoughts and he charged down the hill, racing for the harbour. His heart rode in his throat, the fear and guilt choking him. Was this his fault? Had he caused this? He didn't understand enough about the church to know how quickly the effects of his actions would ripple through the world.

He'd promised Gabriel everything would work out. If he'd broken things in a way that harmed him, Lucky could never forgive himself. The thought made him sick. Gabriel had to be all right. He had to. Lucky couldn't bear to think otherwise.

Gabriel had been hurt enough.

The smoke filled the air as he made it to the city streets. It burned his eyes and throat, forcing him to slow down from a run. He pushed through the streets as others fought past him.

He couldn't blame them for wanting to get away from the choking black clouds.

Lucky headed towards the waterfront. People yelled and called, some afraid, some angry. A bucket chain passed water from the harbour up to the church, but many of the smaller burning properties had been left to the flames. The idea turned his stomach, but he couldn't afford to get involved. Not until he knew Gabriel was safe.

The air got a little easier to breathe as he made it out of the narrow streets and into the wide area near the harbour. Beaters guarded the road leading down to the water, armed not only with knives but rifles as well. Fighting them was a risk, but he could see the *Dreamer*, moored alongside a pair of galleons.

Lucky backed away. The other entrances to the harbour were likely to be similarly guarded, and getting shot wouldn't help him get to Gabriel. He needed another way through. He turned around, searching for options, and came across a Beater relieving himself in an alley.

He was oblivious as Lucky crept up on him, and brought the hilt of Captain Haven's knife down on the back of his skull. The Beater crumpled, his eyes rolling back. Lucky caught him and laid him gently on the ground. Whispering hurried apologies, Lucky stripped him of his uniform. He didn't want to cause any more pain, any more violence. He only wanted to go home.

The Beater's uniform sat uncomfortably on him. Everything it represented, everything he'd done while wearing one rankled at him. But he forced down his discomfort and approached the harbour again, keeping his expression neutral, even though his heart pounded. He hoped they wouldn't question him too much as his mouth was dry.

At the entrance, the Beaters gave him a disinterested glance and waved him through before he could even speak. Lucky forced himself to walk until he was out of sight, then ran down to the ships. He let out a sigh of relief seeing the *Dreamer* floating there, with no sign of damage to her. But when he called up, there was no answer.

He made his way on to the ship, shivering. The *Dreamer* was never empty. Even when she was docked, there was always a small contingent on board. Now she was a ghost ship. Lucky hurried to the captain's cabin and banged frantically on the door. No one answered him.

Inside, he found the remains of breakfast and three cups of coffee – one was half drunk, while the others contained only dregs. The captain's bed had been made, while Gabriel's bunk was a disorganised mess, the blankets spilling on to the floor. The iron band around his chest tightened a notch with every step, and his stomach ached as if someone had punched it.

The story was the same all over the ship. The mess was empty, discarded plates and half-eaten food scattered about the place. Poe wasn't sitting on his stool in the galley, and it felt like part of the room was missing. In the bunk room, half-made beds spoke of sailors who had recently slept in them but were now nowhere to be found. The silence of the place set the hairs on the back of his neck to stand up. The *Dreamer* was always full of noise, and now she felt as silent as the grave.

No.

No, he couldn't afford to think like that.

They were probably in the town helping to fight the fire. He should have paid more attention to the bucket line, perhaps he would have recognised a familiar face.

Before he returned to the harbour, he checked his cell. He didn't really know what he was looking for, hoping for, but when he got there, it was as empty as the rest of the ship. The blankets had been folded back on top of the chest, and the lantern was cold. The picture of Gabriel remained on the wall and Lucky reached out and touched the sketch of the outstretched hand.

'I'll find you again. I promise.'

Someone laughed. Lucky froze. The sound had no humour; instead, it was cold and hungry. He spun around, searching for white hair or a crescent smile, but there was nothing. Just the empty ship.

She wasn't real.

Shaken, Lucky headed back down the gangplank and into town. He hurried to the bucket line but none of the people looked familiar. Lucky's heart shrivelled in his chest. Where were they? Where could the crew be?

'What's going on here?' he asked one of the people in the line. The man grunted and shook his head.

'Not now,' he gasped, his face flushed from exertion.

Lucky slipped away, walking down to the beach. His heart ached with worry, and he called out for Gabriel again and again.

'Hey.'

Lucky's heart leapt and he spun around, but it wasn't Gabriel approaching him, it was another Beater. He muttered a curse and made to turn away, but she grabbed his shoulder.

'What are you doing out here? We need you up in the castle.'

'What for?' he asked.

Her eyes widened. 'What for? We've got a crew of heretics to execute, in case you've forgotten.'

Lucky staggered back, his heart seizing in his chest. 'What . . . what?'

The Beater peered at him. 'You moon-touched or something? Did you miss the entire bloody battle that's been raging these last two days?'

'Yes,' Lucky admitted. He struggled to stand, his world tumbling around him. It might not be them, he told himself, but he knew it was. 'I . . . I, er, just got here. I came from . . . Minmouth.' It was the only place he could think of in time.

The Beater relaxed a little. 'Oh, right.'

'Can you tell me what happened?' Lucky asked. 'Has anyone been hurt?'

'A few on both sides. But we rounded them all up now, and we're ready to put an end to this. Maybe if the heretics die, then everything will go back to how it was.' She raised an eyebrow. 'You know about the tapestry, at least, right?'

'I do. And executing anyone isn't going to fix that.'

'How do you know?' The suspicion was back, and Lucky noted her hand on her dagger.

'I met with some Beaters from the mother church,' he admitted. 'The tapestry there just stopped. It's all stopped, all over. This isn't about the water dancers. This isn't their fault. It just happened. We shouldn't be fighting like this. We should be looking to move on with our lives, work out how to live as best as we can now.'

She drew the knife in a smooth movement. 'Who are you? You're no Beater.'

Lucky backed away, and drew Captain Haven's knife. He'd kept her gift unsullied so far, but now he'd drawn it in violence twice. Lucky suspected she wouldn't mind. The Beater came at him, the dagger raised. He ducked her blows, the frantic, harried attacks of someone who had given up trying to make sense of the world and now just wanted to punish someone for her hurt.

Again and again she came at him, driving him back to the drier sand where it was harder to move. Lucky tried to reason, tried to plead, and then tried to flee. He dashed over the sand, kicking it behind him with each step, heading around her and down towards the tideline, where the sand would be firmer. She came after him, growing closer with every step.

Lucky raced between the large rocks, washed smooth by the daily caresses of the sea. The Beater yelled and launched herself at him. Lucky threw himself aside and she tumbled past him. Her foot slipped out from underneath her and she fell sideways, her head slamming into a rock. Her eyes rolled back in her head, and she slumped face down in the water, her blood staining the sand around her.

Lucky thought of his mother and screamed.

A flash of white flicked in his peripheral vision. He turned, spinning on the sand, heart back in his throat, expecting that cold empty smile, but there was nothing but the sand and the sea and the dead Beater.

Lucky turned and fled.

The path to the castle wound around the headland, a steep cobbled road that leaned over the sea as it made its way up. Lucky tried to run, but he was winded by the steepness and the slippery cobbles.

He had no idea what he'd do. He was alone. Armed with only a knife. He had no idea how many Beaters were up here, but if they were holding the entire crew of the *Dreamer*, there had to be a whole host of them. He pushed his way up to the castle, forcing himself to go as fast as he could.

For Gabriel.

His legs ached and his lungs burned. His heart thumped against the inside of his chest, punishing him.

For Gabriel.

His mouth dry, sides heaving, Lucky pulled himself up to the front of the castle. He'd never seen it from this side. A wide gate stood over the road, two towers on either side of it. The gates were raised, and the iron portcullis hung halfway down. Lucky eyed it suspiciously, half expecting it to fall on him as he passed under.

A stone courtyard lay ahead, the walls to his right over-looking the sea far below. On the other side, the walls built up into the cliff, though what kind of attackers could crawl over the rocks like that, he wasn't sure. A set of gallows had been erected, several nooses swaying in the breeze. Lucky's blood went cold.

Two Beaters stood at the entrance to the main keep.

'Did you bring the priest?' one called to Lucky. 'We need him to get the bloody job done. I'm tired of standing around.'

Lucky shook his head, unsure what to say.

'Where's Annabelle?' the other replied. 'It was her job.'

Lucky thought of the dead Beater on the beach. 'The priest's not coming. He's dead. The fire killed him.' Maybe if there was no priest, there would be no execution.

Both Beaters paled. 'What? The fuck you say.'

'It's true,' he said softly. The breeze caressed his shoulders, weaving in and out of his collar, spreading a chill across his sweat-damp shoulders. 'The priest is dead.' He waited for their reaction, waited for them to tell him the execution was off, or at least stayed.

'That's it, then.' The Beater on the left turned and pushed open the door. 'Come on. No nice gallows for this bunch. We'll just shoot the lot of them.'

Chapter Thirty-Nine

'No!' Lucky shouted. 'No, you can't.'

The other Beater stared at him. 'Why the fuck not? You said it yourself. They've killed the priest. They're heretics. They've got to die, and we don't owe them a quick death at the end of the rope.'

'It's . . .' His mind worked frantically. 'It's . . . bad luck. Bad luck to kill heretics without a priest.'

The Beater raised an eyebrow.

Lucky nodded frantically, feeling dizzy. 'It's true, I swear. That's what happened here a while ago. They took a heretic out to the exercise yard around the back of the castle, and they were going to shoot him there and then and a leviathan attacked, killed a Beater by swallowing them in one mouthful.'

The words tumbled out of him, a waterfall of lies.

'Bullshit,' said the Beater emphatically, but his companion looked a little uncertain.

'It's not. I was there,' Lucky protested. 'How else would I know about it?'

'The leviathan attack is common knowledge,' the Beater scoffed.

'Yes, but the exercise yard isn't,' Lucky replied. He fought the urge to laugh, feeling light-headed and sick. So much depended on them believing him. He couldn't mess it up now. 'How would I know about that if I was making it up?'

The two Beaters looked at each other. 'It was the yard above the dungeons that got destroyed,' one admitted cautiously. The other fixed Lucky with a piercing stare.

'Why would I lie?' Lucky said, trying desperately to keep the tremor out of his voice. 'I'm a Beater like you. I don't care about heretics. I care about not being eaten by a leviathan. I lost a companion that day, and I still have nightmares. Have you ever seen a leviathan up close? Their eyes are dead, just flat discs of yellow that glare down at you. Their mouths are full of rows and rows of needle-like teeth, so if they get hold of you, they pierce through your bones and pin you there. And their slime makes you numb, so you can't even feel it. You're still conscious as you go down their throats.'

He was rambling, but the words were having an effect, as the Beaters both shuddered in unison.

'Fuck that,' one announced, and the other made an emphatic noise of agreement.

'So what do we do?' the first one asked.

'Stay as we are, I'd suggest,' Lucky said. His heart raced and he couldn't believe his luck was holding. 'Send someone to get a priest from another town. We'll just have to hold the prisoners until then.'

'Ugh, tedious.'

'But better than being eaten,' Lucky added.

'Fine. What's your name? I haven't seen you before.'

'Robin,' Lucky replied. 'I haven't lived here for a while.'

'Not surprised you left after a bloody leviathan took a bite out of the place,' the Beater said sympathetically.

'I'm going to check on the prisoners, and then I'll come and relieve one of you. The other should head off to Minmouth.' It was three days' walk there, and then back again. That would buy Lucky some time at least. That is, presuming the real priest didn't show up anytime soon. Sneaking forty-five sailors out of the castle couldn't be that hard, could it?

Lucky stepped into the castle.

The thick stone walls pushed in on him, immediately making him long for the open sea and sky. It was funny how things changed. To his left, a staircase curled up and around to the next floor, but Lucky didn't want up. He wanted down.

He passed through a hall with a large table, though only one seat at the far end. The fireplace was cold and empty. Lucky moved onwards. He had no idea where he was going; he only knew that the dungeons were on the far side of the castle. He never really considered who lived here, but it didn't seem to be anyone right now. Perhaps whoever it was had fled when the leviathan attacked.

Eventually he came across a set of steps that awoke memories. They rushed up, as if they'd been trapped underwater and were now coming up, desperate for air. He remembered his panic and confusion, the cold eyes of the leviathan, the water rushing in around his legs from the gaping hole in the castle wall.

The steps were dry now, but the hole remained, water lapping at the corridor below. He stepped down cautiously, half afraid another leviathan would burst through again. *You were supposed to be released in three days,* Yale had told him. Three days later and Lucky would've been freed from jail and on his way to becoming a Weaver. He'd never have met Gabriel, probably never have had the courage and strength to break the threads and set himself free. Strange as it was to say, the leviathan had done him a favour.

You're welcome, the voice of his dreams said. Lucky froze, his heart seized in his chest. He looked around wildly, but just like on the beach, he was alone.

She wasn't real.

He took a moment to calm the frantic beat of his heart, and proceeded down the rest of the steps, into the cold seawater pooling on the floor. He forced down a shudder, as his memories threatened to combine with his reality. There was no leviathan, and he was no longer a prisoner. He was Lucky and he was here to rescue his Gabriel.

They were going to go home. Together.

The Beaters were gathered in the guard room. Seven of them. That didn't seem too many. Even if they were armed, the crew of the *Dreamer* had the overwhelming numbers. They could do this, he told himself. They could do this.

'Who are you?' one of the Beaters called.

'I'm Robin, from Minmouth,' he answered. 'I was sent to fetch the priest, but I couldn't find him.' He didn't want to risk provoking the same reactions as he had with the Beaters on the door. 'I guess he's still trying to put out the fire at the church. It was burning steady as I came past. I'm sure he'll be along in a bit.'

'He better hurry,' another replied. 'They're getting rowdy in there.'

'How many of you are there? In case there's any trouble,' he added, hoping the question felt reasonable.

'On top of us? There's another twenty further up out of the wet,' she replied.

Lucky's heart sank. That put their numbers much closer. So much for overpowering the Beaters. From down the corridor came shouts and banging. The Beater rolled her eyes.

'Who wants to go and yell at them this time?' she asked. 'I suppose when you know you're going to die imminently, the need to play nicely goes out the window.'

'Let me try,' Lucky said. 'I've had some experience with heretics.' That at least wasn't a lie, and the words flowed out much more easily. The Beater shrugged and gestured to the passage.

Lucky walked back towards his old home. Walking down towards his cell felt so strange, a mixture of nostalgia and fear. He could almost see himself ahead, hunched and broken. He reached out, wanting to touch the man he was, wanting to comfort him and tell him one day he'd be free.

The cells were all full. Only built for one, each had six or seven crew members. Some jeered and spat at him, seeing only the Beater's uniform, until he passed Poe.

'It's you!' he called, and Lucky clutched the bars.

'I've come to get you out,' he hissed.

Poe gave him a smile, warm and rich as his cooking. 'That's generous of you, lad. And just in time to save our necks, too.'

Lucky noticed he was holding his side, his face several shades paler than it normally was. 'You're hurt.'

'Maybe a scratch,' Poe replied. 'It wasn't going to matter much shortly.'

'I'll get you out,' Lucky promised. 'I . . . don't know how, but I'll get you all out.'

'Captain and Gabe are in the last cell,' he said, inclining his head. He put a hand against Lucky's. 'Gabe's . . . He's in a bad way, Lucky. Prepare yourself.'

Lucky felt as if someone had crushed his heart. Reached into his chest and squeezed it to pulp. He pulled away and moved down towards the cell at the end, his cell, but pulled up short. How did you prepare yourself for something like that? He took a deep breath, fighting down waves of fear and nausea.

'Gabriel?' The word came out choked and cracked. Broken. Like Lucky. Was Gabriel broken too? Hurt? Dying?

'Lucky.'

He looked up but it wasn't Gabriel's voice. Instead, Captain Haven stood at the bars. He looked past her, saw the shape of the first mate sitting on his bunk at the back of the cell, and beside her . . .

Gabriel sat next to her, his hands in his lap, his head down. There was a nasty cut on his forehead, but he was sitting up and conscious, which was better than Lucky had expected.

'Gabriel!' he called, his heart picking up, fluttering now. 'Gabriel, it's me.'

Gabriel lifted his head and regarded him, his expression blank.

'Gabriel?' The fluttering turned to panic, erratic, flighty. 'It's Lucky. I've come back for you.'

Captain Haven stepped in front of him and shook her head. Her eyes were red and raw. 'He doesn't know you. He doesn't know anyone now. The sacrifice finished taking its price and now he doesn't remember anything from the previous day. For the last nine days, I've told my son I'm his mother and I love him and every night he goes to sleep and forgets that. I thought I suffered enough when the sacrifice took from me. I think this might be worse.'

She sounded exhausted. Cracked. Ready to give up. He'd never expected Captain Haven to be the first to give up on fighting.

'Is there anything we can do?'

'No!' Her eyes flashed. 'The sacrifice is permanent. It can't be undone. I told him, I told him it was too much. That it shouldn't be entered into lightly, but he thought he could cheat it, give it something without paying the cost.' Her hands gripped the bars, knuckles white. 'You can't do that. I should know. I tried.'

Lucky touched her hand gently, a butterfly-light touch, and she sniffed, gave him a sad smile.

'He's too young. He shouldn't have had to face this for years. It isn't fair.' The last word came out in a choked sob.

It wasn't fair. None of it was fair. None of them deserved any of this.

'Can I talk to him?'

'Let him be,' she replied and there was some of her fierce maternal nature back in her voice. 'You're a stranger to him, Lucky. He doesn't understand what's happening, just that he's locked up and awaiting a death sentence. And he has to learn that fact again each morning we're here. Don't compound his hurt. Please.'

The pain in his chest spread, twisting around his guts, but he pushed it down. One fight at a time. He couldn't think about Gabriel's situation now. The more pressing matter was getting everyone out.

'What happened?'

'Two Beater galleons caught up with us. Seems someone in Ciatheme saw Gabe on board, recognised him as the heretic who tried to stop the augury.' She squeezed her hands into fists, her shoulders shaking. 'A fucking child sold us out. The Beaters took Gabe and I, and the rest of the crew went to get us back. At the time, something was happening in the church and people were panicking. In the chaos, we were winning, we were going to escape, but we were caught between the Beaters pursuing us and a burning building. I surrendered rather than face anyone else getting shot.'

'Anyone else?' He didn't think he could feel any colder. There was ice in his veins, tearing at his skin from the inside.

'Grace's dead. Another four sailors. Sienna took a bullet, but Poe says the noose will probably kill her before the wound does.'

Lucky staggered, gripping the bars to prevent himself falling. 'No.'

'Yes,' she replied grimly. 'We were so close, Lucky. I swear. We could have got back to the ship, held them off from there, but that building just went up suddenly, flames spreading so quickly. I've failed.'

'There's still time. There's still hope.' This was right. 'I'll find a way to get you out.'

'I wish you the best of luck,' she replied, in a tone that told him she'd lost hope long ago. 'I'm going to spend my last hours with my son, make sure he knows he's loved if nothing else. I can't do much, but I can do that for him.'

Lucky gave one last look at Gabriel, quiet, hunched in the corner of the cell where Lucky had spent ten years of his life.

The sight awoke a rage in his chest. This wasn't right. He'd had enough of prisons. Had enough of walls and bars and choices thrown away by higher powers. He'd find a way to end this.

He stalked past the Beaters in the guard room and headed up the stairs. He needed weapons. Keys. A plan. He needed to get them out before more Beaters came back. Before the priest arrived or they decided they didn't need him. He knew he didn't have long, but he would have enough time. He'd save them.

This was right.

'You're finally here.'

He recognised the voice instantly. Heard that cold smile in every word. Lucky yelped. The voice wasn't in his head. It was real.

She was real.

He closed his eyes. No. Not now. She wasn't real, couldn't be real. She was a ghost, a fallen statue, a child's tortured memories twisted around by a terrible event.

She wasn't real.

'I am.'

His head jerked up, eyes open. He couldn't stop himself. The girl stood at the top of the stairs, exactly as he remembered her. And he did remember her. Her flyaway white hair. Her crescent smile. Her eyes, cold and hungry and cruel and old. So very old.

'Who are you?' he stammered, his voice shaking. His body shaking. His heart curled up and quivered like an animal in a trap.

'Wrong question,' she replied with a smile, and her voice was a storm wave, a rock grinding against itself, down to sand. Her voice was the wind and the sand and the water and it was older than all of them. She held out a hand. 'Remember.'

Lucky let her touch his forehead. And he remembered.

Chapter Forty

Two boys walk along an empty beach. They hold hands, their fingers laced tightly around each other. They're about fourteen, young, but old enough to understand a few things. Old enough to be afraid of the future.

One has blond hair, tied at the back of his head. It's long, well past his shoulders, blowing in the wind. His eye is black, his lips bloodied. He's cleaned the blood a bit, but there's still a smear of it, on his jaw. He holds his free hand to his chest.

The other has brown hair, short, rippling in the sea breeze. He's uninjured, but his face is lined with worry. He leads the way, walking fast across the sand, as if he could outpace their troubles. In his free hand, he carries a small pail.

'When are you going?' the blond boy asks.

'Tomorrow,' his friend replies.

'Will you come back?'

'I will. If I can.' He kisses the boy's cheek, a soft, innocent gesture. No passion in it, only a youthful fondness. 'I want to come back.'

'I'm scared,' the blond boy says. 'I'm scared next time he won't stop. If you don't knock at the door, he might not stop.' He curls in on himself, his battered face pale, bloodied lip trembling.

The other boy stops. 'You're Lucky, remember? You'll be all right.' He licks his thumb. 'Can I?'

The blond boy nods and he gently wipes away the smear of blood. There's a soft blond fuzz on the blond boy's jaw, and he smiles.

'You'll be a man soon and then he won't be able to put a finger on you. You've just got to stay Lucky until then.'

They walk on in silence, turning over the stones, looking for crabs to put in the pail, to sell for bait to the fishing boats. A few coins they can use to share a meal, a drink, or put away to help them leave for a better life.

That's all they want: a better life.

The tide is out right now, and not just out to its normal levels. The water has retreated more than usual, leaving an expanse of speckled sand, pools, and smooth rocks. The pickings are good, and for a while, they're both content, catching the crabs and laughing with each other. For a while they can forget.

It's the blond boy who spots it first. A dark, jagged crack in the rocks, normally buried deep beneath the waves. He points and shouts, jumping up and down on the sand, his hair bouncing.

'Rob! Rob, come look at this.'

The brown-haired boy drops the rock he'd been looking under and hurries over.

'It's a cave. Do you think it goes in deep? Let's take a look.'

The other boy, Rob, looks over his shoulder at the sea. It's still a way out, but he knows how fast the tide can come in.

'Please,' the other boy begs. 'I bet no one has been in there for years. Who knows what we might find.'

Rob nods. It's their last day, after all. Tomorrow, his mother is sending him away with the church. He'd had a fit during service yesterday and a man dressed in black had spoken to his mother, promised her lots of money. His mother had cried and cried but Rob understood she was hungry, all the time. Every day she watches him eat, and he knows she doesn't always eat later like she claims. So he'd agreed. If the church pays him well, he'll save up and come back after a few years, come back to his mother and his friend and everything will be fine.

They'll be happy.

The blond boy squeezes through the crack. He's skinny, lithe, but taller than Rob. He has to crouch to get in, whereas Rob can almost remain upright. The rocks press in on him, and he feels like they're stealing his breath, squeezing it out as they scrape along his skin.

After a painful ten feet, they find themselves in a wider chamber. The rocks here are marked with the passage of water, channels and runnels, round depressions. Barnacles cover their surface, like little white scars. The sea plays in here every day, normally. He stands in the centre, looking around him, enjoying the sensation of being a human where humans aren't normally allowed.

'Look at this!' the blond boy calls. His voice rings around the chamber, amplifying his excitement. 'Steps!'

'What? Don't be silly. This is a cave.'

'Steps,' he says again, grabbing Rob's hand and pointing.

And there are. He didn't see them at first, hidden behind a protrusion of rock. But when the blond boy leads him, he finds them, little carved steps, leading upwards into the cliff.

The sound of the waves outside grows louder, and the blond boy looks nervous.

'Perhaps we should go back,' he suggests, shivering.

But Rob is already climbing the steps. They have time, he thinks. And this cave could be lost for another ten years or more. Next time they might not be able to squeeze in.

'Rob . . .' his friend calls, voice wheedling. He starts up the steps after him.

Rob emerges into another chamber and this one takes his breath away. The walls and ceiling are decorated with thousands of small tiles, in hundreds of shades of blue and green. It's like standing underwater, looking up at the sun.

At the back of the chamber, there is a statue. The figure looks female, but has been worn down by the waves over time. Only her smile is still visible, cold and hungry. She stands on a plinth decorated with seashells. When Rob brushes a finger against the stone, it sets off tingles that race up his arm.

The blond boy gasps as he enters.

'Look at this place!' He spins around on the spot, mouth open.

'*Our place,*' *Rob says fondly.* '*You're right. No one has been here for hundreds of years, probably.*'

'*I wish . . .*' *He pulls his arms around him.* '*I wish things could be different.*' *He caresses the bruises on his wrist, dark finger marks printed in pain on his skin.*

'*They will be,*' *Rob tells him.* '*Look, let's promise each other.*'

The boy gives him a shy smile. '*I promise we'll meet again in the future.*'

'*No, something bigger.*' *Rob is gripped by a strange energy, a thunderstorm on his chest. Maybe it's the pressure of their last day. Maybe it's the beauty of the place. Maybe it's the weight of guilt of leaving his closest friend, one who might be more than a friend.*

He reaches out, places his hand on the statue, looks at the other boy to do the same. '*Let's promise . . . let's promise that when we're adults, we'll live together in the castle, how about that?*'

The boy grins. He looks hopeful for the first time and Rob's heart lifts. They stand, hand in hand, each touching the worn statue, and intone their promise. An innocent moment, two youths who simply want to believe in a better future.

But innocence doesn't matter to her.

Chapter Forty-One

Lucky staggered back, clutching his head as the memories rushed back in.

'That was you,' he gasped.

She fixed him with a cold smile, her eyes blank and baleful as a leviathan, and didn't dignify that with an answer.

'You . . . you've been doing all this.' She killed his mother. All this time, his memories had been right. Lucky had never been a murderer. 'The one who branded the leviathans was you, too, wasn't it? You've been dragging me back here. Did you do the same to Gabriel? Is that how Captain Haven was in the right place to save him from his father?'

The smile grew.

'You've been manipulating us. Driving us towards the castle all this time.' Things finally started to make sense, and the revelation left him feeling weak and wobbly. He had promised, he and Gabriel. Neither of them remembered the event. Gabriel hadn't even known about Lucky's mother's death. He'd just spent ten years thinking his best friend had gone off to the church without saying goodbye.

Gabriel had promised twice in his life, but Lucky had been owned by both fate and Promise.

'Claimed by two forces,' she said, her voice ancient and crumbling. 'Fate and Promise. Unusual. Unlikely. Rare.'

'Lucky,' Lucky spat.

Her mouth turned up, the humour genuine now. 'Lucky indeed.'

'Well, you've done it, now. Thank you.' He gave her a deep bow. 'We're both in the castle. The promise is fulfilled. Now it's time for us to leave.'

'The promise was to live in the castle.' Somehow her voice came from her mouth and also echoed in his head.

Lucky tensed. 'For how long?'

'As long as I choose.'

The castle was broken and drafty, an empty shell of whatever it had once been. It wouldn't be fair to leave Gabriel in a place like this. Not when he was suffering already. He needed his family.

'No.'

'You can't escape me. I've driven you this far. If you leave, I'll drive you back.'

He saw his mother's body in his mind's eye. He saw Gabriel's father, a bullet between his eyes. The guard, swallowed by the leviathan. The city of Ciatheme, burning. Grace, dead. Sienna, bleeding.

'A small price to fulfil your promise. How many more will you allow to die for your stubbornness?'

'I stopped fate.' Lucky crossed his arms.

She laughed and it was the sound of drowning. 'Fate is passive. Fate is walls. A prison in your mind. There are far more terrifying things than prison.'

In his mind, Lucky knew she was right. She'd never stop. She'd kill everyone he cared about, everyone Gabriel cared about, until she'd driven them right back to the castle. They'd promised, and she'd hold them to it.

'We were children,' he begged. 'We didn't know what we were doing. We just wanted a little hope. A dream of a better time. Was that really so wrong?'

'It's not a matter of right or wrong. It's a matter of promise.'

'And there's no way out?' His voice was dull, dejected. Broken.

'Of course there is.'

He lifted his head.

'You can die. He can die. Then it is over.'

Lucky shook his head. 'It's not fair.'

She came closer, bringing with her the smell of blood and seawater. 'It's not about fair or unfair. It's about promise.'

That was it then. Lucky sank to his knees. Live in the castle, or he or Gabriel could die. Else everyone around them would die like his mother. And that wasn't going to happen. 'There are nearly thirty Beaters in the castle. They want to execute Gabriel. How can we live in the castle if they hang him?'

'You have to live in the castle.' She said it as if it was the most obvious thing, like fish have to live in the sea. 'It is promised.'

'Right then.' He got to his feet. 'Let's free our home from Beaters then.'

It wasn't the home he'd chosen, wasn't the home he wanted. But if it was a home with Gabriel, then perhaps that would be enough.

She faded away, though the scent of blood and salt lingered in the corridor. He didn't know what he was going to do when he found the Beaters, but he had the feeling whatever it was, she'd be behind him. And the Beaters would die. He felt bad for that. He had no love for them, but they lived in a prison as much as he did. Lucky had opened the door, but like a caged animal, they needed time to leave on their own.

He found them on the second floor, lounging around, playing dice. Forty-five people waited to die at their hands, and they were sprawled around as if this was a tavern and they were on shore leave.

A rage burned in his gut, fire racing through his veins. They'd hurt his crew; his family. His Gabriel.

'Get out,' he snarled.

Heads snapped up.

'Who are you?' someone called.

'Is the priest here? Is it time for the execution?' another asked and there was an excited murmur of voices that fanned the flames of Lucky's rage.

'I said get out!' He strode into the room. 'All of you, leave this place, now.'

'Are you going to make us?' A man stood up, towering over Lucky. He was not only taller, but broader too, and Lucky suspected that if the man picked him up, he'd be able to snap Lucky over his knee like a twig.

'You need to leave,' he said, more softly now. 'Or you'll die.'

There was a moment of silence, then laughter rippled around the room. He could understand – he was one man. But they didn't know he was promised. They didn't understand what that meant.

The big man lunged for him. Lucky ducked under his grasp, but that only put him further into the room. Another Beater punched him, and he couldn't quite avoid the blow. The man's fist hit him in the jaw, sending him pinwheeling backwards. Someone else caught him a jab to the kidneys, and another kicked the back of his knee.

Lucky fell to the floor. More blows rained down on him. There was nothing he could do but curl up, protect his head as much as possible.

'Bring some light,' someone called. 'Let's get a better look at him.'

The blows let up for a moment as someone came forwards with a lantern. Lucky tensed, biding his time. The lantern came closer. When he felt the warmth of it on the back of his neck, he rolled over and pushed himself to his feet. He threw himself at the Beater, knocking him back against a low table. The lantern cracked, spilling oil over the table and the Beater. The spark raced across the surface, lighting up the wood and chewing into the Beater's black uniform. He screamed, beating at the flames racing up him with his bare hands.

The fire spread, consuming a tapestry hanging on the wall, climbing it like a red vine, reaching for the ceiling.

More Beaters moved to help the burning one, trying to smother the flames with a heavy cloth. The Beater's screams went from fear, to pain, to agony, and despite Lucky's anger at the guard's bloodlust, his screams tore through Lucky's soul.

'Get out!' he yelled. 'Get out while you still can.'

She lurked at the side of the room. He could see her shape in the shifting smoke, hear her laugh in the crackle of the flames. The burning Beater's screams turned to sighs as he lost consciousness. He'd be dead soon, the first of them.

Lucky hadn't killed him, but it was his fault.

His promise.

Above them, there was an ominous crack from the ceiling as a beam blackened. Some of the Beaters fled then. The large man who'd first threatened Lucky picked up his unconscious companion and slung him over his shoulders.

But not all the Beaters saw sense. Someone leapt at Lucky, pinning him down. Lucky struggled in their grip as a second Beater raised a knife. He twisted as they brought it down and it grazed along his rib. He bit back a cry as a third Beater stepped in to hold him in place.

The dagger paused over his heart.

Lucky closed his eyes.

The ceiling beam cracked.

A huge chunk of burning wood tumbled down. It struck the Beater with the knife, caving in his skull. He let out a wet gurgle as he toppled and lay still. The other Beaters let go of Lucky as they turned to stare in horror. Lucky rolled out of the way, grabbing the fallen knife. He came up in a crouch, holding the blade out in front of him.

'You're all going to die!' he yelled. The smoke curled into his mouth, choking him, but he had to try. Had to make them understand. 'She'll kill all of you if you don't leave me alone.'

Another beam fell, hitting the floor and taking out some of the boards. A Beater disappeared into the hole before they could even call out. A sickening crack made Lucky curl up. It might have just been wood snapping, he tried to tell himself, but he couldn't believe it.

The remaining Beaters were looking uncertain now. Smoke filled the room, thick and heavy, forcing everyone to crouch or choke. More floor gave way, making a woman leap for safety. That seemed to be the signal needed, and the whole group fled the room.

Lucky crawled for the doorway. His eyes burned, tears streaking down his face. He coughed and gagged as his body tried to expel the smoke, but there was little point when he just breathed it straight back in again.

She wouldn't care if he died here.

As he struggled to reach the exit, that was the thought that went around and around his head. If he died here in the castle, she'd still achieved her goal. It was only anyone trying to make him leave that would attract her ire.

The same went for Gabriel.

Half blind, half mad, completely desperate, Lucky fought his body's desire to curl up and sleep. He staggered out of the room as the rest of the floor gave way. As he struggled for the stairs, she laughed in his ear.

Lucky ran down the stairs, and then down again into the water. It sloshed around his ankles, pulling at him.

'Get out!' he yelled at the Beaters. 'The castle's on fire. It will fall down any minute.'

They stared at him, but there was no denying the smoke smudges on his face and hair, or the way his voice cracked from the coughing.

'I can smell smoke,' one of the Beaters agreed.

'Leave me the keys, get to safety. I'll deal with the prisoners.'

'Deal how?' She raised an eyebrow.

'Does it matter?' Exhaustion chewed at Lucky, wearing him thin. 'It's over. You know what's happened with the church. Executing a group of dancers isn't going to bring everything back. It's over.'

She fixed him with a stare, her hand going to her knife.

'Or fight me?' Lucky shrugged. Black spots flicked at the edge of his vision. He was so damn tired. Tired of running and fighting. Tired of arguing. Tired of death.

She lunged at him, and he half stepped, half staggered out the way, moving back into the waterlogged passage. She pursued him, and Lucky backed away down towards the cells. Lucky spotted Promise lurking behind the Beater.

The other Beaters were watching from the doorway as the woman lurched for him. Lucky dodged back but instead of taking another swipe at him, her foot slipped in the water. She plunged forwards, face first into the murky seawater. The ghost stepped forwards and held the woman's head underwater.

Lucky turned away, but he couldn't block out the sound of her thrashing and choking. Another life snuffed out. He'd tried to warn her, but he still felt responsible. The Beater's thrashing slowed, and then she went still, and Lucky took the keys off her belt. The ghost smiled at the remaining Beaters, who ran. He watched them go for a moment, then turned to the cells.

He worked his way down the length, unlocking and opening the doors, ending with his old cell.

'Lucky.' Captain Haven stood up from the bed 'I take it you found a solution to the Beaters?'

He rubbed the back of his head. 'I . . . I burned the castle down and convinced the Beaters it was haunted.' It was, in a way.

Her eyes widened. 'I see. Well, I suppose that works.' She knelt in front of Gabriel. 'Gabe, we're free. We're going to go back to the ship now. That's where you live, on a ship called the *Dreamer*. Let's get you back home, son.'

Gabriel lifted his head, a frown on his face. Lucky's heart ached.

'No,' he said softly. 'Gabriel has to stay here.'

She crossed the cell in a flash, standing in front of him, hands on her hips, face close to his. 'Say that again, I dare you.'

'It's important. Gabriel has to stay here with me.'

'I'm not leaving my son in the burned-out shell of a ruined castle,' she snapped back. 'Not at the best of times and especially not when he's . . . unwell,' she finished. 'He's staying with me and if you try otherwise, I'll put you down.'

'Mel.'

They both turned to see Poe approaching, pushing through the milling crew members. Behind him, Cass supported Sienna, who was slumped against their shoulder.

'Mel, I think we should listen to Lucky's story,' he said. 'I saw the way that Beater died. There's something going on.'

The captain glared at both of them but waved a hand at Lucky. 'You better make this convincing.'

So Lucky told her the story he'd learned just recently, of two scared boys and an innocent promise corrupted by an ancient force that managed to escape detection for hundreds of years.

'I saw the thing,' Poe said as Lucky finished. 'It killed a Beater. If you try and take Gabriel away from here, it will find a way to bring him back, and it won't care a clam if you die in the process.'

She looked over her shoulder. 'I don't want to leave him.' Her voice ached. 'You can't ask me to leave my son. I'll stay too.'

Lucky glanced over his shoulder at Promise. She shook her head, her smile wide and hungry. Captain Haven hadn't promised. She wasn't part of this. Lucky wasn't sure what would happen, but nothing about Promise suggested it would end well. Perhaps she'd decide the captain had to die. Or perhaps Captain Haven would try and leave and Gabriel would follow her. Or perhaps she'd stay, and having to explain to Gabriel every morning would grow too much for her.

He shook his head. 'I don't think that's a good idea.'

Amala came over, wrapping her arms around her wife. 'Lucky will take care of him. And we can still visit, right, Lucky?'

'I don't think we promised anything that would affect that.'

Captain Haven broke down, sobbing against her wife, her anguished wailing filling the narrow passage. Gabriel raised his head, his expression concerned. He held out a hand, then pulled it back again. Lucky's heart ached. Even now, all Gabriel wanted to do was help.

Poe clapped his hands. 'Come on, move out. Everyone back to the ship. Watch out for each other, take care of the injured.'

The crew shuffled off, giving their captain some privacy. Amala stroked her hair, whispering softly in her ear. In the back of the cell, Gabriel watched uncertainly. Lucky felt caught in the middle of her grief, but he didn't want to retreat too far. Eventually she quietened, and stood up straight, wiping her nose on her hand.

'I'm sorry,' she muttered.

Lucky gave her a sad smile. 'Never apologise for caring about Gabriel. I will look after him. I promise. I'll take care and keep him safe. Do my best to make sure he's happy.'

'I know. He should be on the *Dreamer* where he belongs. But if you're there, I think he'll be all right. He . . . he might not be able to say it, but he loved you. He'd go to sleep holding your pendant, saying your name. Yours was the last name he forgot.'

Lucky fought back the sobs that bubbled up in his chest. She put a hand on his shoulder.

'We'll be back soon.' She said a tearful farewell to Gabriel, promising to return, and then left, marching down the passage with Amala scurrying at her heels.

Lucky let them leave and stepped into the cell. Gabriel looked up at him.

'Who are you?' he asked. His voice was cautious, and Lucky remembered he was still dressed as a Beater.

'I'm Lucky.' He walked over to the bed and sat down, not quite close enough for their shoulders to touch. 'I'm Lucky and I love you. Let me tell you a story.'

Chapter Forty-Two

The mornings were the worst. Lucky couldn't imagine what it was like to wake up each morning, not knowing where you were, who anyone was, even your own name. The first mornings together had been a panicked mess, but as time passed, he learned little tricks.

Routine helped, so he made sure he woke first each day. The *Dreamer* had left a bag of coffee beans in the supplies, but there was no way to grind them, so Lucky put a few on a plate next to the cup of hot water he brought Gabriel each morning. He'd start by saying good morning, telling Gabriel his name, and explaining that he was Lucky, and he was here to help.

Soft words, gentle words, calm words. But more than that, confident words worked best. Gabriel woke scared and confused each day, so Lucky tried to be the voice of reassurance, to always have an answer, even if he wasn't always sure. He didn't allow his mask to break until he was fully confident Gabriel was asleep again at night. Then he let the fears and frustrations come rushing out of him in great sobs.

He was back in a prison again, but as far as prisons went – and Lucky had experienced a few – this wasn't the worst. There were no guards, and his time was his own. He could cook his own meals, make his own leisure time, and he had Gabriel. Gabriel would never love him again; he couldn't learn to love someone in a day. Not Gabriel, who loved souls not bodies. But Lucky loved him. Painfully, distantly, maybe, but it was still love.

They had a life together and perhaps that was enough.

Their days depended on Gabriel's mood. Sometimes he was good-natured and curious. Those were the best days. They'd go down to the beach, and Lucky would show him all the things in the rock pools, all the wading birds stalking the tideline, point out the dolphins that sometimes came into the bay. He didn't know the real names for everything, but that didn't matter, because whatever word he used, Gabriel would forget it again by the next day.

Sometimes he wanted to know their story, and Lucky would spend all day talking about their lives together, from childhood, to the fire in the castle. He'd try to keep the worst of the story to himself, but he'd often find his voice choked and hoarse before the end. On those days, Gabriel would put his hand next to Lucky's so their fingers touched and it was harder than ever to keep himself from breaking down.

Sometimes nothing he could do or say would be enough. Gabriel would yell or cry or hide from him. Once he ran from the castle altogether and Lucky spent a frantic hour searching Ciatheme for him. No one died that he was aware of, but he couldn't help panicking about it for days afterwards.

No one bothered them. The castle was mostly ruins, and the rumours of the ghost spread easily. The room Lucky had passed on that day with the long table and single chair was the only one with an intact roof and walls, so he and Gabriel spent most of their time in there.

It was a life together and every day was enough.

While Gabriel slept, Lucky had another routine. First, he'd make his way to the ruins of the exercise yard. There he'd call for Promise and ask her if they'd lived there long enough. Every day, she'd laugh and tell him to ask her again tomorrow. He never had any hope, but the routine in itself gave him a little comfort, a little crumb of control.

Once a week he'd light a pyre, and throw a handful of powder on it. Captain Haven had left him three. The white one meant things were continuing as normal. Red meant an emergency, come quickly. And black . . . well, he never expected to use the black powder.

Sometimes he'd go to bed, but most of the time rest didn't come easily to him. He'd sit and watch Gabriel sleep, listen to the quiet rise and fall of his breathing. Other times he'd take himself to a far corner of the castle, and weep and shout and bang his fists against the stone until his hands were bloody.

Mostly, he sketched. As the days went on, the castle walls became covered in images of birds, fish, animals. He sketched the crew of the *Dreamer*, Captain Haven and her wife, Poe, Sienna, Cass and Erin. Sometimes he'd talk to them, ask them for advice. They always stayed silent. He supposed that was a good sign, really. If they spoke back, it would mean his mind had snapped and he'd be no good to Gabriel then.

The *Dreamer* came once a month, and he looked forward to the company, but the visits were always stilted, awkward. As the months passed, they grew shorter and shorter.

But it was a life together, the only one they'd have.

One year, sixteen days after they'd first come to live in the castle, Lucky awoke and looked out the window and everything changed.

'Gabriel!' he called, pulling on his clothes. 'Gabriel, wake up, we need to get up.'

Gabriel stirred, turning towards him and blinking. Yesterday had been a good day, and he'd let Lucky braid his hair.

'Who . . .' Gabriel started.

'I'm Lucky,' Lucky said, holding out a hand. 'I'm Lucky and I love you so much. You're Gabriel, and I'm going to fix things.' He was babbling now, but it didn't matter. 'Please, just trust me. I need you to come with me. We're going down to the beach. You like it there.'

He threw Gabriel's clothes at him.

'I don't understand. Where am I? I don't remember anything,' Gabriel protested, but he started dressing. Lucky bounced on his heels. Perhaps this was what three cups of coffee felt like? His heart raced in his chest and his nerves fluttered.

He stopped off in the ruins of the kitchen, looking for what he needed. He ended up taking a solid metal pole from over the fireplace. Then he led Gabriel down to the beach.

The tide was out. Not just low tide out, but far, far further out than it normally went. Lucky hadn't seen it that far out in over ten years. He set out across the sands at a brisk walk, sending wading birds scattering.

'Where are we going?' Gabriel asked. 'What's going on?'

'I'm going to fix things,' he said again, and Gabriel frowned. Lucky was grateful he was willing to follow at least. He didn't know how much time they had, and if Gabriel had had a bad day, he might have lost their one opportunity.

The crack in the cliffs looked exactly as he remembered it. Squeezing through as a grown man was much harder, though. Gabriel paused at the entrance.

'I . . . I don't want to go in there,' he murmured. 'I don't like that.'

'Stay there, then,' Lucky said gently. 'I'll be out shortly. I promise. Just wait for me. Then everything will be fine.'

Gabriel pulled his arms around himself, and Lucky pushed further into the crack. The rock pressed in on him, biting at him, catching at his clothes and hair. It didn't want to let him through.

Lucky wasn't going to be stopped.

He burst through into the first chamber and hurried straight for the steps. The sea had left them smooth and slippery as glass. He fell twice before crawling up on all fours, the steel bar clamped tightly in his fist.

Then he was in the shrine room. It looked just as it had to his fourteen-year-old self. The tiles were just as bright and colourful as they had been then. The statue stared blankly at him and he waited.

'What are you doing?'

Her voice echoed around the chamber, echoed in his head. It was storms lashing against the cliffs. It was ships breaking up in the waves. It was angry.

Lucky kept his calm. He was practised now.

'I remembered something,' he said, hefting the pole against his palms. 'I remembered that when the Beaters killed the other Promises, they did it by destroying their shrines. Do you want to be a leviathan?'

'You wouldn't.'

Lucky took the pole in both hands, ready to swing it at the statue. 'Want to try me?'

'I'll kill you,' she hissed like the air leaving a drowning man's lungs. 'I'll kill him.'

He shook his head. 'I don't think so. You'd have stopped us from leaving the castle if you could do that. We're promised to you. We can die, but you can't kill us.' He drew the pole back.

'Wait!'

Lucky smiled. 'I'm waiting.'

'I'll let him go.' The rage in her voice was quiet, but present, lurking under the surface.

'Let us both go,' Lucky replied. 'And give Gabriel back his memories.'

'I can't do that.' Sulky. Petulant. A thousand-year-old goddess with her arms crossed like a child.

'You commanded a leviathan to attack a castle,' Lucky replied. 'I think you can. Or else you can become a leviathan yourself. What's it to be?'

She hung there, glaring at him, forcing him to wait. Lucky could wait. He had time. Either way, it would be over soon.

'I will do it, for a cost.'

Lucky raised the pole higher and she hissed.

'A sacrifice was made. A sacrifice must be paid.'

'What are you asking?' He'd do it for Gabriel. Whatever she asked, if it would make him whole again, he'd do it.

'Memories for memories. I'll return his memories, and I'll return yours.'

'I don't have any missing memories,' he replied. He remembered their promise, and that was the only piece that was missing from his life.

'Really?' She touched his forehead and vanished.

Lucky gasped as a rush of memories broke the dam and flooded his mind. Ten years of incarceration. Ten years of boredom, fear, frustration, anguish, guilt. Too much to bear as a whole thing. His mind had wrapped it up, bundled it all together as a self-contained thing, with only a few moments poked free.

He dropped to his knees, feeling every moment all at once. Every chill of air. Every lump on the hard bunk. Every unkind word, every slap, every poke and prod. Every dehumanisation. Every time he'd wept for his mother, every time he'd woke up screaming about the promise. Every mouthful of seawater he'd swallowed getting sucked out.

Lucky panted, pressing his hands into the stone of the shrine room. This was right. He could bear it. He breathed in the sea salt, struggling not to vomit. This was right. He'd bear his past and he'd claim his future.

His Gabriel.

The assault on his mind eased. He'd never forget those moments. Unlike his other memories, they'd never fade, never be eased away into a tidy corner. They'd come back when his guard was down, when he slept, every fever dream from now to his death. But he had them under control now, and he could move. Could leave.

Lucky left the pole at the base of the statue. Maybe someone else would need it one day. He hoped not. Before he left the lower chamber, he took out Captain Haven's knife and scratched into the walls.

LEAVE THIS PLACE, ONLY DEATH AWAITS

Then he stepped out to see if she'd kept her word.

The vast sky sucked at him as he emerged. He gripped the rocks, fingernails cracking as he dug them in. His stomach swooped, his heart racing. The iron band trapped his lungs, squeezing out his breath.

'Hey.'

The voice filled his heart, lifted his soul. That one word, the one he'd been dreaming of for so long.

'Gabriel?' He opened his eyes, focusing on the sand. He wanted to believe so badly, but he'd been hurt so much. 'Gabriel, my Gabriel?'

'I'm real,' Gabriel said softly. 'You're real.'

Lucky took a breath, counting to five in his head. He raised his gaze, taking in Gabriel slowly, drinking him in, hoping with every fibre of his soul.

Gabriel held out a hand towards him. 'Hey,' he said again, and the sound burst in Lucky's heart. His eyes filled with tears. 'I remember. I remember all of it.'

Lucky's heart leapt so hard he was worried it would burst from his chest. He pushed his own hand out towards Gabriel. 'Can I touch you? Can I kiss you?'

Gabriel nodded frantically. 'We've got so much time to make up.'

Lucky wrapped his arms around him, kissing him hungrily. They fell back, arms around each other, lying in the sand, enjoying the touch and taste of each other.

'What . . . what did you do in there?' Gabriel asked.

'I fixed it,' Lucky said with a laugh that was a little wild, a little too high. 'I told you I would.'

Gabriel ran a hand down his cheek. 'You always said everything would work out. I should have never doubted you, Lucky.'

Lucky shook his head. 'No, not Lucky. Neither of us need to be Lucky anymore. Call me Rob, like you used to.'

Gabriel leaned in close, and Rob lost himself in those deep brown eyes. 'Rob,' he said softly, and then his lips were busy.

They walked back, hand in hand, just as they had as teenagers. Back in the castle, Rob led the way to the exercise yard, and the pyre. He pulled out the bag of black powder and threw a handful into the fire. Black smoke leapt up into the blue sky, summoning the *Dreamer*. Saying everything was all right again.

She came two days later as he and Gabriel walked along the shore. Rob caught sight of sails on the horizon and knew it was her.

Gabriel paced on the sand. 'What am I going to say to everyone? What if I say the wrong thing? I . . . I got my sacrifice back, what if they hate me for that?'

Rob laughed. 'No one could hate you. You're impossible to hate.' He held out a hand, letting Gabriel take it. Gabriel's fingers tightened around his, pulling Rob close. 'You're adorable, Gabriel Haven.'

'I suppose I am,' Gabriel replied with a grin.

The ship weighed anchor and a dinghy rushed across the water towards the beach. Rob counted three people on board.

'Golden boy!' Sienna raised an arm as the dinghy slid on to the sand. The other arm was missing, ending at a stump below her shoulder.

'Sienna!' Gabriel called back. 'I'm so glad you're all right.'

She leapt out of the boat first, leaving Captain Haven and Amala to get out at a more sedate and dignified pace.

'Course I'm all right. Had to survive so I could come and kick your arse for making everyone worry.' She pantomimed swinging her leg back for a kick, then stopped and turned her attention to Rob. 'I guess your kidneys are safe for now.'

Gabriel raised an eyebrow and Rob shook his head. 'I'll explain another time.'

Gabriel turned to his parents, his hand tightening around Rob's. Amala was already crying, and Captain Haven failed to suppress the quiver in her lip.

'Hello, Ma, Mum,' Gabriel said.

Amala choked back a sob. 'It's so good to see you again, Gabe. Are you feeling up for a hug?'

He held out his arms. Rob turned away, letting the three of them have a moment together.

'Poe's putting on a feast tonight,' Sienna commented. 'Gonna go to bed with a belly like this.' She mimed a mound over her stomach.

'Bet I can out-eat you,' he replied, and she grinned.

'Bet Gabe out-eats both of us,' she replied.

'Yeah, not putting money on that.'

She looked him up and down. 'Living for Lucky looks good on you.'

'Not Lucky.' He shook his head. 'I'm living for Rob.'

Her eyes widened and she gave him a hug. 'Rob. It suits you.'

The dinghy flashed across the water, driven by the water dancers. Even with his memories back, Gabriel still had his abilities, and Sienna seemed to do well enough with one arm. The moment merged with memories of escaping his cell, a dizzying déjà vu that didn't quite line up. But one thing in particular stood out as different.

This time, he knew he was going home.

Epilogue

Ten years later.

The leviathan breached, its long sinuous neck reaching over the waves as its body twisted and rolled. For a moment, a wide yellow eye stared across the sea and straight into Rob's soul. Then it came down with a splash, disappearing back under the water.

The *Dreamer* carried on, keeping a respectful distance from the creature. Close enough to act if needed, but not to put any pressure on the leviathan. It was only an animal, after all.

No matter what it had been once before.

Across the deck, Sienna, now the first mate, conversed with the twins. Probably discussing tactics if they had to act against the leviathan. There were three more dancers on board, though one of them was too old and weary to do much these days.

Despite all the changes over the last decade, there was always someone willing to make an offering at the shrine. Always more misfits and dreamers.

Sienna caught him watching and gave him a wave. 'Tell the captain we've still got eyes on her and she's following the same course. Shouldn't be any need to pursue her much longer, unless she turns back in land.'

'Will do,' he called back.

'There better be plenty of that for me,' she said, pointing at the tray in his hands.

'Of course. Seen Poe?'

She pointed to the stern, where a group of sailors sat playing dice. Rob gave her a nod of thanks, and she turned back to the twins.

'You don't need to fetch my meals,' Poe grumbled as Rob set half the dishes down beside him.

'Don't have to, no,' he replied, smothering a smile. 'How are your fingers?'

The old cook held up his hands. 'Not so bad today.'

'Certainly not stopping him taking our money,' one of the other sailors commented and there were several groans of agreement.

'I'll leave you to it, then.' Rob walked away as Poe broke into a tale about the time he'd accidentally caught a shark when fishing. Each time he told the story, the length of the shark jumped up another foot. It would be the size of a leviathan before long.

At the captain's cabin, he fought down the ingrained need to knock. Old habits died hard. He let himself in and set the rest of the food down on the table. Gabriel sat at the desk, bent over a page of writing. He stared intently at the words he'd written, worrying at his lip. For a moment, Rob just stood watching, drinking in the man he loved.

'Come and eat.'

'Is it that time already?' Gabriel laced his fingers together and stretched his hands over his head.

'It was that time a while ago,' Rob teased. 'The writing going well?'

Gabriel took off his reading glasses and rubbed a hand over his face. 'I think I'm nearly finished.'

'I'm proud of you.' Rob held out his hand as Gabriel stood. 'But you still need to take a break and eat.'

Gabriel took his hand and pulled them close together. Rob kissed him, tasting the lingering coffee and sea salt on his lips. He glanced down at the stack of paper, sat on top of several letters from Gabriel's mothers. They were mostly written by Amala, with a couple of lines from Mel, mostly about the fish she'd caught. Rob wondered if they were as embellished as Poe's tales.

Retirement seemed to be suiting them well.

Just as captaincy suited Gabriel.

'When you're finished with the writing, I'll illustrate it,' he told Gabriel as they sat down at the table. 'It will be the finest book in the Sea Hall library.'

Gabriel's eyes shone with pride at the idea. Since taking over the running of the *Dreamer*, he'd been documenting every observation and understanding he'd made about the leviathans, their anatomy, their behaviours, and feeding patterns, along with techniques for water dancers to work effectively with the creatures.

'I think you're a better cook than even Poe was,' Gabriel commented.

'You're biased.' Rob waved a spoon at him, and Gabriel grinned. 'And don't let Poe hear that. He still considers himself the cook, even if the arthritis doesn't let him do much directly.'

'Ma tried to get him to retire too, but he wasn't having any of it.'

'He seems happy enough, fleecing sailors of their wages at dice,' Rob said. 'And it's nice to have someone to bounce ideas off and ask for help when I need it. He knows so much more than me. Maybe we should write down his knowledge, too.'

Gabriel reached a hand across the table, and Rob entwined his own with Gabriel's. Four fingers. Familiar. Safe.

Where he belonged.

THE END

Acknowledgements

My second book! A massive thank you to anyone who has already picked up TIL DEATH DO US BARD, or who goes on to read it after reading this one. Speaking of BARD, I described that book as a warm hug. This one is more of holding your loved one's hand at the top of a roller coaster. (Once I was on a roller coaster that broke down at the top of the highest point and I nearly broke my partner's hand, so maybe don't hold them *too* tight!) PROMISING SEAS is tenser, darker, than BARD. Where Logan and Pie were stubborn and difficult, Lucky and Gabriel have been beaten down by the world already. But like BARD, this book is full of found family, of people you can build a home around, of love in all its forms.

To my partner and my son, I love you so much.

Thank you to my editor Natasha Qureshi who helped to take a story that possessed me on a random October Tuesday and shape it into something special. To Lydia Blagden and Mia Carnevarle for another stunning cover. And my amazing agent Becca Podos who has been a rock at every step of the process.

Thanks to Camp Helicon and especially Cass for the sprints that pushed me into completing my first draft.

My army of beta readers: Alex, Cat, Pragnya, Beckett, Liana, Sophie, Jude, Sage, Juli, JB Levi, and Jo, thank you for helping bring my messy first draft under control.

And thanks to my many, many wonderful friends. My beloved PitSquirrels – Liv, Janet, Becks, Ameila, Ariana, Kim, and Noreen, I'm proud of all of you. Doom, Aubrey, and Beggs for the group chats. And the Jar – Kal, CJ, Miriam, Ollie, Kit, MJ, Chloe, Birdie, Cam, Aaron, Benny, and Robert Loans for your endless support and love.

WANT
MORE?

If you enjoyed this
and would like to
find out about similar
books we publish,
we'd love you to
join our online Sci-Fi,
Fantasy and Horror
community, Hodderscape.

Visit hodderscape.co.uk for
exclusive content from our authors, news, competitions
and general musings, and feel free to comment, contribute
or just keep an eye on what we are up to.

See you there!